CRAVEN

HER GREEK GROOM

THE *Sara* CRAVEN COLLECTION

August 2016

September 2016

October 2016

November 2016

Sara
CRAVEN
HER GREEK GROOM

MILLS & BOON

First Published in Great Britain 2016
By Mills & Boon, an imprint of HarperCollins*Publishers*
1 London Bridge Street, London, SE1 9GF

HER GREEK GROOM © 2016 Harlequin Books S.A.

The Tycoon's Mistress © 2000 Sara Craven
Smokescreen Marriage © 2001 Sara Craven
His Forbidden Bride © 2003 Sara Craven

ISBN: 978-0-263-92239-4

09-0916

Our policy is to use papers that are natural, renewable and recyclable products and made from wood grown in sustainable forests.
The logging and manufacturing processes conform to the legal environmental regulations of the country of origin.

Printed and bound in Spain
by CPI, Barcelona

THE TYCOON'S
MISTRESS

Former journalist **Sara Craven** published her first novel 'Garden of Dreams' for Mills & Boon in 1975. Apart from her writing (naturally!) her passions include reading, bridge, Italian cities, Greek islands, the French language and countryside, and her rescue Jack Russell/cross Button. She has appeared on several TV quiz shows and in 1997 became UK TV Mastermind champion. She lives near her family in Warwickshire – Shakespeare country.

CHAPTER ONE

CRESSIDA FIELDING turned her Fiat between the two stone pillars and drummed it up the long, curving drive to the house.

She brought the car to a halt on the wide gravel sweep outside the main entrance and sat for a moment, her hands still tensely gripping the steering wheel, staring up at the house.

The journey from the hospital had seemed endless, through all the narrow, winding lanes with the glare of the evening sun in her eyes, but she'd have gladly faced it again rather than the situation that now awaited her.

Her mind was still full of the image of her father in the intensive care unit, his skin grey under the bright lights and his bulky body strangely shrunken.

Lips tightening, Cressida shook herself mentally. She was not going to think like that. Her father's heart attack had been severe, but he was now making good progress. And when his condition was sufficiently stable, the surgeons would operate. And he would be fine again—in health at least.

And if it was up to her to ensure that he had a life to come back to, then—so be it.

With a sudden lift of the heart, she noticed her uncle's Range Rover was parked by the rhododendrons. At least she wasn't going to be alone.

As she went up the short flight of steps the front door opened to reveal the anxious figure of the housekeeper.

'Oh, Miss Cressy.' The older woman's relief was obvious. 'You're here at last.'

'Yes, Berry, dear.' Cressida put a comforting hand on Mrs Berryman's arm. 'I'm back.' She paused in the hall, looking round at the closed doors. She drew a deep breath. 'Is Sir Robert in the drawing room?'

'Yes, Miss Cressy. And Lady Kenny's with him. A tower of strength he's been. I don't know what I'd have done without them.' She paused. 'Can I bring you anything?'

'Some coffee, perhaps—and a few sandwiches, please. I couldn't eat on the plane.'

She watched Berry hurry away, then, with a sigh, walked across the hall. For a moment she halted, staring at herself in the big mirror which hung above the pretty crescent-shaped antique table.

She was a cool lady. Her boss said it with admiration, her friends with rueful smiles, and would-be lovers with exasperation bordering on hostility.

It was a persona she'd carefully and deliberately constructed. That she believed in.

But tonight there were cracks in the façade. Shadows of strain under the long-lashed grey-green eyes. Lines of tension tautening the self-contained mouth and emphasising the classic cheekbones.

It was the first time she'd had the chance to take a good look at herself, and the emotional roller-coaster of the past few weeks had left its mark.

Her clothes were creased from travel, and her pale blonde hair seemed to be sticking to her scalp, she thought, grimacing as she ran her fingers through it. She stopped for one deep, calming breath, then went into the drawing room.

She halted for a moment, assimilating with shock the

over-stuffed sofas, with their heavy brocade covers, and matching drapes, which managed to be expensive and charmless at the same time—all new since her last visit.

The lovely old Persian rugs had been replaced by a white fitted carpet, and there were gilt and crystal chandeliers instead of the graceful lamps she remembered, and mirrors everywhere.

It all looked like a stage setting, which had probably been exactly the intention, with Eloise playing the leading part—the nearest she'd ever come to it in her entire career. Only she'd quit before the end of the run...

Sir Robert, perched uneasily on the edge of a chair amid all this splendour, sprang to his feet with open relief when he saw Cressida.

'My dear child. This is a bad business.' He hugged her awkwardly. 'I still can't believe it.'

'Nor can I.' Cressida shook her head as she bent to kiss her aunt. 'Has there been any word from Eloise?'

'None,' Sir Robert said shortly. 'And we shouldn't expect any. She practically ransacked the house before she left.' He frowned. 'Berry says she's taken all your mother's jewellery, my dear.'

'Dad gave it to her when they were married,' Cressida reminded him evenly. 'She was entitled. And as least we're rid of her.'

'But at a terrible price.' Sir Robert pursed his lips. 'Of course, I could never understand what James saw in her.'

'Which makes you quite unique, darling,' his wife told him drily, drawing Cressida down to sit beside her. 'Eloise was a very beautiful, very sexy young woman and she took my unfortunate brother by storm. He was besotted by her from the moment they met, and probably still is.'

'Good God, Barbara, she's ruined him—she and her—paramour.'

'That's the trouble with love,' Cressida said slowly. 'It blinds you—drives you crazy...'

I never understood before, she thought painfully. But I do now. Oh, God, I do now...

She pulled herself together and looked at her uncle. 'Is it really true? It's not just some terrible mistake?'

Sir Robert shook his head soberly. 'The mistake was your father's, I'm afraid. It seems he met this Caravas man when he and Eloise were in Barbados two years ago. He claimed to be a financial adviser, produced adequate credentials, and gave them a few bits of advice which were perfectly sound.' His mouth tightened. 'I think they call it salting the mine.'

'When did he first mention the Paradise Grove development?'

'Several months later,' her uncle said grimly. 'They happened to run into him at the ballet, it seems, except there was nothing random about the encounter. There were a couple of other meetings—dinner, an evening at Glyndebourne which he paid for—then he started talking about this exclusive hotel and leisure complex, and what an investment opportunity it was. He said it would make them millionaires many times over, but only a really high investment would bring a high return.'

Cressy drew a painful breath. 'So Dad put all his money into it? And remortgaged this house? Everything?'

Sir Robert's nod was heavy. 'If only James had told me what he was planning, I might have been able to talk him out of it. But by the time I found out what was troubling him, it was too late.'

'And, of course, it was a sting.' Cressy looked down

at her clasped hands. Her voice was level. 'Paradise Grove was a mangrove swamp in the middle of nowhere. No one was ever going to build anything there.'

'Yes. But it was clever. I've seen the plans—the architects' drawings—the documentation. Including the apparent government licences and permissions. It all looked very professional—very official.'

'Like all the best confidence tricks.' Cressy shook her head. 'And the clever Mr Caravas? When did he and Eloise get together?'

'I imagine quite early on. There's no doubt she pushed James into the scheme for all she was worth. And now she and Caravas have completely vanished. The police say that they'll have new identities and the money safely laundered into a numbered account somewhere. Their plans were carefully made.' He paused. 'Your father wasn't the only victim, of course.'

Cressy closed her eyes. She said, 'How on earth could Dad have taken such an appalling risk?'

Sir Robert cleared his throat. 'My dear, he was always a gambler. That was part of his success in business. But he'd had some stockmarket losses, and—other problems. He saw it as a way of ensuring his long-term security in one big deal. He's never taken kindly to retirement. He wanted to be a key player again.' He paused. 'Quite apart from the personal pressure.'

'Yes,' Cressida said bitterly. 'And now I have to see if there's anything that can be saved from this ghastly mess.' She looked around her. 'I suppose this house will have to go.'

'It seems so,' Barbara Kenny said unhappily. 'I doubt if James will have much left apart from his company pension.'

Cressy nodded, her face set. 'I've brought my laptop

down with me. Tomorrow I'll start looking—finding out how bad things really are.'

There was a tap on the door and Mrs Berryman came in with a tray. The scent of the coffee, and the sight of the pile of ham sandwiches, the plate of home-made shortbread and the rich Dundee cake accompanying them, reminded Cressy how long it was since she'd eaten.

She said warmly, 'Berry—that looks wonderful.'

'You look as if you need it.' The housekeeper's glance was searching as well as affectionate. 'You've lost weight.'

'Berry's right,' her aunt commented when they were alone again. 'You are thinner.'

Cressy was pouring coffee. 'I expect it's an illusion created by my Greek suntan. Although I did do a lot of walking while I was out there.' *And swimming. And dancing…*

'My dear, I'm so sorry that your holiday had to be interrupted like this,' Sir Robert said heavily. 'But I felt you had to be told—even before James collapsed.'

Cressy forced a smile. 'It was time I came back anyway.' Her mouth tightened. 'You can have—too much of a good thing.' She handed round the coffee and offered the plate of sandwiches. 'I'd have been here sooner, but of course it's the height of the holiday season and I couldn't get a flight straight away. I had to spend a whole day in Athens.'

It had been a nervy, edgy day—a day she'd spent looking behind her constantly to see if she was being followed. She'd joined a guided tour of the Acropolis, mingled with the crowds in the Plaka, done everything she could to lose herself in sheer numbers. And all the time she had been waiting—waiting for a hand on her shoulder—a voice speaking her name...

'Cressy, I worry about you,' Lady Kenny said forthrightly. 'You don't have enough fun. You shouldn't have your nose stuck to a computer screen all the time, solving other people's tax problems. You should find yourself a young man. Start living.'

'I like my job,' Cressy said mildly. 'And if by "living" you mean I should be swept away by some grand passion, I think we've seen enough of that in this family.' Her face hardened. 'Watching my father make a fool of himself over someone as worthless as Eloise taught me a valuable lesson. I've seen at first hand the damage that sex can do.'

'He was lonely for a long time,' her aunt said quietly. 'Your mother's death hit him hard. And Eloise was very clever—very manipulative. Don't be too hard on him, darling.'

'No,' Cressy said with sudden bitterness. 'I've no right to judge anybody. It's all too easy to succumb to that particular madness.' *As I know now.*

For a moment she saw a cobalt sea and a strip of dazzling white sand, fringed with rocks as bleached as bones. And she saw dark eyes with laughter in their depths that glittered at her from a face of sculpted bronze. Laughter, she thought, that could, in an instant, change to hunger...

Suddenly breathless, she drove that particular image back into the recesses of her memory and slammed the door on it.

She would not think of him, she told herself savagely. She could not...

She saw her aunt and uncle looking faintly surprised, and went on hurriedly, 'But I shouldn't have let my dislike of Eloise keep me away. Maybe if I'd been around I could have done something. Persuaded Dad, somehow, that Paradise Grove was a scam. And he might not be in Intensive Care now,' she added, biting her lip hard as tears stung her eyes.

Sir Robert patted her shoulder. 'Cressy, you're the last person who could possibly be blamed for all this. And the doctor told me that James's heart attack could have happened at any time. He had warning signs over a year ago. But he wanted to pretend he was still young and strong.'

'For Eloise,' Cressy said bitterly. 'Oh, why did he have to meet her?'

Lady Kenny said gently, 'Sometimes fate works in strange ways, Cressy.' She paused. 'I've prepared a room at our house if you'd like to come back and stay. You shouldn't be on your own at a time like this.'

'It's sweet of you,' Cressy said gratefully. 'But I must remain here. I told the hospital it was where I'd be. And I shan't be alone with Berry to look after me.'

'Ah, yes.' Sir Robert sighed. 'I'm afraid Berry may be another casualty of this debacle.'

'Oh, surely not,' Cressy said in swift distress. 'She's always been part of this family.' One change that Eloise had not been allowed to make, she added silently.

Sir Robert finished his coffee and put down his cup. 'My dear.' His tone was sober. 'I think you must accept that nothing is ever going to be the same again.'

He was right, Cressy thought as she stood on the steps an hour later, waving her aunt and uncle an approximation of a cheerful goodbye.

Everything had changed quite momentously. Beginning with herself.

She shook herself mentally as she went back into the house.

She had to forget about those days of golden, sunlit madness on Myros, and how near she too had come to making a disastrous mistake.

That urgent summons back to England, although devastating, had been in another way a lifeline, dragging her back to reality. Waking her from the dangerous seductive dream which had enthralled her and could have led her to total ruin.

A holiday romance—that was all it had been. As trivial and tawdry as these things always were, with a handsome Greek on one side and a bored tourist on the other. Just for a while she'd allowed herself to indulge a risky fantasy, and then real life had intervened, just in time, returning her to sanity.

For a moment she found herself wondering what would have happened if her uncle's message had not been waiting at the hotel. If she'd actually called Draco's bluff and gone back to Myros...

She stopped herself right there. Speculation of that kind was forbidden territory now. Myros, and all that had happened there, was in the past, where it belonged. A memory that one day, in years to come, she might take out, dust down and smile over.

The memory of desire and being desired...

But not now. And maybe not ever, she thought, straightening her shoulders.

Now she had to look to the immediate future, and its problems. She'd have an early night, and tomorrow she would start to sift through the wreckage, see if anything could be salvaged.

And tonight, she told herself with determination, she would sleep without dreaming.

*   *   *

But that was more easily said than done. Cressida's night was restless. She woke several times, her body damp with perspiration, haunted by images that left no trace in her memory. Nothing that she could rationalise, and then dismiss.

Perhaps it was simply coming back to this house, where she'd been a stranger for so long, and finding herself in her old room again. The past playing tricks with her unconscious mind.

At least this room hadn't undergone the high-priced makeover inflicted on the rest of the house.

Eloise had been determined to erase every trace of her predecessor, Cressy thought, more with sorrow than with anger. And no expense had been spared in the process—which could explain how James Fielding might have found himself strapped for cash and been tempted to recklessness.

Although, in fairness, this wasn't the first time her father had sailed close to the wind. Only this time his instinct for disaster seemed to have deserted him.

But that, she thought, can happen to the best of us.

She pushed back the covers and got out of bed, wandering across to the window. Light was just beginning to stain the eastern sky, and the cool morning air made her shiver in her thin cotton nightgown and reach for a robe.

She'd never needed one in Greece, she thought. The nights had been too hot except in the hotel, which had had air-conditioning. Each evening the chambermaid had arranged her flimsy confection of silk and lace in a fan shape on the bed, with a rose on the bodice and a hand-made chocolate on the pillow.

Later, in the taverna on Myros, she'd slept naked, kicking away even the thin sheet to the foot of the bed, her body grateful for the faint breeze sighing from the Aegean sea through the open window.

Moving quietly, she went downstairs to the kitchen and made herself a pot of coffee which she carried to the study.

She'd brought in the computer and set it up the night before, and if she couldn't sleep then she might as well start work. Begin to probe the real extent of the financial disaster facing her father.

Because it could be faced. She was convinced of that. James Fielding was a survivor. He would get over this heart attack, and the ensuing operation, and take up his life again. And somehow she had to salvage something from the wreckage—make sure there was something to give him hope.

She'd done some preliminary calculations of her own on the plane, partly to prevent herself thinking of other things, she realised, her mouth twisting, and had worked out how much she could afford to contribute. But the outlook was bleak. Even if she sold her London flat, and worked from this house, she'd struggle to pay the new mortgage.

Besides, she wasn't sure whether she could endure to live under this roof again for any length of time. There were too many bad memories.

Cressida had been a teenager, still mourning her mother, when she had learned of her father's decision to remarry. And her sense of shock, almost betrayal, had doubled when she'd discovered his choice of wife.

Looking back, she could see that she'd responded intolerantly to the newcomer, staring at her with resentful eyes.

Eloise had been a bit-part actress, her chief claim to fame as hostess on a second-rate TV quiz show. She was tall and full-breasted, her lips permanently set in a beguiling pout, her violet eyes wide, almost childlike.

Until she was crossed, Cressida thought wryly. And then they would narrow like a rattlesnake's.

As they'd done when she first met her new step-daughter. The hostility had not been one-sided by any means. Eloise had made it plain that she had little time for other women, and especially for a young girl just beginning to blossom out of gawkiness, although there was no way Cressy could ever have rivalled her voluptuous charms.

Chalk and cheese, Cressy thought with sadness. And I was just a nuisance, someone to be sidelined, if not totally ignored.

And even when, urged by her father, she'd tried a few awkward overtures, she'd found herself completely rebuffed. Eventually she had acquired a reputation for being 'tricky', if not downright difficult. And James Fielding, unable to see he was being manipulated, had made his displeasure known to his daughter, creating a rift that had widened slowly but surely over the years.

Cressida had soon realised she was no longer welcome in her own home. Even at Christmas Eloise had usually organised a ski-ing holiday for her husband and herself.

'Darling,' she'd said coaxingly when the first one was mooted. 'Cressida doesn't want to spend her vacations with a couple of old fogies. She has her own friends. Her own life.' Her steely gaze had fixed her stepdaughter. 'Isn't that right?'

It had been easier to swallow her hurt and bewilderment and agree. She *had* had friends she could go to, and Uncle Robert and Aunt Barbara had always been there for her, their comfortable, untidy house a second home.

For a long time Cressida had convinced herself that the scales would eventually fall from her father's eyes and that he'd see Eloise's greed and self-absorption. But it had never happened. He'd been carried away by his passion for her—a passion that she had been careful to feed.

As for Eloise herself, Cressida was sure she'd looked at James Fielding and seen only a successful business-man, with a settled background and an attractive Georgian house not too far from London.

What she hadn't understood was that James's com-pany had struggled to recover from the big recession of the eighties, or that James himself had faltered more than once as chairman, and was being encouraged to take early retirement.

Eloise had been too busy entertaining, enjoying weekend parties with amusing people, and being seen in all the right places.

Even after James's actual retirement she'd seen no need to scale down their style of living or their expen-diture.

Alec Caravas had been a younger man with a fool-proof scheme for making them both instantly wealthy. Cressida could see how easily Eloise would have been seduced.

After all, she thought, I was planning to give up my job, my lifestyle, my independence. I shouldn't judge anyone else.

Her own meetings with her father over the past two years had been mainly confined to lunches in London, with the conversation constrained.

Perhaps I should have made more of an effort,

Cressida thought as she drank her coffee. Perhaps I should have played the hypocrite and pretended to like her. Even looked for her good points. Told myself that, whatever my personal feelings, she loved Dad and was making him happy.

Only, I never believed that. I just didn't want to be proved right quite so comprehensively.

She sighed, and turned resolutely to the computer screen. It was little use rehashing the past, she told herself forcibly. She had to try and salvage something from the present to ensure her father had a future.

She worked steadily for a couple of hours, but found little to comfort her.

Her father's company pension was indeed all that was left. All his other assets had been liquidised to make him a major shareholder in Paradise Grove. And he'd borrowed heavily too.

If he recovered from his heart attack, it would be to find himself insolvent, she realised unhappily.

His whole way of life would have to be downsized. She'd have to rent a larger flat, she thought, or even a house. Make a home for him—and Berry, who'd be needed more than ever. But how could she afford it?

I won't worry about that now, she told herself, glancing at her watch.

It was time she took a shower and dressed, and got over to the hospital again.

As she pushed back her chair, she noticed for the first time the small icon at the bottom of the screen indicating there was an e-mail message for her.

Someone else believes in an early start, Cressida thought wryly, as she clicked on to the little envelope and watched the message scroll down.

I am waiting for you.

The words were brief, almost laconic, but they had the power to make her stiffen in shock and disbelief.

She twisted suddenly in her chair, staring over her shoulder with frightened eyes.

The room was empty. And yet she felt Draco's presence as surely as if he was standing behind her, his hand touching her shoulder.

She said, 'No,' and again, more fiercely, '*No*. It's not true. It can't be…'

And heard the raw panic that shook her voice.

CHAPTER TWO

THERE was a rational explanation. There had to be.

Someone, somewhere, must be playing a trick on her, and had accidentally scored a bullseye.

All the way to the hospital Cressy kept telling herself feverishly that this was the way it had to be. That it must be one of her colleagues…

Except that they were all under the impression that she was still sunning herself on an island in the Aegean. She hadn't told anyone from work that she was back.

And, anyway, the message was too pointed—too personal to have come from anyone else but Draco. Wasn't it?

But how the hell did a Greek fisherman with one small, shabby boat and a half-built house manage to gain access to a computer, let alone have the technical know-how to send electronic mail halfway across Europe?

It made no sense.

Besides, he only knew my first name, she reminded herself with bewilderment. He can't possibly have traced me with that alone.

Her mind was still going round in ever decreasing circles as she went up in the lift to the Intensive Care Unit. But she steadied herself when the sister in charge met her with the good news that her father's condition had greatly improved.

'He's asleep at the moment, but you may sit with him.' Calm eyes looked squarely into Cressida's. 'You can be relied on not to make emotional scenes, Miss Fielding? He really doesn't need that kind of disturbance.'

'Of course not.' Cressy said steadily. 'I just want him to get better.'

She fetched some coffee from the machine in the corridor, then quietly took up her vigil, forcing herself to composure. She couldn't afford to send out any negative vibrations.

And she hadn't time to worry about mysterious e-mail messages or who might have generated them. Her father was her priority now, and nothing else could be allowed to matter.

That worrying grey tinge seemed to have gone from James Fielding's face. He looked more his old self again, she thought, surreptitiously crossing her fingers.

If he continued to make good progress he could soon be moved to a private room, she told herself. The premiums on his private health insurance had been allowed to lapse, but she would pay.

She said under her breath. 'I'll look after you, Daddy—whatever it takes. I'll make sure you're all right.'

He woke up once, gave her a faint smile, and fell asleep again. But it was enough.

Apart from the hum of the various machines, the unit was quite peaceful. And very hot, Cressy thought, undoing another button on her cream cotton shirt.

Almost as hot as it had been in Greece.

For a moment she could feel the beat of the sun on her head, see its dazzle on the water and hear the slap of the small waves against the bow of the caique as it took her to Myros.

* * *

Myros...

She noticed it the day she arrived, when she walked across the cool marble floor of her hotel bedroom, out on to the balcony, and looked across the sparkle of the sea at the indigo smudge on the horizon.

As she tipped the porter who'd brought up her luggage, she asked, 'What is that island?'

'That, *thespinis*, is Myros.'

'Myros.' She repeated the name softly under her breath.

She stayed where she was, fingers lightly splayed on the balustrade, lifting her face to the sun, listening to the distant wash of the sea and the rasp of the cicadas in the vast gardens below.

She could feel the worries and tensions of the past months sliding away from her.

She thought, with bewilderment and growing content, I really need this holiday. I didn't realize it, but Martin was quite right.

Her work was always meticulous, but she'd made a couple of mistakes in the last few weeks. Nothing too dire, and nothing that couldn't be swiftly put right without inconvenience to the client, but disturbing just the same.

Martin had looked at her over his glasses. 'When was the last time you took a break, Cress? And I don't mean Christmas and the usual Bank Holidays. I mean a real, live, away-from-it-all, lie-in-the-sun break. The sort that ordinary people have.'

'I have time off,' she had said. 'Last time I decorated my sitting room at the flat.'

'Exactly.' He'd sat back in his chair, his gaze inflexible. 'So you take the rest of the afternoon off, you visit a travel agent and you book yourself at least three weeks of total relaxation in some bit of the Mediterranean. Then get yourself some sun cream and a selection of pulp fiction and go. And that's an order,' he had added as Cressy had begun to protest pressure of work.

She'd obeyed mutinously, agreeing to the travel company's first suggestion of an all-inclusive trip to the latest in the Hellenic Imperial hotel chain.

'They're all the last word in luxury,' the travel clerk had enthused. 'And there's a full programme of sport and entertainment on offer. This one only opened recently, which is why there are still a few rooms available.'

'Anything,' Cressy had said, and had put down her gold card.

She might have arrived under protest, but she couldn't pretend she wasn't impressed.

For the first few days she simply relaxed under an umbrella on one of the sun terraces, swam in each of the three pools, had a couple of tennis lessons, and tried her hand, gingerly, at windsurfing. She also sampled all of the restaurants on the complex.

For once the brochure had spoken nothing but the truth, she thought wryly. The Hellenic Imperial was the height of opulence. The service was excellent, and no element of comfort had been overlooked.

But by the end of the first week Cressy was beginning to feel that it was all too perfect.

Most of the other guests seemed perfectly content to stay on the complex and be waited on hand and foot, but Cressy was restless. She rented a car, and took in the sights. The island's capital, with its harbour full of glamorous yachts and its sophisticated shopping facilities, left her cold. She much preferred driving up throat-tightening mountain roads to see a church with famous frescoes, sampling dark, spicy wine in a local vineyard, or drinking tiny cups of thick, sweet coffee in *kafeneions* in remote villages.

But, more and more, she found herself looking across the glittering sapphire of the Aegean and wondering exactly what lay there on the horizon.

One morning, when she was changing some money at Reception, she said casually, 'How do I get to Myros?'

The clerk could not have looked more astonished if she'd asked what time the next space ship left for the moon.

'Myros, *thespinis*?' he repeated carefully.

Cressy nodded. 'It's not that far away. I presume there's a ferry.'

He pursed his lips. 'There are boats,' he said discouragingly. 'But tourists do not go there, Kyria Fielding.'

'Why not?'

He shrugged. 'Because everything they want is here,' he returned with unshakeable logic.

'Nevertheless,' Cressy said equably, biting back a smile, 'I'd like to know where the boats leave from.'

The clerk looked almost distressed. 'You don't like this hotel, *thespinis*? You find it lacking in some way?'

'Not at all,' she assured him. 'I'd just like a change.'

'But there is nothing on Myros, *kyria*. It has no hotels, no facilities. It is a place for farmers and fishermen.'

'It sounds perfect,' Cressy said, and left him in midprotest.

She was aware of curious glances as she sat in the bow of the caique watching Myros turn from an indistinct blur into a tall, mountainous ridge, the lower slopes softened by patches of greenery. She was without question the only foreigner on the boat, and the skipper, who looked like an amiable pirate, had initially demurred over accepting her fare.

As the caique traversed the shoreline, Cressy saw long stretches of pale sand, sheltered by jagged rocks.

The fishermen and the farmers have been lucky so far, she thought. Because this place looks ripe for exploitation to me.

The harbour was only tiny, with no smart boats among the battered caiques. Row upon row of small white houses seemed to be tumbling headlong towards the narrow waterfront where fishing nets were spread to dry.

Somewhere a church bell was ringing, its sound cool and sonorous in the hot, shimmering air.

Cressy found her heart clenching in sudden excitement and pleasure.

Her canvas beach bag slung over her shoulder, she scrambled ashore.

There was a sprinkling of tavernas and coffee shops on the harbourside, most of them frequented by elderly men playing a very fast and intense form of backgammon.

Cressy chose a table under an awning at the largest, waiting while the proprietor, a stocky man in jeans and a white shirt, finished hosing down the flagstones.

'Thespinis?' His smile was cordial enough, but the black eyes were shrewdly assessing.

Cressy asked for an iced Coke, and, when he brought it, enquired if there was anywhere she could hire a car.

The smile broadened regretfully. The only vehicles on Myros, she was told, were Jeeps and pick-up trucks,

and none were for rent. The roads, the *kyria* must understand, were not good.

Well, I knew they didn't cater for tourists, Cressy
reminded herself philosophically. But it was a setback.

She said, 'I saw beaches, *kyrie*. Can I reach them on
foot?'

He nodded. 'It is possible, *thespinis*. Our finest beach
is only a kilometre from here.' He paused thoughtfully,
fingering his heavy black moustache. 'But there is a
better way.' From a storeroom at the back of the taverna, he produced an ancient bicycle. 'It belonged to
my sister,' he explained. 'But she is in Athens.'

'And you'll lend it to me?' Cressy raised her eyebrows. 'That's very kind.'

He shrugged. 'She will be happy for you to use it. It
is an honour for her.'

'But how do you know I'll bring it back?'

The smile became almost indulgent. 'When the *kyria*
wishes to leave Myros, she must return here. Also, she
must eat, and my taverna has good fish. The best.' He
nodded. 'You will come back, *thespinis*.'

Cressy hadn't ridden a bicycle for years. She waited
while the proprietor, whose name was Yannis, ceremoniously dusted the saddle for her, then mounted awkwardly.

She said, 'I hope it lasts the distance, *kyrie*.'

'A kilometre is not too far.' He paused. 'I do not
recommend that you go further than that, thespinis.'

'We'll see,' Cressy said cheerfully. 'Once I get the
hang of it, I may do the grand tour.'

Yannis's face was suddenly serious. 'Go to the beach
only, *thespinis*. I advise it. Beyond it the road is bad.
Very bad.'

Now, why did she get the feeling that Yannis was

warning her about more than the state of the road? Cressy wondered, as she wobbled away.

But he hadn't been exaggerating. Outside the small town, the road soon deteriorated into a dirt track, with olive groves on one side and the sea on the other, and Cressy had to concentrate hard on keeping her eccentric machine upright, and avoiding the largest stones and deepest potholes.

Apart from the whisper of the sea, and the faint breeze rustling the silver leaves of the olive trees, Cressy felt as if she was enclosed in a silent, shimmering landscape. She was glad of the broad straw hat protecting her blonde hair.

The beach was soon reached, but, she saw with disappointment, it was only a narrow strip of sand with a lot of pebbles and little shade.

The others I saw were much better, she thought. Yannis can't have meant this one.

In spite of the road, she was beginning, against all odds, to enjoy her unexpected cycle ride, and decided to press on to one of the secluded coves she'd glimpsed from the ferry.

Ten minutes later, she was beginning to regret her decision. The gradient on her route had taken a sharp upward turn, and her elderly bone-shaker was no mountain bike.

This must have been what Yannis meant, she thought grimly. Certainly it warranted a warning.

She halted, to have a drink from the bottle of water which he'd pressed on her and consider what to do next.

Myros was only a small island, she argued inwardly, and the next beach couldn't be too far away. So, it might be better to leave the bike at the side of the track—after all, no one in his right mind would steal it—and proceed on foot.

She laid the ancient machine tenderly on its side in the shade of an olive tree, blew it a kiss, and walked on.

She'd gone about five hundred yards when she first heard the music, only faint, but unmistakably Greek, with its strong underlying rhythm. Cressy paused, breathless from her continued climb, and listened, her brows drawing together.

She swore softly under her breath. 'I don't believe it,' she muttered. 'I've come all this way in this heat, only to find someone else's beach party.'

She was going to walk on, but then sudden curiosity got the better of her, and, letting the music guide her, she moved quietly through the scrub and stones to the edge of the cliff. There was a track of sorts leading down to the pale crescent of sand below, but Cressy ignored that, moving to slightly higher ground where she could get an overall view of the beach.

The first thing she saw was a small caique, with faded blue paint and its sails furled, moored just offshore. But that appeared to be deserted.

Then she looked down, and the breath caught in her throat.

Below her, alone on the sand, a man was dancing.

Arms flung wide, head back, his face lifted to the sun, he swayed, and dipped to the ground, and leapt, his entire body given over to the sheer joy of living— and the raw power of the music.

And totally absorbed in his response to it, thought Cressy. Clearly nothing else existed for him at this moment.

She dropped to her knees in the shelter of a dried and

spindly shrub and watched, amused at first, but gradually becoming more entranced.

She'd seen demonstrations of *syrtaki* at the hotel, of course, but never performed with this wild, elemental force.

This man seemed completely at home in his solitary environment, Cressy told herself in bewilderment, as if he was somehow part of the sea, and the rocks, and the harsh brilliant sunlight, and shared their common spirit. Or the reincarnation of some pagan god…

She halted right there.

Now she was just being fanciful, she thought with self-derision.

He might be a wonderful dancer, but what she was actually seeing was a waiter from one of the hotels on the other island, practising his after-dinner routine for the tourists.

But not from my hotel, she thought. Or I'd have remembered…

Because he wasn't just a beautiful dancer. He was beautiful in other ways, too.

He was taller than average, and magnificently built, with broad, muscular shoulders, narrow hips and endless legs, his only covering a pair of ragged denim shorts which left little to the imagination.

The thick, dark hair, curling down on to the nape of his neck, gleamed like silk in the sunshine, and his skin was like burnished bronze.

To her shock, Cressy found her mouth was suddenly dry, her pulses drumming in unaccustomed and unwelcome excitement. She realised, too, there was an odd, trembling ache deep within her.

What the hell am I doing? she asked frantically, as she lifted herself cautiously to her feet and backed away. I'm an intelligent woman. I go for brains, not brawn. Or I would if I was interested in any kind of involvement, she reminded herself hastily.

Besides, this brand of obvious physicality leaves me cold. I'm not in the market for—holiday bait.

She was being unfair, and she knew it as she walked on, her pace quickening perceptibly.

After all, the lone dancer could have no idea he had an audience. He'd created his own private world of passion and movement, and if its intrinsic sensuality had sent her into meltdown then that was her problem, not his.

All the same, she was glad when the music faded from earshot. Although the image in her mind might not be so easy to dismiss, she realised ruefully.

'I don't know what's happening to me, but I don't like it,' she said under her breath, lengthening her stride.

A further five minutes' walk brought her to another cove, and this one was deserted, she noted as she scrambled thankfully down to the sand.

She stood for a moment, listening to the silence, then spread her towel in the shade of a rock, kicked off her canvas shoes, and slipped out of her navy cotton trousers and shirt to reveal the simple matching bikini beneath.

The sea was like cooling balm against her overheated skin. She waded out until the water was waist-high, then slid gently forward into its embrace, breaking into her strong, easy crawl.

When she eventually got tired, she turned on her back and floated, her eyes closed against the dazzle of the sun.

She felt completely at peace. London, the office and its problems seemed a lifetime away. Even the rift with her father no longer seemed quite so hurtful—or so insoluble. Eloise had driven a wedge between them, but—with care—wedges could be removed. Maybe she'd needed to distance herself in order to see that.

Back under her rock, she towelled herself down, applied sun cream with a lavish hand, drank some more water, then lay down on her front. She reached behind her and undid the clip of her bikini top. A suntan might not be fashionable, but it was inevitable that she would gain a little colour in this heat, and she didn't want any unsightly marks to spoil the effect in the low-backed dresses she'd brought.

She felt bonelessly relaxed, even a little drowsy, as she pillowed her cheek on her folded arms.

There's nothing I can't handle, she told herself with satisfaction as she drifted off to sleep.

She would never be certain what woke her. There was just an odd feeling of disquiet—a sudden chill, as if a cloud had covered the sun—that permeated her pleasant dream and broke its spell.

Cressy forced open her unwilling eyelids. For a moment she could see nothing, because the dazzle of the sun was too strong.

Then, slowly, she realised that she was no longer alone.

That there was someone lying on the sand beside her, only a few feet away. Someone tall and bronzed in denim shorts, who was—dear God—smiling at her.

She wanted to scream, but her throat muscles seemed suddenly paralysed. And she couldn't move either because she'd undone her top.

When she found her voice, it sounded small and husky. 'What do you want?'

His smile widened. His mouth, she saw, was firm, although his lower lip had a betrayingly sensuous curve, and his teeth were very white. For the rest of him, he had a straight nose, just fractionally too long for classical beauty, strongly accented cheekbones, and deepset eyes the colour of agate flecked with gold.

He also needed a shave.

He said, 'Why did you not come down and dance with me?' His voice was deep, with a distinct undercurrent of amusement, and he spoke in English.

It was the last thing she'd expected him to say, and for a moment she was stunned. Then she rallied.

'I don't know what you mean.'

'Ah, no.' He shook his head reprovingly. 'You should not tell lies—especially when you are so bad at it. Your eyes will always give you away.'

'That's ridiculous,' Cressy said with hostility. 'And also impertinent. You know nothing about me.'

'I know that you were watching me from the cliff, and then you ran away.' The return was imperturbable.

'I didn't run,' Cressy said with as much dignity as she could evoke when she was lying, prone, wearing only the bottom half of a bikini. 'I just wanted to find some peace and quiet. And I didn't mean to disturb you. Please go back to your—rehearsal.'

'That is finished for the day. Now it is time to eat.' He reached behind him and produced a small rucksack.

Cressy groaned inwardly. How on earth was she going to get rid of him, she wondered wildly, without insulting his Greek machismo? She was uneasily aware of how isolated this little beach was. And that they were both almost naked. The last thing she needed to do was provoke him in any way. Even to anger.

She made a business of looking at her watch. 'So, it

is. Well, I must get back to the village. Yannis is expecting me to eat at his taverna.'

'But not in the middle of the day,' he said. 'In the middle of the day he likes to drink coffee and play *tavli*. He'll cook for you tonight.'

'I don't think so.' Cressy made a discreet effort to fasten the hook on her bikini top: 'I have to get the evening ferry back to Alakos.'

Her unwanted neighbour watched her struggles with interest, but didn't volunteer his assistance as she'd been half afraid he might. 'You are staying in a hotel on Alakos?'

'Yes.' At the third attempt, Cressy managed the hook, and felt marginally more secure. 'At the Hellenic Imperial.'

'The Imperial? *Po po po.*' His dark brows lifted. 'You would need to be very rich to stay at such a place.'

'Not at all,' Cressy said with a certain crispness, wondering if he was planning to kidnap her and hold her to ransom. 'I work for my living like everyone else.'

'Ah—you are a model, perhaps—or an actress?' He produced a paper bag from his rucksack and opened it. Cressy saw that it contained pitta bread with some kind of filling.

'Of course not,' she denied swiftly. 'I work in an office—as a taxation accountant.' She reached for her shirt. 'And now I must be going.'

'It is a long time until evening—and your ferry.' He divided the envelope of pitta bread into two and held out half to her, using the paper bag as a plate.

'No,' Cressy said. 'It's very kind of you, but I couldn't—possibly.'

He leaned across and put the improvised plate on the corner of her towel.

'Why are you frightened?' He sounded as if he was merely expressing a friendly interest.

'I'm not.'

He sighed. 'You are lying again, *matia mou*. Now eat, and tell me about your work in England, and later we will swim. And do not tell me you cannot swim,' he added, as her lips parted in negation, 'because I too was watching.'

Cressy sat very upright. She said, quietly and coldly. 'Does it occur to you, *kyrie*, that I might not want to spend the afternoon with you? That I prefer to be alone?'

'Yes,' he said. 'But that will change when you know me better. And no one so young and so lovely should wish to be alone. It is a sad thing.'

There was lamb tucked into the pitta bread. The scent of it was making her mouth water.

She glared at him. 'I've no taste for meaningless compliments, *kyrie*.'

He said, 'Nor do I, *thespinis*. You know that you are young, so accept that you are also beautiful. And my name is Draco.' He smiled at her. 'Now eat your food, and don't be afraid any more.'

But that, thought Cressy, looking down at the pattern on the towel—or anywhere rather than at him—that was easier said than done.

CHAPTER THREE

IN SPITE of all Cressy's misgivings about the risks of her situation—and they were many and various—she supposed she had better accept Draco's offer of food. One placatory gesture, she told herself, and then she would go.

If she was allowed to, said a small, unpleasant voice in her head. She'd seen his athleticism when he was dancing. She might be able to out-think him, but did she really imagine she could outrun him up that lethal track?

So much for striking out and being independent, she derided herself. She should have stayed safely in the hotel precincts.

She had expected she would have to force a few mouthfuls past the unremitting tightness of her throat, but to her astonishment the lamb, which had been roasted with herbs and was served with a light lemon dressing and sliced black olives, tasted absolutely wonderful, and she finished every bite.

'It was good?' Draco asked as Cressy wiped her lips and fingers on a tissue.

'It was terrific,' she admitted. She gave him a taut smile. 'You speak English very well.'

His own smile was slow, touched with overt reminiscence. 'I had good teachers.'

'Women, no doubt,' Cressy heard herself saying tartly, and could have bitten her tongue in half. The last thing she needed to do was antagonise him, and his personal life was none of her business anyway, so what had possessed her to make such a comment?

She saw his face harden, the firm mouth suddenly compressed. For a moment she felt the crackle of tension in the air between them like live electricity, then, totally unexpectedly, he began to laugh.

'You are astute, *thespinis*.' Propped on one elbow, he gave her a long and leisurely assessment, missing nothing, making her feel naked under his agate gaze. 'But my grammar—my pronunciation—are not perfect. I am sure there is room for improvement—with the right help.'

Cressy was burning from head to foot, and it had nothing to do with the sun.

She said, 'I'm afraid that you'll have to find another tutor, *kyrie*. I'm not in the market.'

'Life has taught me that most things are for sale, *kyria*—if the price is right.'

There was real danger here. Every instinct she possessed was screaming it at her.

She said coolly and clearly, 'But I am not. And now I think I'd better go.'

'As you wish.' The powerful shoulders lifted in a negligent shrug. 'But understand this. I take only what is freely given. Nothing more. And, in any case, you are the stranger within my gates, and you have eaten my bread, so you have nothing to fear.'

He lifted himself lithely to his feet. 'Now I am going to swim. Naturally, I hope you will still be here when I return, but the choice is yours, *kyria*.'

For a moment he stood looking down at her. He said softly, 'So beautiful, and such a sharp tongue. And yet so afraid of life. What a pity.'

The damned nerve of him, Cressy seethed, watching

him lope down the sand. Translating her natural caution into cowardice.

And, for all his assurances, it was quite obvious that he was just another good-looking Greek on the make. She'd seen it happening at the hotel. Watched them targeting the single women, the divorcees, the ones with hunger in their eyes.

Cressy had avoided their attentions by being busy and absorbed.

But I should have known I couldn't escape for ever, she thought angrily.

Except that she could. Draco was swimming strongly away from the beach. She could see the darkness of his head against the glitter of the sea.

All she had to do was grab her things, put on her shoes, and she would be free.

Free to go back to the village and wait for the evening ferry, at any rate, she reminded herself with an inward groan. Where Draco would know exactly where to find her…

She was caught in a trap of her own making, it seemed. And to sneak away as if she was genuinely scared appeared oddly demeaning anyway.

It would certainly be more dignified to stay where she was. To treat any overtures he might make with cool and dismissive courtesy. And then return to the village in time for a meal at the taverna and her homeward boat trip exactly as she'd planned.

Maybe Draco needed to learn that, for all his good looks and sexual charisma, not all tourists were pushovers.

And he'd virtually guaranteed that she was safe with him, that traditional Greek hospitality would remain paramount, and, in a strange way, she believed him.

Unless, of course, she chose differently. And there was no chance of that.

So she would stay—for a while. Because she was in control of the situation.

But only because he's allowing you to be, niggled the small, irritating voice.

Ignoring it, Cressy reapplied her sun cream, put on her dark glasses and reached for the book she'd brought with her.

When Draco came back he'd find her composed and occupied, and not prepared to be involved in any more verbal tangles.

Distance was the thing, she told herself. And this beach was quite big enough for both of them.

She did not hear his return up the beach—he moved with the noiseless, feline grace of a panther—but she sensed that he was there, just the same. She kept her shoulder slightly turned and her eyes fixed rigidly on the printed page, a silent indication that the story was too gripping to brook interruption.

At the same time she'd expected her signals to be ignored. That he'd at least make some comment about her decision to remain. But as the soundless minutes passed Cressy realised she might be mistaken.

She ventured a swift sideways look, and saw with unreasoning annoyance that Draco was lying face down on his towel, his eyes closed, apparently fast asleep.

She bit her lip, and turned her page with a snap.

But it was all to no avail, she realised five minutes later. She simply couldn't concentrate. She was far too conscious of the man stretched out beside her.

She closed her book and studied him instead. She wondered how old he was. At least thirty, she surmised. Probably slightly more. He wore no jewellery—no me-

dallions, earrings or other gifts from grateful ladies. Just
an inexpensive wristwatch, she noted. And no wedding
ring either, although that probably meant nothing. If
part of his livelihood involved charming foreign woman
holidaymakers, he would hardly want to advertise the
fact that he was married.

And she could just imagine his poor wife, she thought
with asperity, staring up at the sky. Dressed in the ubiq-
uitous black, cooking, cleaning and working in the
fields and olive groves while her husband pursued his
other interests on the beaches and beside the swimming
pools on Alakos—and nice work if you could get it.

'So what have you decided about me?'

Cressy, starting violently, turned her head and found
Draco watching her, his mouth twisted in amusement
and all signs of slumber fled.

There was no point in pretending or prevaricating.
She said flatly, 'I don't have enough evidence to make
a judgement.'

His brows lifted. 'What can I tell you?'

'Nothing.' Cressy shrugged. 'After all, it's unlikely
that we'll meet again. Let's be content to remain strangers.'

'That is truly what you want?' His tone was curious.

'I've just said so.'

'Then why did you stare at me as if you were trying
to see into my heart?'

'Is that what I was doing?' Cressy made a business
of applying more sun cream to her legs. 'I—I didn't
realise.'

He shook his head reprovingly. 'Another foolish lie,
matia mou.'

Cressy replaced the cap on the sun cream as if she
was wringing someone's neck.

'Very well,' she said. 'If you want to play silly games. What do you do for a living, *kyrie*?'

He lifted a shoulder. 'A little of this. A little of that.'

I can imagine. Aloud, she said, 'That's hardly an answer. I suppose the caique moored in the next cove is yours, and I've seen you dance, so I'd guess you're primarily a fisherman but you also do hotel work entertaining the guests. Am I right?'

'I said you were astute, *thespinis*,' he murmured. 'You read me as you would a balance sheet.'

'It really wasn't that difficult.'

'Truly?' There was slight mockery in his tone. 'Now, shall I tell you about you, I wonder?'

'There's very little to say,' Cressy said swiftly. 'You already know what my work is.'

'Ah.' The dark eyes held hers steadily for a moment. 'But I was not thinking of work.' He got to his feet, dusting sand from his legs. 'However, you have reminded me, *thespinis*, that I cannot enjoy the sun and your company any longer. I have to prepare for this evening's performance.' He slung his towel over his shoulder and picked up his rucksack.

He smiled down at her. *'Kalispera, matia mou.'*

'You keep calling me that, *kyrie*,' Cressy said with a snap, angrily aware of an odd disappointment at his departure. 'What does it mean?'

For one fleeting moment his hand brushed her cheek, pushing back an errant strand of silky hair.

He said softly, 'It means "my eyes". And my name, if you recall, is Draco. Until we meet again.'

He'd hardly touched her, Cressy repeated to herself for the fourth or fifth time. There was nothing to get upset about. He'd pushed her hair behind her ear, and that

was all. He hadn't touched her breast or any of her
exposed skin, as he could so easily have done.

All that time she'd carefully kept her distance. Built
the usual invisible wall around herself.

And then, with one brief, casual gesture, he'd invaded
her most personal space. And there hadn't been a
damned thing she could do about it.

Oh, there'd been nothing overtly sexual in his
touch—she couldn't accuse him of that—yet she'd felt
the tingle of her body's response in the innermost core
of her being. Known a strange, draining languor as he
had walked away. And a sharp, almost primitive need
to call him back again.

And that was what she couldn't accept—couldn't
come to terms with. That sudden dangerous weakness.
The unexpected vulnerability.

God knows what I'd have done if he'd really come
on to me, she brooded unhappily.

But the most galling aspect of all was that he'd been
the one who'd chosen to leave, and not herself.

I should have gone the moment I woke up and saw
him there, Cressy told herself in bitter recrimination. I
should have been very English and very outraged at
having my privacy disturbed. End of story.

For that matter, the story was over now, she admitted
with an inward shrug. She just hadn't been the one to
write *Finis*, that was all. And, while she might regret it,
there was no need to eat her heart out either.

When she'd heard the thrum of the caique's engine
as it passed the cove she'd tried hard to keep her attention fixed on her book. When she'd finally risked a
quick glance she had found, to her fury, that he was
waving to her from the tiller.

But at least he had been sailing in the opposite di-

rection to the harbour, and she wouldn't run the risk of
bumping into him there while she was waiting for the
ferry.

And now she had the cove to herself again, just as
she'd wanted. Except that it was no longer the peaceful
sanctuary that she'd discovered a few hours before.
Because she felt restless, suddenly, and strangely dis-
satisfied.

She wanted to cry out, It's all spoiled, like an angry,
thwarted child.

But there was nothing to be gained by sitting about
counting her wrongs, she thought with a saving grace
of humour.

She went for a last swim, relishing the freshness of
the water now a slight breeze had risen, hoping wryly
that it would cool her imagination as well as her body.

She collected the bicycle and stood for a moment,
debating what to do next. It was too early for dinner
and, now that the searing afternoon heat had abated, she
decided she might as well see what remained of Myros.
It was only a small island, and the circular tour would
probably take no more than an hour.

It was very much a working island, she soon realised.
The interior might be rocky and inhospitable, but on the
lower slopes fields had been ploughed and vines and
olives were being cultivated, along with orchards of citrus fruits. The scattered hamlets she passed through
seemed prosperous enough, and the few people she encountered offered friendly smiles and greetings.

And, contrary to what Yannis had suggested, the road
to the north of the island even had some sort of surface.

So Cressy was disconcerted to find her path suddenly
blocked by tall wrought-iron gates and a stone wall.

It seemed that the public road had suddenly become private.

Cressy dismounted and tried the gates, but they were securely locked and she could only rattle them in mild frustration. Beyond them she could see a drive winding upwards between olive groves, then, intriguingly, curving away out of sight, making it impossible to guess what lay further on.

She walked along the side of the wall for a while, but it seemed to stretch for ever, and eventually she was forced to retrace her steps.

Apparently, a whole section of the island had been turned into a no-go area. And all she could do was turn back.

After that disappointment, the puncture was almost inevitable.

Cressy brought her untrustworthy steed to a juddering halt and surveyed the damage, cursing herself mentally for having been lured into such an extensive trip.

Now she was faced with a long walk back to the port, pushing the bicycle.

The breeze had strengthened, whipping up the dust from the road and sending irritating particles into her eyes and mouth. She'd finished her water some time before, and she felt hot, thirsty and out of sorts. What was more, she suspected she was getting a blister on her foot.

From now on, she promised herself, she'd confine her activities to the grounds of the Hellenic Imperial.

She'd limped on for another quarter of a mile when she heard the sound of a vehicle on the road behind her.

'More dust,' she muttered, dragging herself and the bicycle on to the stony verge.

A battered pick-up truck roared past, but not before Cressy had managed to catch a glimpse of the driver.

She said a despairing, 'Oh, no—it can't be…' as the truck braked sharply and began to reverse back to where she was standing.

He said, 'How good to meet again so soon. I did not expect it.'

She said crisply, 'Nor I. You were on board a boat, *kyrie*. Now you're driving a truck. What next, I wonder?'

'Probably my own two feet, *thespinis*—like you.' Draco slanted a smile at her through the open window. 'Get in, and I will drive you back to the port.'

'I'm enjoying the walk,' Cressy said regally, and he sighed.

'More lies, *matia mou*. When will you learn?' He swung himself down from the truck, picked up the bicycle and tossed it onto a pile of sacks in the back of the vehicle, then gave Cressy a measuring look. 'You wish to travel like that, or with me?'

Glaring at him, Cressy scrambled into the passenger seat. 'Do you always get your own way?'

He shrugged. 'Why not?'

She could think of a hundred reasons without repeating herself, but she said nothing, sitting beside him in mutinous silence as the pick-up lurched down the track.

At least he'd changed out of those appalling shorts, she thought, stealing a lightning glance from under her lashes. He was now wearing clean but faded jeans and a white shirt, open at the neck with the sleeves turned back over his tanned forearms. And he seemed to have shaved.

All ready for the evening conquests, no doubt.

After a while, he said, 'You are not in a very good mood after your day on the beach.'

Cressy shrugged. 'It started well,' she said stonily. 'Then went downhill fast.'

'As you tried to do on Yannis's bicycle?' He was grinning. 'Not wise.'

'So I discovered,' she admitted tautly. 'Now all I want is to get back to Alakos.'

'You don't like my island?'

'It isn't that at all,' she denied swiftly. 'But I'm hot, dusty, and my hair's full of salt. I need a shower, a cold drink and a meal.'

'*Katavaleno*. I understand.' He swerved to avoid a major pothole. 'So, tell me what you think of Myros?'

'I like what I've seen.' Cressy paused. 'But some of it seems to be cordoned off.'

'Ah,' he said. 'You have been to the north of the island. Some rich people have their houses there.'

'They clearly like their privacy.' She frowned. 'Don't the islanders mind?'

'There is enough room for all of us.' He shrugged. 'If they wish to stay behind high walls, that is their problem.'

There was a silence, then he said, 'When I saw you, you were limping. Why?'

Cressy fought back a gasp.

She said curtly, 'You don't miss much, do you? My foot's a little sore, that's all.'

'You have sprained your ankle?'

'No—nothing like that.'

'What, then?'

Cressy hesitated. 'It's just a small blister.' She forced a smile. 'I seem to have lost the knack of walking.'

He nodded. 'And also of living, I think.'

Cressy flushed. 'So you keep saying. But it's not true. I have a terrific life. I'm very successful, and very happy. And you have no right to imply otherwise,' she added hotly. 'You don't know me, or anything about me.'

'I am trying,' he said. 'But you don't make it easy.'

'Then perhaps you should take the hint,' she flashed. 'Find a more willing subject to analyse.'

She was suddenly thrown across the seat as Draco swung the wheel, turning his ramshackle vehicle on to the verge, where he stopped.

'What are you doing?' Cressy struggled to regain her balance, feeling her breath quicken as Draco turned slowly to face her.

'You think you are unwilling?' The agate eyes glittered at her. 'But you are wrong. You are only unaware.'

He allowed that to sink in, nodding slightly at her indrawn breath, then went on, 'As for the happiness and the success you speak of, I see no such things in you. A woman who is fulfilled has an inner light. Her eyes shine, her skin blooms. But when I look into your eyes I see sadness and fear, *matia mou*.'

He paused. 'And not all high walls are made of stone. Remember that.'

Cressy's back was rigid. She said raggedly, 'I'm sure this chat-up line works with some people, but not with me, *kyrie*. You're insolent, and arrogant, and I'd prefer to walk the rest of the way.'

Draco restarted the truck. 'You will hurt no one but yourself, *thespinis*. And you will walk nowhere until that blister has received attention,' he added curtly. 'So don't be a fool.'

She had never been so angry. She sat with her arms

wrapped round her body, damming back the words of fury and condemnation that threatened to choke her. Fighting back tears, too, unexpected and inexplicable.

She didn't move until the truck stopped outside Yannis's taverna, and she turned to make a measured and final exit, only to find herself fighting with the recalcitrant door catch.

Draco had no such problems, she realised with gritted teeth as he jumped out of the driving seat and appeared beside her. In a second the door was open, and Cressy found herself being lifted out of the passenger side and carried round the side of the taverna to a flight of white-painted stone steps.

Gasping, she began to struggle, trying vainly to get her arms free so that she could hit him. 'How dare you? You bastard. Put me down—put me down now.'

She saw Yannis in a doorway with a plump, pretty woman in a faded red dress standing beside him, their faces masks of astonishment. Heard Draco bark some kind of command in his own language as he started up the steps with Cressy still pinned helplessly against his chest.

The door at the top of the stairs was standing open, and Cressy was carried through it into a corridor lined by half a dozen doors in dark, carved wood.

Draco opened the nearest and shouldered his way in. It was a large room, its pale walls tinged with the glow of sunset from the half-open shutters at the window.

The floor was tiled and there was a chest of drawers, a clothes cupboard and a large bed covered in immaculate white linen, towards which she was being relentlessly carried.

And her anger gave way to swift, nerve-shredding panic.

As Draco put her down on the coverlet, she heard herself whisper, 'No—please...' and hated the note of pleading in her voice.

Draco straightened, his face cold, his mouth a thin line. 'Do not insult me. I have told Maria to come to you. Now, wait there.'

As he reached the door, he was met by the plump woman carrying towels, a basket containing soap and shampoo, and, most welcome of all, a bottle of drinking water.

She rounded on Draco, her voice shrill and scolding, and he grinned down at her, lifting his hands in mock surrender as he went out, closing the door behind him.

Maria looked at Cressy, her dark eyes unwelcoming. She said in slow, strongly accented English, 'Who are you, *kyria*, and what are you doing here?'

Cressy said wearily, 'I don't think I know any more.' And at last her precarious self-control slipped, and she burst into a flood of tears.

CHAPTER FOUR

SHE hadn't intended it, but it was probably the best thing she could have done. Because next moment she'd been swept into Maria's embrace and was being cooed at in Greek, while a surprisingly gentle hand stroked her hair.

When the choking sobs began to subside, she was urged into the little tiled shower-room.

'All will be well, little one,' Maria said as she left her alone. 'You will see. Men,' she added in a tone of robust disapproval.

The warm water and shampoo provided a healing therapy of their own, and Cressy felt almost human again as she wandered back into the bedroom with the largest towel wrapped round her like a sarong.

She checked in surprise because her discarded clothing seemed to have vanished. True, she hadn't been looking forward to putting it on again, but, apart from a change of underwear in her bag, it was all she had. And she could hardly travel back to Alakos in a towel.

Then she saw that there was something lying on the bed—a dress in filmy white cotton, with a full skirt and a square neck embroidered with flowers.

She heard a sound at the door, and turned eagerly. 'Oh, Maria,' she began, and stopped, her breath catching in her throat, as Draco strode into the room.

She swallowed, her hand instinctively going to the knot that secured the towel in place.

She said icily, 'Get out of here—now. Or I'll scream for Maria.'

'You will need strong lungs. Maria is busy in the kitchen.' He put down the bowl he was carrying on the table beside the bed. 'And I am here on an errand of mercy. Let me see your foot.'

'My foot is fine.'

'You wish to have an infection?' His tone was inflexible. 'And spend the rest of your vacation in hospital?' He pointed to the bed. 'Sit down.'

'You have an answer for everything,' Cressy said as she mutinously obeyed. 'I suppose you trained as a doctor between fishing and dancing in restaurants.'

His mouth twisted. 'No, *thespinis*. I took a course in common sense.'

He knelt in front of her and lifted her foot gently to examine it. His fingers were gentle and cool, and she felt a strange shiver of awareness glide between her shoulder blades and down her spine. He glanced up.

'I am hurting you?'

'No.' Cressy bit her lip, trying to appear composed. But it wasn't easy. The clean, male scent of him seemed to fill her consciousness, and she found herself breathing more deeply, inhaling the faint fragrance of soap and clean linen. The silky black curls were inches from her hand, and she wondered how they would feel as her fingers caressed them.

Beneath the towel, she could feel her skin warming in swift, unbidden excitement. Feel her hardening nipples graze against the rough fabric...

Oh, God, what am I doing?

Aloud, she said urgently, 'Look—there's no need for you to do this. I can manage—really.'

'You don't like to be touched?'

'I've never thought about it.' She found herself startled into honesty.

'Then think now.' He paused, and there was a sudden harshness in his voice. 'Do you like to be in the arms of your lover?'

'Of course,' she said, and was glad that his head was bent, and that this time he could not look into her eyes and see that she was lying again.

She was expecting more questions, but he was suddenly silent, concentrating, presumably, on what he was doing.

There was disinfectant in the bowl that he'd brought, and Cressy tried not to wince as he swabbed the blister.

'What's that?' she asked dubiously as he uncapped a small pot of pale green ointment.

'It is made from herbs,' he said. 'It will help you to heal.'

When he'd finished, Cressy had a small, neat dressing held in place by a strip of plaster.

'*Efharisto,*' she said unwillingly. 'Thank you. It—it feels better already.'

'Good,' he said, getting to his feet. 'Then you will be able to dance with me tonight.'

'No,' Cressy said, feeling her heart thud painfully against her ribcage. 'No, I couldn't possibly.'

'Why not? Because your lover would not like it if he knew?'

'Perhaps.' Cressy examined her plaster with renewed interest. This non-existent boyfriend was proving useful, she thought. She had a dress ring in her luggage at the hotel. From now on she would wear it—on her engagement finger.

'Then why is he not here with you—making sure that no other man's hand touches his woman?'

She shrugged. 'He didn't want to come. He—he doesn't like very hot weather.'

'He has ice in his veins—this Englishman.' The harshness in his tone was inlaid with contempt.

'On the contrary.' Cressy moved her foot cautiously. 'But we have a modern relationship, *kyrie*. We don't have to spend every minute of every day together. We—like our space.'

He said slowly, 'If you belonged to me, *matia mou*, I would not let you out of my sight.'

She raised her eyebrows. 'Isn't that a little primitive?'

'Perhaps.' His mouth smiled but the agate eyes were oddly hard. 'But it is also—effective.'

He picked up the bowl and the roll of plaster. 'Come down when you are ready, *thespinis*. Yannis is waiting to cook your dinner.'

'I can't come down,' she said. 'I have nothing to wear.'

Draco indicated the dress that was lying on the bed. 'You call this nothing? Maria has put it here for you. It would honour her for you to wear it. And be an honour for you, too,' he added sharply. 'It was her wedding dress.'

'Oh.' Cressy swallowed. 'I had no idea. Then of course I must...' Her voice tailed away.

He replaced the dress carefully, then went to the door.

He said, 'I will tell them to expect you—to dine, and then to dance.'

And was gone.

Maria must have been very much slimmer at the time of her marriage, Cressy reflected, for the dress was almost a perfect fit.

Of course, the canvas shoes didn't really do it justice, but they'd have to suffice.

She'd brushed her damp hair until it hung, sleek and shining, to her shoulders, and applied a touch of colour to her mouth.

Now, she circled doubtfully in front of the long narrow mirror fixed to the wall. No one at her City office would have recognised her, she thought. She hardly recognised herself.

I look about seventeen, she thought. Except that I never looked like this when I was seventeen.

It wasn't just the dress. There was something in her face—something soft, almost wistful, that was new and unfamiliar. Under their fringe of lashes, her eyes were dreaming.

My eyes. That was what he had called her. Matia mou.

Only she wasn't going to think about that any more—what he'd said, or done. She was going to eat her meal, get on her ferry, and go back to the sanctuary of her expensive hotel. And if he turned up there, Security would know how to deal with him.

She nodded fiercely, and went down to the courtyard of the taverna.

Yannis welcomed her with extravagant admiration, and Maria appeared in the kitchen doorway, smiling mistily.

But Draco, as a cautious glance round soon revealed, was nowhere to be seen.

Perhaps the mention of a boyfriend had produced the desired result, Cressy told herself, firmly quashing an unwelcome tingle of disappointment.

To her surprise, the taverna was busy, and not just with local people. One of the tour companies had brought a crowd over from Alakos, it seemed, and most of the tables had been rearranged in a long line under the striped awning, and people, laughing and talking, were taking their seats there.

Yannis took Cressy to a secluded corner, protected by latticework screens covered, in turn, by a flowering vine.

He brought her ouzo, followed by dishes of taramasalata and houmous, and juicy black olives, with a platter of fresh bread.

As she sampled them, Cressy saw that a group of bouzouki players had arrived and were tuning their instruments.

For the dancing, thought Cressy with sudden unease. She sent a restive glance at her watch.

'There is a problem?' No mistaking that deep voice. Cressy looked up, shocked, to see Draco depositing a bottle of white wine on the table and taking the seat opposite.

Her warning antennae had let her down badly this time, she thought, biting her lip.

She hurried into speech. 'I was wondering about the ferry. What time does it leave?'

He sent an amused glance at the exuberant holiday-makers. 'When these people are ready to go. There is no hurry.' He paused. 'Or are you so anxious to leave us?'

She kept her voice even. 'I think it's time that I got back to the real world.'

'Or what passes for reality at the Hellenic Imperial hotel,' he said softly.

'You don't approve of such places?'

He shrugged. 'The islands need tourists, and tourists need hotels. They can prove—lucrative.'

'Especially,' Cressy said waspishly, 'for someone like you.'

His grin was unabashed. 'I do not deny it.' He picked up her glass to fill it with wine.

She said, 'I didn't order that.'

He smiled at her. 'It is a gift.'

'I didn't expect that either.'

'You ask for so little, *matia mou*. It is one of your many charms.'

Cressy flushed. 'If you really want to do me a favour, *kyrie*, you'll stop calling me *matia mou*.'

His brows lifted. 'Why?'

'Because it's—inappropriate. In my country it could be construed as harassment.'

She couldn't believe how prim and humourless she sounded.

He said quietly, 'But you are in my country now. On my island. And things are different here.'

'Is that a warning?' She stiffened.

'Do you feel that you are in danger?'

Yes, she wanted to scream. Yes—and I don't understand what's happening to me. I don't want this.

Aloud, she said lightly, 'I'm the stranger within your gates, *kyrie*. Isn't that what you told me? I've eaten your bread, and now I'm drinking your wine.' She lifted her glass towards him, then took a mouthful. It was cool and crisp against her dry throat. 'So why should I be afraid?'

He raised his own glass. '*Stin iyia sas*. To you, *thespinis*, and to your beauty in that dress. If your lover was here, he would beg on his knees to make you his bride.' He drank, and put down his glass.

He said softly, his gaze holding hers, 'I will make a bargain with you. I will not call you "my eyes" until

your eyes promise me that I may. And, in return, you
will tell me your given name.'

Under the cool white cotton, her skin felt as if it was
on fire.

She lifted her chin. 'Very well, *kyrie*. I'm called
Cressida.'

'Cressida,' he repeated thoughtfully. 'The golden
one—who was faithless to her lover Troilus.'

'According to Shakespeare, and the other men who
wrote about her,' Cressy said crisply. 'She, of course,
might have had a different viewpoint. And, if it comes
to that, your own namesake isn't much to brag about—
a tyrant imposing laws that no one could live under.
Although that shouldn't surprise me,' she added with
warmth.

'Quarrelling?' Yannis arrived with two plates of
grilled swordfish, Greek salads, and a big bowl of fries.
'Not while you eat my food, or you will get bad stom-
achs.' He wagged an admonishing finger at them both,
and went off.

Draco grinned at her. 'He is right. Let us begin
again.'

He held out his hand. '*Hero poli*, Cressida. I am
pleased to meet you.'

Reluctantly, she allowed her fingers to be enclosed in
the warmth of his. '*Hero poli*—Draco.'

'And your name is very beautiful,' he added.

Cressy wrinkled her nose. 'I used to hate it,' she confessed. 'But then I hated everything about being a girl.
I wanted so badly to be a boy when I was little that my
father used to call me Sid as a joke. My mother was
very cross about it, so he'd never use it in front of her.
Only when we were on our own.'

'And does he still call you—Sid?' His brows lifted.

Cressy looked down at her plate. 'Not for a long time,' she said quietly.

'I am not surprised.' He gave a faint smile. 'I must tell you, Cressida, that you are no boy.'

She met the sudden intensity of the dark eyes and flushed, reaching hurriedly for her knife and fork.

The swordfish was succulent and delicious, and she ate every scrap, even conducting a laughing battle with Draco over the last few fries.

'It is good to meet a woman who does not wish to starve herself,' he told her as he refilled her glass.

She shook her head. 'One of these days all these calories will suddenly explode, and I'll turn into a mountain.'

'No.' The dark eyes travelled over her in smiling, sensuous appraisal. 'For me, you will always look as you do now, *agapi mou*.'

Cressy frowned. 'What does that mean?' she asked suspiciously.

He laughed. 'It is best that you don't know.'

Cressy felt her colour deepen helplessly. To cover her confusion, she turned to watch the bouzouki players, tapping her fingers on the table to the music.

Draco was watching her. 'You like bouzouki?'

'I don't know very much,' she admitted. 'Just "Zorba's Dance", like everyone else.' She hesitated. 'I liked what you were dancing to this morning.'

'That was also by Theodorakis.' He smiled faintly. 'He is still very much a hero. A man whose music spoke to the people.'

She said, 'I—I hope you're going to dance tonight.'

'Only if you will promise, just once, to be my partner.'

'But I couldn't,' Cressy protested. 'I've never done any Greek dancing.'

'I did not mean that. When the entertainment is over, Yannis plays other music.' The agate eyes glittered at her. 'We will choose something very slow—very sweet—so that you won't hurt your foot.'

'Oh.' Cressy felt hollow inside, but she mustered a smile. 'Thank you.'

'Would you like some dessert? Halva, perhaps—or baklava?'

'Just coffee, please.'

He said, 'I'll fetch it.'

She watched him lithely threading his way between the tables, and saw without surprise that several of the woman holidaymakers from the large party were watching him too, nudging each other and exchanging whispered comments and giggles.

I could always send a note over saying, 'He's available,' Cressy thought sourly. Only people might get killed in the rush.

She'd come away on holiday to relax, yet she'd never felt so edgy and restless in her life.

She'd had her day and her evening neatly planned, but here she was, in another woman's wedding dress, having dinner with a man who supplemented his income by 'befriending' lonely women.

And she wasn't lonely, she told herself vehemently. Yes, she missed her father's company, but she had plenty of friends. She could go out every night, if she wanted. And there were plenty of men who'd be keen to escort her.

Which was fine. It was when they tried to get closer that warning bells started to ring and she felt herself freeze.

No man was prepared to be held at arm's length for ever. She understood that perfectly well. She'd always assumed that one of her casual friendships would eventually bloom into something deeper. Something based on liking and respect, rather than casual physical attraction.

She'd always sworn she'd never be caught in that trap.

So a holiday romance had never been on the cards.

Draco was good-looking, with a sexual aura as powerful as a force field, but this time he'd chosen the wrong target, she told herself with determination.

Their acquaintance would end with dinner, as she would make clear.

I'll pay Yannis for the meal, she thought, and ask him to tell Draco goodbye for me.

And then she'd never set foot on Myros again. She would arrange for the hotel to launder and return Maria's dress and collect her own things. And that would be an end to it.

She looked round for Yannis, but at the same moment the bouzouki players struck up again, and she saw that he and three other men had formed a line and begun to dance, their hands resting on each other's shoulders. It was a slow, intricate dance, but their movements were perfectly synchronised, and strangely dignified, Cressy thought, watching, entranced.

This wasn't just a cabaret act, as it was at the hotel, she realised as she joined the rest of the audience in clapping in time to the music. These were men to whom their own culture was a living, breathing thing.

The music quickened its pace. The dance changed to include Maria and a couple of other women, and, gradually, the crowd from Alakos were persuaded to join in too, weaving their way between the tables in a long, twirling chain.

A waiter appeared at her side with coffee. 'For you, *thespinis*. Kyrios Draco says he is to dance next.'

Giving her an ideal chance to slip away, thought Cressy. As the waiter moved off, she stopped him. *'O logariasimos, parakolo?'* Adding, 'May I have the bill, please?' in case he didn't understand her attempt at Greek.

But he didn't seem to have much grasp of English either, because he shrugged, smilingly spread his hands, and kept on walking.

The dance finished and everyone sat down, laughing and talking.

When the music started again, it was slow and haunting, almost plaintive.

Cressy knew that Draco had appeared, because the chattering voices were stilled suddenly, and there was a new tension in the air. She stared down at her coffee, not wanting to look up—not wanting to watch, but eventually impelled to.

Across the distance that divided them, above the heads of the crowd, his eyes met hers—held them steadily. He inclined his head in silent acknowledgement. Then he began to dance.

Yannis and the other men knelt in a half-circle around him, clapping the rhythm. Tonight, there was none of the exuberance she'd seen that morning. The movements were as passionate, but they spoke of pain and isolation. The music seemed to wail and weep, emphasising the yearning expressed by his taut body.

Cressy, totally enthralled, saw weariness and suffering. And every so often a dangerous flicker of wildness.

She thought, with an odd certainty, This is about love—and the loss of love…

When it stopped, there was silence for a moment, and then the applause broke out, wave after wave of it, and people were standing to take photographs.

When disco music began to play over the sound system it was almost a shock. But no one else could have followed Draco, she thought.

Everyone was up on their feet, joining in, jigging around vigorously. Glad, she thought, to dispel some of the emotion of the last few minutes.

Cressy noticed the girl at once. She was red-haired and pretty, wearing a tiny Lycra skirt and a skimpy top displaying a generous amount of cleavage. Her hand was on Draco's arm and she was smiling up at him, moving closer, her whole body an invitation.

Cressy put down her coffee cup, aware that her hand was shaking. She knew an overwhelming impulse to rush over to them—to drag the redhead away—to slap her—scratch her nails down that simpering face.

But she wasn't a violent person, she told herself vehemently. She never had been.

Except that she'd never been jealous before. And that made all the difference.

The resentment she felt for Eloise didn't even feature on the same scale, she thought, closing her eyes, conscious that she felt slightly sick.

She and Draco came from two different worlds. So how could she possibly feel these things for a total stranger—someone she didn't want? That she couldn't want…

The soundtrack had changed to something soft and dreamy, and Cressy kept her eyes shut, because she didn't want to see the red-haired girl in Draco's arms.

His voice, soft and amused, said, 'It is too soon to sleep, *agapi mou*. You have a bargain to keep.'

She looked up at him, feeling her stomach muscles clench in unwelcome excitement and longing.

She said coolly, 'Shouldn't you be spending time with your adoring public?'

His grin was appreciative. 'She was beautiful, *ne*?' He whistled. 'Such a mouth—such breasts.' Lazily, he scanned Cressy's indignantly parted lips, then let his gaze travel slowly downwards. That was all he did, yet for one dizzy, scared moment she knew how his mouth would feel on hers—recognised the intimate touch of his hands on her body.

He went on quietly, 'But I am here with you, my golden one, so don't disappoint me.'

He held out his hand, and, silently, she rose from her seat and went with him. Felt his arms close round her, drawing her against him. Cressy surrendered, sliding her own arms round his firm waist and resting her cheek against his chest as they moved quietly together to the music, one tune fading effortlessly into another.

She was not an accomplished dancer, yet in Draco's arms she seemed to drift in perfect attunement, as if she was part of him. It might have been a dream, except that she was only too aware of the physical reality of his nearness.

She was trembling inside, her body tingling as the warmth of his skin invaded her thin layers of clothing, giving her the helpless impression that she was naked in his arms. Shocking her by the sudden scalding heat of desire.

There were no pretences anymore. He was as aroused as she was.

He whispered against her ear, his voice raw and urgent, 'You feel it too, *ne*, my girl, my heaven? This need we have for each other?'

She pulled away, staring up at him, her eyes wide, the pupils dilated as she met the glint of golden fire in his.

She said hoarsely, 'I—I can't do this. I have to go—have to...'

And stopped, as she realised they were alone. The courtyard was deserted. Yannis and his helpers had vanished into the taverna, the glass doors discreetly closed behind them, and the crowd from Alakos had gone.

She said on a little sob, 'The ferry—oh, God, the ferry...'

She ran out of the courtyard and down the street towards the harbour, but Draco caught her before she'd gone more than a few yards.

'The ferry has gone,' he said.

'But you knew I had to catch it. You knew that.' Her voice shook. 'Now I'm stranded. Oh, *hell*. What am I going to do?'

'You stay here,' he said calmly. 'It's not a problem.'

'Yes,' she said bitterly. 'Oh, yes, it is. You don't understand...'

'I know more than you think.' He put his hands on her shoulders, looking down into her angry, frightened face. 'You believe I have kept you here to share my bed tonight, but you are wrong. I shall sleep at my own house, and you will stay here with Yannis and Maria.'

Cressy gasped. 'When was this decided?'

'When we realised that there would be no room for you on the ferry. An overcrowded boat is not safe, particularly when many of the passengers have been drinking Metaxa. It is better to wait for tomorrow.'

She bit her lip. 'Very well.' She paused. 'But the hotel. They'll know I haven't come back...'

'Yannis has telephoned them, so all is well.'

She said quietly, 'Then there's nothing left to say.'

The music had stopped when they came back to the courtyard, and the lights were out.

Draco walked beside her, his tread as quiet as a cat's. He did not touch her, but she felt him in every fibre of her being.

He would kiss her, she thought confusedly, and she wanted him to. In fact, she ached for him. But she'd betrayed too much already, while they were dancing. And when his mouth touched hers she would have no defences left.

No strength to say no when he walked up the moonlit stairs beside her to the quiet, cool room with the wide bed. No power to resist when he drew her down into his arms.

His for the taking, she thought. And he would know that, and would take...

They reached the foot of the stone steps and she paused uncertainly, waiting for him to reach for her.

He said softly, 'Until tomorrow—Cressida the golden. But now—*kalinichta*. Goodnight.' And she felt the brush of his lips against her hair, as swift and tantalising as a butterfly's wing.

And then she was free, walking up the stairs alone, and bewildered. She turned at the top of the stairs and looked down at him, the still shadow waiting there. Watching her go.

She said huskily, 'I don't understand. What do you want from me?'

'I want everything, *agapi mou*.' There was a strange

harshness in his voice. 'All you have to give. And nothing less will do.' He paused. 'But I can wait.'

He turned away into the darkness, leaving Cressy standing motionless, her hand pressed to her trembling mouth.

CHAPTER FIVE

'MISS FIELDING—are you all right?'

Cressida started violently, and looked up to see one of the senior nurses standing beside her.

'Yes,' she said. 'I'm fine. I'm sorry—I was miles away.'

A thousand miles, she thought, and another world...

'I'm going to ask you to go to the visitors' room for a little while. The consultant is coming to see your father, and he'll talk to you afterwards.'

'Of course.' She almost stumbled up from her chair and along the corridor. It wasn't a comfortable room. There was a table in the middle of the room with magazines, and a few moulded plastic chairs ranged round the walls.

She went over to the window and looked out at a vista of rooftops.

She felt ashamed. She was supposed to be here for her father, trying to infuse him with her own youth and strength, and instead she'd allowed herself to daydream—to remember things far better forgotten. A time that was past and done with.

Except...

The memory of that enigmatic e-mail message would not be so easily dismissed.

I am waiting for you.

It can't be him, she denied, almost violently. I won't believe it.

She grabbed a magazine from the table and sat down,

only to open it at a page recommending Greek holidays. She looked at the crescent of bleached sand fringed by turquoise water in the picture and realised bleakly that there was no refuge from her memories.

They crowded her mind, filling it. Drawing her inexorably back to Myros.

She'd hardly slept that first night at the taverna. She had been too aware of the danger threatening her to be able to relax. And Draco was the most danger she'd ever encountered in her life.

No wonder he was a fisherman, she had thought, turning over restlessly and thumping the flat pillow with her fist. He knew exactly how to keep a woman hooked and helpless.

But he wouldn't reel her in. She wouldn't allow it to happen. She was her own person, and her plan didn't include casual sex. It never had.

Draco had to learn that no matter how attractive he might be he was not always going to win.

And he'd soon find consolation. Every time he danced there'd be a queue of eager and willing girls vying for his attention. He wouldn't have time to remember the one that got away.

She had nodded fiercely, and closed her eyes with determination.

When she'd awoken, early sun had been spilling through the slats in the shutters across the tiled floor.

The first thing she had seen was that all the things she'd used yesterday, including the beach towel, were lying pristinely laundered and neatly folded on the chair, and the white dress, which had been carefully draped there, had gone. Maria, it seemed, had performed a dawn raid.

Which I didn't intend, Cressy had thought, as she slid out of bed and headed for the shower.

When she had gone down the outside stairs, Maria had been sweeping the courtyard. To Cressy's embarrassment, it had been made immediately clear that she would be allowed to pay nothing for her night's lodging or her meal. Nor would she be permitted to have the white dress cleaned.

'It is my pleasure to do this for you,' Maria declared. 'Everyone say how beautiful you look in the dress.'

Cressy flushed a little. 'Oh?'

'Ah, yes.' Maria gave her a roguish look. 'And one person in particular, *ne*?' She pointed to the table Cressy had occupied the night before. 'Sit there, *kyria*, and I will bring you breakfast. Rolls and coffee, and some of the honey from my sister's bees.' She bustled off, leaving Cressy to take a careful look around, but she had the courtyard to herself, she realised with relief.

She consulted the list of ferry times in her bag, and saw that the first one ran in just over half an hour. She should make it easily.

Her meal also included fresh orange juice and a bowl of creamy yoghurt. By the time she got up from the table she was replete.

'I can't thank you enough,' she told Yannis and Maria when they came to say goodbye to her.

'You are welcome.' Yannis's hand closed over hers. 'Welcome at any time. Your room will always be waiting.'

Cressy's smile was a little taut. 'Maybe—one day,' she said. She hesitated. 'And please would you thank Draco for me? He's been—kind.'

She picked up her bag and headed down to the harbour, determined to be the first one on the ferry. But it wasn't moored at the landing point she'd used yesterday. In fact she couldn't see it anywhere, she realised frantically, shading her eyes and staring out to sea.

'So you did not intend to say goodbye.' Draco got up from the stack of wooden crates he'd been sitting on. The shorts he was wearing were just as disreputable as the previous pair, and he'd topped them with an unbuttoned white cotton shirt.

Cressy lifted her chin. 'I—I left a message with Maria.'

'Now you can give it to me in person.'

Exactly what she hadn't wanted. She said stiltedly, 'Just—thank you, and good luck.'

'I believe in fate more than luck.' He looked her over, smiling faintly. 'Last night you were Cressida,' he said. 'But today you are Sid again. What will you be tomorrow, *agapi mou*?'

She shook her head. She said, almost inaudibly. 'I don't think I know any more.'

'Perhaps you are being reborn,' he said. 'Rising like a phoenix from the ashes of your former life.'

She threw back her head. 'But I don't want that. I'm quite content with things as they are.'

'Content?' There was scorn in his voice. 'Is that the most you can wish for? What a small, narrow word, when there is excitement, passion and rapture to be experienced.'

'Perhaps,' she said, 'I like to feel safe.'

'There is no safety, *agapi mou*. Not in life. Not in love. As you will discover when you stop running away.' He shrugged. 'But if you wish to return to Alakos and the comfort of your hotel, I will take you.'

'Thank you,' she said. 'But I'll wait for the proper ferry.'

'Then you'll wait a long time,' he said drily. 'Kostas drank too much Metaxa last night on Alakos. There will be no ferry until tonight.'

Cressy gasped indignantly. 'Is he allowed to do that?'

Draco grinned. 'He does not usually wait for permission. It is my boat or nothing, *pethi mou*.'

She gave him a fulminating glance, then sighed. 'All right. Your boat. Just as long as I get back to Alakos.'

'Why the hurry? Are you so sure that Myros has nothing more to offer?' There was an undercurrent of mockery in his tone.

'I'm paying to stay at the Hellenic Imperial,' she reminded him tautly.

'Ah, money,' he said. 'That concerns you deeply?'

'I like to get my money's worth. But I'm sure you're far above such considerations.'

He lifted a negligent shoulder. 'It's easier not to think about it, I promise you.'

Cressy bit her lip, aware that she'd been ungracious about his undoubted poverty.

She said, 'You must let me pay you for the trip.'

He sent her a quizzical look. 'Did Yannis and Maria ask you to pay for the meal last night—or your room?'

'No,' she said. 'They didn't. But…'

'And I am no different. There is no charge.' And there was a note in his voice which told her not to argue.

She sat tensely in the bow as the caique pushed its way through the sparkling sunlit water. The faint early haze was clearing and it was going to be another scorching day, she thought, lifting her hair away from the nape of her neck.

Draco said from the tiller, 'You are too warm? There is an awning…'

'No, I'm fine,' she assured him quickly. 'It's just so—beautiful.'

'I think you are falling in love, *agapi mou*, with my country. You will never want to go home.'

She stared at the horizon. 'I think my boss would have something to say about that.'

'You are indispensable?'

'Hardly. I don't think anyone really is. We just fool ourselves, then we go, and our space is filled, and no one even remembers we were once there.'

'That is a sad thought for such a lovely day,' Draco said after a pause. 'But you will be remembered always.'

She shook her head. 'I don't think so.'

'Ah, but you will,' he said. 'By your lover, for one—and your father, for another. And I—I will remember too.'

'You will?' She sent him a look of disbelief. 'That's nonsense.'

'Of course I'll remember. It is not every day I meet a girl with hair like the sun, and moonlight in her eyes, who is called Sid.'

Her heart twisted slowly and painfully. To cover the sudden emotion, she pulled a face. 'I knew I'd regret mentioning that.'

'There is nothing to regret. It is good that your father had this special name for you.' He smiled at her. 'Sometimes when I look at you I can see the little girl you were.'

Cressy turned away and stared at the sea. She said flatly, 'She's been gone a long time.'

'You will find her again when you hold your own daughter in your arms.'

How simple he made it sound, Cressy thought, her throat aching. And how unlikely it really was.

She straightened her shoulders. 'Alakos doesn't seem to be coming any closer.'

He said, 'I thought you would wish to pay a last visit to our beach.'

'And I thought I'd made it clear I wanted to go straight back.' There was sudden ice in her voice as she turned on him, but Draco did not appear chilled.

His eyes met hers steadily. 'You offered to pay for your trip. This is the price—that you swim with me just once.'

She said acidly, 'Dancing last night. Swimming today. Do you set up a full fitness programme for all your women?'

He spoke very quietly. 'That is a suggestion that demeans us both. But if it is really what you think, then there is no more to be said.'

She watched him move the tiller, heading the caique out into the open sea.

Then she looked back at the horizon and found it suddenly blurred with unshed tears.

It was a miserably silent journey. To Cressy's surprise, Draco avoided the main harbour and sailed round to the hotel's private bay, bringing his craft skilfully alongside the small jetty.

In a subdued voice, she said, 'I don't think you're meant to be here.'

He shrugged. 'Does it matter? I shall soon be gone.'

His touch completely impersonal, he helped her ashore, and put her bag on the planking beside her.

She said in a sudden rush, 'Draco—I'm sorry—I didn't mean what I said. I—I don't want us to part bad friends, but I'm just so confused. I can't seem to get my head together...'

He nodded, but the bronze face showed no sign of softening.

'Then start listening to your heart instead, Cressida. And when you do, you know where to find me.' He pointed towards Myros. 'I shall be there—waiting for you.'

She stood on the jetty and watched until the boat was a mere speck, but he never looked back.

Cressy jumped as the door to the visitors' room opened and the consultant came in.

'Miss Fielding.' His handshake was limp for such an eminent man. 'You'll be pleased to hear that your father is making good progress. If it continues, we should be able to send him home next week.'

'Oh.' Cressy sat down on one of the uncomfortable chairs. 'Oh, that's such a relief. And the operation?'

'As soon as we consider he's fit enough.' The consultant looked vaguely round. 'Is your mother not here? I should speak to her about his future care.'

Cressy said evenly, 'My stepmother is—away.'

'Of course,' he said. 'Building up her strength to nurse the invalid at home, no doubt. Admirable.'

Cressida bent her head. 'Now may I go back to my father, please?

'You're going to be all right, Dad,' she whispered to the still figure in the bed. 'Isn't that wonderful news? I just wish you'd give some sign that you can hear me. Although I do understand that you've got to rest.

'And I can work for you, Daddy. I can deal with the bank, and the mortgage company, and everyone. I can't get your money back, but maybe I can stop you losing everything else. I'll talk to them—I'll make them listen. Because I need to work—to stop me from thinking. Remembering…'

In spite of the heat, she shivered.

She had gone straight up to the hotel, she recalled, and lain down on the bed in her air-conditioned room and stared up at the ceiling…

There was a vast, aching emptiness inside her. A trembling, frightened nothingness.

She thought, What am I doing? What have I done?

Draco's face seemed to float above her, and she closed her eyes to shut him out. But she couldn't dismiss her other senses so easily. Her skin burned as she remembered the sensuous pressure of his body against hers. She seemed to breathe the scent of him. To feel the brush of his lips on her flesh.

A little moan escaped her. She was consumed by bewildered longing, her body torn apart by physical needs that she'd never known before.

She twisted restlessly on the bed, trying to find peace and calm, but failing.

She got up and went out on to the balcony, but the indigo shimmer of Myros on the horizon drove her inside again.

She stayed in her room until midday, when she made herself go down and join the queue at the lavish buffet on the hotel's terrace.

She'd never realised before how many couples seemed to be staying at the hotel, wandering around hand in hand, or with their arms round each other.

Making her blindingly—piercingly aware of her own isolation—her own loneliness.

Making her realise that she couldn't bear it any

longer. And that she didn't have to—that she too could choose to be happy for a little while.

A few days—even a few hours, she thought. I'd settle for that. Whatever the ultimate cost.

She could tell herself a thousand times that she was crazy even to contemplate such a thing, but it made no difference. Her will power—her control didn't seem to matter any more. The ache of yearning was too strong, too compelling, and it was drawing her back.

When she told them at Reception that she was going back to Myros to stay for a while she half expected they would try to dissuade her, but her decision was accepted almost casually.

Down at the harbour, she didn't wait for the ferry, but paid one of the local boatmen to take her across to the other island.

She was trembling as she walked up from the quay towards the taverna. This was madness, and she knew it, and it would serve her right if she walked in and found Draco with someone else, she thought, pain twisting inside her. But one swift glance told her that he wasn't there.

Yannis was playing *tavli*, and his jaw dropped when he saw her. Then he recovered himself, and got to his feet smiling broadly.

The *thespinis* was welcome. It was good that she had come back. Especially as he had mended the wheel on his sister's bicycle.

Up in her room, Cressy changed into a black bikini, topping it with a scooped neck T-shirt in the same colour and a wraparound skirt in a black and white swirling print.

All the way to the beach she was straining her ears to hear music, but there was only silence and solitude.

She left the bicycle on the clifftop and scrambled down to the sand. The heat was intense, but she felt cold with disappointment.

She had been so ridiculously sure that he'd be there— waiting for her.

Was it really only twenty-four hours? she wondered, spreading her towel in the same spot. It seemed more like a year.

She slipped off her skirt and top, kicked off her sandals, and ran down to the sea, welcoming its cool caress against her overheated skin.

She needed to work off some of this emotion somehow, and a long, strenuous swim would do the trick. If only it could restore her common sense at the same time.

She drove herself on, pounding up and down as if she was covering lengths in a pool, until her arms and legs were heavy with tiredness and she knew it was time to go back.

She put a foot down, finding sand and shingle, and began to wade towards the beach, wringing the excess water out of her hair.

Out of the dazzle of the sun she saw him, standing motionless on the edge of the sea, small waves curling round his bare feet.

She began to run, cursing the pressure of the water which held her back.

He was holding her towel, she realised, and as she reached him he wrapped it round her, pulling her into his arms. She lifted her face mutely, and for the first time experienced the hungry demand of his mouth on hers.

The kiss seemed to last an eternity, as if, with that first taste, they could not get enough of each other.

He was not gentle, nor did she require him to be. His mouth clung, burned, tore at hers as if he was trying to absorb her into his being.

Her own lips parted breathlessly, welcoming the thrust of his tongue, inciting the dark, heated exploration to go deeper still. Offering herself without reserve.

Sun, sea and bleached sand were performing a crazy, spinning dance around her, and she put up her hands to grip his bare shoulders. She was trembling under this wild onslaught on her senses, her legs shaking under her.

Just as she thought she might collapse on the sand at his feet, Draco lifted her into his arms and carried her up the beach. He'd spread a rug in the shadow of some rocks and he lowered her on to it, coming down beside her, seeking her mouth again, his hand tangling in her damp blonde hair.

She surrendered her lips eagerly to the sensuous rapture of his possession. She felt as if she was drunk—or that she'd entered some other undreamed of dimension.

Her hands caressed his back, holding him to her as his mouth travelled downwards, questing the curve of her throat and the small hollows at its base.

His tongue found the cleft between her breasts and lingered, and she gasped, her body arching involuntarily, her nipples hardening in excitement under the damp fabric.

His lips brushed each soft swell of flesh above the confines of the bikini top as one hand stroked down her body to find and cup the delicate contour of her hip with total mastery. Making no secret of his intention.

He lifted his head and stared down at her, the dark eyes slumbrous, a flush of deeper colour along the high cheekbones, as if he was waiting for some sign from her.

Watching him, Cressy raised a hand and undid the halter strap of her bikini, then released the little clip, freeing the tiny garment completely.

Draco bent his head and with great precision took it from her with his teeth.

He tossed it aside and lowered his mouth fully to her bare breasts, paying them slow and languorous homage, his lips moulding their soft fullness. As she felt the provocative flicker of his tongue across the puckered rose of her nipples a little moan of surprise and longing escaped her.

His mouth enclosed each hot, excited peak in turn, pleasuring them softly and subtly. Eyes closed, Cressy gave herself up to delight, feeling her last remaining inhibitions sliding away.

At the same time his fingers were feathering across her thighs, brushing the delicate mound they guarded, and her body responded with a rush of scalding, passionate heat.

His mouth moved down her body slowly, almost druggingly, paying minute attention to each curve and hollow. He murmured softly in his own language, resting his cheek against the concavity of her stomach.

She was dimly aware that at some point he had discarded the swimming trunks that were his sole covering, but it was only when she felt the glide of his fingers against the heated, throbbing core of her womanhood that she realised that she too was now naked.

He kissed her mouth again, his tongue teasing hers as his hands continued their gentle erotic play, taking her ever closer to some brink she'd never known existed.

As her breathing quickened she felt him move slightly, his body covering hers, his hands sliding under her to lift her for his possession.

For a fleeting moment she experienced the heated pressure of him against her, seeking her. And then there was pain, and she heard her voice, muffled against his shoulder, crying out in shock and sudden panic.

He was instantly still. Then he rolled away from her almost frantically, his breath rasping in his throat.

When she dared look, he was sitting a few feet away, one leg drawn up, his forehead resting on his knee. There was a faint sheen of perspiration gleaming on his skin, and his chest heaved as he fought for control.

She whispered his name, and when there was no response reached across and put her hand lightly on his arm.

He shook her off almost violently. His voice was a snarl. 'Do not touch me. It is not safe.'

She said in a whisper, 'What is it? I don't understand…'

As the silence lengthened between them she said, more urgently, her voice shaking a little, 'Talk to me, please. Tell me what's wrong. What I've done.'

Draco turned and looked at her, his dark eyes hooded, the firm mouth compressed.

He said, 'You have done nothing wrong. The mistake, God help us both, is mine.'

He reached for his trunks and pulled them on, his face taut.

Colour stormed into her face and she grabbed clumsily for her towel, holding it in front of her defensively, just as if there was an inch of her that he'd left undiscovered.

'You lied to me, Cressida. Why?' His voice was harsh.

'Lied?' she repeated uncomprehendingly.

'You let me think you had a lover. But it is not true. So why did you pretend.'

'What did you expect me to do?' Her eyes blurred with humiliated tears. 'It was what you wanted to hear—wasn't it? And it seemed—safer.'

'No,' he said. 'It was not safe. It was a stupid lie, and a dangerous one. You thought I would not know?'

She bent her head. 'I—I didn't think so. I didn't realise it would make any difference...'

She heard him whisper something sharp and violent, then he was beside her again. He drew her towards him, cupping her face gently between his hands, making her meet his searching gaze.

He said quietly, 'It makes all the difference in the world, *agapi mou*. But I am also to blame. I should have realised that you were claiming a sophistication you did not possess.'

She said tautly, 'Of course, you know so much about women.'

'More than you know of men, certainly.'

Cressy bit her lip, unable to deny his curt response. Her voice shook slightly. 'Draco—I'm so sorry...'

'Sorry?' he repeated, his voice incredulous. 'You offer me the ultimate gift—and say you are sorry?'

She said flatly, 'But it's a gift you don't seem to want.'

His mouth relaxed into the shadow of a smile. 'You think I don't want you, *agapi mou*?' He took her hands and carried them fleetingly to his body. 'You are wrong. But a woman's innocence should not be thrown away to feed the hunger of the moment. You deserve better.'

His lips touched hers, swiftly and gently. 'Now dress yourself, and we will go back to the town, where there are more people and less temptations.'

He got to his feet and walked down the beach, where he stood, his back turned, gazing at the sea, while Cressy huddled into her clothing.

When he came back to her, she said, 'I think I'd better go back to Alakos.'

'Why should you do that?' His dark brows drew into a frown.

'Because I'm very embarrassed.' She made a business of folding her towel. 'I've made a real fool of myself.' She added carefully, 'And I'd just be in the way if I stayed.'

'Ah,' Draco said softly. 'You feel you might hinder my search for the next willing body.' He cast a despairing look at the heavens. 'Is that truly what you think of me?'

She said, 'Draco—I don't know what to think. I don't *know* you.'

'Then why did you come back?' He spoke gently, but there was an inflexible note in his voice. 'Just so that I could rid you of your unwanted virginity? I don't believe that.'

She bit her lip. 'Because I found I couldn't stay away. And now I've ruined everything.'

He sighed. 'Nothing is spoiled—unless you wish it to be.' There was a silence, then he stroked the curve of her face with one long finger. 'Is that what you want, *pethi mou*? Or shall we begin all over again? Start to learn about each other, not just with our bodies, but our minds?'

She said on a little sob, 'Oh, Draco, please.'

'Then so be it.' He took her hand, held it in his, his

fingers strong and warm. 'But understand, Cressida, that this changes everything. And if you leave me now, I shall follow. However long, however far.' He paused. 'You accept this?'

And, from some great distance, she heard herself answer, 'Yes.'

CHAPTER SIX

IT HAD just seemed a romantic thing to say on a beach, Cressy told herself as she drove home from the hospital. After all, they'd both known that their time together was going to be limited. That sooner or later the idyll would end, and she would fly back to real life.

What she hadn't foreseen was that it would indeed be much sooner.

At first, as the sunlit days had passed, she'd felt she was living in a dream, or under a spell that Draco had cast around her.

Most of her waking hours had been spent in his company, and even when she'd been asleep the image of him had never been far from her mind.

The first part of the morning she'd usually spent alone. She'd assumed that Draco was out in his boat, fishing, but when she'd mentioned this to Yannis he'd shrugged and said, 'I think he is at his house, Kyria Cressida. He is having some building done.'

Cressy understood. A lot of local houses seemed to be built in instalments, the owners occupying the ground floor until they could afford to add further storeys.

Draco had clearly made enough money to build another floor on to his, and if there was a vaguely troubling query at the back of her mind as to exactly where that money came from, she dismissed it. Nothing was allowed to impinge on her happiness.

Sometimes she wondered wistfully whether she

would ever be asked to see his house, but assumed it would never happen. These close-knit village communities might not be pleased to see one of their number with an *anglitha*, especially if he'd been earmarked for one of their daughters, she thought with a pang.

Anyway, if Draco wished to keep his private life to himself, that was his concern. He would have to go on living here after she'd gone...

She sighed. The realisation that her time in Greece was running out was causing her real pain.

I didn't really want to come here, she thought, grimacing. Now I don't want to leave.

It was hard to separate one day from another, when all of them were touched with gold. Sometimes they went out on the boat, landing on some quiet beach to swim, and cook the fish they'd caught over a wood fire.

At other times Draco drove the pick-up to the island's peaceful beauty spots, along the coast, or up into the high bare hills. And at night they danced together.

She was relaxed with him now. They shared a lot of laughter, but they could be quiet together too. When he teased her, she teased back. They had, she thought, become friends—and that was good.

But she couldn't deny the painful, ecstatic lift of her heart that happened each time he strode into the courtyard of the taverna to find her. Or the sweet, sensual ache that any physical contact with him seemed to evoke.

For much of the time he kept her at a distance, and she knew it. Just sometimes, in the drowsy afternoons, he would draw her into his arms and explore her mouth gently with his. Her hair seemed to entrance him. 'Like pale silk,' he would whisper, winding strands round his fingers and carrying them to his lips.

But—so far and no further, it seemed. The merest touch of his lips could ignite her desire, making her burn and melt with longing for the intimacy of his touch, for the consummation that her aroused flesh had been denied, but if he was aware of that, he gave no sign.

Just once, when he'd kissed her goodnight, she'd tried to hold him, pressing herself against him, her lips parting in mute invitation beneath the pressure of his. Longing to spark the passion that she knew lay just beneath the surface.

But he'd gently detached her clinging hands and stepped back, bending his head to drop a kiss on each soft palm before he let her go. And she had walked away up the stairs, knowing that he would not follow.

His control seemed to be total—and yet there were occasional moments when she felt him watching her. Was aware of a strange tension quivering along her nerve-endings, as if her body had somehow discerned the naked hunger in his and was responding to it.

Someone else was watching her too, she thought. Maria. The older woman was still warmly friendly, but once or twice Cressy had caught an anxious glance, or a little worried frown, and she wondered why.

But not too deeply. Her only real concern was the moment when she would see Draco again—would hear his voice and feel his smile touch her own mouth.

And that was all that mattered.

She didn't realise, of course, how swiftly and how finally things could change.

She woke early that day on Myros, to the bleak realisation that there was just over a week of her holiday left. She sat up in bed, hugging her knees, frowning a little. Maybe this was the time to walk away—while she still could. Before she was in too deep and reduced to begging.

Draco had told her the previous evening that he would come for her just after breakfast.

'So for once you're not going to work on your house.' Cressy had raised her eyebrows. 'I'm honoured.' She'd paused. 'How's it getting on—the house, I mean?'

He had shrugged. 'It is almost finished. It has taken longer than I thought.'

She'd been tempted to say, I'd love to see it, simply to test his reaction, but she had remained silent.

When she considered, the house was the least of it. There were so many things she still didn't know about him, she thought, her frown deepening. He had never spoken of his family, or mentioned friends apart from the crowd at the taverna, and even there he seemed to be treated with a certain respect rather than the usual raucous camaraderie.

But then he was incurious about her background too, she acknowledged.

She knew all kinds of little details about him, of course. She knew that his lashes were long enough to curl on his cheek when he slept. That there was a scar on his thigh, a relic from his boyhood when he'd gashed himself on a rock while swimming.

She was also aware that he could only relax for a certain time before he became restive, and that he secretly preferred her to wear dresses rather than trousers.

There'd been times recently, too, when he'd appeared to retreat so deeply into his own thoughts that it had been impossible for her to reach him, and this had made her feel oddly helpless and a little on edge.

Perhaps he was trying to find a humane way of telling

her that it was over and suggesting she went back to
Alakos, she thought desolately as she went to her
shower.

'Today we'll do something different,' he told her as
they walked down to the harbour. 'There is something
I want you to see.'

She felt a little surge of pleasure. Maybe at last she
was going to see the mysterious house—or even meet
his family.

She said lightly, 'That sounds intriguing.'

They sailed past their usual beach, heading north.

'Where are we going?'

'You have never been all round the island. I think
you should.' Draco gave her the tiller.

'Oh.' Cressy masked her disappointment. After a moment, she said slowly, 'Myros is so lovely, Draco. It's
like part of a different world. I—I shall hate to say
goodbye.'

'So enjoy it while you can,' he said casually. 'And
don't run us on to the rocks, *pethi mou*.'

To the north of the island the coastline became more
dramatic, with one high promontory standing out from
the rest. And on this jutting headland, clinging to it like
a lizard on a rock, was the massive sprawl of a villa,
white-walled and roofed in terracotta.

'My God.' Cressy shaded her eyes. 'So that's what
was behind the stone wall. It's absolutely vast. Who
does it belong to?'

'The head of the Ximenes Corporation.' His tone was
indifferent. 'You've heard of that?'

'I think so.' Cressy wrinkled her nose. 'They're in
shipping, aren't they?'

'And banking, and a hotel chain. The founder of the
dynasty was called Alexandros. Like his namesake, he

wished to conquer the world before he was thirty.' Draco put his hand over hers to alter the tiller. 'Do not go too close, *agapi mou.*'

'Because intruders aren't welcome?' Cressy pulled a face. 'Poor rich man.'

'You despise money?' His sideways glance was curious.

'On the contrary. I work long hours to earn as much as I can.'

'And that is important to you?'

'Well—naturally.'

'More important than being a woman, perhaps?'

Cressy bit her lip, sudden bewilderment battling with hurt. 'That's a cruel thing to say.'

Draco shrugged a shoulder. 'You are not a child,' he said. 'You live in a society where sexual freedom is accepted, and yet you are still a virgin. Why?'

She removed her hand from beneath his. 'I don't think it's any of your concern.'

'We said we would learn about each other,' he said. 'Yet you refuse to answer a simple question. One that would solve the mystery about you. Why won't you explain?'

'You dare say that to me?' She was angry now. 'You're the one with the secrets. You tell me nothing about yourself.'

'You don't ask.'

'All right.' She drew a deep breath. 'Are your parents alive?'

'No,' he said. 'But I have aunts and uncles and a great many cousins. Now, answer my question.'

Cressy hesitated. 'Perhaps I'm out of touch with today's morality,' she said. 'Or maybe I just haven't met the right man.'

'Ah,' he said softly. 'This great love of which every woman dreams. So, you believe in that.'

I never did before.

Her need for him, her longing, was an aching wound which only he could heal. And it was impossible for him not to know that. So why did he torment her by holding back?

She kept her voice light. 'We're all entitled to our dreams.'

'So, what do you dream of, Cressida *mou*?'

'Oh, dreams are like wishes.' She twisted round, pretending to take a last look at the villa on the headland. 'If you talk about them, they don't come true.'

'Then tell me this,' he said. 'Why did you come back here?'

Cressy swallowed. 'I—I wanted to see more of Myros.'

He sighed impatiently. 'Must I look into your eyes to know the truth, *agapi mou*?'

She said, almost inaudibly, 'And because you asked me…'

'Even though you knew that I wanted you—what I would ask?'

She swung back, tears stinging her eyes. 'Yes,' she said. 'Is that what you want to hear, Kyrios Draco? That I wanted you so much I came back to offer myself…' The stumbling words choked into silence.

'Yes,' he said quietly. 'I—needed to hear that, *agapi mou*.'

His arm encircled her, drawing her against him. 'Don't cry, my golden one—my treasure,' he whispered against her hair as she buried her face in his shoulder. 'And don't be ashamed of what you feel.'

'How can I help it?' Her voice was muffled.

'You imagine I do not want you—because I have been patient?' His voice sank to a whisper. 'I have had to force myself to remain cool, but no longer. I have to speak—to tell you everything in my heart.'

He paused. 'My life is yours, Cressida *mou*. Be my wife and stay with me for ever. Work beside me each day and lie in my arms at night.'

His body was shaking against hers. As she lifted her head she saw the proud face strangely anxious, the firm mouth incredibly vulnerable.

She put up her hand and touched his cheek, brushing her thumb softly across his lips.

She whispered, 'I'll stay...'

He kissed her once, his mouth hard, almost fierce on hers. Telling her beyond doubt how precarious that taut control really was.

'I must wait for more,' he told her as he reluctantly released her, his mouth twisting. 'I want to live with you, my bride, not drown with you.'

She laughed, leaning back in his embrace, the breeze from the sea lifting her hair, happiness warming her like her own private sun.

Lips touching her hair, Draco whispered words of love and need, his voice raw as he switched to his own language.

'I wish I could understand what you're saying,' Cressy sighed, her fingers lightly caressing the strong arm that held her so securely.

'I will tell you one day.' There was a smile in his voice. 'But only when we are married.'

In the hour it took to return to Myros harbour, they also made some practical plans.

It was agreed that Cressy would catch the midday ferry to Alakos, to pack the rest of her things and check out of the Hellenic Imperial. And make a few necessary phone calls, she thought, with a sudden bump of nervousness.

'I would take you myself,' Draco said, frowning. 'But there are things I must do at my house, arrangements I must make.' He paused. 'You'll stay there with me until our marriage, *pethi mou*? You'll trust me?'

'Is that really necessary?' Flushing slightly, Cressy met his gaze directly. 'Draco—I love you. I want to belong to you.'

'And so you will,' he said gently. 'In our house, in our bed, on our wedding night. That is how it must be, Cressida *mou*.'

She shook her head. 'You have a will of iron, *kyrie*.'

His gaze caressed her. 'When you look at me like that, *kyria*, I have no will at all.'

At the taverna, she went up to collect her things, leaving Draco to talk to Yannis.

As she fastened her travel bag she heard a sound behind her, and looked round to find Maria standing in the doorway.

'Maria.' Cressy smiled at her a little shyly. 'You've heard the news? I'm hoping very much that you'll lend me your wedding dress again.'

'Kyria Cressida.' Maria took a step forward, her face troubled. 'Are you sure about this? Kyrios Draco—how well do you know him?'

'I know that I love him.'

'You should take care,' Maria said quietly. 'This is not a marriage of equals.'

Cressy bit her lips. 'I understand what you're trying to say. That we'll have to make more adjustments than other couples. But...'

Maria gestured impatiently. 'That is not what I mean. There are things you do not know.'

Cressy stared at her. 'What sort of things?'

Yannis shouted Maria's name from below and she turned to go. 'I cannot say more. But you must be careful.' She left Cressy staring after her.

She was quiet as she walked down to the ferry with Draco at her side.

'Already regrets?' He smiled at her.

'No,' she denied, a little too quickly. She wanted to ask about Maria's warning, but it needed an oblique approach, and there wasn't time because people were already boarding the ferry.

He kissed her mouth, and she felt his thumb trace the sign of the cross on her forehead.

'Come to me soon,' he whispered. 'I shall be waiting for you, my beloved.'

As she collected her key from Hotel Reception, Cressy wondered what the deferential concierge would say if he knew she was planning to marry one of his countrymen.

She'd had time to think on the ferry trip, but hadn't come to any firm conclusions.

Perhaps Maria simply doubted that Draco had sufficient means to support a wife. After all, Cressy had little real idea of what he did for a living, she realised with a touch of unease.

Or had there been something more cynical in her warning? Did Maria suspect that Cressy's real attraction for Draco was as an affluent tourist?

But I'm not rich, and he knows it, Cressy thought. I'm well paid, but when I stop working that'll be it.

And I've still got rent to pay, and bills to settle back in England.

On the other hand even quite modest savings might seem a fortune to an impecunious fisherman.

She found herself remembering the silences—all the times she hadn't known what he was thinking. And, in spite of herself, began to wonder.

That total certainty about the future—her inner radiance—had taken a jolt, but a few doubts were perfectly natural, surely.

Anyway, she and Draco couldn't get married immediately, she reminded herself. There were all kinds of legal and religious formalities to be completed first.

And plenty of time for any lingering qualms to be assuaged.

She was halfway through her packing when the telephone rang.

'Cressy, my dear.'

'Why, Uncle Bob.' She sat down on the edge of the bed. 'What a surprise. I—I was actually planning to call you—'

'Cressy,' he interrupted firmly, 'I'm afraid you must listen carefully. I've got bad news.'

Ten minutes later she replaced the receiver. Her face was colourless and she felt deathly cold.

Her wonderful golden dream had gone, to be replaced by bleak and frightening reality. A chilling reminder of exactly who she was. Not some silly, lovesick child swept away by a handsome face, but a woman with a career, duties and obligations. A woman with a life far removed from some half-finished shack on a piece of Mediterranean rock.

Her father was not only ruined, but alone and ill. He might even be dying. Their recent estrangement was suddenly meaningless. She had to go back to England at once.

For a moment Draco's face seemed to swim in front of her. Gasping, she wrapped her arms round her body. She couldn't let herself think about him, or the folly of the last ten days. She had quite deliberately to wipe him from her mind, and her memory. There was no place for him in her life now, and never had been outside a crazy dream. He was a luxury she couldn't afford, she thought, biting her lip until she tasted blood.

As it was, no real harm had been done, and she had to be thankful for that.

It made her wince to think how naive she'd been— how easily she'd been beguiled to near disaster.

Draco had been so clever, using his sexuality to keep her in a torment of frustration and longing. All those kisses, she thought bitterly. The fleeting caresses that had aroused without satisfying.

And all leading to what? Not marriage, she was certain. He was probably bluffing about that. No, he was counting on her walking away once he'd shown her the life she could expect. But not until she'd handed over a hefty payment for his injured feelings, no doubt.

It was fate, she told herself as the plane took off from Athens. Fate intervening to stop her making the most hideous mistake of her life.

She had to see it like that or she'd go mad. She had to block the pain or she'd moan aloud. Had to tell herself that Draco was just a beach boy on the make or she'd mourn him for ever.

And she had her father's problems to sort out. She had no time for her own.

All very reasoned, Cressy thought now, as she brought her car to a halt in front of the house. Very rational. If only there hadn't been an unknown factor in her equation. A factor that still seemed to be pursuing her.

Cressy spent most of the afternoon on the telephone and sending e-mails, informing her father's creditors that she'd be negotiating on his behalf during his stay in hospital. But if she'd hoped for instant response or co-operation, she was disappointed.

She was just reluctantly deciding to call it a day when she heard the sound of a car outside and her uncle appeared, accompanied by Charles Lawrence, her father's legal adviser.

Sir Robert spoke without preamble. 'Cressy—have you spoken to the bank?'

She shook her head. 'They put me off with polite noises. Why—have you heard something?'

'I was contacted this morning.' Charles Lawrence was speaking. 'It's an extraordinary business, Cressida. They've had an offer to pay off the mortgage on this house, and your father's other debts. Someone's prepared to—take them over.'

'Just like that?' Cressy stared at both men. 'But that's impossible.'

Mr Lawrence nodded. 'So I thought. But I've since spoken to the other party, and the offer has been confirmed.'

Cressy mentally reviewed her father's close friends. There were several millionaires among them, but she wouldn't have credited any of them with that level of generosity.

She said doubtfully, 'Is it Dad's old company—have they put together a rescue package for him?'

'Nothing like that, I fear. The offer has come from

the Standard Trust Bank. They are based in New York, but they're owned by the Ximenes Corporation. I expect you've heard of it.'

'Yes.' Her voice sounded odd, suddenly, almost distorted. 'Yes—it was mentioned to me quite recently.'

'Well, I don't understand any of it,' Sir Robert said bluntly. 'Who are these people, and what on earth have they to do with James? I wasn't aware he'd had any dealings with them.'

'I'm sure he didn't.' Charles Lawrence shook his head. 'It's a complete mystery, but I hope Cressida may be able to solve it.' He gave her a bleak smile. 'It seems they wish to negotiate with you personally, my dear.'

'Did they give any particular reason?' Cressy felt hollow as weird, incredible suspicions continued to ferment in her mind.

No, she thought. It's not true. It can't be. It's just an odd coincidence. It has to be—*has to*…

'No, but I got the impression that the chairman—a chap called Viannis—is a law unto himself.' He consulted some notes. 'He's staying in London at the Grand Imperial—occupies the penthouse, apparently. You're to phone for an appointment.'

'Well, I don't like the sound of it,' Sir Robert said restively. 'You're James's solicitor. He should be talking to you.'

'I suggested as much, but they were adamant. It has to be Cressida. Although she can always refuse,' he added quickly.

'No,' Cressy said. 'If this Viannis is prepared to throw my father a lifeline, then I'll talk to him, or anyone. I'll call tomorrow and fix up a meeting.'

'Well,' Sir Robert said dubiously, 'if you're quite sure, my dear.'

After their departure Cressy sat for a while, staring into space. Then she rose and went over to the desk and her laptop.

The e-mail icon was waiting for her, as she'd suspected it would be.

Swallowing, she clicked on to the message.

'Sid,' she read. 'I am waiting for you. Come to me.'

And that meant there could no longer be any doubt at all.

'Oh, God,' she whispered, her clenched fist pressed against her mouth. 'What am I going to do?'

CHAPTER SEVEN

As the gates closed and the lift began its smooth rush to the penthouse, Cressy drew a deep breath.

Whatever—whoever—was waiting for her, it was essential that she appear composed and in control. She couldn't afford to let the mask slip for a moment and reveal the turmoil of emotion inside her.

She had dressed carefully for this meeting. Her navy blue suit was immaculate, the skirt cut decorously to the knee. The heavy cream silk blouse buttoned to the throat, and she wore neat navy pumps with a medium heel and carried a briefcase. Her hair had been brushed severely back from her face and confined at the nape of her neck with a gilt clip.

Her make-up had been meticulously applied to cover up the tell-tale signs of another sleepless night.

She looked, she thought, cool and businesslike. She hoped she was going to be treated accordingly.

She thought, not for the first time, her throat tightening uncontrollably, Oh, let him be a stranger. Please—*please* let me be wrong about this...

She was met on the top floor by a tall blonde man with a transatlantic accent, who greeted her unsmilingly and introduced himself as Paul Nixon, Mr Viannis's personal assistant.

He led her down the thickly carpeted corridor and knocked at the double doors at the end.

He said, 'Miss Fielding is here, sir,' and stood aside to allow Cressy to go in.

The room was full of light. There were huge windows on three sides, permitting panoramic views all over London.

But Cressy was only aware of the tall, dark figure silhouetted against the brightness. For a moment she was scarcely able to breathe, and she halted abruptly, feeling as if a giant fist had clenched in her stomach, all her worst fears finally and inevitably confirmed.

He was very still, but with the tension of a coiled spring. Across the room, his anger reached out and touched her, and she had to fight an impulse to flinch. Or even run...

He said softly, 'So, you have come to me at last—Cressida, my faithless one.'

There was a note in his voice which sent a shiver between her shoulder blades, but it was vital not to seem afraid.

She lifted her chin. 'Mr Viannis?'

'What charming formality.' The mockery in his tone was savage. 'You feel it's appropriate—under the circumstances? After all, how do you address your ex-fiancé—someone you've so signally betrayed?'

She said steadily, 'I came here to negotiate a deal for my father, not indulge in useless recriminations.'

'No,' he said. 'You came here to accept my terms. There is nothing to negotiate.'

She'd hoped to find a stranger and in some ways her wish had been granted, because this wasn't Draco. This man had never worn scruffy denims or danced in the sunlight. Had never kissed her, or smiled at her with lazy desire. Could never, even for a few breathless moments, have held her naked in his arms.

This man looked thinner—older, she thought, her eyes scanning him with sudden bewilderment. His charcoal suit with its faint pinstripe was exquisitely cut, his tie a paler grey silk.

The tumbled black hair had been tamed and trimmed. And there was no golden light in the dark eyes that met hers. They were cold—impenetrable.

Even his voice was different. Now he spoke with hardly any accent at all.

She thought, How could I not have seen it—the ruthlessness behind the golden sunlit charm?

He walked over to the big desk in the centre of the room and sat down, curtly indicating that she should occupy the chair set at the opposite side.

She obeyed reluctantly. Her legs were shaking and her heart was thudding unevenly.

She said, struggling to keep her voice level, 'How did you find me?'

'You were staying in one of my hotels, so that provided the basic information.' He shrugged. 'After that, I had enquiries made.'

'You checked up on me?' Her voice was taut. 'Was this before or after you asked me to marry you?'

His smile did not reach his eyes. 'Oh, long before. When we first encountered each other. I needed to be sure that you were just as you seemed.'

'I'm glad I measured up to your exacting requirements.' She spoke with deliberate disdain, trying to cover her growing unease.

'That was then,' he said. 'This is now.'

Cressy touched the tip of her tongue to her dry lips, realising too late that Draco had seen and marked that tiny act of self-betrayal.

She hurried into speech. 'And that's how you discovered my father's—difficulties, I suppose?'

'Yes,' he said. 'But they are hardly "difficulties". Your father is facing total ruin.'

'I know that,' she said. 'Which is the reason I'm here today.'

'No,' he said. 'You are here because you ran away. Because you left me without a word. You are here to explain.'

'My father collapsed,' she said flatly. 'He was in Intensive Care. I—had to come back.'

'Without one word to the man you had just promised to marry?' His voice bit.

Cressy's hands were clenched so tightly in her lap that her fingers ached. She said, 'I didn't think that either of us took that seriously. A lot of women have—flings on foreign holidays.'

'Ah.' Draco leaned back in the tall leather chair. 'So you saw our relationship as some trivial, transient affair. A thing of no consequence.' His tone suggested courteous interest, but she wasn't fooled.

'In some ways,' she said uncertainly.

He said slowly, 'If that was true, I would have taken you on the beach that first afternoon and you would have spent the rest of your holiday in my bed.'

'And eventually gone on my way with a diamond necklace, I suppose,' Cressy flashed.

'Perhaps.' He sounded indifferent. 'If you'd pleased me sufficiently.'

'I can't think why you held back.'

'Because I was fool enough to respect your innocence, Cressida *mou*.' His tone was harsh. 'I did not see it was just a physical attribute. That, in reality, you were just as calculating and heartless as your namesake.'

Cressy leaned forward. 'You think I've treated you badly,' she said hotly. 'But you weren't honest with me either. You deliberately let me think you were poor. Why?'

'An unaccountable need to be wanted for myself only, and not for my worldly goods,' he drawled. 'It was so refreshing to meet someone who had no idea who I was, *pethi mou*.'

'And how long did you plan to go on deceiving me?' She realised now why Maria had tried to warn her. To tell her that she was involved with a man who was not only very rich, but powerful. A man who would live up to his name if crossed.

'It would have been over as soon as you returned from Alakos. You see, *agapi mou*, I had planned a big party for our engagement at my house.'

She stared at him. 'It belongs to you, doesn't it? That wonderful villa on the headland?'

'Yes,' he said. 'My family and friends were flying in from all over the world to meet you—my future wife—there.'

'Oh.' Cressy felt sick.

'At first I thought you had simply missed the ferry,' he went on, as if she hadn't spoken. 'I called the hotel, and they told me you had checked out, so I waited for a message. I waited a long time. I cannot remember the precise moment I realised you were not coming back.'

'My father needed me,' she said desperately. 'I had to get to Athens—to go to him.'

'And it never occurred to you to turn to me—the man you'd professed to love?' His mouth twisted contemptuously. 'What a mistake, Cressida *mou*. My helicopter would have flown us to Athens. My private plane would have taken us on to London. You would have been there in half the time.'

'But I had no means of knowing that,' she protested.

'If you had come to me you would have known. Only you didn't. And that is the worst thing of all. To know that you were in trouble—in pain—yet you didn't want to share this with me. Even if I'd been as poor as you thought, at least I had the right to put my arms around you and hold you.

'As it was, I could have taken you straight to your father and been with you to comfort and care for you, as a man should with his woman.' He paused, the dark eyes merciless. 'Tell me, *pethi mou*, had you any intention of contacting me again—ever? Or was I simply to be—erased, like an unfortunate mistake in a calculation?'

Cressy shook her head, feeling tears thickening in her throat. 'Draco—I don't know—I was worried—confused...'

'Then let me tell you the answer,' he said. 'You didn't love—and you didn't trust either. That was the bitter truth I had to learn. I was poor, so I could be discarded, as if I had no feelings. And one day you will discover how that feels. Because I shall teach you.'

He smiled at her. 'You will discover, Cressida *mou*, that I am not so easily forgotten.'

She said in a low voice, 'I suppose you mean to use my father's problems against me. Well—I'm prepared for that.'

'Are you?' he asked softly. 'I had originally intended to present the settlement of his debts as a gift to you when we announced our engagement. Since then I have had time to think again.'

She said urgently, 'Draco—whatever you think of me—please don't punish my father any more. He's a sick man.'

'And when he leaves hospital he will need a home

to go to,' he said. 'The house that now belongs to me. Is that what you're trying to put into words?'

She said on a note of desperation, 'I could pay rent...'

'Yes, you will pay,' he said quietly. 'But not with money. I have enough of that already.'

'Then how?' Her voice was barely more than a whisper.

'Don't you know?' he said. 'Don't you understand that I still want you?'

The room was very still suddenly. She stared across the desk at him. At the hard bronze face and the cool mouth that looked as if it would never smile again. Watched and waited for some softening—some warmth. But in vain.

She swallowed. 'You mean—in spite of everything— you're going to marry me?'

His laugh was harsh. 'No, not marriage, my sweet. I will not be caught again. This time I'm offering a less formal arrangement.' He added cynically, 'And spare me the pretence that you don't understand my offer.'

'I understand.' Her voice seemed to come from a long way away. 'You're saying that if I—sleep with you— you won't enforce the mortgage or my father's other debts.'

'Yes,' he said softly. 'I am saying exactly that. And what is your answer?'

She said hoarsely, 'Draco, you can't mean this. If you loved me, you wouldn't...'

'I said that I wanted you, Cressida *mou*. I did not mention love.'

Pain ripped at her, tearing her apart. She hadn't realised it was possible to hurt so much. Or to be so afraid.

She said, her voice shaking, 'Is this your idea of revenge? To rape me?'

'No,' he said. 'Because you will come to me willingly, Cressida, as we both know.'

'Never.'

He shrugged. 'Then regard it simply as a business transaction. You understand those better than you know yourself, I think.'

'Business?' Her voice cracked. 'How can it be that?'

'I have something you want.' His smile mocked her. 'You have something I want. That's how deals are made.'

'You make it sound so simple.'

'It is hardly complicated.' His voice was cool, and oddly impersonal. 'You will come to me, and stay with me as long as I require. When our liaison ends, I will hand over the mortgage and other papers—instead of a diamond necklace,' he added, his mouth twisting.

'And if I refuse this—degrading offer?'

He leaned back in his chair. He said quietly, 'We have already established that your father's well-being is your sole priority. So I do not think we need consider that possibility—do you?'

'No.' Her voice was barely audible. 'No, I don't—really—have a choice.'

He smiled thinly. 'You've made the right decision.' He got to his feet and came round the desk to her side. He took her hand, pulling her out of the chair.

He led her across the room to a door, which he opened, revealing a large and luxurious bedroom.

'You mean—now?' Her voice rose, and she recoiled, swinging round to face him. 'Oh, God, you can't be serious.'

His brows lifted. 'Why not?'

She said wildly, 'Because it's the middle of the morning.'

He began to laugh. 'How conventional you are, *agapi mou*,' he mocked. 'When we were on Myros there was not one minute of the day or night that we did not want each other.'

She bit her lip. 'That was different.'

'Did you expect me to seduce you over dinner with flowers and moonlight?' His tone was cynical. 'It is too late for that. Once, perhaps, I would have made it beautiful for you. Now—' he shrugged '—regard it as the signature on a contract.'

'Draco.' Her voice broke. 'Please—don't do this to me—to us.'

'Us?' he echoed contemptuously. 'There is no "us". I have bought you, Cressida *mou*. That is all. And this time you will not have the opportunity to run away.' He glanced at his watch. 'I have a couple of calls to make. I will join you in a few minutes.'

She said bitterly, 'You're enjoying this, aren't you?'

'I intend to,' he said. 'Whether or not you share my pleasure is your own concern. But I think you will.'

He pulled her towards him, his arm a steel band forcing her compliance. His dark face swam momentarily in front of her startled eyes. Then he bent his head and kissed her breast.

The sudden heat of his mouth scorched through her thin blouse and lacy bra as if she was already naked. His lips found her nipple, tugging at it, creating a sharp, exquisite pain that triggered a scalding flood of need in return.

Surprised and shamed at the physical fierceness of her response, Cressy gasped, her hands curling into impotent fists at her sides.

When he lifted his head he was smiling faintly. He reached for one small clenched hand and raised it to his lips with insolent grace.

His other hand slid down over her hip to her thigh, and lingered there suggestively.

He said softly, 'Nothing has really changed between us, Cressida *mou*. Only the terms of our coming together. Shall I prove it to you? Show you exactly how much you still want me?'

Helpless colour warmed her face. She shook her head, staring down at the carpet, not daring to meet the intensity of his gaze. Scared of what else she might betray.

She had not bargained for the overwhelming force of instinct. But that could be harnessed, she told herself. Hidden.

For her own sake, she had to try.

She found herself impelled gently but inexorably into the bedroom. She began a last protest, but Draco laid a finger on her parted lips, silencing her.

He said, 'I shall try not to keep you waiting too long.'

The door closed behind him, shutting her in. She stood, her arms wrapped defensively across her body, staring round.

It was a big room, and the bed was its dominant feature, wide and low, with a dark green cover tailored in heavy linen, matching the drapes at the windows.

A very masculine room, she thought, comfortable but impersonal. A suitable place for a bargain, but not for love. Never for love.

She walked across and tugged at the cords, swinging the curtains across to block out the brilliant sunlight. She wanted shadows, she thought. Shadows and darkness to hide in.

She needed, too, to blot out the searing memory of those other golden days on Myros when she had turned to him, eagerly offering her mouth—her body.

Her whole body seemed to stir in sudden yearning, and regret, and she stiffened, bringing her rebellious senses back under control once more. She could not allow herself such weakness.

Whatever Draco did to her—no matter how he made her feel—somehow she had to stay aloof—and endure.

Presently, she thought, I shall wake up and find all this was just a nightmare.

She looked back, dry-mouthed, at the bed, pain searing through her as she realised how different it could have been.

But she'd made her choice—a whole series of choices—and she had to live with the consequences. Starting now...

She left her clothes in the adjoining dressing room. The carpet was soft under her bare feet as she walked to the bed. The percale sheets felt crisp and cool against her burning skin as she lay tensely, waiting for the door to open.

Which, eventually, just as her nerves had reached screaming point, it did.

'Shy, *agapi mou*?' He was a dark shape at the end of the bed. He turned away, walking over to the windows and flinging back the drapes again, flooding the room with sudden light.

Draco came back to the bed. For a moment he stood staring down at her, then he reached down, twitching the covers from her outraged fingers and tossing them to the foot of the bed.

He said softly, 'A man likes to look, as well as touch.'

Teeth set defiantly, Cressy withstood his lingering scrutiny, deliberately not covering herself with her hands, nor looking away, even when he began, almost casually, to remove his clothes.

Only when he came to lie beside her on the bed and drew her into his arms did she finally close her eyes, her body rigid against his naked warmth.

The scent of his skin, once so familiar and so precious, now admixed with a trace of some expensive cologne, pervaded her mouth and nose, so that she seemed to be breathing him, absorbing him into every atom of her consciousness.

She remembered one day on the beach, kissing his shoulder, tasting the heat of the sun and the salt of the sea on its curving muscularity. But she couldn't afford those kind of memories. She had to lie still and unyielding—and hate. Resentment would be her only salvation.

But it wasn't easy, not when his hands had begun to caress her, the warm fingers skimming over her flesh in exquisite, tantalising exploration.

As they softly brushed her taut nipples Cressy had to bite back a gasp, her body clenching in hot, shamed excitement.

Where his hands touched, his mouth followed. He kissed her breasts softly, his tongue unhurriedly circling each puckered rose peak in turn. Sensation, knife-sharp and honey-sweet, pierced through her, making her quiver and arch towards him involuntarily, and she felt his lips smile against her skin.

His hand parted her thighs and began to stroke her, delicately, subtly, making her moan and writhe against the intimate play of his fingers as they promised—tantalised—and then denied.

Every sense, every atom of consciousness was focused painfully on that tiny, pulsating centre of her being as she felt herself being drawn slowly and exquisitely to some undreamed of brink. As she felt her breath quicken and heard the frantic drumming of her own heart.

She made a small, wounded sound in her throat. A wordless plea for him—somehow—to end this beautiful torment.

'Not yet.' His tongue caressed the whorls of her ear. 'Not yet, but—soon...' And his hand moved fractionally, deepening the caress. Imposing a more compelling demand.

She was blind, deaf—mindless. Aware of nothing but the fierce concentration of pleasure that he was creating for her. As if the sun, beating against her eyelids, was blooming and growing inside her.

And when, at last, he gave her the release she craved, she cried out in harsh animal delight as ripple upon ripple of pure feeling engulfed her—convulsed her. As she was flung out into space, where she fell into the centre of the sun and was consumed.

She was totally relaxed, her body still throbbing with pleasure, as Draco moved above her, and, with one deep thrust, into her.

For a fleeting instant she was scared by the memory of pain, then shocked by its absence. Because now there was only joyous acceptance, and a sense of completion.

As if, she thought, this was the moment she had been made for.

She raised her languid lids and stared up at him, letting herself enclose him. Hold him.

Allowing herself to savour how alien it felt, yet at the same time how totally familiar—and precious.

The bronze face was stark, his eyes like pits of darkness as he began to move, slowly and powerfully, inside her.

Instinct lifted her hands to his shoulders and clasped her legs round his lean hips, so that she could partner him completely. Could mirror each compelling stroke.

As the rhythm and intensity increased, Draco groaned something in his own language. She kissed his throat, licking the salt from his skin, feeling the thunder of his pulse against her lips.

At the same time, deep within her, she was aware of the first flutterings of renewed delight. Incredulous, gasping, she held him closer, her sweat mingling with his as the spiral of pleasure tautened unbearably, then imploded.

Her whole body rocked as the tremors of rapture tore through her, echoed by the wild spasms of his own climax.

When it was over, he lay very still, his face against her breasts.

She wanted to hold him. To put her lips against the damp, dark tangle of hair and whisper that she loved him. That as he'd been the first, so would he be the last.

As his cherished bride, it would have been her right to open her heart to him. As his mistress—she sank her teeth into her swollen lower lip—she had no rights at all. And that was something she must never forget. That her role in his life was at best transient.

At last he stirred, lifting himself away from her. He reached for his watch from the night table, grimaced at the time, and fastened the thin gold bracelet back on his wrist. Then he turned and looked down at Cressy, his dark eyes almost dispassionate.

'Thank you.' His voice was cool, even faintly

amused. 'I had not expected such—enchanting co-operation. You learn quickly.'

'Is—is that all you have to say?' Her voice shook. She felt as if she'd been slapped.

'No, but the rest must wait. I have a meeting in the City. But you don't have to leave,' he added swiftly as Cressy half sat up. 'No one will disturb you if you wish to sleep.'

'I don't,' she said curtly. 'I haven't visited my father today. I need to get back there.'

He nodded, unfazed. 'Paul will contact you with your instructions.'

'Instructions?'

'I shall soon be returning to Greece. I require you to accompany me.'

'But my job—my father,' Cressy protested. 'I can't just—go.'

'You will find that you can. Your employer has been most understanding. Your—services are on temporary loan to me. I did not explain the exact nature of the services,' he added with a shrug. 'So you can tell him as much or as little as you wish.'

She swallowed. 'My God,' she said. 'You don't allow much to stand in your way, do you? Suppose I'd turned you down.'

'I was certain you wouldn't.' His mouth twisted. 'Apart from other considerations, your sexual curiosity had been aroused, *agapi mou*, and needed to be satisfied.' His hand touched her shoulder, then travelled swiftly and sensuously down her body. It was the lightest of caresses but it brought her skin stinglingly alive.

Draco's laugh was soft. 'You see, Cressida *mou*, even now you are eager for your next lesson. How sad that I have not more time to devote to you.'

Cressy reached down and dragged the discarded sheet up over her body. She recognised that it was basically a meaningless gesture, but it made her feel marginally better.

She forced herself to meet his gaze. She said, 'You mentioned I was on loan to you. For how long, exactly?'

Draco swung his long legs to the floor. 'I said three months initially.'

She said, 'I—see.'

The blissful euphoria which had followed their love-making had gone. In its place, pain and shame were dragging her apart.

'I suggest you see a doctor as a matter of urgency,' he tossed over his shoulder as he walked to the bathroom. 'Today I used protection, but even so we must ensure there's no chance of you becoming pregnant.'

Cressy was suddenly very still, her eyes enormous as she stared after him.

With a few casual words, she thought, he'd relegated her to the status of a non-person.

Yet this was the reality of the situation. She was no longer his golden love. She was a temporary sexual partner. And the skill and artistry he'd brought to her initiation had simply been a means to an end. Draco had ensured her pleasure merely to increase his own.

And if she'd hoped in some secret corner of her mind that the glory of their coming together would soften his attitude towards her, she knew better now, and disappointment twisted inside her like a claw.

There were tears crowding in her throat, stinging the backs of her eyes, but she would not shed them in front of him.

She said quietly. 'No—of course not.'

The bathroom door closed behind him, and presently she heard the sound of the shower running.

She released a trembling breath. Somehow she had to come to terms with the relationship that he'd offered her, and all its limitations, when the most she could hope for was that it would soon be over.

'Oh, God,' she whispered brokenly. 'How can I bear it?'

And she turned her face into the pillow and lay like a stone.

CHAPTER EIGHT

SHE pretended to be asleep when Draco came back into the bedroom, lying motionless, her eyes tightly shut, as she listened with nerves jangling to his quiet movements, the rustle of clothing as he dressed.

When, at last, he came across to the bed, she forced her tense body into deep relaxation, keeping her breathing soft and even.

She thought she heard him sigh as he turned away, but she couldn't be sure.

It was some time after she heard the bedroom door click shut behind him that she ventured to sit up, and make sure she was really alone.

She thought, I have to get out of here. I don't want anyone to see me—to know…

She knew she was being ridiculous. That there wasn't a member of Draco's staff who wouldn't be perfectly aware of the situation. She just didn't want to find herself face to face with any of them.

She was scared, too, that if she gave way to sleep she might still be here when Draco returned.

She showered swiftly, but if she hoped to wash away the touch and taste of him it was in vain. His possession had been total. He was irrevocably part of her now, and there was nothing she could do about it.

She shivered as she towelled her damp hair.

What had happened to all her high-flown plans about fighting him—about remaining indifferent? she wondered bitterly.

115

One kiss—his hand on her breast—and all her resolution had crumbled. Indeed, she could hardly have made it easier for him. She wanted to hate him for the way he had made her feel, but she hated herself more.

There were mirrors all round the bathroom, throwing back images of a girl whose eyes were heavy with newly learned secrets. The cool lady she'd been so proud of had vanished for ever, swept away on a frantic tide of passion.

Yet the encounter had left no visible marks on her skin, she thought, with detached surprise. Her mouth was reddened and slightly swollen, and she ached a little, but that was all.

I got off lightly, she told herself. But she knew in her heart that it wasn't true.

When she was dressed, she looked at herself and winced. All those carefully chosen garments—the business suit and prim shirt—had been worn as armour, yet they'd proved no protection at all.

She went back to her flat and changed into a plain black shift, sleeveless and severe, stuffing the discarded clothing into a refuse sack. She never wanted to see any of it again. She thrust her bare feet into sandals and grabbed a simple cream linen jacket before going down to her car.

It was a nightmare journey, a battle between her need to concentrate on the road and the storm of bewildered emotion within her. But at last she reached the hospital.

In one piece, but only just, she thought grimly.

As she waited for the lift to take her up to the ICU, she was waylaid by a nurse.

'Your father's been moved, Miss Fielding. He's made such good progress over the last twenty-four hours that he's in a private room on "A" wing now.'

'You mean he's getting better? But that's wonderful.' Cressy's mouth trembled into a relieved smile. 'Because he looked so ill when I was here last.'

'Oh, he's still being carefully monitored, but everyone's very pleased with him.' The older woman beamed. 'Mind you, I think all the goodies he's been receiving—the fruit and flowers from Mrs Fielding—have cheered him up a lot.'

'Eloise has sent fruit and flowers?' Cressy repeated incredulously.

'Well, there wasn't an actual card, but he said they must be from her. He was so thrilled.' She paused. 'Is Mrs Fielding not with you today? What a shame.'

When she reached her father's room, it looked like a florist's window.

As she paused in the doorway, admiring the banks of blooms, James Fielding turned an eager head towards her, his welcoming smile fading when he saw who it was.

'Cressy, my dear.' He spoke with an effort, failing to mask the disappointment in his voice. 'How good to see you.'

'You look marvellous, Daddy.' She went to the bed and kissed his cheek. 'I've never seen so many flowers. I'd have brought some, but they didn't allow them in ICU, and now everyone else has beaten me to it.' She was aware she was chattering, trying to cover up the awkward moment. Attempting to hide the instinctive hurt provoked by his reaction.

He didn't want it to be me, she thought with desolation. He hoped it was Eloise. That she'd come back to him.

'Those lilies and carnations over there, and the fruit basket, came without a card,' her father said eagerly.

'But I think I know who they're from.' He smiled tenderly. 'In fact, I'm sure. I just wish she'd signed her name. But perhaps she felt diffident about that—under the circumstances.'

Diffident? Cressy wanted to scream. Eloise hasn't an insecure bone in her body.

Instead, she forced a smile as she sat down beside his bed. 'Yes—perhaps…'

He played with the edge of the sheet, frowning a little. 'Has she been in contact—left any message at all?'

Cressy shook her head. 'There's been nothing. Daddy. Don't you think I'd have told you?'

'I don't know,' he said with a touch of impatience. 'Certainly there's never been any love lost between you.'

'Well, that's unimportant now.' She put a hand over his. 'All that matters is that you get well.'

'The consultant says I can go home soon, if I keep up this progress. But he wants me to have a live-in nurse for a while. He feels it will be too much for Berry.'

His frown deepened. 'I wasn't sure that my insurance covered private nursing, but he says it's all taken care of.' He paused. 'What I need to know is—do I still have a home to go to?'

She said gently, 'Yes, you have, darling. I've managed to do a deal with your creditors. You can go on living at the house.'

He nodded. 'That's good. I'd have hated Eloise to find the place all shut up, or occupied by strangers, and not know where to find me. Because it won't last—this Alec Caravas thing. She's had her head turned by a younger man, that's all.'

Cressy's lips parted in a silent gasp of incredulity.

For a moment she could feel the blood drumming in her ears and felt physically sick.

Was that really his only concern—providing a bolt-hole for his worthless wife—if she chose to return? Didn't he realise she'd been Alec Caravas's full accomplice—and that the police would want to interview her if she ever dared show her face again?

She'd expected her father to ask all sorts of awkward questions about the exact accommodation she'd reached over his debts, but he didn't seem remotely interested. Instead he just took it for granted that she'd managed to get things sorted.

Just as he'd tacitly accepted the estrangement between them that Eloise had imposed, she realised with a sudden ache of the heart.

And he would never have any conception of the terrible personal price she'd been forced to pay on his behalf.

I've ruined my life to get him out of trouble, Cressy thought with anguish. And he doesn't even care. Nothing matters except this obsession with Eloise.

She got clumsily to her feet. 'I—I'd better go. I promised the nurses I wouldn't tire you.'

'Perhaps it would be best.' He leaned back against his pillows, reaching for the radio headphones.

She took a deep breath. 'But there's something I must tell you first. I—I have to go abroad very soon—to work. It's a special contract. It may take a few months.'

'Well, that's excellent news.' His smile held some of the old warmth. 'I hope it means more money—or a promotion. You deserve it, you know.'

She said quietly, 'I'm not sure what I deserve any more. And I'm not certain if I should go—if I should leave you.'

'Nonsense, darling. Of course you must go. We both have our own lives to lead. We can't be dependent on each other. And the last thing I want is you fussing round me. Berry and this nurse will be bad enough.'

'No,' she said. 'You're probably right. I—I'll see you tomorrow.'

She went quietly to the door and let herself out. In the corridor, she stopped and leaned against the wall, aware that her legs were shaking so badly she thought she might collapse. She closed her eyes as a scalding tear forced its way under her lid and down her cheek.

She thought brokenly, Oh, Daddy...

'Miss Fielding—is something wrong?' A nurse's anxious voice invaded her torturous thoughts.

Cressy straightened quickly. 'No—it's all right.' She tried a little laugh. 'I think the worry of the past few days has just caught up with me, that's all.'

'I'm not surprised. Oh, and talking of surprises...' The girl felt in the pocket of her uniform. 'You know the fruit and flowers that arrived for your father with no name on them? Well, they've just found this card in Reception. It must have fallen off when the delivery was made.' She beamed. 'One mystery solved.' She lowered her voice significantly. 'Although I think he was hoping they were from Mrs Fielding.'

Cressy held out her hand. 'May I look?'

The signature was a slash of black ink across the rectangle of pasteboard. *'Draco Viannis.'*

She wasn't even surprised. She closed her hand on the card, feeling its sharp edges dig into her palm. Wanting it to hurt. Needing a visible scar to counterbalance all the inner pain.

She said quietly, 'Thank you. I'll—see that he gets

it. Now, is it possible for me to have a word with the consultant?'

She didn't go straight back to the house. There was a National Trust property a few miles away, whose grounds were open to the public. There was an Elizabethan knot garden, and a lake with swans, and Cressy had always loved it there.

She found an unoccupied bench and sat, gazing across the sunlit waters with eyes that saw nothing and a heart without peace.

Her father had needed her, she thought, so she'd turned her back on the love that Draco was offering and gone running to him. She'd wanted, just once more, to be the cherished only daughter—to bask in the old relationship. To be important to him again.

But that was always going to be impossible, she realised wearily. Because they were not the same people any longer. Life had moved on for both of them.

So why this last vain attempt to cling on to her childhood?

She looked down at her hands, clenched in her lap. She remembered other hands, dark against her pale skin, and shivered.

She thought, Was I really so afraid of becoming a woman? Was that the true reason I ran away from Draco?

Under the circumstances, her reluctance to face the challenge of her own sexuality was ironic. Because Draco himself had changed all that in one brief, but very succinct lesson.

And now she was left stranded, between his desire for revenge and her father's indifference.

I've wrecked everything, she told herself desolately.

Sacrificed the only chance of real happiness I've ever been offered.

But she couldn't let herself think about that, or she would break down completely. And she had to be strong to get through the next few weeks or months, living on the edge of Draco's life. Strong enough, too, to walk away with her head high when it was over.

And before that she had other problems to deal with.

Her father might be too preoccupied with the loss of his wife to question this 'job abroad' too closely, but her aunt and uncle might not be so incurious. They would want a full explanation, and she couldn't imagine what she would say to them—or to Berry, who would find it unthinkable for her to leave her father in this way.

And how could she explain why her father's debts were now in abeyance, and the house reprieved, without mentioning the precise terms of her 'contract' with Draco?

Her conversation with the consultant had been uncomfortably revealing. Over the years her father's health cover had been reduced to a minimum. The top-grade private room he was occupying, and the services of the live-in nurse, were being paid for by Draco.

'I thought you knew and approved, Miss Fielding,' the consultant had told her, frowning. 'He described himself as a close friend of the family.'

'Yes,' she'd said, dry-mouthed. 'Yes, of course.'

It seemed there was not a part of her life that Draco didn't control. And the fact that in this instance his influence was totally benign somehow made it no better.

Oh, God, she thought. It's all such a mess.

And began, soundlessly and uncontrollably, to cry until she had no more tears left.

It was the sudden chill of the evening breeze across the lake and the clang of the bell announcing that the grounds were closing that eventually roused her from her unhappy reverie.

It was more than time she was getting back. Berry would have dinner waiting for her and would be worried about her non-appearance, she thought, sighing, as she returned reluctantly to her car.

The hall lights were on when she let herself into the house, but there was no sign of the housekeeper—or of dinner either. No place laid in the dining room or welcoming aroma of food in the air. Just—silence.

She called, 'Berry—I'm home,' and waited, but there was no response.

Maybe she'd gone into the garden, to pick some last-minute fruit for dessert or bring in some washing, Cressy thought, subduing an unwelcome tingle of apprehension.

She walked to the drawing room door, twisted the handle, and went in.

Draco was standing beside the fireplace, one arm resting on the mantelshelf as he stared down at the empty grate. He turned slightly, the dark eyes narrowing as Cressy paused in the doorway, her hand going to her throat in shock.

He said softly, 'So here you are at last, *agapi mou*. I have been waiting for you.'

She said shakily, 'So I see. Where's Berry? What's happened to her?'

His brows lifted. 'Naturally, I have murdered her and buried her body under the lawn,' he returned caustically. 'Or so you seem to think.'

She bit her lip. 'I don't think anything of the kind,' she denied curtly, aware that her heart was hammering in a totally unwelcome way at the sight of him. But then he'd startled her—hadn't he?

'I was just a little anxious about her,' she added defensively.

'So many anxieties about so many people.' His smile did not reach his eyes. 'What a caring heart you have, my golden girl. The truth is that I gave your Mrs Berryman the evening off. I believe she means to go to a cinema.'

'You gave Berry the evening off?' She stared at him, open-mouthed. 'And she agreed?'

His mouth twisted. 'She was a little reluctant at first, but I can be very persuasive.'

'To hell with your powers of persuasion,' Cressy lifted her chin. 'You had no right to do anything of the sort.'

'I have all kinds of rights, Cressida *mou*.' His tone hardened. 'And I mean to enjoy all of them.' He held out a hand. 'Now come and welcome me properly.'

Mutinously, she walked forward and stood in front of him. When he kissed her she stood unmoving, unresponding to the warm, sensuous pressure of his lips on hers.

After a moment, he drew back.

'Sulking?' he asked. 'What's the matter? Did I hurt you, perhaps, this morning?'

Colour rushed into her face. She stared down at the carpet. 'I don't know.'

He said, 'Look at me, *matia mou*. Look at me and say that.'

Cressy raised her eyes unwillingly to him. His smile was faintly mocking, but there was an odd watchfulness in his gaze which she found unnerving.

She said, 'No—no, you didn't. As you know quite well.'

'Where you are concerned, my beautiful one, I suspect I know very little.' His tone was dry. 'But I am glad you did not find your first surrender too much of an ordeal.'

She threw her head back defiantly. 'Your words, *kyrie*. Not mine. And now perhaps you'd tell me what you're doing here.'

'I thought I should pay a visit,' he said. 'To make sure that all was well with my property.' He paused. 'But I see it is not.' He took her chin in his hand, studying her, ignoring her gasp of outrage. 'You have been crying, *pethi mou*. Why?'

'Do you really need to ask that?' She freed herself stormily and stepped back. 'Or did you imagine I'd be turning cartwheels for joy because the mighty Draco Viannis had sex with me today.'

His mouth tightened. 'Would you have wept if Draco the fisherman had taken you that day on Myros?'

'He didn't exist,' she said. 'So how can I know?'

'You could always—pretend.'

She shook her head. 'There's been too much pretence already. Now we have a business arrangement.'

'Ah, yes,' he said softly. He removed his jacket, tossed it over the arm of one of the sofas and sat down, loosening his tie.

He smiled at her. 'Then perhaps you would take off your dress—strictly in the line of business.'

Her skin warmed again, hectically. 'My—dress?'

'To begin with.' His tie followed the jacket, and he began, unhurriedly, to unbutton his shirt.

She said, 'You—you actually expect me to strip for you?'

'It is hardly a novelty.' His tone was dry. 'After all, Cressida *mou*, the first time I saw your beautiful breasts it was your own idea.'

Her voice trembled. 'I—hate you.'

He laughed. 'That should add an extra dimension to the way you remove your clothes, my lovely one. I cannot wait.'

She said, 'But someone might come...'

He grinned at her. 'More than one, I hope, *agapi mou*.'

To her fury, she realised she was blushing again. 'You know what I mean.'

'Yes,' he said. 'And why do you think I gave the housekeeper leave of absence? Precisely so we should not be disturbed. Now, will you take off your dress, or do you wish me to do it for you?'

'No.' Her voice was a thread. 'I'll do it.'

She unfastened the long zip, slid the dress from her shoulders and let it pool round her feet.

'Tell me,' she said. 'If we'd been married, would you have degraded me like this?'

'And if we'd been on our honeymoon, Cressida *mou*, would you have expected either of us to remain fully clothed for very long?'

'You,' she said bitterly, 'have an answer for everything.'

'And you, my lovely one, talk too much.' Draco leaned back, watching her through half-closed eyes. 'Now take off the rest—but slowly.'

They lay together on the thick rug in front of the fireplace, his hands making a long, lingering voyage of rediscovery.

This time, she thought fiercely, she wouldn't let it happen. She wouldn't become some mindless—thing, subject to his every sexual whim. She had a will of her own and she would use it.

But it wasn't easy. Not when he was kissing her slowly and deeply, his tongue a flame against her own. Not when her breasts were in his hands and the tight buds of her nipples were unfurling slowly under his caress. Or when he was stroking her flanks, cupping the roundness of her buttocks in his palms.

And not when she needed him so desperately, so crazily, to touch her—there—at the very core of her womanhood.

He whispered against her lips. 'This time you have to ask, *agapi mou*. You have to tell me what you want.'

Her voice cracked. 'Draco—please…'

'Not good enough, my sweet one. Is it this?' He kissed her breasts, taking each soft, scented mound into his mouth in turn.

'Yes,' she said. 'No. Oh, God…'

'Or this?' His fingertips brushed her intimately, as lightly as a butterfly kiss and as fleeting.

Her only answer was a soft, involuntary whimper of yearning.

'Or even—this?' His voice sank to a whisper as he bent his head and his mouth found her.

She cried out, and for a moment her body went rigid, all her inhibitions rearing up in shock.

But her one prim attempt to push him away was unavailing. He simply captured her wrists in one strong hand and did exactly as he wanted.

Which, Cressy realised, as her whole body began to shake in sudden wanton delight, was exactly what she wanted too.

The last vestiges of control were dissolving under the warm, subtle flicker of his tongue. She was going wild, her head twisting from side to side, the breath bursting hoarsely from her lungs. Pleasure was filling her like a dark flame, driving her to the limits of her endurance. And beyond.

Her whole being seemed to splinter in a rapture so intense she thought she might die.

As awareness slowly returned, she realised she was kissing him, her parted lips clinging to his in abandoned greed. She had marked him too, she saw. There were small crescents on the smooth skin of his shoulders that her nails had scored in those final fainting seconds.

She felt bewildered—and ashamed that her resistance could be so easily and swiftly destroyed. And she was angry, too, because she didn't want to be Draco's creature, locked into this—sexual thrall.

He raised his head and looked down at her.

He said, his voice slurred, 'I couldn't concentrate at my meeting for thinking of your loveliness—your sweetness. I should be at a dinner tonight with a group of other bankers, but I had to find you—to be with you...'

She turned her head, avoiding his gaze. 'Am I supposed to be grateful?'

'No,' he said with sudden harshness. 'Just willing.'

He lifted her hips towards him, and smoothly and expertly joined his body to hers.

She could not fight him physically—she was no match for his hard, virile muscularity—but she could close her mind against him. Force herself to lie passive and unresponsive beneath him—refuse herself the delicious agony of consummation that his powerful body was offering her once more. That, she discovered with shock, her own sated flesh was incredibly, impossibly eager to accept.

And Draco knew what she was doing. Because he too was holding back, deliberately tempting her to abandon her self-denial and join him on the path to their mutual delight.

His mouth touched hers, softly, coaxingly, then brushed her closed eyelids. His lips tugged at the lobe of her ear and explored the vulnerable pulse in her throat. He whispered her name almost pleadingly against her breast.

And, in spite of everything, her iron resolve was beginning to falter, her aroused body making demands she could no longer ignore.

But Draco's patience had cracked too. He was no longer teasing, or even very gentle. Instead, he was driving himself with a kind of grim determination towards his own climax.

At its height, he cried out something in his own language, his voice harsh, almost broken.

When it was over, he rolled away from her and lay, one arm covering his eyes, as his rasping breath slowly returned to normal.

Cressy sat up slowly, pushing her hair from her eyes. She supposed she had scored a small victory, but it seemed a barren, sterile thing, especially when her newly awakened body was aching for the fulfilment she'd spurned.

She felt cold, and a little frightened. She didn't dare look at him, or say anything, even when, a long time later, he got to his feet and walked to the sofa and his discarded clothing. A brooding silence enclosed them both.

At last he said, 'You made me use you. Why?'

She said, 'I assumed you wished to be repaid for my

father's medical bills. You can't always choose the currency.'

He whispered something under his breath, and the controlled violence of it made her flinch. He picked up her dress and tossed it to her. 'Cover yourself.'

She slipped it over her head, but didn't fasten it. She didn't trust her shaking hands to deal with the zip.

He was fully dressed when he spoke again, his tone clipped, remote. 'You will find food in the kitchen. I brought a hamper from London. There is chicken, and champagne and peaches.'

She ran her tongue across her dry lips. 'Aren't you hungry?'

'I find I do not wish to eat with you,' he returned curtly. 'Besides, I think it best if I go before I do something I shall regret.'

He walked to the door and she followed him, barefoot, holding the slipping dress against her.

She said, her voice faltering a little, 'Did you drive yourself here? I didn't see another car.'

'I parked at the back of the house. The housekeeper directed me.'

'In my father's place?' Her voice rose. 'Oh, God, how could she do such a thing?'

'Because, unlike you, Cressida *mou*, she seems able to accept that I am the master here now.'

Hurt exploded inside her, and an odd sense of desolation.

She said thickly, 'Damn you,' and swung back her hand. She wanted to hit him—to drive the expression of cold mockery from his face.

But he was too quick for her, grabbing her wrist with hard fingers, shaking her slightly, so that the damned dress slid off her shoulders again, baring her to the waist.

She saw his face change, become starkly intent. He said softly, 'There is only one way to deal with a woman like you.'

He swung her round so that her back, suddenly, was against the closed door. She tried to cover her breasts with her hands, but his fingers closed round her wrists, lifting them above her head and holding them there.

He said, 'It is a little late for such modesty. Rage suits you better.'

She said breathlessly, 'Let me go—you bastard...'

'When *I* choose,' he said. 'Not you.'

She heard her dress tear as it fell to the floor. He took her quickly, his anger meeting hers in an explosive fusion that stunned the senses.

She thought, This is an outrage... And then she stopped thinking altogether.

Because his hands were under her thighs, lifting her so that she had to clamp her legs round his waist, join the driving rhythm of his possession.

His mouth was crushing hers passionately, drinking the salty, angry tears from her lips. She was moaning in her throat, gasping for breath, dizzy and drowning in the merciless forces he had released in her.

She tried to push him away, but it was already too late. Deep within her she could feel the first harsh tremors of her approaching climax. As the pulsations overwhelmed her, tore through her, she sobbed her release against his lips, then hung in his arms, limp as a rag doll, incapable of speech, hardly able to think.

Draco stepped back from the door and carried her across the room, dropping her almost negligently on to the sofa.

Cressy lay, staring up at him, her face hectically flushed, her hair wildly dishevelled and her eyes wide and enormous.

His smile was mocking as he casually fastened his clothing. He reached into the inside pocket of his jacket for his wallet.

A shower of fifty-pound notes fluttered down on her.

He said softly, 'I think I have ruined your dress, *agapi mou*, so buy yourself a new one. Something that does not make you look as if you are in mourning for your virginity, hmm?'

He paused. 'And do not ever try to reject me again.'

She wanted to reach out to him, to say his name, to ask him to stay with her, but she was too shattered by the impact of the last few minutes to be able to move or formulate coherent words.

She could only watch helplessly as he turned and walked to the door, where he paused.

'And do not wait for me to apologise,' he flung back at her. 'Because I find, after all, I do not regret a thing.' And he went out, slamming the door behind him.

CHAPTER NINE

'I'M GOING to hire a detective,' said James Fielding. 'Someone who knows what he's doing. He'll find her— persuade her to come home. Of course it will cost a great deal of money, but that's not a problem. It's time I was back in the workplace, anyway. I was a damned fool to be talked into early retirement.'

There was an awkward silence. Cressy saw the swift, worried glance exchanged by her aunt and uncle, and looked down at her hands gripped together in her lap.

Every day it was the same, she thought wearily. Schemes to make new fortunes. Plans to win Eloise back. Her father could talk of nothing else. He seemed to have lost all touch with reality.

His financial difficulties—the fact that the house no longer belonged to him—were simply brushed aside as temporary difficulties.

But then who am I to criticise? she wondered. With the nightmare I've created for myself?

It had been a week since Draco had slammed out, and since then she hadn't heard a word from him.

And she was scared.

After he'd gone, she'd lain on the sofa for a long time, limbless, weightless in the aftermath of that raw, savage ecstasy. She'd never dreamed she was capable of such a primitive intensity of feeling. Was stunned by her capacity for passion.

It was as if she'd lived her life only knowing half of herself.

When she'd been able to move again, and think, she had gone up to her room, showered, and changed into jeans and a thin sweater. She had burned the torn dress, along with the money, in the kitchen range, and had thrown away the food and wine. She'd felt too numb to eat. Besides, it had all been too reminiscent of the picnics they'd shared on Myros, and she hadn't been able to bear to remember the uncomplicated happiness of those days.

Days, she'd thought, when I was falling in love…

And could have wept for the innocence and tenderness of that lost time.

She had recalled the way his arm had held her, fitting her to the curve of his body. The beat of his heart under her cheek. How he'd smiled at her. The reined-back hunger in his eyes. The huskiness in his voice when he'd asked her to marry him.

Everything, she'd thought bleakly, that she'd thrown away with both hands.

And no amount of sex, however mind-blowing, would ever make up for that.

By the time Berry had returned she'd managed to regain some kind of composure. She'd spent the evening in the study, working on her computer, tying up some loose ends from work and listening to music.

'Has your visitor gone, Miss Cressy?' Berry looked around her as if she might find him hiding in a corner. 'You could have knocked me down with a feather when he told me he was the new owner and showed me the papers.' She lowered her voice. 'I didn't really want to leave him here, but he was so persuasive.' She shook her head. 'Not an easy gentleman to say no to. But did I do the right thing?'

'Yes, of course.' Cressy smiled at her with a tranquillity she was far from feeling. 'I suppose he thought it was time he saw what he was getting for his money.'

'And he told me Mr Fielding will be renting the house from him and we won't have to move out. Oh, that's such a relief, Miss Cressy. I've been so worried.'

So have I, Cressy thought bleakly. And my worries aren't over yet.

As each long day passed, she felt as if she was living on a knife-edge, waiting for the phone to ring. Scanning her e-mail box for messages.

But the nights were even worse. She lay awake for hours, staring into the darkness, her body aching for him—longing for him. She felt bereft—like a child crying unheard for comfort.

Perhaps he'd decided to cut his losses and shut her out of his life altogether. That was the thought that tortured her every waking moment.

She told herself that she was concerned for her father. Because if Draco had really decided to finish their relationship, it did not follow that he would write off her father's debts.

But in her heart she knew it would never be as simple as that. That she was using her father's problems as a barrier—as self-protection against a hurt that might tear her in pieces. Against feelings she dared not examine too closely in case they destroyed her.

'Cressy, dear.' Her aunt's voice reached her from some far distance. 'I think it's time we went, and let James rest.'

'Yes, of course.' She rose, reaching for her bag, aware that Lady Kenny was watching her with a faint frown.

'Coffee, I think,' Sir Robert said when they were in the corridor.

In the hospital cafeteria, he joined the queue at the counter while Cressy and Barbara Kenny found a corner table.

'It doesn't get any better, does it?' Lady Kenny said abruptly. 'Poor James is like a dog with a bone. He won't let go.'

Cressy shook her head. 'And he gets so agitated when he talks about her. I know it's not good for him. What he'll be like when he gets home...'

'I wonder if that's such a good thing.' Her aunt played with her wedding ring. 'Whether he wouldn't be better living somewhere with no memories. But he'll have the nurse to keep an eye on him, and dear Berry, so we must hope for the best.' She gave Cressy a searching glance. 'Now tell me about this new job of yours.'

'There's nothing to tell,' Cressy hedged. 'I'm not even sure it's happening.'

'I gather it's connected with the Standard Trust Bank,' Lady Kenny went on, as if she hadn't spoken. 'And that the head of the bank—some Greek tycoon— has made himself personally responsible for your father's debts. Isn't that a little unusual?'

Cressy shrugged. 'I suppose so. I haven't really thought about it.'

'Even when he insisted on conducting the negotiations with you personally?' Her aunt's tone was acerbic. 'And when you'd only just come back from Greece?' She gave an exasperated sigh. 'Cressy, I'm not a fool. Are you involved with this man?'

Cressy bit her lip. 'Not in the way that you think, Aunt Bar.'

Which was no more than the truth, she thought unhappily. No one would believe the complexities of her relationship with Draco.

'I have a short-term contract,' she continued, 'which necessitates my working abroad. After what he's done for Dad, I could hardly refuse. And I can look after myself,' she added, infusing her tone with brightness.

Lady Kenny snorted. 'Oh, really? Have you looked in a mirror lately? You're all eyes and cheekbones.' She leaned forward. 'Darling, men like Draco Viannis are not philanthropists. You don't know what you're getting yourself into. Your uncle and I are both worried sick. And if your father would come down to earth for a few minutes, I know he'd put a stop to it.'

'It's for three months,' Cressy said quietly. 'If I go at all.' She swallowed. 'Mr Viannis may be having second thoughts.'

'I can't vouch for this coffee.' Sir Robert deposited a tray on the table and sat down, fixing his niece with a penetrating look. 'Now then, Cressy, I want a word about this Viannis chap. Are you sure you know what you're doing?'

They were both so kind, Cressy thought as she drove home later, and so anxious about her. And she knew she'd done nothing to set their minds at rest.

But what could she say—what reassurance could she possibly give? Especially when she herself felt as if she was operating in some kind of vacuum.

There was a strange car, large, powerful and glossy, parked in front of the house, and Berry was waiting to open the door for her.

'You've a visitor, Miss Cressy. I've shown him into the drawing room.'

Cressy's heart thudded, and her throat tightened painfully as she walked towards the drawing room. Ever since her last encounter with Draco she hadn't been inside the room, unsure if she could handle the memories it would evoke. In fact, she'd made a point of using her father's study instead.

Now she had to face him there. Brave whatever he had to tell her.

Swallowing, she twisted the handle and went in.

The anticlimax when she found herself confronted by a stranger was almost ludicrous.

Except that she did know him, she realised after a stunned moment. It was Paul Nixon, who worked as Draco's PA. She'd seen him briefly in London.

She felt sick. Draco wasn't even going to break their agreement in person.

'Miss Fielding. I'm sorry I didn't make an appointment, but Mr Viannis called from New York last night to say he'll be returning to Myros next week and wishes you to meet him there. And that doesn't leave much time.'

She felt as if she'd been reprieved from a death sentence, and was ashamed of the relief and joy that flooded through her.

She said quietly, 'I understand. Won't you sit down? Can I offer you some tea or coffee?'

'Your housekeeper already did that, ma'am.' He delved into a briefcase. 'I have a file here, with your itinerary. You'll fly first class to Athens, and transfer to Myros by helicopter. Also details of the personal allowance that you'll receive while you remain Mr Viannis's—companion, and the final settlement he is prepared to make.'

Caught on the raw, Cressy took the folder he handed her.

'What a lot of paperwork,' she said coolly, hiding her hurt. 'All to get a man into bed with a woman.'

Paul Nixon's solemn face reddened uncomfortably and he gave Cressy an austere look. 'The details of Mr Viannis's private life are no business of mine, Miss Fielding. I'm just here to do a job.'

'You do it well,' she said. 'But I'm sure you've had plenty of practice.'

He looked more po-faced than ever. 'You'll also be requested to sign a contract of confidentiality,' he went on. 'Guaranteeing that no details of your time with Mr Viannis will ever be made public.'

'In case I write a kiss-and-tell story for the tabloids?' Cressy asked with disbelief. 'My God, I'm the last person in the world who'd want to go public.'

'I'm sure that's how you feel now, ma'am. But things can change, and Mr Viannis would not wish any future marriage he might contract to be compromised by unwelcome revelations.'

She felt as if she'd been punched in the stomach, but she recovered and managed a taut smile. 'In other words, hell hath no fury, Mr Nixon. Tell your boss I'll sign his guarantee.'

She took the pen he handed her, and wrote her name where indicated.

Then she showed him to the door, wished him a pleasant drive back to London, and returned to the drawing room.

The folder was lying on the coffee table. The next three months of her life all spelled out for her in clauses, sub-clauses and settlements.

She picked it up, weighed it speculatively for a moment, then, with a small choking cry, threw it across the room as hard as she could. It hit the wall and fell, disgorging its contents on to the carpet.

And then she burst into tears.

Cressy finished rubbing sun screen on to her legs, and put the cap back on the bottle.

It would be tempting, she thought with detachment, to allow Draco to arrive and find her burned to a crisp, and consequently unavailable, but she could not risk the damage to her skin.

The sky above Myros was cloudlessly blue, the sun relentlessly hot, and the swimming pool beside her deliciously cool. If only she could relax and enjoy it...

But that was impossible.

She found herself stealing another glance at her watch, and swore under her breath. He would be here only too soon. She didn't have to mark the passage of every minute until then.

She'd arrived the previous day, leaving rain and a chill, unseasonal breeze in England.

Her father, immersed in the letters he was writing to various companies offering his services as a consultant, had wished her an almost casual goodbye.

At one time she would have been wounded by his self-absorption. Now she had her own immediate problems to deal with.

The resident nurse, a Miss Clayton, was a kind, sensible woman, and Cressy had liked her at once. But it was clear she had a struggle on her hands to induce James Fielding to rest.

'It's not just a question of medication,' she'd told Cressy as they shook hands. 'He needs to relax more.'

Don't we all? thought Cressy, with irony, reaching for the iced lemonade on the table beside her. She might be in the equivalent of Eden, but she was like a cat on hot bricks just the same.

However disapproving Mr Nixon might be, there had been nothing wrong with his travel arrangements. It had been VIP treatment all the way.

The villa was just as beautiful as she'd imagined, with large airy rooms and exquisitely tiled floors, and a magical view of the sea from every window. And although it was luxurious, it wasn't stridently so. The furniture tended to be on the heavy, old-fashioned side, suggesting it had been passed down over several generations, and Cressy found it charming.

And the service was faultless, she thought. Courteous and unobtrusive.

If Vassilis, Draco's elderly major-domo, had reservations about his employer's choice of guest, he gave no sign of it.

She knew now what building work Draco had found it necessary to supervise, because she was living in it.

It was a guest bungalow, completely separate from the villa itself, with its own garden and pool, tucked away in a corner of the grounds.

It had a large living room, where her meals were served, a bathroom, with a big sunken tub as well as a conventional shower, and a huge bedroom, with walls painted in pale gold and a king-size bed with an ivory cover, draped in matching filmy curtains.

The perfect love nest, she'd thought, lips twisting, as Vassilis had shown her round it. All that was lacking was the perfect love.

But at least she was the first one to stay there. She hadn't had to spend her first sleepless night speculating on the women who'd occupied this bed before her. Her successor could worry about that.

Pain knifed at her, but she couldn't let that matter. She had to keep reminding herself of the tenuous nature of her position. Accustom herself to the idea that she had no permanent role in Draco's life.

And perhaps by the time it ended she would have learned to live with the pain.

In the distance, she heard the sound of a helicopter. She scrambled off the cushioned lounger and stood, staring upwards, her hand shading her eyes, her heart thumping against her ribcage.

It came in low enough for her to be aware of a figure—a face looking down at her—then descended towards the pad on the far side of the main house.

She took a deep, steadying breath, and thought, He's here.

And now, as Vassilis had tactfully indicated, she must wait to be summoned.

Fright and excitement warred inside her for control. After a moment, she resumed her place on the lounger. She didn't want to be found standing beside the pool as if she was planning to drown herself.

She picked up the magazine she'd been glancing through and tried to concentrate on it as the minutes dragged by.

It was over an hour later when Vassilis's upright figure appeared in the gap in the high flowering hedge that divided the bungalow from the rest of the grounds.

He said in his careful English, 'Mr Viannis presents his compliments to you, madam, and asks if you will dine with him this evening. He suggests ten o'clock.'

Six hours to go, Cressy thought. Draco was playing it cool. Whereas she might well become a nervous wreck.

Aloud, she said sedately, 'Please thank Mr Viannis,

and tell him I'd be delighted.' She paused. 'Am I to join him at the main house?'

'Yes, madam. I shall conduct you there.' He made her a small half-bow, and turned away.

Well, what had she expected? she asked herself with self-derision as she went back to her magazine. That Draco was going to rush to her side and smother her with kisses?

She was being taught her place, she thought, in one unequivocal lesson.

But, she told herself forlornly, she would have preferred the kisses.

She spent a lot of time that evening deciding what to wear. In the end she chose a cream silk shift, with boot-lace straps and a deeply slashed neckline that skimmed the inner curves of her breasts. The minimum of underwear and a pair of cream strappy sandals with high heels completed the outfit.

Dressing the part, she thought, as she brushed her hair to fall in a silky curtain on her shoulders. But wasn't that what he was paying for?

She noticed that Vassilis kept his eyes discreetly lowered when he came to collect her.

It was a warm, sultry night, and the cicadas were busy as she walked through the garden. There were lights on inside the villa, and on the terrace which surrounded it.

One massive pair of sliding glass doors stood open, leading, she knew, to the *saloni*, and Vassilis paused outside, indicating politely that she should precede him into the lamplit room.

Lifting her chin, she obeyed, aware of him closing the doors behind her. Shutting her in.

He was standing at a side table, pouring himself a

drink. He was wearing jeans, and a dark polo shirt, unbuttoned to reveal the shadowing of hair on his chest, and for a brief moment her heart lifted as she saw the lover she'd first met.

Then he turned and studied her, the firm mouth unsmiling, and she knew she was mistaken.

He said softly, 'So, here you are.'

'As you see,' she said, masking her real emotions with flippancy. 'Stripped, bathed, and brought to your tent.'

His tone was flat. 'You are not amusing.' He pointed to the cloudy liquid in his glass. 'I am drinking ouzo. May I get you some?'

'I'd prefer plain water.'

He gave her a cynical look. 'How abstemious of you, *agapi mou*,' he drawled. 'You don't feel that alcohol might dull the edge of your coming ordeal?'

'Is that how you regard it?'

Draco shrugged. 'I want you very badly.' The dark eyes met hers in a frankly sensual challenge. 'And I am not in the mood to make allowances.'

Her throat tightened. She was aware that her skin was tingling, her entire body stirring with irresistible excitement under its thin silken covering.

Faint colour rose in her face, but she didn't look away.

She said, 'I'll take the risk.'

He lifted a sceptical brow, then turned back to the table, dropping ice cubes into a tumbler and filling it with water.

When he came across to give her the glass, Cressy felt her pulses surge. She thought that he would touch her, run his fingers down her bare arm, take her hand, kiss her mouth.

But he stepped back, lifting his own glass in a mocking salute. 'To courage, *pethi mou*,' he said, and drank.

They had dinner on the terrace, the table lit by glass-shaded candles. Vassilis brought them a light creamy soup, delicately flavoured with lemon, then fish baked with herbs, served with tiny potatoes and a green salad.

The food was delicious but Cressy had to force herself to eat. She was too aware of the shadowed face of the man who sat opposite her. Conscious of the caress of his dark eyes on her lips, her shoulders, her breasts. And she felt deep within her the slow ache of anticipation.

The silence between them was electric—alive with tension. As if, she thought, a storm was brewing.

She said, trying to introduce an element of normality, 'How was New York?'

'Like an oven. I prefer to go there in the fall.'

'Was your trip successful?'

'Thank you, yes.' There was faint amusement in his voice.

'And was the flight back tiring?'

'Yes, but I have amazing powers of recovery.' He was grinning openly now, and she felt herself blush.

After a pause, he said, 'You sound as if you have been taking lessons.'

'In what?' She sent him a puzzled look.

'Polite conversation for difficult situations,' he said silkily. 'And don't glare at me like that, or Vassilis will think we have quarrelled,' he added as the older man came soft-footed along the terrace.

He brought dessert—a bowl of fresh peaches and glossy black grapes—and when he had filled tiny cups with strong, bitter coffee, he discreetly vanished.

Cressy said, constrainedly, 'He's been very kind.'

His mouth twisted. 'He is paid to be.'

She drank some of the smoky brew. 'Is that what I'm paid for, too?'

He said harshly, 'No, it is not kindness I want from you. And you know it.'

'Then what?'

His smile was crooked. 'For tonight, *agapi mou*, I want you naked in my arms, and I cannot wait any longer. Come with me now.'

Her high heels made it difficult for her to keep up with his stride as they went through the moonlit garden, so she kicked off her sandals and ran beside him, barefoot.

Instantly he lifted her into his arms and carried her the rest of the way. As they reached the bungalow he stopped and kissed her, his mouth fierce and hungry, and she put her arms round his neck and held him, her lips parting eagerly beneath his.

A lamp had been lit in the bedroom, the covers were turned back, and a bottle of champagne on ice had been placed on the night table.

She thought, The stage is set, and wished it hadn't been. That no outsider had intruded on their first night together.

And then Draco kissed her again, and she forgot everything as her need for him surged through her.

He undid the single button which held her dress at the back, and it slid down her body to the floor. He knelt, stripping off her remaining covering, then buried his face against the slight concavity of her abdomen.

He whispered, 'I have dreamed of this, Cressida *mou*, of the scent of your skin—the taste…'

He picked her up and put her on the bed, shrugging

off his own clothes as he came down beside her. He kissed her mouth, and her breasts, then entered her, and she was so very ready, her body opening sweetly for him.

His taking was strong and powerful, and she gave without reserve, glorying in the muscled heat that filled her, taking him deeper and deeper, her mouth soft and moist under his, her fingers grazing his spine.

The final dark rapture took them both unawares. She cried out against his mouth, startled by the force that convulsed her, and heard his deep groan of pleasure in reply.

There were tears on her face, and his eyelashes were wet, but his lips were warm and sure against hers, and the fingers that stroked her body were endlessly tender.

And it was the most natural thing in the world to fold herself into the strong curve of his body and sleep.

But some time later, when she stirred drowsily and reached out to him, the place beside her was empty. And cold, too, as if he'd been gone a long time.

She had expected him to be there. Had counted on waking to the new day in his arms. Instead, loneliness was an icy hand at her throat.

She could just catch the fragrance of the cologne he used on his pillow. It was all that was left of him in the moonlit room, so she pulled the pillow into her arms and held it tightly, breathing the scent of him as she waited for the dawn alone.

CHAPTER TEN

CRESSY turned at the end of the pool, and cut back through the turquoise water with her clean, easy stroke. She'd already completed ten lengths, hoping that strenuous exercise would clear her mind and calm the agony of emotional confusion raging inside her.

Last night when she made love with Draco she had felt that it wasn't just a mating of their bodies, but their spirits too. And she was sure he'd been as moved by their attunement as she had.

She'd expected—she'd needed to sleep in his arms, and wake to feel his mouth warm and drowsy against hers. She'd hoped he would feel the same.

But he'd walked away. And realising that, for him, it had just been another sexual encounter—enjoyable, but soon forgotten—had been a cruel lesson to learn.

Vassilis had brought her breakfast as usual to the little vine-covered pergola, and it had taken all her resolve not to ask where Draco was, if he would be joining her. Or even if he'd sent her a message...

Well, she knew the answer to that too. Because he had not.

Underlining yet again that she had no real importance in his life, apart from the fact that he found her body desirable.

And perhaps she'd needed that kind of reminder, or she might have allowed the euphoria of the previous night to betray her into saying something really stupid. Something he would not want to hear.

She reached the other end of the pool and paused, shaking the drops of water from her face. As she did so she felt strong hands slide under her arms and draw her bodily up out of the water.

'*Kalimera,*' Draco said, as he set her down on the tiled surround. He was wearing elegant pale grey pants, and a white shirt, open at the neck.

'I—I didn't know you were there.' She made a business of wringing the excess water from her hair.

'I have been watching you,' he said. 'Tell me, *pethi mou*, are you training for the next Olympic Games?'

She shrugged. 'Swimming is good exercise.'

He said softly, 'I know another,' and pulled her towards him.

She hung back. 'I'm soaking. Your clothes will be ruined.'

'Then I'll take them off,' he said, and began to unbutton his shirt.

'Your staff...'

'Know better than to interrupt us. Besides, the maids have finished.'

She knew that. She had seen them leave while she was having breakfast, carrying the unwanted champagne and talking and giggling together. No doubt mulling over the fact that Kyrios Draco had found nothing to celebrate during his night with his *anglitha*. She'd felt stung, and his casual reference galled her all the more.

She said breathlessly, 'Is this what you expect? That I just—perform to order at any hour of the day and night?'

His shirt went to join the grey suit jacket and silk tie which, together with a briefcase, were already lying on one of the sun loungers.

He said, 'I was not aware, *agapi mou*, that I had asked you to perform at all.' He unzipped his trousers and stepped out of them, revealing brief black swimming trunks.

He regarded her bleakly. 'I have been in a meeting on Alakos since early morning. Perhaps I should have stayed there rather than hurry back to be with you. Or maybe you would prefer me to return to the main house for my swim?'

She said, stumbling a little, 'No—stay—please.' She looked at him appealingly. 'Draco, try to understand. This—isn't easy for me.'

His voice was cold. 'It was not intended to be.' He walked to the edge of the pool and dived in.

Cressy towelled herself down, then retired rather miserably to her lounger under the sun umbrella. Somehow he'd managed to wrongfoot her again, she thought.

When Draco eventually emerged from the pool, he dried himself quickly, then stretched out on one of the spare loungers a few feet away. He did not speak, or look at her, but busied himself with some papers he took from his briefcase.

With a smothered sigh, Cressy reached for the sun screen and began to apply it to her legs, aware that Draco's eyes had flickered briefly in her direction.

Making her wonder at the same time exactly how much of his attention it would be possible to attract.

He had put her firmly in her place, but how strong was his resolution to keep her at a distance?

She spent a long time smoothing on the lotion, lifting each slender leg in turn and running her hands slowly over her calves and up to her thighs, aware that his gaze was straying for longer and longer periods in her direction.

When she'd finished her legs, she began on her abdomen, using just her fingertips and upward circular movements until her bikini bra got in the way.

She unhooked it, and dropped it to the tiles, and began gently and very delicately to rub sun screen on to her breasts, paying particular attention to her nipples.

A lightning glance from under her lashes at Draco revealed that he'd abandoned all pretence of studying his papers, and instead was lying on his side, propped up on one elbow, watching her with undisguised appreciation.

He said softly, 'For a lady who does not perform, you're putting on quite a show, Cressida *mou*.'

She said, 'I don't want to burn…'

'No,' he said. 'You wish me to do so, instead.'

She gave him a small, cool smile, lifting her hands to push her hair back from her face, so that her breasts tilted upward in deliberate provocation.

'I thought you liked to look at me.'

'I do. You are very lovely. That is why I had your bedroom designed in gold and ivory—so that it would match your hair and your skin. Even if, as I thought then, I could only enjoy the picture you'd make in my imagination. Or on our wedding night,' he added almost casually.

She winced inwardly. She said, 'I hope I didn't disappoint you.'

'Not physically, *agapi mou*. Your body is all that a man could dream of.' His smile did not reach his eyes.

'But?' Cressy lifted her chin. 'Isn't that what you were going to say?'

He said, 'I was going to quote from your Shakespeare's *Troilus and Cressida*—when Troilus realises he has been betrayed.' His voice was quiet, almost reflective. '"If beauty have a soul, this is not she".'

Colour flared in her face. She reached for her discarded towel and pulled it across her body.

She said quietly, 'That's—cruel...'

'Perhaps,' he said. 'I am not in the mood for kindness.' He stood up, stretching indolently, then picked up his clothes.

He said, 'However, I'm hungry and I'm tired. I'm going up to the house to have some food, and then sleep for an hour or two. *Herete*, Cressida *mou*.'

She said quickly, before her courage deserted her, 'You don't have to go. You could have lunch here, and then we could—sleep together—in the beautiful room you made for me.'

There was a silence, then Draco shrugged, his eyes hard. 'I fear that is not possible. You see, to me, sleep is the ultimate surrender between a man and a woman. It signifies trust—mutual dependence, commitment. And I swore a long time ago that it was an intimacy I would only share with my wife.'

She hadn't known it was possible to hurt so much. She said, 'I see,' and was astonished that her voice didn't break.

His smile grazed her skin. 'But if you feel inclined to "perform" again at some time, you have only to let me know. I will be delighted to join you.'

And he walked away, leaving her staring after him, her eyes blurred with tears.

I suppose, Cressy told herself drearily, that this is what's known as stalemate.

She'd found her way out of the garden and was standing on the headland itself, staring out to sea, her hair whipping about her face.

The wind had risen in the night, and below her the water had been stirred into little foam-capped waves.

There was no way down to the shore that she could see, but it was good just to get away from the immediate vicinity of the bungalow.

There were times, she thought restively, when she felt as if she was in solitary confinement.

She hadn't seen Draco for nearly a week now. True, he wasn't always there. The helicopter had been buzzing backwards and forwards regularly. But when he was at home he made no attempt to seek her company.

And pride, as well as fear of another rejection, prevented her from asking him to come to her.

'Kyria Fielding.' She looked round to see Vassilis hurrying towards her. 'I could not find you. I was concerned.'

'Did you think I'd run away again—or that I was going to throw myself over?' Cressy asked drily.

'That is not a subject about which to make jokes,' he said reprovingly, and she sighed.

'I'm sorry, Vassilis. Is there a problem?'

'I have brought your lunch, *kyria*. It will be getting cold.'

She sat, as she always did, at the small table he'd laid for her on the terrace. Her napkin was spread on her lap, and wine was poured into her glass.

The service remained impeccable, she thought, wondering if Vassilis found it strange that his employer's mistress should be spending her days and nights alone. Whatever his views, he was too well-trained to betray them.

He took the lid from a dish and served her a tiny

boned chicken stuffed with a delicately savoury rice. It was delicious, as usual, but as she ate Cressy thought with nostalgia of the meals she'd eaten at Yannis's taverna.

Instead of this evening's gourmet treat, she wondered if she could persuade Draco to take her out to eat. Spit-roasted lamb, she thought, and a Greek salad, and some rough red wine.

And maybe he would dance for her, and smile at her because he saw once more the girl he'd fallen in love with.

It was worth trying, anyway. Anything, she thought, was better than this limbo she was currently occupying.

She began to plan. She would ask Vassilis to arrange transport for her to Myros town, so that she could tell Yannis and Maria they were coming and get them to reserve the usual corner table.

She would also get her hair trimmed, she thought, combing its tangles with her fingers. She might even buy something to wear—something demure, and pretty, and very Greek.

But first she had to see Draco, and invite him formally to have dinner with her. And when he arrived at the bungalow that evening she would tell him he was driving her to Myros instead.

All she needed now was an excuse to go up to the house.

The telephone, she thought, with sudden inspiration. She could say she needed to call her family in England, which was no more than the truth. She'd rung home on her first evening, to tell them all she'd arrived safely, but she'd been reluctant to call again, in case she was faced with questions she couldn't answer.

I'll just have to risk it, she told herself.

She changed into a pair of slim-fitting white trousers, topping them with a dark blue cotton knit sweater with short sleeves and a discreet neckline.

Neat, she thought, as she brushed her hair and tied it back at the nape of her neck with a scarf, but not over-seductive.

Vassilis was clearly surprised to see her when she presented herself at the main door a few minutes later, but he nodded when she mentioned the telephone.

'I will ask for you to use the one in Kyrios Draco's study, madam. It is more private there.'

He led the way to a thick, heavily carved wooden door, and tapped. There was a moment's low-voiced conversation in Greek, then he stood back.

'Go in, madam, if you please.'

So far so good, thought Cressy, pinning on the casually pleasant smile she'd been practising.

But it wasn't Draco who rose with formal politeness as she entered, but Paul Nixon.

'Miss Fielding.' His tone held faint surprise. 'If you're looking for Draco, he's in Athens.'

Disappointment was like a slap in the face.

She said, 'I didn't realise. I didn't hear the helicopter.'

'He went very late last night,' he said. 'I guess you were asleep.' He paused. 'I understand you wish to use the phone?'

No, she thought. I want to make an assignation with my lover.

She said, 'Yes, if that's possible. I'm feeling guilty about my family.'

'And we can't have that.' There was something in his tone, as he gathered up the papers he was working on, which needled her. At the door, he paused. 'You know the code for the UK? Then I'll leave you to it.'

She spoke to her aunt first. 'Aunt Bar—how's everything going? How's Dad?'

'I'm not altogether sure,' Lady Kenny said slowly. 'Your uncle and I went to lunch there yesterday, and he seemed quiet, almost subdued. And he didn't mention Eloise once.' She sighed. 'I think he's finally coming to terms with the fact that she's never coming back.'

'But that's a good thing—isn't it?'

'We must hope so.' Her aunt paused. 'And you, Cressy—how are things with you?'

'Oh, fine,' she said brightly, crossing her fingers in the folds of her skirt. 'You don't have to worry about me.'

When she rang her home, Nurse Clayton told her that her father was proving a model patient, if a little low-spirited.

'A call from you could be just what he needs to cheer him up,' she added.

Her father's voice sounded quiet and tired. He said, 'Sid, darling, I was hoping you'd ring. I've been doing a lot of thinking, and I realise I haven't been very fair or very kind to you for a long time now.'

'Oh, Dad.' Her throat constricted. 'You don't have to say this. Not now.'

'Yes,' he said. 'I must. I don't even know how much personal responsibility you've taken for my financial mess. No one seems prepared to give me any straight answers.' He paused. 'And it matters, because you're all I've got, and you're precious. So, tell me the truth, Sid. This Viannis—is he treating you well?'

'Yes,' she said steadily. 'Yes, he is. And I'll be home very soon now. We'll talk properly then.'

'It's good to hear your voice,' he said. 'I just needed to tell you I was sorry. Bless you, Sid, and take care always.'

She replaced the receiver, frowning a little. She'd never heard him like that before, speaking as if every word was an effort.

She thought, I'll arrange with Draco to ring each day from now on.

She found Paul Nixon waiting in the big square entrance hall.

She said, 'Thank you for the use of the room. I wonder if I could put you to some more trouble.'

'You can always ask.'

It didn't sound particularly hopeful, she thought, bewildered, but she pressed on.

'I was wondering if someone could drive me to Myros town?'

'For what purpose?'

This time his curtness was undisguised.

She flushed. 'Because I haven't been outside the grounds of this villa since I got here.' She ticked her reasons off on her fingers. 'Because I need a hairdresser, and because I'd like to visit Yannis and Maria at the taverna again. I hope that's all right,' she added with a touch of sarcasm.

He said, 'I'll arrange for a beautician from the hotel to visit you here.'

She stared at him. 'I said I'd like to go out.'

'I'm afraid that's not possible, Miss Fielding. Draco wishes you to remain in the environs of the Villa Hera.'

She laughed disbelievingly. 'You mean I can't even go for a walk? But that's ridiculous.'

'This is a small island, Miss Fielding,' he said quietly. 'With traditional views and values, which Draco respects. And your status has changed since you were last here.'

She stiffened as she realised what he was implying. 'You mean Maria might not want to meet Draco's whore?'

'Precisely. Also your presence here is a matter of total discretion. Draco does not wish that compromised—largely for your own sake. One day you won't have his protection. And as his discarded mistress you'd be a fair target for the gutter press.'

There was a note almost like relish in his tone.

The breath caught in her throat. She said. 'You don't like me very much, do you?'

'I work for Draco, Miss Fielding. I don't judge how he chooses to amuse himself.'

'Really?' Cressy raised her eyebrows. 'I get the impression you've been judging me ever since I stepped out of that penthouse lift in London.'

He looked at her icily. 'Okay, Miss Fielding. You want to hear it—you'll get it. Draco and I go way back. We were at school together in the States, and at college. He was best man at my wedding, and I planned to stand up for him when he married this shy Aphrodite that he'd found on a beach. A girl he worshipped, and who loved him for himself alone. Someone he'd thought he'd never find.

'Only there was no wedding, and you know why. My wife and I were right here when he realised you'd dumped him and run.'

He drew a harsh breath. 'I had to watch my best friend go to pieces in front of me, and it wasn't pleasant. He was torn apart—going crazy. You damn near destroyed him, and if you're suffering a little in return, that's fine with me.'

He shook his head. 'I never wanted him to get involved with you again, but I guess this is his way of finally getting you out of his system, so I sure hope it works.

'And don't bother running to him to get me fired when he comes back tonight, lady,' he added curtly. 'My letter of resignation will already be on his desk.'

She made herself meet the cold accusation, the hostility in his eyes.

She said tonelessly, 'Why should you lose your job for telling the truth? I—I shan't say anything to Draco. And I hope you'll stay and go on being his friend.'

She walked past him towards the door and the sunshine beyond, then turned. Her voice trembled. 'And, for the record, you can't possibly blame me more than I do myself.'

The breeze was still strong, so she spent the remainder of the afternoon inside the bungalow, curled up in a corner of the big, deeply cushioned sofa which dominated the living area, her arms wrapped round her body in a vain attempt to stop herself shaking.

Paul Nixon's words had brought home to her as never before exactly what she'd done. She thought of Draco, scorned and humiliated, like an eagle brought low, and pain tore at her.

I'm no better than Eloise, she thought. I left, too, without considering the ruin and desolation I was leaving behind. And I did that to the man I loved, whereas I don't believe she ever cared for my father.

But her father had forgiven. Had gone on loving Eloise in spite of everything.

Which Draco had not. And once his need for revenge was satisfied, she would be out of his life for ever.

'I'd go to him on my knees,' she whispered. 'If I thought it would do any good. If he'd hold me just once more as if he was keeping me safe against the world. But it's too late.'

A short while later she heard the helicopter passing overhead. And fifteen minutes afterwards became aware of approaching footsteps striding swiftly across the terrace.

She scrambled to her feet, and waited for the door to open.

The wind had ruffled his dark hair. As she looked at him, she felt her heart contract with helpless yearning.

He said, 'Paul tells me you were asking for me.'

'Only to get your permission to telephone England.'

He frowned slightly. 'Naturally, you have it. You do not need to ask. I will arrange to have a phone installed here for your personal use.'

'That's kind,' she said. 'But there's no real need.'

He said quietly, 'Please allow me to do this for you.' He paused. 'Was your call satisfactory?'

'I suppose so.' It was her turn to hesitate. 'I'm worried about my father.'

'I'm sorry.'

'It's probably nothing,' she said. 'He just sounded so defeated somehow.' She sighed. 'But he called me Sid. And he hasn't done that for a very long time.'

He looked her over, smiling slowly. 'And is that who you are now?'

'Only until the sun goes down.' She met his dark gaze. 'Will you have dinner with me this evening?'

'Why, *agapi mou*?' he drawled. 'Is this your way of telling me that you're available again?'

No, she thought, it's my way of telling myself that if

a few hours of lovemaking are all I'm allowed of you, then I'll settle for that.

She shrugged, watching him through her lashes. 'Find out for yourself, *kyrie*—after dinner.'

His brows lifted in mocking acknowledgement. He walked across to her and pulled her against him, his lips exploring hers in warm, sensuous appreciation. At the same time he untied the scarf confining her hair, separating the silky strands with restless fingers and drawing them forward to frame her face.

She laughed and shook her head. 'It needs cutting.'

'I forbid it,' he said huskily. 'It would be a crime against humanity.'

He drew her down to sit beside him on the sofa. He said, 'I have to go away again tomorrow.'

'Must you?' She moved slightly so that his fingers could more easily cup her breast. 'Where this time?'

'New York.'

'I thought you didn't like it there in summer.'

'I have no choice. I have business to settle, and a possible merger to arrange.'

'Tell me about it.' She slipped a hand into the open neck of his shirt, her fingers tracing patterns among the crisp dark hair.

He shook his head. 'I never talk about deals before they are concluded.'

'My father used to say that.'

'Presumably before his business acumen deserted him.' His tone was faintly acerbic.

'It wasn't entirely his fault,' she protested. 'He was under pressure from my stepmother, and he could never refuse her anything. She helped con him out of the money, and now she's gone off with the man who ruined him, and he'd still have her back if he could.'

He gave her a cynical look. 'Love drives you crazy, *pethi mou*. Didn't you know?' He kissed her again. 'I'll go now. I need a shower and a drink before dinner, and I have some calls to make.'

'Is it always like this?' she asked. 'Phone calls and meetings, and dashing from city to city?'

'Not always.' He ran a caressing hand down her spine. 'And when I come back I shall make sure I have some free time to devote to you alone.' He paused. 'Do you miss me when I'm away?'

She wriggled away from his hand and the question at the same time. 'I've never been to New York.'

He was silent for a moment. 'I have too hectic a schedule for you to accompany me this time,' he said quietly. 'There'll be other trips.'

She put on one of her favourite dresses, a simple button-through style in dark green linen, with a square neck and a skirt that flared slightly. She brushed lustre on to her lips, and mascara on to her long lashes, and stroked scent on to her throat and breasts. Preparing herself for love, she thought, her mouth twisting sadly.

When she emerged from her bedroom, she was confronted by a procession of people with table linen, cutlery and glassware, all milling round in the living room.

She beckoned to Vassilis. 'Will you tell them all to go, please?'

'To go, madam?' He was clearly shocked. 'But we must make things ready for Kyrios Draco.'

'I can do that myself,' Cressy said briskly, ignoring his horrified expression. 'I can lay a table, arrange flowers and light candles.'

'But the *kyrie*…'

'The *kyrie* wants peace and privacy, and so do I.'

Cressy offered him a winning smile. 'Please make them understand I wish to be alone with him.'

He was clearly scandalised by such candour—the fiction that she was just another guest and this was an ordinary dinner party had to be maintained somehow—but he had the room emptied in minutes.

As she moved round the table, putting the final touches, Cressy let herself pretend that she was back in London, in her own flat, waiting for Draco to arrive. That once again they were lovers, with a wedding to plan and a future to dream about.

As it could have been, she thought. Only I was too much of a coward to take the risk.

When everything was as good as she could make it, she sat down and tried to compose herself. It was impossible that she should still feel shy with Draco, yet she did. Because in many ways he was still an enigma.

He made love to her with breathtaking skill and artistry, but that was such a minor part of his life. And the doors to the rest were closed to her.

Restlessly, she reached for the pile of magazines that Vassilis provided on an almost daily basis. They were mostly high-fashion glossies, which didn't interest her greatly, but there was the odd news magazine sometimes, reminding her that there was a real world outside Myros.

She picked up the latest edition and began to flick through the politics and reviews which made up most of its content.

She turned to the business pages and stopped, her whole body suddenly rigid, because Draco was there. And not alone. The full-length photograph of him in evening dress, taken outside some restaurant, also featured the beautiful girl clinging to his arm. She was tall and dark, with sultry eyes and a pouting mouth, and her spectacular figure was enhanced by a piece of designer glamour that had probably cost more than a thousand dollars per square centimetre.

'Draco Viannis with shipping heiress Anna Theodorous', ran the caption, and, numbly, Cressy turned to read the accompanying story.

Insiders, expecting to hear that the Ximenes Corporation's bid for the Theodorous tanker fleet has been successful, were intrigued last week by rumours of a more personal merger between the two giants.

Draco Viannis seems likely to surrender his bachelor status at last when his engagement is announced to Dimitris Theodorous's lovely twenty-year-old daughter Anna.

While boardroom negotiations were said to have temporarily stalled, the couple seemed inseparable at a series of fashionable Manhattan niteries, and a Ximenes source confirmed they were close.

Maybe all Dimitris has to do is wait for his rival to become his son-in-law.

Someone was moaning, a small, desolate sound in the stillness.

It was a moment before she realised that the noise was coming from herself, and pressed a hand to her mouth to stifle it.

She closed the magazine and thrust it back into the middle of the pile, as if she could somehow, by so doing, make it disappear altogether.

But there would be other stories in other newspapers and magazines that she would have to confront eventually. This would be a big business marriage, and it would not be celebrated quietly.

A whimper escaped her. But she couldn't let herself go to pieces.

It would be pointless anyway. He had made it coldly clear all along that he would marry eventually. She just hadn't expected it to be so soon. But it was none of her business. She'd forfeited all rights the day she'd agreed to his terms.

Nor was it any use telling herself that this was a political marriage rather than a love match. How many men with his money and power did follow their hearts, anyway? And Draco wouldn't risk being caught in that trap again.

Besides, having Anna Theodorous as a wife would be no hardship to any red-blooded man.

She'll be the one, thought Cressy, to sleep in his arms and be the mother of his children.

And I shall have to remember that every day for the rest of my life.

CHAPTER ELEVEN

'YOU are very quiet.' Draco watched her meditatively across the candlelit table.

She smiled at him. 'I thought you might like to eat in peace.'

'And I thought perhaps you were worn out by domesticity, *agapi mou*.' He indicated the table. 'Vassilis tells me you did all this yourself.'

'Yes,' Cressy said lightly. 'I'm amazing, aren't I? Imagine knowing where knives and forks go.'

His lips twitched. 'Can you cook as well? Does my chef have to worry?'

'I'm a very good cook, but I wouldn't dare invade his domain.'

How can I do this? she asked herself. How can I sit and chat about trivia when my heart is breaking?

He said softly, 'There seems no end to your talents, my beautiful one.'

She leaned back in her chair, letting her fingers play gently with the long stem of her wine glass, caressing the slender shaft with sensuous enjoyment. 'I try to please.'

Draco watched what she was doing with undisguised amusement. He said gently, 'Behave, Cressida *mou*.'

She let her lashes sweep down to veil her eyes. 'That's for wives, *kyrie*. Mistresses are allowed to do as they like. It goes with the territory.'

'You seem to know a great deal about it.'

'I've had to learn fast. After all, I don't want your successor to feel I'm lacking in any respect.'

'My successor?' His fork clattered to his plate. 'What in hell do you mean?'

She shrugged. 'Well, this certainly beats accountancy. I expect a long and lucrative career. Of course, I shall need you to introduce me to your friends when my three months is up,' she added casually.

He said with a snap, 'I'll make a note in my diary.'

'You sound put out.' Cressy raised her eyebrows. 'But I have to be practical. And I really should become more demanding too. After all, I'm still wearing my own clothes,' she added, frowning. 'Why wasn't there a wardrobe full of top designer gear waiting for me?'

'Perhaps because I felt you would almost certainly throw it in the sea,' he said.

'I wouldn't throw jewels in the sea,' she said. 'Or furs.'

'I admit I did not think of furs.' Draco picked up a peach and began to peel it. 'But the average temperature on Myros may have affected my judgement.'

'I could always save them,' she said. 'For New York in the fall.'

'But if you want jewels, you shall have them,' he went on, as if she hadn't spoken. 'Do you prefer diamonds or pearls?'

'Both,' she said.

His brows lifted. 'Take care, *pethi mou*. You may price yourself out of the market.'

'I'll be careful,' she said. 'And I'll be very selective next time, too, about my choice of benefactor.' She looked thoughtfully into space. 'A lonely widower, perhaps—whose daughter's just got married...'

'What is this nonsense?' There was no amusement in his voice now.

She shrugged. 'You'll be going on to the next lady. I'll have to go on to the next man.' She paused on the very edge of the abyss. Then jumped. 'You will introduce me to Dimitris Theodorous, won't you?'

Draco put down the knife he was using very carefully. 'What are you talking about?' His tone was ice.

'The merger,' she said. 'I've been reading all about it.'

'It's no secret,' he said. 'Ximenes has been negotiating for those tankers for a long time.'

'I wasn't,' she said, 'talking about tankers.'

'I did not think so.' The agate eyes glittered at her.

'Miss Theodorous photographs beautifully,' she went on recklessly. 'I loved her dress—what there was of it. Do tell her so.'

He leaned back in his chair. 'With pleasure,' he drawled. 'Which particular dress did you have in mind? She has so many.'

She had to guess. 'The Versace.'

He smiled reminiscently. 'Ah, yes.'

Cressy brought her fist down on the table. 'You bastard.' Her voice shook. 'You were with her every night in New York. Then you came back here—to me.'

He shrugged. 'What good is a woman in New York when I am on Myros?' His voice was silky.

'You're despicable.'

'No,' he said. 'Practical—like you.' His eyes blazed at her suddenly. 'And you forfeited the right to dictate to me about other lovers when you ran out on our wedding.'

She said fiercely, 'And you forfeited the same right when you forced me into bed with you.'

'You think I used force?' His chair grated across the tiled floor as he stood up. 'You are a child, Cressida *mou*. But perhaps it is time you learned another lesson. Perhaps I should show you what to expect when you find yourself in the bed of Dimitris Theodorous or any of his type.'

He strode round the table, and pulled her up from her chair by her wrist. She tried to struggle free and failed.

'Let go of me…'

'No,' he said. 'You obey orders, not give them.' He took hold of the neckline of the green dress and tore it apart, the strong fingers negligent.

She said breathlessly, 'Draco—what are you doing?'

He said, almost conversationally, 'When Theodorous goes cruising on his yacht, he takes three girls at a time. As soon as they get on board their clothes are removed, and they spend the rest of the voyage naked, even in front of the crew. Is that how you wish to be treated? Because I am willing.'

He picked her up and carried her into the bedroom, dropping her on the bed.

She stared up at him, trembling, as he began to unfasten his clothing.

She said, 'Draco—you're frightening me.'

'But this is only a demonstration, Cressida *mou*.' His smile seared her. 'The reality would be infinitely worse, I promise you.'

She shrank, sudden tears hot in her throat. 'Draco—no, please.'

There was an endless, terrible silence, then she heard him sigh. He sat down on the bed beside her and took her chin in his hand, making her look at him.

He said quietly, 'One night with Theodorous, *agapi*

mou, and you would never feel clean again, I promise you.'

He put her into the bed and drew the sheet gently over her.

Her clenched fist was pressed against her mouth. She said, 'What will happen to me when you're married?'

'Hush,' he said. 'Get some rest. We will talk about it when I get back from New York.'

He half rose, and she caught at his hand. 'Stay with me—please.'

He hesitated. 'For a little while, then.' He lay down beside her, on top of the covers, sliding an arm round her shoulders and drawing her against him.

'Aren't you going to undress?'

'No.'

'Don't you—want me?'

'Yes,' he said. 'But I do not trust myself with you, Cressida *mou*. Too much has happened tonight.'

'Oh.' She closed her eyes and put her head against his chest, soothed by the strong beat of his heart. When she spoke again, her voice was quiet. 'Are you leaving very early tomorrow?'

'Around five. I have a meeting in Athens before my plane leaves.'

She said, 'Can I see you off?' and felt him smile.

'You will be asleep.'

'No,' she said. 'No, I'll be there. I promise.'

His lips touched her forehead, and he began to talk to her very softly in his own language. She did not know what he was saying, but it didn't seem to matter, because his arms were holding her, and she felt so safe—so secure that her eyelids began to droop...

She awoke with a start, and lay, watching the grey light stealing through the shutters. She was alone, but then she'd expected to be. And who was to say that she might not soon be alone for the rest of her life?

She peered at her watch, and realised with shock that it was almost five a.m., that he would be leaving.

There wasn't time to dress or even get to the helicopter pad. She grabbed a thin white cotton robe and thrust her arms into the sleeves, fastening its sash as she ran. The tiles were icy under her bare feet, and the stones on the path outside were painful, but she didn't falter.

She flew down through the garden, her lungs on fire, as at last she panted out on to the chill, damp grass of the headland.

The sun was a sullen red disc on the horizon. Behind her, coming over the house, she heard the beat of the rotors, and she swung round, staring up into the sky, waving frantically, willing him to look down and see her.

The noise was earsplitting. The chopper was right overhead now, but she could see him, and knew that he saw her too as he lifted his hand in greeting.

And she put her hands to her mouth and shouted, 'I love you,' into the vibrating air, knowing as she did so that he couldn't hear her. That her words would be eaten, fragmented and thrown away by the machine that was taking him away from her.

She stood watching, and waving, until the helicopter was just a speck in the distance, then she turned and went slowly back to the bungalow.

'You do not eat enough, madam,' Vassilis said sternly. 'You will make yourself ill.'

'It's too hot to eat,' said Cressy.

The temperature had soared in the last few days, and the sea looked like glass, the horizon shrouded in a permanent haze. Even the big parasols near the pool were no defence against the sun's fierceness, and after her swim Cressy preferred to retreat to the shade of the terrace.

She wondered if it was equally warm in New York, but didn't dwell on it. What might or might not be happening on the other side of the Atlantic was a no-go area for her. It had to be if she was to retain any peace of mind.

And when he came back they would talk…

She watched as Vassilis, clucking, removed the remnants of her half-eaten lunch, then settled back in her chair. She hadn't slept well the previous night. She'd had a series of small hateful dreams which still hung over her like a pall, and made her feel restless and uneasy.

Or maybe a storm was brewing somewhere which would end this still, brazen heat.

She found herself wishing that the newly installed telephone would ring, and she'd pick up the receiver and hear Draco's voice saying *agapi mou*. But she knew she might as well cry for the moon. He'd called twice since he'd been away, each time asking briefly and politely if she was all right. She'd said, 'Yes' and 'Thank you' and that had been that.

He hadn't mentioned when he was coming back, and she hadn't dared to ask. Or if he would be alone when he came…

She heard the sound of footsteps and sat up with sudden incredulous hope, only to see Paul Nixon approaching.

Since their confrontation up at the Villa Hera she

hadn't set eyes on him, and as far as she knew he'd never come down to the bungalow before. Now he walked up to the terrace, and halted awkwardly in front of her.

He said, 'Miss Fielding—Cressida—there's been a phone call. I have some bad news for you.'

She felt sick, her eyes scanning his grave face. She said, 'It's Draco, isn't it? Something's happened—I knew it...'

'No,' he said quickly. 'No, Draco's fine. The call was from England—from your uncle. I'm afraid your father's had another heart attack.'

She scrambled to her feet. 'Oh, God—when? Is he back in hospital? I must go to him...'

He took both her hands in his, which was odd of him, when he disliked her so much.

He said, 'He's not in hospital. He was at home when it happened.'

Her voice seemed to belong to a stranger. She said, 'He didn't make it—did he?' And saw him bow his head in acquiescence.

He said, 'I've spoken to Draco, and I'm to escort you back to England for the funeral at once.'

She moved sharply. 'There's no need for that.'

'Yes, there is,' he told her firmly. 'You can't face this alone. If you'll pack what you need, I'll start making our travel arrangements.'

'I knew there was something wrong,' she said, her voice shaking. 'I—I dreamed it.'

'Can I get you something? Some brandy, maybe, or some tea if you'd prefer?'

She shook her head. 'I don't want anything. I'd just like to be on my way. My aunt will need me.'

'Yes.' He patted her shoulder clumsily. 'Miss Fielding—I'm truly sorry.'

She tried to smile. 'Just now you called me Cressida. If we're going to be travelling companions, perhaps you should stick to that.'

He nodded. 'I'll send one of the maids to help you pack.'

She stood watching him walk back up the path. She wanted to cry, but no tears would come.

She thought, It's over. It's all over. And, in spite of the intense heat, she shivered.

When she reached home the following day, her aunt and uncle were waiting for her.

'Cressy.' Lady Kenny took her in her arms. 'My poor darling. What a terrible homecoming.'

Cressy kissed her cheek. 'I think I was expecting it,' she said quietly. 'He sounded so different lately—like a shadow of himself. As if he'd given up.'

Her aunt hugged her, then turned to Paul Nixon, who was waiting in the doorway.

She held out her hand. 'I don't think we've met. I'm Barbara Kenny.'

'This is Paul,' Cressy said, offering him a strained, grateful smile. 'He's a friend of Draco's, and he made all the arrangements for me. He's been very kind. I—I couldn't have managed without him.'

'Yes,' Sir Robert said, shaking hands with him, 'Mr Viannis said he'd look after you.'

'You've spoken to Draco?' He seemed to have been in contact with everyone but herself, she thought painfully.

'I could hardly avoid it, my dear. He's in the drawing

room. Took an overnight flight from the States, I understand.'

Draco was standing by the window as she went in. He came towards her quickly, and she waited for him to enfold her in his arms, but instead he embraced her formally, with a kiss on each cheek, leaving her feeling faintly chilled.

'You are well?' The dark face was concerned.

She nodded. 'I didn't know you'd be here.'

'I thought I should come,' he said. 'For all kinds of reasons. I hope you will tell me what I can do to help.'

She thought, You're with me, and that's enough…

He stepped back. 'Now I will leave you with your family,' he added, and, making them all a slight bow, he went out.

A little later she saw him walking in the garden with Paul Nixon, both of them deep in conversation.

'I didn't expect to like him,' Barbara Kenny said abruptly. 'But I can't deny his charm. I gather he proposes to stay here, so you'd better come to us.'

Cressy smiled at her wearily. 'Aunt Bar,' she said, 'you know quite well that I've been living with him in Greece. It's a bit late to consider the conventions. Besides,' she added with a touch of constraint, 'this house does belong to him.'

'Well, yes.' Lady Kenny flushed slightly. 'But you're in mourning—he can hardly expect…'

Cressy bent her head. She said quietly, 'You don't have to worry, Aunt Bar. I don't think he's expecting anything.'

The door opened and Berry came in, pushing a trolley laden with tea things. Her eyes were red and puffy, and her mouth trembled when she saw Cressy.

'Oh, Miss Cressy, my dear. Poor Mr Fielding. It

shouldn't have happened. He should have had many more years—seen his grandchildren born.'

Cressy bit her lip, aware that Lady Kenny was staring at her in sudden horrified speculation.

She gave a slight, almost wistful shake of her head, then turned back to the housekeeper, her voice gentle. 'It's terrible for us, Berry, but I really don't think he wanted to go on living.'

'No, he didn't,' Berry said forcefully. 'Not after he got that awful letter from *her*.'

Cressy was startled. 'Did Daddy hear from Eloise?'

'Nancy—Nurse Clayton took the post into him. She wasn't to know, of course, but if I'd seen Mrs Fielding's writing I'd have held it back, that I would. Given it to Sir Robert first.'

'What did it say?'

'I don't know, Miss Cressy. Mr Fielding burnt it in an old ashtray in the study, so that no one else would see it. All he'd say was that she was never coming back. White as a sheet he was too, and looked as if he'd been crying. And he was never the same, after.'

'Whatever we all thought of Eloise,' Cressy said, 'Daddy truly loved her. And he didn't want to go on living without her.' She swallowed. 'I really think it's that simple.'

And I, she thought, as pain tore at her, I am my father's daughter.

It was a quiet funeral. None of James Fielding's former colleagues attended, but all the neighbours paid their respects, and the little church was full.

Draco stayed at Cressy's side throughout, which raised a few eyebrows, and she knew there were already various rumours spreading about his ownership of the house, but she didn't care.

Whatever anyone thought about their relationship, they were wrong, she told herself unhappily.

Apart from taking her arm in church, he hadn't touched her at all during the past difficult days.

At night, she remained in her old room, while Draco slept on the other side of the house. And he'd never given the slightest hint that he wished to change these arrangements.

She thought, It's over, and realised that when she'd thought the same words on Myros, she hadn't simply been referring to her father.

She felt sick and empty inside. Grief for James Fielding was now commingling with the agony of this other loss, draining the colour from her face and haunting her eyes.

She supposed he had already asked Anna Theodorous to marry him before he came away, but she wished he would tell her openly rather than leave her in limbo like this.

He promised he'd talk to me when he came back from New York, she told herself. And talk to me he will.

Nearly everyone who'd been to the church had come back to the house afterwards, and Cressy was ashamed at her own impatience when some of them showed a disposition to linger.

The last of them had just gone, and she was collecting the used sherry glasses in the drawing room, when Paul Nixon came in. He was carrying a large buff envelope.

He said, 'Draco's had to go back to London, Cressida, but he asked me to give you this.'

'He's gone?' She stared at him, the colour draining

from her face. She put the glasses down carefully. 'But he can't have done. And without even saying goodbye?'

Paul sighed. 'I guess he felt it was for the best.' He put the envelope in her hands and gave her a constrained smile. 'After all, you're a free woman now.'

'A free woman?' God, she thought, I sound like an echo.

He said, 'Look in your package.' He bent and gave her a quick peck on the cheek. 'Goodbye, honey, and good luck.'

When he'd gone, she tore open the envelope, letting its contents spill out on to the sofa. The first document was the deeds to the house, and there was a note from Draco attached to it which she seized upon.

Your father's debts died with him, Cressida, and with them any obligation to me. So you are free to take up your own life again, and forget, if you can, all the unhappiness I have caused you.

Perhaps we were fated to make each other unhappy, my beautiful one.

I am also giving you back the house, with the hope that you will make your home there and find some true joy at last. I ask God to bless you.

She lifted the note and held it against her heart, staring silently, sightlessly into space.

Lady Kenny came in. 'Well, I have to confess, darling, I'm glad that's over.' She sat down with a heavy sigh. 'It's been such a horrible time for everyone. Your uncle thinks it would do us all good to go away for a few days, so what do you think?'

'It's a lovely idea,' Cressy said, putting all the papers

carefully back in the envelope. 'But I'm already going away.'

'You are?' Her aunt stared at her. 'But where?'

'To London first. To New York, maybe—if I have to. Or an island called Myros, Or anywhere.' She forced a smile. 'Wherever Draco is.'

'Oh, my dearest child, do you think that's wise?' Lady Kenny looked distressed. 'I know he's incredibly good-looking—and he's been amazingly sweet and thoughtful—in fact Robert really likes him—and I've grown quite attached myself, but—' She broke off. 'Where was I?'

'I think,' Cressy said gently, 'that you were about to tell me I'm making a big mistake.'

'Well, I have to think so. All that money and power. He can do exactly what he likes, and probably always has. And what if he gets tired of you, and breaks your heart?'

'That's a risk I'll just have to take.' Cressy bent and kissed her. 'Because I love him, Aunt Bar, and I always will. And I don't want to go on living without him either, whatever the terms.'

She saw her aunt's face change suddenly, and glanced round.

Draco was standing in the open doorway, his body as rigid as if he'd been turned to stone, his face bleak and strained.

Across the room, his gaze captured hers. Held it.

He said hoarsely. 'Are they true? Those things you were saying?'

She said, 'You came back...'

'I did not intend to. I wanted to release you completely. But I found I could not go. Not without a word. Or without holding you in my arms one last time.'

He walked slowly forward, halting a few feet away from her, while Lady Kenny rose quietly and tiptoed, unnoticed, from the room. 'I heard what you said, *agapi mou*. Every word. Did you mean it? Do you—can you love me?'

'Yes.' She looked at him pleadingly, her heart in her eyes. 'Draco—don't leave me, or send me away. Take me with you, please. I'll do anything you want. Be anything you want. I won't make waves. I'll live anywhere, if I can just be part of your life sometimes. And I won't be a threat to your marriage, I swear it.'

'You have been a threat to me since I first saw you peeping down at me on that beach on Myros.' He came to her, pulling her into his arms without gentleness. 'If you knew how I have longed to touch you through all these long sad days—to comfort you.'

'But you did.' She put up a hand and touched his cheek. 'You've been there for me all the time.'

'I used to come to your room,' he said. 'Sit in a chair and watch you sleep, counting how many more hours I had to spend with you. Feeling time slipping through my fingers. Telling myself that I had ruined everything, and that you would be glad to be rid of me.'

She said, 'Why didn't you wake me up—make love to me?'

'You were grieving for your father,' he said. 'I could not intrude on that.'

She bent her head. 'I think I did my grieving a long time ago. This time, I was just—letting him go.'

He said softly, 'Ah, *pethi mou*…'

He lifted her into his arms and sat down on one of the sofas, cradling her on his lap.

He said gently, 'Why did you leave me, my dear one? Why didn't you turn to me?'

She drew a deep breath. 'Because I was scared. My father's illness was an excuse to leave, not a reason. I—I didn't believe in love. I'd seen the damage it could do. Saw my father change completely when my stepmother came into his life, and that frightened me. I didn't want that to happen to me. I wanted to stay in control—not be at someone else's mercy for the rest of my life.

'When that call from England came, it seemed like a sign telling me I didn't have to change after all. That I could just go back to my old life and pretend nothing had happened. That I'd be safe that way.

'Only it was already too late.' She beat suddenly on his chest with her fists. 'Why didn't you tell me it was too late? Because you knew—didn't you?'

'Yes,' he said. 'I knew.' He was silent for a moment. 'So, I made you afraid of love.'

'I was more frightened of myself,' she said. 'Of the way you could make me feel. Although I didn't know the half of it then.'

He shook his head. 'How can you still love me, Cressida *mou*, when I've treated you so badly?'

'It could have been worse,' she said. 'You could simply have cut me out of your life.'

'That was never a possibility.' His voice was suddenly harsh. 'Even when I was hurt and angry, you were in my blood. I could not let you go. So I told myself you were just another tramp, who cared only for money and material things. And that I would have you on those terms.'

He stroked her hair back from her forehead. 'After our first time together, I was so ashamed—so angry with myself. You had been so sweet—so giving. You turned my revenge back on me, *pethi mou*—and I suffered.

'Every time I came to you it became more difficult to pretend. That's why I could never stay with you afterwards—hold you in my arms all night as I longed to do—because I knew I might break down and tell you how I truly felt. And you might not care.'

He sighed. 'And because I knew how temporary an arrangement it was. That your father might have another fatal attack at any time. And you would be free to walk away again, and this time I would have no power to bring you back.'

'You always had power over me.' She pressed a kiss to his tanned throat. 'The power of love—right from the first. Even when you offered me your bargain. I—I wanted to hate you, but I couldn't.'

'That last morning on Myros,' he said, 'you promised you would say goodbye to me, but you didn't come, although I delayed the takeoff. And then something made me look down, and you were there, waving to me, all in white, like the bride I'd dreamed of.

'And I told myself that when I came back from New York I would go on my knees to you if necessary, and beg you to forgive me—and to marry me.'

Her heart missed an incredulous, joyous beat. She said, 'I thought you were going to marry Anna Theodorous.'

'That was her father's plan, not mine. And he leaked the story to the newspapers to pressure me over the tanker deal.' His mouth tightened. 'He is a man who regards women as commodities, *agapi mou*. Even his own child.'

The hands that cupped her face were trembling suddenly. He said, 'Cressida—can you forgive me—after all that has happened between us? Will you be my wife?

She said wonderingly, 'Do you doubt it? Draco—you must know how you make me feel.'

'You do not have to love someone to like being in bed with them, *pethi mou*,' he told her quietly. 'As it was, each time we made love I could only think of how much happiness I had thrown away.'

'And I thought the same. Oh, why didn't you tell me?'

'I did tell you.' He smiled into her eyes. 'On our last night together on Myros. You must learn to speak Greek, my love, then you would know.'

She slid her arms round his neck, pressing herself against him. 'Can I have my first lesson now?'

He groaned. 'No, Cressida, because I have to find your aunt and arrange for you to stay at her house until the wedding. You see—I am belatedly trying to do the right thing,' he added wryly.

She said, 'Won't it be awkward for you to take me back to Myros as your wife? Perhaps we should leave things as they are. I mean—you don't *have* to marry me...'

He kissed her softly, and lingeringly. 'But you are so wrong, my heart. I do have to marry you, and very soon. I cannot wait any longer. Besides, Vassilis requires it. He told Paul while I was away that you did not eat because you were pining for me.'

'Oh,' she said. 'So you're marrying me just to please your staff.'

'And because I cannot go many more nights without sleep,' Draco added, straight-faced.

'And those are your only reasons?' Cressy sat up in mock outrage.

'There are others.' He pulled her back into his arms.

'Which we will discuss when we are less likely to be interrupted,' he added, his mouth softly exploring hers.

'What a pity,' she whispered against his lips. 'Because I have some wonderful memories of this room...

'But I want to make one thing clear,' she went on, when he allowed her to speak again. 'I'm staying with you, not Aunt Bar.'

'You will do as you're told, Cressida *mou*.' He sounded like the autocrat again, and she ran a loving finger across his lips.

'Then I shall sue you for breach of contract.' She smiled up at him. 'You bought me for three months. There are still two left—and I want them. I want *you*. Besides,' she added, 'if you'd really been going to marry Anna, you wouldn't have stopped making love to me. So why should you stop because you're marrying me instead?'

'I think there is something wrong with your logic,' Draco said, trying not to laugh. 'But I don't think I care. I am certainly not going to argue.'

She reached up and kissed him in turn, letting her tongue flicker softly along his lower lip. 'So will you dine with me tonight, Kyrios Draco? And after dinner will you please take me to bed and make love to me for hours?'

'I will.' His mouth took hers with a deep, sensual yearning that made her body melt against his. 'And after we have made love, Kyria Cressida, will you sleep in my arms for what is left of the night?'

She took a deep breath. 'Oh, yes, darling. Yes, I will.'

His arms tightened round her. 'Then it seems, my bride, that we have a bargain.'

'For three months?' Her smile was misty.

'No.' Draco looked deep into her eyes, shining for him with love and trust. 'For the whole of our lives, *matia mou.*'

SMOKESCREEN
MARRIAGE

CHAPTER ONE

THE room was in deep shadow. Moonlight pouring through the slats of the tall shuttered windows lay in thin bands across the tiled floor.

The whirr of the ceiling fan gently moving the warm air above the wide bed was barely audible against the ceaseless rasp of the cicadas in the garden below the room.

Once, she'd found these sounds alien. Now, they were the natural accompaniment to her nights in this house.

As was the firm masculine tread approaching the bed. The warm, husky voice, touched with laughter, whispering 'Katharina *mou*.'

And she, turning slowly, languidly, under the linen sheet that was her only covering, smiling her welcome, as she reached up to him with outstretched arms, her body alive with need—with longing…

With a gasp, Kate sat up in the darkness, throat tight, heart pounding violently.

She made herself draw deep calming breaths as she glanced round the room, seeking reassurance. Her bedroom, in her flat. Curtains masking the windows, not shutters. And, outside, the uneasy rumble of London traffic.

A dream, she thought. Only a bad dream. Just another nightmare.

At the beginning, they'd been almost nightly occurrences, as her stunned mind and bruised senses tried to rationalise what had happened to her.

She had never really succeeded, of course. The hurt, the betrayal had cut too deep. The events of the past year were always there, in the corner of her mind, eating corrosively into her consciousness.

But the bad dreams had been kept at bay for a while. It was now almost two weeks since the last one.

She had, she thought, begun to heal.

And now this...

Was it an omen? she wondered. Tomorrow—the next day—would there be some news at last? The letter—the phone call—that would bring her the promise of freedom.

God knows, she'd made it as easy as she could, going right against the advice of her lawyer.

'But, Mrs Theodakis, you're entitled...'

She'd stopped him there. 'I want nothing,' she said. 'Nothing at all. Kindly make sure the other side is—aware of that. And please don't use that name either,' she added constrainedly. 'I prefer Miss Dennison.'

He had assented politely, but his raised brows told her more loudly than words that no amount of preference could change a thing.

She had taken off her wedding ring, but she couldn't as easily erase the events of the past year from her tired memory.

She was still legally the wife of Michael Theodakis, and would remain so until she received his consent to the swift, clean-break divorce she had requested.

Once she was free of him, then the nightmares would stop, she told herself. And she could begin to put her life back together again.

That was the inner promise that had kept her going through these dark days and endless nights since she'd fled from Mick, and their charade of a marriage. From the images that still haunted her, waking and sleeping.

She drew her knees up to her chin, shivering a little. Her cotton nightgown was damp, and clinging to her body. She was tired—her job as a tour guide escorting parties of foreign tourists round the British Isles was a demanding one—but her body was wide awake, restless with the needs and desires she'd struggled so hard to suppress.

How could the memory of him still be so potent? she wondered despairingly. Why couldn't she forget him as easily as he seemed to have forgotten her? Why didn't he answer her solicitor's letters—or instruct one of the team of lawyers who served the mighty Theodakis clan to deal with them for him?

With all his money and power, it was the simplest thing in the world to rid himself of an unwanted wife. He was signing papers all day long. What would one more signature matter?

She lay down again, pulling the covers round her, in spite of the warmth of the August night. Cocooning herself so that the expanse of the bed beside her would not seem quite so empty—so desolate.

And knowing that nothing would ever make any difference to the loneliness and the hurt.

It was nearly eight when she reached home the following evening, and Kate felt bone-weary as she let herself into the narrow hall. She had spent the day showing a party of thirty Japanese tourists round Stratford-on-Avon. They had been unfailingly polite, and interested, absorbing information like sponges, but Kate was aware that she had not been on top form. She'd been restless, edgy all day, blaming her disturbed night for her difficulties in concentration.

Tonight, she thought grimly, she would take one of the pills the doctor had prescribed when she first returned from Greece.

She needed this job, and couldn't afford to lose it, even if it was only temporary, filling in for someone on maternity leave.

All the winter jobs for reps with tour companies had already gone when she came back to Britain, although her old company Halcyon Club Travel were keen to hire her again next summer.

And that's what she planned to do, although she'd stipulated that she would not return to any of the Greek islands.

On her way to the stairs, she paused to collect her mail from the row of rickety pigeon-holes on the wall.

Mostly circulars, she judged, and the gas bill—and then stopped, her attention totally arrested as she saw the Greek stamp.

She stared down at the large square envelope with its neatly typed direction, her eyes dilating, a small choked sound rising in her throat.

She thought, 'He's found me. He knows where I am. But how?'

And why was he making contact with her directly, when she'd made it clear that all correspondence was to be conducted through their lawyers?

But then, when had Mick Theodakis ever played by any rules except his own?

She went up the stairs slowly, aware that her legs were shaking. When she reached her door, she had to struggle to fit her key into the lock, but at last she managed it.

In her small living room, she dropped the letter on to the dining table as if it was red-hot, then walked across to her answerphone which was blinking at her, and pressed the 'play' button. Perhaps, if Mick had written to her, he'd also contacted her lawyer, and the message she was hoping for might be waiting at last.

Instead Grant's concerned voice said, 'Kate—are you all right? You haven't called me this week. Touch base, darling—please.'

Kate sighed inwardly, and went across to the bedroom to take off the navy shift dress, and navy and emerald striped blazer that constituted her uniform.

It was kind of Grant to be anxious, but she knew in her heart that it was more than kindness that prompted his frequent calls. It was pressure. He wanted her back, their former relationship re-established, and moved on to the next stage. He took it for granted that she wanted this too. That, like him, she regarded the past year as an aberration—a period of temporary insanity, now happily concluded. And that when she had gained her divorce, she would marry him.

But Kate knew it would never happen. She and Grant had not been officially engaged, when she'd gone off to work as a travel company rep on Zycos in the Ionian Sea, but she knew, when the season was over, he would ask her to marry him, and that she would probably agree.

She hadn't even been sure why she was hesitating. He was good-looking, they shared a number of interests, and, if his kisses did not set her on fire, Kate enjoyed them enough to look forward to the full consummation of their relationship. And during her weeks on Zycos she had missed him, written to him every week, and happily anticipated his phone calls planning their future.

Surely that was a good enough basis for marriage—wasn't it?

Probably Grant thought it still was. Only she knew better. Knew she was no longer the same person. And soon she would have to tell him so, she thought with genuine regret.

She unzipped her dress, and put it on a hanger. Underneath she was wearing bra and briefs in white broderie anglaise, pretty and practical, but not glamorous or sexy, she thought, studying herself dispassionately.

And totally different from the exquisite lingerie that Mick had brought her from Paris and Rome—lacy cobwebby things that whispered against her skin. Filmy enticing scraps to please the eyes of a lover.

Only, there was no lover—and never had been.

She slipped on her pale-green gingham housecoat and tied its sash, then put up a hand and removed the barrette that confined her red-gold hair at the nape of her neck during the working day, letting it cascade down to her shoulders.

'Like a scented flame,' Mick would tell her huskily, his hands tangling in the silky strands—lifting them to his lips.

She stiffened, recognising that was a no-go area. She could not afford such memories.

She wanted to move away from the mirror but something kept her there, examining herself with cold critical attention.

How could she ever have imagined in her wildest dreams that she was the kind of woman to attract and hold a man like Mick Theodakis? she asked herself bleakly.

Because she had never been a classic beauty. Her nose was too long and her jaw too square for that. But she had good cheekbones, and long lashes, although the eyes they fringed were an odd shade between green and grey.

'Jade smoke,' Mick had called them...

And she was luckier than most redheads, she thought, swiftly refocusing her attention. Her creamy skin didn't burn or freckle, but turned a light, even gold. The tan she'd acquired in Greece still lingered. She could see quite plainly the white band of her finger where her wedding ring had been. But that was the only mark, because Mick had always encouraged her to join him in sunbathing nude beside their private pool.

She froze, cursing inwardly. Oh, God, why was she doing this to herself—allowing herself to remember these things?

Well, she knew why, of course. It was because of that envelope ticking away like a time bomb in the other room.

Her throat tightened uncontrollably. She turned away from the mirror and went into the kitchen and made herself a mug of coffee, hot, black and very strong. If she'd had any brandy, she'd have added a dollop of that too.

Then, she sat down at the table, and steeled herself to open the envelope.

It was disturbing to realise how easily he'd been able to pinpoint her whereabouts—as if he was demonstrating his power over her from across the world. Showing her that there was nowhere she could run and hide. No refuge that he could not find.

Only he had no power, she told herself fiercely. Not any more. Not ever again. And she tore open the envelope.

She found herself staring down at an elegantly engraved

white card. A wedding invitation, she thought in total bewilderment, as she scanned it. And the last thing she'd expected to find. She felt oddly deflated as she read the beautifully printed words.

So—Ismene, Mick's younger sister was marrying her Petros at last. But why on earth was she being sent an invitation?

Frowningly, she unfolded the accompanying note.

'Dearest Katharina,' it read. 'Papa finally gave his permission and I am so happy. We are to be married in the village in October, and you promised you would be there for me on my wedding day. I depend on you, sister. Your loving Ismene.'

Kate crumpled the note in her hand. Was Ismene crazy, or just naïve? she wondered. She couldn't really expect her brother's estranged wife to be part of a family occasion, whatever rash commitment Kate might have made in those early days when she was still living in her fool's paradise.

But I'm not that person any more, Kate thought, her face set, her body rigid. I'll have to write to her—explain somehow.

But why had Mick ever allowed the invitation to be sent? It made no sense. Although the wilful Ismene probably hadn't bothered to seek his permission, she acknowledged with a faint sigh.

And she was astonished that Aristotle Theodakis, the all-powerful patriarch of the family, had agreed to the marriage. While she'd been living under his roof at the Villa Dionysius, he'd been adamantly opposed to it. No mere doctor was good enough for his daughter, he'd roared, even if it was the son of his old friend and *tavli* opponent. And slammed doors, furious scenes, and the sound of Ismene's hysterical weeping had been almost daily occurrences.

Until Mick had flatly announced he could stand no more, and had insisted that he and Kate move out of their wing of the main building, and out of earshot, down to the comparative seclusion of the beach house. Where they'd remained…

She drank some of the scalding coffee, but it did nothing to melt the ice in the pit of her stomach.

Those weeks, she thought, had been the happiest of her life. Day had succeeded sunlit day. Night followed moonlit night. Raised voices were replaced by birdsong, the whisper of the breeze in the pine trees, and the murmur of the sea.

And, above all, Michael touching her—whispering to her, coaxing her out of the last of her natural shyness, teaching her to take as well as give in their lovemaking. And to be proud of her slim, long-legged body with its narrow waist and small high breasts.

And she'd been an eager pupil, she thought bitterly. How readily she'd surrendered to the caress of his cool, experienced hands and mouth, sobbing out her breathless, mindless rapture as their naked bodies joined in passion.

So beguiled, so entranced by the new sensual vistas that Mick had revealed to her, that she'd mistaken them for love.

Whereas all she'd really been to him was a novelty—a temporary amusement.

The smokescreen he'd cynically needed to divert attention from his real passion.

The coffee tasted bitter, and she pushed it away from her, feeling faintly nauseous.

She couldn't afford to tear her heart out over Ismene, she told herself curtly. They'd become close over the months, and she knew that the younger girl would be missing her company with only Victorine to turn to. In fact, the note had almost sounded like a cry for help.

But she couldn't allow herself to think like that. And in particular she couldn't permit her mind to dwell on Victorine, the Creole beauty who now ruled Aristotle Theodakis, without releasing any of her hold over his son.

She would write a brief and formal expression of regret,

and leave it there. Keep it strictly impersonal, although Ismene might be hurt to have no response to her note.

But then, Kate thought, I also have the right to some re-action to my request for a divorce. After all, it's been a month since my lawyer sent off the papers.

Impatiently, she pushed the invitation away and rose. It was no wonder she was feeling flaky. She ought to have something to eat. She'd only had time to grab a sandwich at lunch time, and there was cold chicken and salad in the fridge, only her appetite seemed to have deserted her.

And she had a hectic day tomorrow—a group of reluctant French schoolchildren to chivvy around the Tower of London.

Perhaps she would just have a warm shower, wash her hair, and go to bed early. Catch up on some of that lost sleep.

Her bathroom was small, and the shower cubicle rather cramped, not tempting her to linger. She towelled down quickly, and resumed her housecoat before returning to the living room with her hair-drier.

She was just plugging it in when, to her surprise and ir-ritation, someone knocked at the door.

Kate sighed, winding a towel round her wet hair. It was bound to be Mrs Thursgood, the elderly widow who lived on the ground floor, and accepted parcels and packets in-tended for other tenants who'd left for work before the mail arrived.

She was a kindly soul but gossipy, and she would expect a cup of tea and a cosy chat in return for her trouble of trailing up to the top floor with Kate's book club selection, or whatever.

I really, truly, don't want to talk, Kate thought grimly, as she pinned on a smile and flung open the door.

And stood, lips parting in a soundless gasp, eyes widening in shock, feeling the blood drain from her face.

'My beloved wife,' Michael Theodakis said softly. '*Kalispera*. May I come in?'

'No,' she said. Her voice sounded hoarse—distorted above the sudden roaring in her ears. She was afraid she was going to faint, and knew she couldn't afford any such weakness. She took a step backwards.

'No,' she repeated more vehemently.

He was smiling, totally at ease, propping a dark-clad shoulder against the doorframe.

'But we cannot conduct a civilised conversation on the *door*step, *agapi mou*.'

She said thickly, 'I've got nothing to say to you—on the doorstep or anywhere else. If you want to talk, speak to my solicitor. And don't call me your darling.'

'How unkind,' he said. 'When I have travelled such a long way at such inconvenience to see you again. I'd hoped some of our Greek hospitality might have rubbed off on you.'

'That isn't the aspect of my life with you that I remember most clearly,' Kate said, her breathing beginning to steady. 'And I didn't invite you here, so please go.'

Mick Theodakis raised both hands in mock surrender. 'Easy, Katharina *mou*. I did not come here to fight a war, but negotiate a peaceful settlement. Isn't that what you want too?'

'I want a quick divorce,' she said. 'And never to see you again.'

'Go on.' The dark eyes glinted down at her from beneath hooded lids. 'Surely you have a third wish. All the best stories do, I believe.'

Kate drew a quick, sharp breath. 'This,' she said gratingly, 'is not a fairy story.'

'No,' he said. 'To be honest, I am not sure whether it is a comedy or a tragedy.'

'Honest?' Kate echoed scornfully. 'You don't know the meaning of the word.'

'However,' he went on as if she hadn't spoken. 'I am quite certain I am not leaving until you have heard what I have to say, *yineka mou*.'

'I am not your wife,' she said. 'I resigned that dubious honour when I left Kefalonia. And I thought I'd made it clear in my note that our so-called marriage was over.'

'It was a model of clarity,' he said courteously. 'I have learned every word of it by heart. And the fact that you left your wedding ring beside it added extra emphasis.'

'Then you'll understand there is nothing to discuss.' She lifted her chin. 'Now, go please. I have a heavy duty tomorrow, and I'd like to go to bed.'

'Not,' he said softly. 'With wet hair. That is something that *I* remember from our brief marriage, Katharina.' He stepped into the room, kicking the door shut behind him.

There was no lock on her bedroom door, and one dodgy bolt on the bathroom. With nowhere to run, Kate decided to stand her ground.

'How dare you.' Her face was burning as she glared at him. 'Get out of here, before I call the police.'

'To do what?' Mick asked coolly. 'Have I ever struck you—or molested you in any way, *agapi mou*, that you did not welcome?' He watched the colour suddenly deepen in her shocked face, and nodded sardonically. 'Besides, all police are reluctant to intervene in domestic disputes. So, why don't you sit down and dry your hair while you listen to what I have to say?'

He paused, then held out his hand. 'Unless you would like me to dry it for you,' he added softly. 'As I used to.'

Kate swallowed convulsively, and shook her head, not trusting her voice.

It wasn't fair, she raged inwardly. It wasn't right for him to remind her of all the small, tender intimacies they'd once shared.

The way she'd sat between his knees as he blow-dried her hair, combing it gently with his fingers, letting the soft strands drift in the current of warm air.

And how her efforts to perform the same service for him had always been thwarted, as he loosened the sash on her robe, and drew the folds slowly apart, pressing tiny sensuous kisses on her naked body as she stood, flushed and breathless, in front of him. Until her attempt at hairdressing was forgotten in the sweet urgency of the moment.

Oh, she did not need to remember that.

Her cotton housecoat was long-sleeved and full-skirted, buttoned chastely to the throat, but she was still blazingly aware that she was naked under it—and that he knew it too, and was enjoying her discomfort.

The room seemed suddenly to have shrunk. His presence dominated it, physically and emotionally. Invaded her space in the worst way. Dried her throat and made her legs shake under her.

Even as she turned away and walked across to the dining table, every detail of him was etched on her mind, as if she'd touched him with her fingers.

Yet she did not have to do that—to remember.

She knew that the black curling hair was brushed back from his face with careless elegance. That his dark eyes were brilliant, but watchful beneath their heavy lids, or that the cool, firm mouth held a hint of sensuality in the slight fullness of the lower lip.

It was a proud face, strong and uncompromising, but when he smiled, its charm had twisted the heart in her body.

He was formally dressed, the charcoal business suit accentuating the tall, lean body which moved with such arrogant grace. His olive skin looked very dark against the immaculate white shirt. His tie was silk, and there were discreet gold links in his cuffs matching the narrow bracelet on his watch and, she noticed with a sudden painful thud of her heart, the plain band on the third finger of his right hand.

The ring which matched hers, inscribed inside with their names and the date, which she had slipped on to his finger on their wedding day...

How could he still be wearing it? How could he be such a hypocrite? she asked herself numbly.

He said, 'Aren't you going to ask me to sit down—offer me some coffee?'

'You're not a guest,' Kate said, keeping her voice level with an effort. 'And this is not a social call.' She frowned. 'How did you get in, anyway?'

'A charming lady on the ground floor.' He paused. 'She seemed pleased you were having a visitor.'

Mrs Thursgood, Kate thought, grinding her teeth. Who normally guarded the front door like Cerberus at the gates of Hell.

She said, 'She allows her imagination to run away with her sometimes.'

She loosened the towel that was swathed round her head, and her damp hair tumbled on to her shoulders. Then she switched on the drier, and picked up the brush.

Mick stood by the old-fashioned fireplace watching every movement, his whole body very still, except for a muscle flickering at the side of his mouth.

He said at last, 'You've received Ismene's invitation.' His tone was abrupt, and it was a statement rather than a question.

'It came today.'

'So you haven't had time to reply.'

'It won't take much time,' Kate said shortly. 'Naturally, I shan't be going.'

'Ah,' Mick said gently. 'But that is what I came to discuss with you. It would mean a great deal to my sister to have you present, so I hope you will reconsider.'

Kate switched off the drier and stared at him, pushing her hair back from her face. 'That's impossible.'

'I hope not. Ismene has missed you very badly, and this is a special time for her.' He paused. 'I would regard your attendance as a favour.'

Kate gasped. 'And that's supposed to make all the difference?' she demanded furiously.

'I thought it might.' He leaned an arm on the mantelshelf,

looking hatefully assured and relaxed. 'In fact, I believed we might exchange favours.'

There was an uncertain silence, then Kate said, 'What do you mean?'

'You want a simple, consensual divorce.' He smiled at her. 'Which you can have—at a price.'

There was another tingling silence.

She said, 'And if the price is too high?'

He shrugged. 'Then I refuse to consent, and we let the legal process run its course.' He added casually, 'I understand it can take several years.'

'That's—blackmail.' Her voice shook.

'Is it?' he said. 'But perhaps I do not agree that our marriage has "irretrievably broken down" as you allege in that document.'

'But you must. It has.' Kate drew a deep breath. 'And you're bluffing. I know you are. You don't wish to stay married any more than I do.'

His mouth twisted. 'You're mistaken, *agapi mou*. I am in no particular hurry to be free.'

No, she thought, with a stab of anguish. Not while your father is still alive, and Victorine is nominally his...

She said slowly, 'So I have to attend Ismene's wedding if I want a quick divorce.'

'Is it really such a hardship? Kefalonia is very beautiful in September.'

'Kefalonia is beautiful all the year round.' Her tone was curt. 'It's only some of the people there who make it ugly.'

'A word of advice, *pedhi mou*.' His smile was mirthless. 'It is better to win an opponent over than to antagonise him.'

Kate lifted her chin. 'I think it's a little late to worry about that.' She hesitated. 'But everyone must know by now that our marriage is over. Won't they find it strange if I'm at the wedding?'

'I am not interested in what people think.' His voice was suddenly harsh. 'Besides, they only know that we have been separated for a short time. You might simply have come back to this country to attend to some family business.'

'Is that what you've been telling people?' She shook her head. 'My God, you can't even be honest about our marriage breaking down.'

'They will know soon enough, when the wedding is over.'

'Well, I hope you don't expect me to take part in some spurious reunion,' Kate said acidly. 'I'm not that good an actress.' She paused. 'Why do you want me there?'

'Did I say wanted?' Mick drawled. 'Don't flatter yourself, my sweet one. I am here on Ismene's behalf, not my own.'

She did not look at him, staring instead at her gingham-covered knee. 'Then I'd be there—just as an ordinary guest? Nothing more?'

He said mockingly, 'Why, Katharina, did you think you had left me all these weeks to sleep alone? That I've been burning for your return. What an innocent you are.'

'Not,' she said, 'any more.' She was silent for a moment. 'I need time to think about this.'

'You have twenty-four hours. I am staying at the Royal Empress Hotel. You remember it?'

'Yes.' It was a painful whisper.

He nodded. 'You can contact me there with your answer.'

He walked to the door, and paused for a final swift look round the room.

He said, 'So this is what you left me for. I hope it is worth it.'

'I don't have to live in the lap of luxury to be happy,' Kate said defiantly.

'Evidently,' he said. 'If happy is what you are.' He looked her over, slowly and thoroughly, a smile curling his mouth.

He said softly, 'Eyes like smoke and hair like flame. What a waste *agapi mou*. What a tragic waste.'

And was gone.

CHAPTER TWO

FOR several long moments Kate stood like a statue, staring at the closed door, pain and disbelief warring within her for supremacy.

Then she gave a little choked cry and ran to her bedroom, flinging herself face down across the bed, her hands gripping the covers as if they were her last hold on sanity.

She said aloud, 'Fool.' And again, more savagely, her voice breaking, '*Fool.*'

Had she really thought she could escape so easily? That Michael Theodakis would simply allow her—the girl he'd taken from nowhere—to walk away from him?

Not that he cared about her, or their marriage, as she had bitter cause to know, but the fact that she'd chosen to expose the hypocrisy of their relationship by leaving, had clearly damaged his pride. And that, of course, was an unforgivable sin.

Her own pride, naturally, didn't count.

He hadn't even asked her why she had left, but then he didn't have to. He already knew. He would have been told...

Nor had he offered one word of apology or explanation for the actions which had driven her away.

No, she was clearly the one who was at fault because she'd failed to turn a blind eye to his cynical infidelity.

After all, she'd had the Theodakis millions to enjoy, and she could not deny Mick had been generous. There'd been the house outside Athens, and the sumptuous apartments in Paris and New York as well as the clothes and jewellery he'd given her, all of which she'd left behind when she fled.

But that had been her choice, and Mick, no doubt, felt he

had bought her silence—her discretion, and, in his eyes, she had reneged on their unwritten bargain.

A bargain she had not realised existed until that terrible afternoon...

She shuddered, pressing her face deep into the bed until coloured sparks danced behind her closed eyelids.

But nothing could drive the image from her brain. Mick sprawled naked and asleep across the bed—their bed. And Victorine sitting at the dressing table combing her hair, clad in nothing but a towel.

And now, in spite of that, he required her to stand meekly at his side during Ismene's wedding celebrations, playing the dutiful wife. As if she owed him something.

But she'd only have to role-play by day, she reminded herself. At least she would not be asked to pretend at night.

And neither would he. Not any longer.

How could a man do that? she wondered wildly. How could he make love to one woman, with his heart and mind committed to another?

And all those precious passionate moments when the dark strength of his body had lifted her to the edge of paradise and beyond—how could they have meant so little to him?

But perhaps sexual fulfilment had also been part of his side of the bargain along with the designer wardrobe and the money he'd provided. One of the assets of being Mrs Michael Theodakis.

But it wasn't enough. Because she'd wanted love. And that was something he'd never offered. At least he'd been honest about that.

Probably, he'd found her inexperience—her naïvete amusing, she thought, lashing herself into fresh anger against him.

Because anger was good. Safe. It kept the frantic tears of loneliness and betrayal at bay. And she couldn't afford any more tears. Any more heartbreak.

She'd wept enough. Now, somehow, she had to move on.

But she couldn't begin to build a new life while her brief

marriage still existed, trapping her in the old one. She needed it to be over, and left far behind her. But for that, of course, she had to have Mick's co-operation. Oh, it would be so good to tell him to go to hell. That she would die sooner than return to Kefalonia and play at being his wife again for however short a time.

Because that meant she would become once more the smokescreen against his father's jealous and totally justified suspicions. And how could she bear it?

Or stand seeing, yet again, the triumph and contempt in Victorine's beautiful face? The look she'd turned on Kate, standing ashen-faced in the doorway that afternoon only a few agonised weeks ago.

'How tactless of you, *chère*.' Her honeyed drawl was barbed. 'Perhaps in future you should knock before entering your husband's bedroom.'

Kate had taken two shaky steps backwards, then run for the bathroom down the passage, her hand over her mouth as nausea churned inside her.

She was violently, cripplingly sick, kneeling on the tiled floor while walls and ceiling revolved unsteadily around her. She had no idea how long she'd stayed there. But eventually some firm purpose was born out of the sickness and misery, making her realise that she had to get out. That her brief marriage was over, and that she could not bear to spend even another hour under any roof that belonged to the Theodakis family.

She had to force herself to go back into that bedroom, bracing herself for another humiliating confrontation, but Victorine had gone.

Mick was still fast asleep. Exhausted by his labours, no doubt, she thought, rubbing salt into her own bitter wounds. And how dared he sleep while her heart was breaking?

She needed to confront him, she realised. To accuse him and see the guilt in his face.

She put her hand on his shoulder, and shook him.

'Mick.' Her voice cracked on his name. 'Wake up.'

He stirred drowsily, without opening his eyes. '*S'agapo*,' he muttered, his voice slurred. 'I love you.'

Kate gasped, and took a step backwards, a stricken hand flying to her mouth. At last he'd said them—the words she'd yearned to hear ever since they'd been together.

Only they were not meant for her, but his secret lover—the woman he'd been enjoying so passionately in her absence. The mistress he'd never actually discarded. It was the final—the unforgivable hurt, she thought as she turned painfully and walked away.

She packed the minimum in a small weekend case, then scribbled him a note which she left on the night table with her wedding ring.

'I should never have married you,' she wrote. 'It was a terrible mistake, and I cannot bear to go on living with you for another moment. Don't try to find me.'

No one saw her go. She drove to the airport, and managed to get a seat on a plane to Athens, and from there to London.

She had sworn that she would never go back.

And I can't, Kate thought, a shudder crawling the length of her body. I can't do it. It's too degrading to have to face her. To see them together, knowing what I know.

But what real alternative did she have?

She couldn't wait for years in limbo until Mick finally decided to let her go.

And, while his father lived, he had no real reason to end the marriage.

She had humiliated him by her precipitate departure, and she was being punished as a consequence. That was what it was all about. She had to be returned to the scene of her anguish—her betrayal—and made to endure all the memories and misery that it would evoke.

She burrowed into the quilt like a small wounded animal seeking sanctuary, her mind rejecting the images forcing themselves relentlessly on her inner vision.

Oh, how could he do this? How dared he simply—appear in her life again and start making demands?

Because he's without shame, she told herself, bitterly. And without decency. He's rich enough to do without them.

But I'm not. And somehow I have to find my way through this, and keep my own integrity in the process. And lying here with my eyes shut isn't going to change a thing.

She sat up slowly, pushing her still-damp hair back from her face with a slight shiver.

Meanwhile she had a job to do tomorrow, and preparations to make for that. Normal life was there to be got on with, even if the safe wall she'd thought she'd built around herself had suddenly come crashing down.

She trailed back into the living room, and switched on her hair-drier, staring unseeingly into space as she dealt with the tangled red waves, restoring them to some kind of order.

As, in the fullness of time, she would restore her life. Find a new calm—a new security.

There had never been any safety with Mick, of course. He'd appeared on her horizon like some great dark planet, and she'd been the moon drawn helplessly into his orbit. And by the time she'd realised the danger she was in, it was already too late.

But from the first time she'd seen him, she'd been in too deep, out of her depth and sinking.

As the drier hummed, Kate let her tired mind drift back over the months to where it had all begun...

'Oh, come on, Katie, don't let me down. It'll be a laugh.' Lisa's tone was cajoling. 'After all, when do we get a chance to get inside a hotel like the Zycos Regina? Don't you want to see how the other half live? Besides, I really need you to make up the foursome.'

Kate bit her lip. It had been a long season on the Greek island of Zycos, and, although on the whole she'd enjoyed being a tour rep for Halcyon Club Travel, she felt bone-weary now that it was over.

All she wanted to do that evening was complete her packing for the following day's flight, have a hot shower, and an early night. But Lisa, the fellow rep with whom she'd shared a small apartment all summer, wanted a night on the town.

She said cautiously, 'Who did you say was going?'

'His name's Stavros,' Lisa said. 'And he's the disc jockey at the Nite Spot down on the waterfront.'

'Oh,' Kate said. 'That place.'

Lisa tossed her head. 'You're such a snob,' she accused.

Kate sighed. 'Not at all. It just hasn't got a very good reputation, and you know it. It's always being raided.'

'Well, we're not taking clients there,' Lisa said. 'And Stavros just plays the music. He's gorgeous.' She rolled her eyes lasciviously. 'The other guy's his cousin Dimitris from Athens.'

Kate began, 'I don't think…' but Lisa cut across her.

'Oh, come on, Katie. Let your hair down for once. It's an evening out, not a lifetime commitment, for God's sake. And we'll be out of here tomorrow.'

Well that was true, Kate acknowledged. It was just one evening, and she could always invent a diplomatic headache if things got heavy.

Besides, if she was honest, she'd always had a sneaking curiosity about the Zycos Regina, the largest but also most exclusive hotel on the island, and set in its own private grounds well away from the lively coastal resorts favoured by the majority of tourists.

She knew that it was part of a chain of equally prestigious hotels dotted round the Mediterranean, their standards of luxury and service putting them out of the reach of the package tour market.

It might be fun, she thought, not just to see how the other half lived, but join them too for a brief while.

She smiled at Lisa. 'All right,' she said. 'You talked me into it.'

She chose carefully from her limited wardrobe that evening, opting for a black linen shift, knee-length, sleeveless and discreetly square necked. Lisa, blonde and bubbly, favoured the outrageous look out of uniform, and would be wearing something skimpy and cut-off, but Kate felt that restraint was her best bet.

For that reason, she twisted her hair into its usual tidy pleat instead of leaving it loose on her shoulders, as she'd originally intended. And she applied just a modicum of makeup, darkening her long lashes, and applying a light coral glow to her mouth.

She slipped on a pair of strappy sandals, then stood back to view herself in the mirror.

The evening was warm and still, but she suddenly found herself shivering as if a small chill wind had penetrated the shutters of her room.

And heard a warning voice in her head say quietly, 'Be careful.'

Oh, for God's sake, she thought impatiently as she turned towards the door. What can possibly happen in such a public—and eminently high-class—place?

Stavros, she disliked on sight. His coarse good looks might attract Lisa, but held no appeal for her. He looked her up and down smilingly, and she felt as if she'd been touched by a finger dipped in slime.

And Dimitris, with his flashy clothes and abundance of gold jewellery, set her teeth on edge too. As did the way he looked at her, as if he was mentally stripping her.

Oh, well, she thought with a mental shrug. The evening won't last forever. It will just seem like it.

The club at the Zycos Regina impressed her immediately with its understated elegance, and subdued lighting. The clientele, mostly couples expensively dressed, were seated at tables set round an oval dance floor, and, on a corner dais, a quartet was playing soft dance music interspersed with interesting jazz.

'It's not very lively,' Lisa complained loudly, twisting round in her chair to survey the other patrons. 'If they're all so rich, why aren't they happier?'

Kate, uncomfortably aware of raised eyebrows and disapproving glances from adjoining tables, winced as she took a sip from the lurid cocktail that had been served to them all by an impassive waiter, and thought how much she'd have preferred a glass of wine.

It embarrassed her to see Dimitris flourishing a wallet full of notes, and clearly believing an extravagant tip allowed him to treat the staff like dirt.

It crucified her too to see Stavros stroking Lisa's exposed skin with a proprietorial hand and leering into her cleavage, then finding Dimitris leaning towards her, murmuring throatily with a suggestive smile, and reaching for her hand.

Deliberately, Kate edged her own chair away, feeling as if she'd woken to find herself in the middle of her worst nightmare.

We don't belong here she thought, with a sigh, as she began to plan her own strategic withdrawal. And we'd better leave before they ask us to go.

She wasn't sure of the moment when she knew she was being watched, but she felt the impact of the glance like a hand on her shoulder.

She drank some more of the unpleasant cocktail, then risked a swift look round, wondering resignedly if the management had already been summoned.

It was a corner table, set slightly apart from the others, and occupied by three men.

And the man watching her sat in the middle. In his early thirties, he was clearly younger than the other two, and, equally obviously, he was the one in control.

Even that first lightning assessment told her that he was good-looking, although not classically handsome. The dark face was strong, the lines of nose and jaw arrogantly marked. But more than that he exuded power, a charismatic force that could reach across a crowded room and touch its object like the caress of a hand.

She knew she should look away, but it was already too late. For an electrifying moment their eyes met, and locked, and Kate felt her breathing quicken and her throat tighten in an odd excitement.

But there was no warmth in his gaze. His expression was cool and watchful, his brows drawn together in a slight frown, as if something had displeased him.

And no prizes for guessing what that was, Kate thought, as she turned back to her companions, her face hot with embarrassed colour.

'Who's that?' Lisa had noticed the direction of her gaze, and was staring herself with open interest. 'Do you know him?' She giggled. 'Have you been holding out on me, Katie?'

'Not in the least,' Kate said crisply. 'Nor do I want to know him. I think he feels we're lowering the tone of the establishment.'

The fact that she thought exactly the same herself seemed paradoxically to increase her resentment.

'But I know him.' Stavros leaned forward, eyes gleaming. 'That is Michalis Theodakis. His father owns the whole Regina chain of hotels, and a great deal more, but the son now runs the company.'

Kate's brows lifted. 'Really?' she asked sceptically. 'What's he doing here?'

'He visits all the hotels,' Stavros explained. 'Checking them at random.'

'So who are the guys with him?' Lisa questioned.

'Who knows?' His minders probably.' His tone was envious. 'He is already a multi-millionaire in his own right, but he will be even richer when he gets control of all the Theodakis holdings. If he ever does,' he added, grinning.

'They say he and his father have quarrelled and Aristotle Theodakis would do anything to prevent him stepping into his shoes.'

He sent Kate a sly glance. 'Do you want him, *kougla mou*? Many women do, and not just for his money. He is quite a stud. You would have to stand in a long line, I think.'

'Don't be absurd,' Kate said coldly, aware that her flush had deepened. 'And do keep your voice down. I think he's planning to have us thrown out.'

That icy considering look had thrown her badly. He had seen her companions and judged her accordingly, so naturally she was honour bound to prove to him that his low opinion of her was entirely justified.

Teeth gritted, she reached for her drink, only to find the whole nasty concoction cascading down the front of her dress as her arm was jogged by a passing waiter.

She gasped and jumped up, shaking her skirt. Stavros and Dimitris were on their feet too, shouting angrily and gesticulating at the waiter, who was apologising abjectly and proffering a clean napkin.

'I'd better go to the powder room,' Kate interrupted, embarrassed at the attention the accident was attracting.

She turned, and cannoned into a tall figure standing behind her. As his hands grasped her arms to steady her, she realised it was Michael Theodakis.

'Allow me to make amends for the clumsiness of my staff, *thespinis*.' He spoke excellent English, she thought, with just a trace of an accent which, allied to his low-pitched drawl, some women would undoubtedly find sexy. 'If you will come with me, my housekeeper will attend to your dress.'

'There's really no need.' She freed herself, and took a small step backwards, her face warming. Because, close to, he was formidably attractive—over six feet in height, broad shouldered and lean-hipped. And prudence suggested she should keep her distance.

'But I think there is.' Somehow, he had repossessed her

hand, and was leading her between the tables towards the exit.

'Will you let go of me, please?' Kate tried to tug her fingers from his grasp. 'I can look after myself.'

'You are deluding yourself, *thespinis*, especially when you keep company like that,' he added with a touch of grimness.

She lifted her chin. 'It's not for you, *kyrie*, to criticise my friends.'

'They are old and dear acquaintances perhaps?' The sardonic note in his voice was not lost on her.

She bit her lip. 'Not—exactly.'

'I thought not.' He walked her across the hotel foyer to the row of lifts and pressed a button.

'Where are we going?' she asked in alarm, as the lift doors opened.

'To my suite.' He steered her inexorably inside. 'My housekeeper will join us there.'

'Take me back to the ground floor, please.' Kate was shaking suddenly. 'I want to go home—now.'

'It will be safer for you to remain at the hotel tonight.' He paused. 'I have a confession to make to you, *thespinis*. I sent Takis to spill your drink deliberately.'

'You must be crazy.' Kate felt dizzy suddenly. 'You can't hope to get away with this—even if you do own the place.'

'Ah,' he said softly. 'So you know who I am.'

'Your fame goes before you. But I'm not interested in being added to your list of conquests.'

He laughed. 'You flatter yourself, my red-headed vixen. My motives, for once, are purely altruistic.'

The lift doors opened, and Kate found herself being marched along a wide corridor towards a pair of double doors at the end.

'No.' There was real panic in her voice. 'I want to go home.'

'So you shall,' he said. 'In the morning when I am sure you have suffered no lasting ill effects.'

'Ill effects?' Kate echoed, as another wave of dizziness assailed her. 'What are you talking about.'

He said flatly, 'Your drink was spiked, *thespinis*. I saw your companion do it.'

'Spiked,' Kate repeated. 'You mean—drugged? But—why?'

He shrugged. 'To make you more amenable, perhaps.' He opened the door, and guided her into the room beyond. 'There is something called the date-rape drug. You may have heard of it.'

She said numbly, 'Heard of it—yes. But you must be mistaken. It can't be true…'

His mouth twisted. 'If the man you were with had asked you to sleep with him tonight, would you have agreed?'

She gasped. 'God—no. He's repulsive.'

'But might not take rejection well, all the same,' he said drily. 'Which is why you must not return to your apartment tonight.'

'But I have to.' Kate was shaking. She put a hand to her forehead, trying to steady herself. Collect her thoughts. 'My—my things are there. I'm going back to England tomorrow. Besides, they may have drugged Lisa too.'

His mouth curled. 'I doubt they would need to.'

She said hotly, 'You have no right to say that. You don't know her.'

He smiled faintly, 'I admire your loyalty, *thespinis*, if not your judgement. Now, I think you should lie down before you fall down,' he added with a slight frown.

'I'm—fine,' Kate said thickly.

'I don't think so,' he said, and picked her up in his arms.

She knew she should protest—that she should kick and fight, but it was so much easier to rest her head against his shoulder and close her eyes, and let him carry her.

She could feel the warmth of his body through his clothing. Could smell the faint muskiness of some cologne he wore.

She sensed a blur of shaded light, and felt the softness of a mattress beneath her. Dimly she was aware of her zip being unfastened and her dress removed, and tried to struggle—to utter some panicked negation.

A woman's voice spoke soothingly. 'Rest easily, little one. All will be well.'

Kate felt the caress of clean, crisp linen against her bare skin, and then the last vestiges of reality slid away, and she slept.

She dreamed fitfully, in brief wild snatches, her body twisting away from the image of Dimitris bending towards her with hot eyes and greedy hands, her voice crying out in soundless horror.

Once, there seemed to be a man's voice speaking right above her in Greek. 'She could solve your immediate problem.'

And heard a cool drawl that she seemed to recognise in the wry response, 'And create a hundred more...'

She wondered who they were—what they were talking about? But it was all too much effort when she was tired—so tired.

And, as she drifted away again, she felt a hand gently touch her hair, and stroke her cheek.

And smiled in her sleep.

CHAPTER THREE

SHE was on fire, burning endlessly in feverish, impossible excitement. Because a man's hands were touching her, arousing her to feverish, rapturous delight. His mouth was exploring her, his body moving against her as she lay beneath him, making her moan and writhe in helpless pleasure. In a need she had not known existed—until then.

And she forced open her heavy lids and looked at the dark face, fierce and intense above her, and saw that it was Michael Theodakis.

Kate awoke, gasping. For a moment she lay still, totally disorientated, then she propped herself up on an unsteady elbow, and looked around her.

Her first shocked realisation was that she was naked in this wide, luxurious bed, her sole covering a sheet tangled round her sweat-slicked body.

In fact, the entire bed looked as if it had been hit by an earthquake, the blue and ivory embroidered coverlet kicked to an untidy heap at its foot, and pillows on the floor.

It was a very large room, she thought, staring round her, with a cream tiled floor, and walls washed in a blue that reflected the azure of the sea and sky. The tall shutters had been opened, and the glass doors beyond stood slightly ajar, allowing a faint breeze from the sea to infiltrate the room and stir the pale voile drapes in the brilliant sunlight.

She shook the sheet loose, restoring it to a more decorous level, as she began slowly to remember the events of the previous night.

She didn't know which was the most extraordinary—the danger she'd been in, or the fact that Michael Theodakis had come to her rescue.

33

He must, she thought, have been watching very closely to have noticed her drink being spiked. But his attention would have been attracted by Stavros whom he'd clearly identified as trouble.

And he'd naturally be anxious to avoid any whiff of scandal being attached to his hotel, however marginal that might be. But whatever his motivation, she couldn't deny she'd had a lucky escape.

Shuddering, Kate sat up, shaking the tangle of red hair back from her face in an effort to dispel the faint muzziness which still plagued her—and paused, her attention suddenly, alarmingly arrested.

Because this room bore signs of occupation which had nothing to do with her, she realised, her heart thumping. Like a brush and comb and toiletries on the mirrored dressing table, a leather travel bag standing on a trestle in one corner, and a man's jacket tossed on to one of the blue armchairs by the window. And she could have no doubt about the identity of their owner.

She whispered, 'Oh God,' and sank back against the pillows, her mouth dry, and her mind working overtime.

Just exactly what had happened during the night? she asked herself desperately. And to be precise, what had happened after Michael Theodakis had carried her up here in his arms? Carried her to his room. His bed.

Because that she did most certainly recall, even if the rest was just a jumble of confused impressions.

But that was the effect of the date-rape drug, she reminded herself. It rendered you insensible. And it was only some time afterwards, if at all, that you remembered what had been done to you. And while she'd been unconscious, any kind of advantage could have been taken of her, she thought, swallowing painfully against her tight throat muscles.

Was it possible that during the hours of darkness, her rescuer could have turned predator?

Slowly, reluctantly, she made herself remember her

dream—that shivering, frenzied erotic ravishment that had tormented her unconscious mind.

But had it really been a dream, she wondered, staring, horrified, at the disordered bed—or stark reality?

Surely she would know—there would be some physical sign—if her body had been subjected to that level of sensual possession.

Or would she? Was this deep, unfamiliar ache inside her induced by physical frustration—or a passionate satisfaction that was entirely new to her?

Kate realised with shock that she could not be sure. And that maybe she never would be, which was, somehow, infinitely worse.

Oh, dear God, she thought, in panic. I've got to get out of here.

But where were her clothes? she wondered, staring fruitlessly round the room. Apart from her shoes, left by the bed, they seemed to have vanished completely.

And, as she absorbed this, a door opened and Michael Theodakis walked in.

Kate grabbed frantically at the slipping sheet holding it against her breasts, as her shocked brain registered that he himself was wearing nothing more than a towel draped round his hips. The rest of him was smooth olive skin, and rippling muscles, and in spite of herself, she found the breath catching in her throat.

He halted, looking her over slowly, brows lifted and eyes brilliant with amusement. He said 'Kalimera. So you're awake at last.'

She stared at him, her pulse rate growing crazy. A sick certainty welling up inside her.

She said hoarsely, 'What—what are you doing here?'

'Shaving,' he said. 'A habit I acquired in adolescence.' He nodded towards the room he'd just left. 'I am sorry that we have to share a bathroom, but now you have it to yourself.'

'Share?' she said. 'A bathroom?'

'This suite only has one.' He seemed totally at ease with the situation, and with his lack of clothing too. But undoubtedly he was used to displaying himself in front of women in a towel, or even without one.

Whereas she—she was strangling in this bloody sheet.

'Which does not matter when I am here alone, as I usually am,' he went on.

'But last night,' Kate said, her voice shaking. 'Was different.'

'Of course,' he said softly. 'Because you were here.' He paused. 'I have ordered breakfast to be served to us on the terrace. Would you like me to run a bath for you?'

'No,' she said. 'I think I've had enough personal services for one lifetime. Like being undressed and put to bed last night.'

'You could not do it for yourself.' He made it all sound so reasonable, she thought in helpless outrage. 'You were barely conscious, *pedhi mou*.'

'I'm aware of that,' Kate said between her teeth. 'And I am not your little one.'

He frowned slightly. 'You have had a shock,' he said. 'But it is over now, and you have come to no harm.'

'Perhaps I don't see it like that.' The sheet was slipping, and she hitched it up, anchoring it with her arms. A gesture that was not lost on him.

There was still laughter in his eyes, but that had been joined by another element. Something darker—more disturbing. Something she had glimpsed in those dark, heated hours in the night, but did not want to recognise again.

Yet, at the same time, she realised that she had to confront him—had to know. Had to...

'Then how do you see it?' The dark eyes moved over her in frank assessment. He was enjoying this, she thought, her anger mounting. 'Maybe we can reach a compromise.'

Kate drew a shaky breath. 'I'd prefer the truth. Did you come to this room during the night.'

'Yes. I came to check that you were all right. So did the housekeeper, and also the hotel doctor. It was quite a procession,' he added drily.

She swallowed. 'But you were also here alone.'

He frowned. 'I have said so.'

She touched her dry lips with her tongue.

'Did you—touch me?'

There was a silence. Then, 'Yes,' he said quietly. 'I did not mean you to know, but I could not resist. Your hair looked so beautiful spread across my pillow. I had this irresistible desire to feel it under my hand.'

She stared at him. 'And was that all—your only irresistible desire, Kyrios Theodakis?'

He sighed. 'There was a tear on your cheek. I brushed it away.'

'And then you left,' she said. 'Is that what I'm supposed to believe?'

The dark eyes narrowed. He said softly, 'What are you trying to say?'

Kate bit her lip. 'Where exactly did you spend the night, Mr Theodakis?'

'This is a suite, Kyria Dennison. There are two bedrooms. I slept in the second. And I slept well. I hope you did too,' he added courteously.

'No,' she said. 'I didn't. I had the strangest dreams.'

The dark eyes narrowed. 'The effect of the drug, perhaps.'

'Perhaps,' she said. 'But this was such a vivid dream. So realistic.'

'You are fortunate,' he drawled. 'I rarely remember mine.'

'I'd give a hell of a lot,' Kate said stormily, 'not to remember this one.'

'You interest me.' He was frowning again, his eyes fixed watchfully on her flushed face. 'You can describe it to me over breakfast.'

'I don't want any breakfast,' she hurled at him. 'And I certainly don't want to eat with you. Because I don't believe it was a dream at all—you unspeakable bastard. Any more than I believe you spent the night in another room.'

His brows lifted. 'You're saying this dream involved me in some way?'

He sounded politely interested, no more. But there was a new tension in the tall figure. A sudden electricity in the room.

'Yes, I am. I'm saying you—used me last night.'

'"Used",' Michael Theodakis said musingly. 'An interesting choice of word. Do you mean that we made love?'

Kate's voice shook. 'I said exactly what I meant. And you took a filthy advantage of me. Oh, you're so damned sure of yourself,' she went on recklessly. 'So convinced that you're the answer to any woman's prayer. I expect you thought I'd be honoured—if I ever remembered.'

'So let us test this memory of yours,' he said softly. 'Tell me, *agapi mou*, exactly what I did to you.'

She said defensively, 'I can't recall the actual details.'

'But was it good for you?' He sounded almost casual. 'You must remember that. For instance, did you come?'

Kate gasped, colour flooding her face. 'How dare you.'

'But I need to know. I would hate to think I had disappointed you in any way.' He walked slowly towards her. 'Perhaps I should—jog your memory a little.'

'Keep away from me.' Kate shrank back.

'But why?' There was danger in his voice. He bent lithely, retrieving one of the pillows from the floor. Tossing it on to the bed beside her. His smile did not reach his eyes as he looked at her. 'When we have already been so close—so intimate? And this time, my beautiful one, I will make sure that you do not forget—anything.'

His hand snaked out, hooking into the folds of linen tucked above her breasts, and tugging them free, uncovering her completely.

Kate gave a small wounded cry, and turned instinctively on to her side, curling into a ball, and sheltering her body with her hands from the arrogance of his gaze, as humiliated tears burned in her throat.

'Why so modest?' His tone lashed her. 'According to you, there is nothing that I have not already seen and enjoyed.'

'Please,' she managed, chokingly. 'Please—don't…'

'But I am an unspeakable bastard, *agapi mou*,' he said softly. 'So why should I listen?'

She couldn't think of a single reason, huddled there on his bed, her breath catching on a sob.

For a moment there was silence and a heart-stopping stillness, then he sighed harshly, and turned away. He picked up a towelling robe from a chair and tossed it down to her.

'Put this on,' he directed curtly. 'You will find it safer than a sheet.'

As she obeyed hurriedly, clumsily, he went on, 'As you have just discovered, I have a temper, *thespinis*, so do not provoke me again. I have never taken a woman in anger in my life,' he added grimly. 'I do not wish you to be the first.'

She wrapped herself in the robe, tying the sash with shaking fingers.

He came to the side of the bed and took her chin in his hands, forcing her to look up at him.

He said quietly, 'The mind can play strange tricks, *pedhi mou*. But I swear I did not share your bed last night. Because if I had done so, you would have remembered, believe me.'

For a fleeting moment, his hands cupped her breasts through the thickness of the robe, his touch burning against her skin, making her nipples harden in sudden, painful need.

She heard herself gasp, then she was free, and he had stepped back from her.

He said, 'I am going to dress. Then you will join me for breakfast.'

She found the remains of her voice. 'My—clothes…?'

'My housekeeper took them to be laundered—after she undressed you last night.' He allowed her to absorb that.

'They will be returned to you after you have eaten.' He paused. 'Shall we say half an hour?'

And left her, staring after him, her bottom lip caught painfully in her teeth.

As she slid down into the scented bubbles of the bath, Kate was almost tempted to go one stage further, and drown herself.

Since the moment she'd opened her eyes that morning, she'd behaved like a crazy woman. But now she was sane again, and hideously embarrassed to go with it.

Oh, God, what had possessed her to hurl those accusations at Michael Theodakis? she asked herself despairingly.

Well, she supposed it had been triggered by him strolling in, next door to naked, and behaving as if it was an ordinary occurrence. As it probably was to him, but not to her...

She stopped right there, her brows snapping together.

What on earth was she talking about? Working as a holiday rep she encountered men far more skimpily clad every day, and had never found it any kind of problem.

So, why had she over-reacted so ludicrously? It made no sense. She bit her lip, as the realisation dawned that it was nothing to do with the way he'd been dressed—or undressed, and never had been.

It was Michael Theodakis himself who'd rattled her—sent her spinning out of control.

From the moment she'd seen him, she'd been on edge, aware of him in a way that was totally outside her limited experience. She'd been on the defensive even before he'd addressed one word to her.

And the dream, she guessed miserably, had simply been a spin-off from being carried upstairs in his arms. Maybe some humiliating form of wish-fulfilment.

So, she'd behaved like an hysterical fool and, in turn, been treated pretty much with the contempt she deserved, she thought, wincing.

She should have stuck to Plan A and just left quietly. After all, she could always have rung the apartment and got Lisa to bring her a change of clothes.

Lisa…

Kate groaned aloud. Until that moment, she hadn't spared her flatmate a thought. And anything could have happened to her.

This, she thought forcefully, is not like me.

Overnight she seemed to have turned into a stranger—and a stranger she didn't like very much.

In spite of her red hair, she'd always been cool, level-headed Kate, and she wanted her old self back. Michael Theodakis might be a devastatingly attractive man with a powerful sexual charisma, but that did not mean she had to go to pieces when she was around him.

Polite, grateful and unreachable. That was the way to handle the next half hour. The only way.

And then she would be gone, not just from this hotel, but from Greece too, and she would never have to set eyes on him again.

She dried herself and reluctantly donned the towelling robe again, knotting the sash for extra insurance. It masked her from throat to ankle, but it didn't inspire the confidence her own clothes would have done, and she needed all the assurance she could get, she thought wretchedly.

She combed her hair with her fingers, and emerged reluctantly into the bedroom, steeling herself to walk to the windows.

Outside, a table had been laid, overlooking the sea. And here Michael Theodakis was waiting, leaning against the balustrade in the sunlight.

Kate drew a deep breath, stuck her hands in the pockets of the robe to hide the fact that they were trembling, and went out to join him.

He was wearing shorts, which showed off those endless legs, she observed waspishly, and a short-sleeved polo shirt, open at the throat and affording a glimpse of the shadowing of body hair she'd already had plenty of opportunity to observe.

He said quietly, '*Kalimera*—for the second time. Or shall we erase the events of the past hour, which do credit to neither of us, and pretend it is the first?'

'Yes.' Kate looked down at the tiled floor, aware that she was blushing. 'Maybe we should—do that.'

'At last,' he said. 'We agree on something.'

She hastily transferred her attention to the table, set with a jug of chilled fruit juice, a basket of crisp rolls, dishes of honey and dark cherry jam, a bowl of thick, creamy yoghurt, a platter of grapes, apricots and peaches, and a tall pot of coffee.

She forced a smile. 'It all looks—delicious.'

'Yes,' he said softly, a quiver of amusement in his voice. 'It does.'

She found she was trembling suddenly, hotly aware that he was still looking at her, and not the food.

'Please sit down,' he went on, and Kate moved round the table, choosing a chair that would be as far away from him as it was possible to get, without actually jumping off the terrace. And she might even try that if all else failed.

'I hope you found your bath soothing,' he said silkily, as he poured the juice into glasses, and handed her one.

'Yes,' Kate said. 'Thank you.'

'But perhaps a body massage might be even more relaxing,' he went on. 'If you would like one, you have only to ask.'

Kate thumped an inoffensive bread roll on to her plate.

'How kind of you,' she said grittily. 'But I'll pass.'

He smiled at her. 'It was not a personal offer, *thespinis*. We have an excellent masseuse at the health spa, who comes highly recommended. But it's your decision.'

Wrong-footed again, thought Kate, taking a gulp of fruit juice and wishing dispassionately that it was hemlock.

'Honey?' Michael Theodakis proffered the dish. 'It might sweeten your disposition,' he added casually.

'My disposition is fine.' Kate spooned some on to her plate. 'Perhaps you just bring out the worst in me, Kyrios Theodakis.'

'My name is Michael,' he said. 'Or Mick, if you prefer. Just as you are Kate, rather than Katharina.'

She put down her knife. 'How do you know my name?' she demanded huskily.

He shrugged. 'Your papers were in the purse you left in the club last night. I did not think your identity was a secret. Besides, the police needed to know.'

'The police.' She stared at him, lips parted in shock, eyes widening.

'Of course.' He sounded matter of fact. 'Your friend Stavros also had ecstasy tablets in his possession when he was searched. Both he and his cousin spent the night in jail. The first of many, I suspect.'

'And Lisa?' Kate asked, with distress. 'Oh, God, they didn't lock her up too, surely.'

'No,' he said. 'I arranged for her to have her freedom. But it is as well she is leaving Zycos today, and I doubt she will ever be permitted to return. She keeps bad company.'

'You—arranged?' Kate said with disbelief. She shook her head. 'How gratifying to have such power.'

'No,' he said, and gave her a cool smile. 'Merely useful sometimes.'

Kate ate some bread and honey, forcing it past her dry throat.

At last she said stiltedly, 'I must sound very ungracious, *kyrie*.' She took a breath. 'I—I have to be grateful, to you, naturally. You saved me from potential disaster, but, for the rest of it, I'm totally out of my depth here.' She shook her head. 'Drug dealers—jail—I've never experienced these things before. I don't know how to handle them.'

He said quite gently, 'You don't have to, *thespinis*. They

have been dealt with for you. Please do not allow them to cloud your memories of Zycos.' He picked up the silver pot. 'Coffee?'

But, as she took the cup from him with a subdued murmur of thanks, Kate knew that it would not be her brush with the horror of Dimitris that would return to haunt her in the days to come, but the thought of this man, and the smile in his dark eyes. The warmth of his body, and the remembered scent of his skin as she'd been carried in his arms.

And, even more disturbingly, that there wasn't a thing she could do about it.

It was not the easiest meal Kate had ever eaten.

The necessity to appear untroubled—to make light, social conversation without revealing her inner turmoil—was an unlooked-for struggle.

'The weather's still wonderful,' she said over-brightly, after a pause. 'But I suppose it can't last forever.'

'Very little does.' He was preparing a peach, his long fingers deft, but he looked across at her and smiled. 'Did you know that the sun turns your hair to fire?'

'I'm aware it's red,' Kate said, with something of a snap. 'You don't need to labour the point.'

'And you should learn to accept a compliment with more grace, *matia mou*,' he said drily. 'Make the most of the sun,' he added. 'Because it will rain soon.'

She looked up at the cloudless sky. 'How do you know?'

He shrugged. 'These are my islands. It is my business to know. And our autumns tend to be damp.'

'Are you from Zycos originally?'

'No.' There was a sudden curtness in his voice. 'I was born on Kefalonia, and my real home was always there.'

'But no longer?' She remembered Stavros mentioning a family dispute.

He was silent for a moment. Then, 'I travel a great deal.

I have no permanent base just now.' He paused again. 'And you?'

'I share a flat in London.'

He frowned. 'With this Lisa?' There was a sudden austerity in his voice.

'Oh, no,' Kate said hastily. 'We were colleagues here for the season, and it just seemed—convenient. My flatmate in London is called Sandy, and she's very different. She works as a researcher on a national newspaper.' She hesitated. 'I shall—miss her when I move.'

'You are planning to do so?' He sounded politely interested.

'Yes,' she said. She took a deep breath. 'Actually—I'm going to be married. Quite soon. So—you see—I have every reason to be grateful for what you did for me. And I do— thank you. Very much indeed.'

There was silence—a slow tingling silence that threatened to stretch into eternity. Expressionlessly, Michael Theodakis looked down at her ringless hands. Studied them. Returned to her face.

He said, 'You are very much in love?'

'Naturally.' Kate stiffened defensively.

'And is it also natural to enjoy erotic fantasies about another man—a stranger?'

Her mouth was suddenly very dry. 'My fiancé is the one who matters. I'm not interested in anyone else.'

'Truly?' he asked softly. 'I wonder.' He pushed back his chair and came round the table to her, pulling her up out of her seat. His arms went round her, pulling her close to his body. Then he bent his head and kissed her, slowly and very thoroughly, his enjoyment of her mouth unashamedly sensuous.

Time stilled. His tongue was slow fire against hers, the practised mouth teaching her things she'd never known she needed to learn. Suddenly, she couldn't breathe—or think.

When he released her at last, he was smiling.

He said, 'I think, *pedhi mou*, that you are fooling yourself.'

Kate took a step backwards. She brushed a shaky hand across her burning lips, her eyes sparking anger at him. Anger she could shelter behind. 'You're despicable,' she flung at him. 'You had no right to do that—no right at all.'

He shrugged an unperturbed shoulder. 'Why not? I am a single man. You are a single woman.'

'But I told you. I'm going to be married.'

'Yes,' he said. 'You did. Be sure to send me an invitation to the wedding. If it ever happens. Because if I was going to marry you, Katharina *mou*, I would make sure you only dreamed of me.'

He lifted her hand, and dropped a brief kiss on to its palm, then turned and walked away into the suite, and out of her life.

Leaving her standing there in the sunlight, looking after him, white-faced and totally defenceless.

CHAPTER FOUR

SHE had a lot to think about on the flight back to Britain.

But her priority was the deliberate, systematic banishment of Mick Theodakis from her mind. Because there was nothing to be gained from remembering the glinting amusement in his dark eyes, or the incredible feel of his mouth on hers. Nothing at all.

So, she made herself contemplate her immediate future instead, which, to her dismay, proved just as tricky.

Because she knew with total and shattering certainty that she couldn't marry Grant. Not any more.

Clearly, he would want to know why she'd changed her mind, she thought wretchedly, and she didn't have a single reason to give that made any real sense, even to herself.

And whatever she said would be bound to hurt him, she thought wincing, and she didn't want to do that. Perhaps she could say that her time in Greece had changed her in some basic way. That she wasn't the same person any longer.

After all, it was no more than the truth.

But she had to recognise that she hadn't harboured a single doubt about her future with Grant until Michael Theodakis had crossed her path. Which was crazy, because you didn't overturn your entire life because of a casual kiss from a seasoned womaniser.

She needed to remember that, for Mick Theodakis, the kiss had been little more than a reflex action, she thought, plus an element of punishment for misjudging him.

All this she knew. So, why didn't it make any real difference?

She was still wondering when she walked into Arrivals

47

and saw Grant waiting for her, smiling, with a bouquet of flowers.

Kate's heart sank. She'd been counting on a slight breathing space before they met.

'Darling.' His arms hugged her close. 'God, I've missed you. From now on, I don't let you out of my sight. We have a wedding to plan, and I can't wait.'

She walked beside him in silence to the car, wondering how to begin.

'So, where's the crazy Lisa?' Grant asked cheerfully, as he stowed her bags in the boot. 'I thought she'd be with you.'

Kate bit her lip, remembering how she'd returned to the apartment to find it bare and empty, with Lisa's keys discarded on the living room table.

She said quietly, 'She decided to take another flight.' She took a deep breath, knowing she couldn't pretend—or hedge any more. 'Grant—I have something to tell you.'

His reaction was every bit as bad as she'd feared. He started with frank disbelief, moved to bewilderment, then to resentment and real anger.

On the whole, she thought, standing outside her flat, watching him drive away, the anger had been the easiest to cope with.

And now she had to deal with Sandy.

'Where's Grant?' was her flatmate's first inevitable question, after a welcoming hug. 'I was going to open a bottle of wine, then tactfully vanish.'

'No need.' Kate squared her shoulders. 'Grant and I are no longer an item.'

Sandy stared at her. 'When did this happen?'

'At the airport. He was making plans. I realised I couldn't let him.'

'Fair enough,' Sandy said equably. 'So—who's the new man?'

'Grant asked that too,' Kate said, aware that she was flushing. 'Why should my breaking up with him imply there's someone else?'

'Because that's the way it generally works.' Sandy poured the wine. 'So don't tell me he doesn't exist.'

Kate paused. 'It was nothing.'

'Then you did meet someone,' Sandy said triumphantly. 'I knew it.'

'No,' Kate shook her head. 'I *encountered* someone. Very briefly. Big difference.'

'Details please?'

'His name was Theodakis,' Kate said reluctantly. 'His family owns the Regina hotel chain, plus the Odyssey cruise fleet, and the Helicon airline. Does that tell you enough?'

'Absolutely.' Sandy gave her a narrow-eyed look. 'And that's a hell of a lot of info for just a brief encounter.'

'He didn't tell me all of it.' Kate's flush deepened. 'I— looked him up on the office computer before I went to the airport.'

'Good move.' Sandy approved. 'When's the wedding, and please may I be bridesmaid? I'd like to meet his friends.'

'I doubt he has any,' Kate said with a snap. 'He's arrogant and totally impossible.'

'Yet he's made you think twice about Grant, who's always been the soul of sweet reason.' Sandy clicked her tongue. 'I spy muddled thinking here, babe.'

'Not at all,' Kate retorted with dignity. 'I simply found out that absence—hadn't made my heart grow fonder.'

'Ah,' said Sandy. 'In that case, you should have no problem getting over Mr Theodakis either.' She raised her glass. 'Good luck,' she added cheerfully. 'You're going to need it.'

When Kate reported for duty at Halcyon's head offices a couple of days later, she was aware of an atmosphere, and sideways looks from other members of staff.

It didn't take her long to discover that Lisa had been fired, and had openly blamed Kate for getting her into trouble with the Greek police.

When the other girl came in to collect some paperwork, Kate confronted her, but Lisa remained obdurate.

'You dropped us all in it,' she accused. 'Now the lads are in jail, and I've got a police record. I'll probably never work in Greece again.'

'Lisa,' Kate said quietly. 'Stavros and Dimitris spiked my drink. They were seen doing it.'

'Rubbish,' Lisa said defiantly. 'It was just a giggle—something to relax you, and take the starch out of your knickers. You—over-reacted.'

'They were also carrying ecstasy tablets.' Kate spread her hands. 'They were drug dealers, Lisa. They could have caused us more trouble than we've ever dreamed of.'

Lisa shrugged, her face hard. She said, 'A word of advice. Whatever you may think of Stavros and Dimitris, they aren't even in the same league as Mick Theodakis. When it comes to ruthless, he invented the word. I don't know why he chose to meddle, but he probably had his own devious reasons. Because Sir Galahad he ain't.'

Kate bit her lip. 'Thanks—but I never thought he was.'

The next two weeks were difficult ones, especially when Grant decided to launch a charm offensive to win her back, turning up at the flat in the evening with flowers, bottles of wine, theatre tickets and invitations to dinner, all of which she steadfastly refused.

Work helped. Halcyon's winter City Breaks programme took her away a lot and, when she was at home, she let the answering machine field Grant's increasingly plaintive calls.

And eventually, her life steadied and found a new rhythm. A new purpose. One which did not include any lingering memories of Michael Theodakis, she told herself determinedly. And certainly no regrets.

After a weekend trip to Rome which had thrown up more than its fair share of problems, she was spending a wet

November afternoon at the office, working on a detailed report, when reception buzzed to say she had a visitor.

Kate groaned inwardly. Surely not Grant, again, she thought glumly as she rode down in the lift. He was beginning to be a nuisance, and she'd have to instruct Debbie to say she wasn't there in future.

She was already rehearsing the words, 'This has got to stop,' when the lift doors opened, and she stepped out into the foyer, to be brought up short, the blood draining from her face as she saw exactly who awaited her.

'Katharina,' Michael Theodakis said softly. 'It is good to see you again.'

Goodness, Kate thought breathlessly, has nothing to do with it.

He was lounging against the desk, immaculate in a formal suit and dark overcoat. Dressed for the City, for meetings and high-powered business deals. Smooth, she thought. Civilised. But she wasn't fooled for a moment.

She felt as if she'd strayed into a pet shop, and found a tiger on the loose.

Her mouth was suddenly dry. 'Mr Theodakis—what are you doing here?'

'I came to find you *matia mou*. What else?' He smiled at her, totally at his ease, the dark eyes making an unhurried assessment of her.

Making her feel, in spite of her neat grey flannel skirt and matching wool shirt, curiously undressed.

She said, her voice barely a whisper. 'I don't understand…'

'Then I will explain.' He straightened. The tiger, she thought, about to leap.

'Get your coat,' he directed. 'I have a car waiting.'

'But I'm working,' Kate said, desperately searching for a lifeline. 'I can't just—leave.'

'Mr Harris says you can, Miss Dennison.' Debbie, who'd been devouring him shamelessly with her gaze, broke in eagerly. 'Mr Theodakis spoke to him just now. I put him through,' she added proudly.

'Oh,' Kate said in a hollow voice. 'I see.'

One mention of the Theodakis name, she knew, would be enough to get the Halcyon boss jumping through hoops. He would dearly love to get exclusive rights at the Regina hotels for his holidays. And, quite suddenly, Kate had become the possible means to that end. Or so he would think.

In the cloakroom, Kate thrust her arms clumsily into the sleeves of her raincoat, but did not attempt to fasten it because her hands were shaking too much. When she tried to renew her lipstick, she ended up dropping the tube into the washbasin. Better not try again, she thought as she retrieved it, or she'd end up looking like a clown.

And she felt quite stupid enough already.

She found herself avoiding Debbie's envious glance as Michael Theodakis took her arm and walked her through the glass doors to the street.

The car was at the kerb, with a chauffeur waiting deferentially to open the door.

What else? Kate thought, as she sank into the luxury of the leather seating. And either I've gone crazy, or this is a dream, and presently I'll be awake again.

But there was nothing remotely dream-like about the man sitting beside her in the back of this limousine. He was living, breathing flesh and blood, and her every nerve-ending was tingling in acknowledgement of this. In terrifying awareness.

As the car drew away, he said, 'You are trembling. Why?'

No point in denial, she realised. He saw too much.

She said, 'I think I'm in shock.' She made herself look at him, meet the lurking laughter in his dark eyes. 'You're the last person in the world I ever expected to see again.'

He grinned at her, the lean body relaxed and graceful. 'Truly? Or did you just hope that I was out of your life?'

Kate lifted her chin. 'That too.'

'Then I am sorry to disappoint you,' he said without any

sign of contrition. 'But it was inevitable. The world is such a small place, Katharina *mou*. I always knew we would meet again. And I decided it should be sooner rather than later.'

Kate sat bolt upright. 'I can't think why.'

'Naturally, I wished to make sure you had recovered from your traumatic experience on Zycos,' he said silkily. 'Have you?'

'I never give it a thought,' Kate said shortly, resisting the urge to ask which particular trauma he was referring to.

'You are blessed with a convenient memory, *matia mou*.' His tone was dry. He looked her over, his glance lingering on the thrust of her breasts under the thin wool. 'You have lost weight a little. Why?'

'I lead a busy life.' His scrutiny brought a faint flush to her cheeks.

'Then you should make time to relax,' he said. 'Taste the wine. Feel the sun on your face.'

Kate sent a dry look towards the drenched streets. 'Not much chance of that today.'

'There is always sun somewhere, *agapi mou*.' He spoke softly. 'You must learn to follow it.'

'Then why aren't you doing so?'

'Because I am here—with you.' He paused. 'It is too early for dinner, so I thought we would go somewhere for tea. I told my driver the Ritz, but perhaps you'd prefer somewhere else.'

'That would be fine, although I can't imagine you'll find afternoon tea very exciting.' Kate tried to speak lightly.

He said gently, 'But you have yet to learn what excites me, Katharina.'

Kate's throat tightened. She felt herself blushing again, and bent her head slightly. A strand of hair fell across her cheek and she lifted a hand to brush it back.

He said, 'Leave it. You should not wear your hair scraped back from your face.'

'It's neat,' she said. 'And tidy. For work.'

'But you are not working now. And I like to see your hair loose on your shoulders. Or across a pillow,' he added softly.

Her face burned. 'But I don't style it to please you, Kyrios Theodakis.'

He smiled at her. 'Not yet, anyway.'

Kate tucked the errant tress behind her ear with a certain stony emphasis.

Immediately, she felt the focus of his attention shift. He moved sharply, his fingers closing round her wrists, capturing her hands while he studied them.

Kate tried to pull away. 'What are you doing?'

'Still no ring, *agapi mou*?' There was an odd note in his voice. 'Your lover cannot be very ardent. He should tell the whole world that you belong to him.'

Kate looked down at her lap. 'I—we decided to wait a little longer. That's all.'

His tone hardened. 'Katharina—look at me.'

Reluctantly, she obeyed, almost flinching at the sudden intensity of his gaze.

'Now,' he said. 'Tell me the truth. Are you engaged to this man? Do you plan to be married?'

She knew what she should do. She should tell him it was none of his damned business, and request him to stop the car and let her out.

The silence seemed to close round them. The air was suddenly heavy. Charged.

Kate swallowed helplessly. She heard herself say, 'I—I'm not seeing him. It's over.'

'Ah,' he said softly. 'Then that changes everything. Does it not, *agapi mou*?' Still watching the bewildered play of colour in her face, he lifted one hand, and then the other to his lips.

At the brush of his mouth, she found herself pierced by such an agony of need that she had to bite down on her lip to stop herself crying out.

Her voice shook. 'No. *Kyrie*—please...'

He made no attempt to release her. The dark eyes glittered at her. 'Say my name.'

'Mr Theodakis…'

'No.' His voice was urgent. 'Say my name as I wish to hear it. As you, in your heart, want to speak it. Say it now.'

Her mouth trembled. 'Michalis—*mou*.'

'At last you admit it.' There was a note of shaken laughter under the words. 'And now I will tell you why I am here. Because there is still unfinished business between us. I know it, and so do you.' He paused. 'Is it not so?'

'Yes.' Her voice was barely audible.

He made a slight, unsmiling inclination of his head, then leaned across and tapped imperatively on the driver's glass partition.

He said. 'The Royal Empress Hotel. And hurry.'

They stood together in the lift as it sped upwards. They were silent, but Kate could hear the sound of her own breathing, harsh, even erratic.

They did not touch, but every inch of her was quivering as if it already knew the caress of his hand.

Her heart was thudding painfully, as he unlocked the door, and ushered her into the large sitting room beyond.

Mutely, Kate allowed herself to be divested of her raincoat, then stood, trying to compose herself as she took stock of her surroundings.

It was a beautiful room, she saw, with elegant, highly polished furniture and large pastel sofas, complementing an exquisite washed Chinese carpet.

One wall seemed to be all glass, giving a panoramic view of the Thames.

And a door standing ajar allowed a glimpse of the bedroom with its king-size bed draped in oyster satin. Bringing her suddenly, joltingly back to a reality.

Dry-mouthed, she thought, 'What am I doing here?'

She knew she was being ridiculous. She was a grown

woman, and she was here of her own free will, but she was still as nervous as a teenager on her first date.

Because the truth was that she didn't really know what to expect. Not this time.

She'd been alone with Grant often, she reminded herself with a kind of desperation, either at her place or his, but she'd never felt like this. Never been so much at a loss, or in this kind of emotional turmoil.

But then her relationship with Grant had been quite different. They'd been finding out slowly and cautiously whether they might have a future together.

But, if she was honest, she'd never burned for him. Craved the touch of his mouth—the caress of his hands on her body. Never been so conscious of his sheer physical presence. She'd assumed that going to bed with Grant would be the final confirmation of their commitment to each other. Settled, even comfortable.

But with Michael Theodakis she could make none of those assumptions.

He would demand total surrender, and the thought of losing control of her body—and her emotions—so completely frankly terrified her.

But that wasn't all.

The brutal reality of the situation was that she'd come here to go to bed with a man she hardly knew. Someone infinitely more experienced than she was, who might well make demands she could not fulfil.

Biting her lip, she took a quick look over her shoulder.

He'd discarded his overcoat and jacket and was on the phone, waistcoat unbuttoned, tugging at his tie with impatient fingers as he talked.

She wandered across to the rainwashed window, and stared out, her thoughts going crazy.

If she told him she'd changed her mind, how would he react? she wondered apprehensively. He'd warned her that he had a temper. Could she risk provoking him again?

He replaced the receiver and came over to her, sliding his arms round her waist and drawing her back to lean against him. He bent his head, putting his lips against the side of her neck where the tiny pulse thundered.

He said softly, 'I hope you like champagne. I've asked them to send some up.'

'Yes,' she said breathlessly. 'That would be—lovely.' She glanced back at the window. 'On a fine day, this view should be spectacular.'

Oh, God, she thought. She was actually making conversation about the weather.

'Then it's fortunate it is raining.' He sounded amused. 'So we do not have to waste time admiring it.'

He turned her to face him, his hand sliding under the edge of her shirt to find the delicate ridge of her spine. Making her shiver in nervous anticipation as his fingers splayed across the sensitive skin.

He pulled her intimately, dangerously close to him, forcing her to the awareness that he was already strongly, powerfully aroused.

She stood awkwardly in the circle of his arms, her heart thudding. She thought, 'I don't know what to do…'

He cupped her face in his hands, making her look up at him.

He said. 'You are shaking. What is there to frighten you?'

She tried to smile. 'There's—you.'

His mouth twisted wryly. 'I am only a man, Katharina *mou*, not a monster. And I ask nothing that you have not given before.'

She said huskily, 'That's just the problem.'

He frowned slightly. 'I don't understand.'

She swallowed. 'Michael—I just don't—do things like this.'

His face was solemn, but his eyes were dancing. 'Is that a matter of principle, *agapi mou*, or do you simply not want to do them with me?'

She said baldly, 'I mean I never have.'

There was a pause. 'But you were seeing a man,' he said quietly. 'A man you planned to marry.'

'Yes,' she said. 'But we weren't—living together. We decided to—wait until I came back from Greece.'

He was very still. 'And before that?'

'There was no one I cared about sufficiently.' She stared rigidly at the pattern on his loosened tie. 'I—I always swore to myself that I'd avoid casual sex. That I'd only ever go to bed with a man if I couldn't help myself. If the alternative was altogether more than I could bear. I—I suppose I felt it should actually mean something…'

Her voice tailed off into silence.

'And now?' he asked.

She shook her head. 'I just don't—know any more.' She looked at him. 'I'm sorry. I should never have come here. I don't know what I was thinking of.' Her voice rose a little. 'I mean, we're strangers, for God's sake.'

'Hardly strangers,' he reminded her, a note of laughter in his voice. 'After all, you have spent one night in my bed already.'

'Yes,' she said huskily. 'But that time I was alone. Now it would be—different.'

'Yes,' he said. 'It would.'

There was another silence, as he looked down at her, his eyes meditative. His thumb stroked her cheek, and moved rhythmically along the line of her jaw, and the curve of her throat above her collar. She caught her breath, her heart juddering frantically.

'You don't want me to touch you?' he asked gently.

'I—didn't say that.'

'Then you think I will be unkind—uncaring in bed? That I will not give you pleasure?'

He sounded completely matter of fact—as if he was asking whether she preferred classical music to jazz, she thought wildly.

She said shakily, 'It's—not that. I'm scared I won't know how to please you. That you'll be disappointed.' She paused. 'You've had so many other women.'

'But never you, *matia mou*,' he said. 'Never until this moment. And while I have been seen with a great many women, I have actually slept with very few of them. Perhaps I think it should mean something too,' he added drily.

'Then—why me?'

He swung her round, so that she could see herself reflected in the window. He pulled the clip from her hair, letting it tumble in a shining mass on her shoulders.

'Look at yourself.' His voice was oddly harsh. 'This is the picture of you that I have carried in my mind—in my heart all these weeks. That has tormented me by day and kept me from sleep at night. And now I want the reality of you, naked in my arms. But, if necessary, I am prepared to wait. Until you are ready.'

She said unevenly, 'And if you have to wait a long time?'

He shrugged. 'I can be patient. But, ultimately, I expect my patience to be rewarded.'

He turned her round to face him, his hands framing her face.

'Do you accept that, Katharina?' His eyes seemed to pierce her soul. 'Do you agree that one day—one night—when you cannot help yourself—you will come to me?'

'Yes.' Her voice was a thread of sound.

He smiled, and released her, stepping back.

He said quietly, 'Then it begins.'

CHAPTER FIVE

AND that was where it should also have ended, Kate told herself bitterly.

She should have taken advantage of the brief respite he'd offered, and vanished. After all, Halcyon owed her leave, and she could have gone anywhere. Stayed away until he'd tired of waiting, and gone back to Greece. And found someone else to act as his smokescreen.

Her hair was dry, so, wearily, she began to make preparations for the night, turning off the fire, extinguishing lights, rinsing her beaker in the kitchen.

She was tired, but her mind would not let her relax from this emotional treadmill.

Oh, she'd been so easy to deceive, she thought, staring into the darkness. So eager to believe anything that he told her—to accept all that he seemed to be offering.

And he'd been clever too, making her think that she was in control—that she was making the choice. When really he'd been playing her like some little fish on his line.

Starting with that first afternoon...

The champagne had arrived with a bowl of strawberries, and a plate of small almond biscuits.

Michael had beckoned to her. 'Come and drink some wine with me,' he invited. 'And let us talk.'

Kate walked reluctantly across the room and seated herself on one corner of the sofa he indicated while he occupied the other.

'Is this a safe distance?' he asked mockingly, as he handed her a flute of champagne. 'I am not sure of the rules in this situation.'

'I expect you usually write your own.' The champagne was exquisitely cool and refreshing in her dry mouth.

'In business, certainly.' His tone was silky. 'But not usually in pleasure.' He let her digest that, then picked a strawberry from the dish, dipped it in champagne, and held it out to her. 'Try this.'

Kate bit delicately at the fruit, feeling self-conscious. 'That's—delicious.'

'Yes.' He was watching her mouth, as he took the next bite himself. 'It is.'

Kate crossed her feet at the ankles, nervously smoothing her skirt over her knees. 'So what do you want to talk about?'

'It occurred to me that we might get to know each other a little better.' He drank some champagne. 'What do you think?'

She shrugged nervously. 'If you wish. What do you want to know?'

'Everything.' He offered her another champagne-soaked strawberry. 'Are your parents living?'

'No,' she said. 'They died five years ago. Their car—skidded on black ice, and hit a wall.'

His brows snapped together. He said quietly, 'I am sorry, *pedhi mou*. Does it still hurt you?'

'Not like it once did.' She shook her head. 'But it meant I had to grow up fast, and make my own life, which I've done. And now I have a job I like which allows me to travel.' She paused. 'Are you an only child too?'

'I was for twelve years, and then my sister Ismene was born. She was only six when our mother died.'

'Oh,' Kate put down her glass. 'That must have been terrible.'

'It wasn't easy, especially for Ismene, although my aunt Linda did her best to take my mother's place.' He paused. 'The Regina hotels were named after her.'

Kate was silent for a moment. Then, 'What's your sister like?'

He considered. 'Pretty—a little crazy—and talks too much.' He shrugged, his mouth slanting wickedly. 'A typical woman.'

'Oh.' Kate's hands clenched into fists of mock outrage, and he captured them deftly, laughing as he raised them to his lips, then turned them so that he could brush her soft palms with his mouth, swiftly and sensuously.

'And she falls in love all the time with the wrong men,' he added softly. 'Something you would never do, I'm sure, *matia mou*.'

No, Kate thought, her heart pounding. But I could come dangerously close…

She removed her hands from his grasp, and picked up her glass again. A fragile defence, but all that was available.

'What—kind of men.'

'While she was at school in Switzerland last year, we had to buy off her art master, and a ski instructor.'

Kate choked back a giggle. 'She sounds quite a girl.'

'You could say that,' Michael agreed drily. 'In the end, my father decided it would be safer to keep her at home on Kefalonia.'

She waited for him to say something more about his father, but instead he took the champagne from the ice bucket and refilled her glass.

'I wasn't going to have any more,' she protested. 'I'm going to be drunk.'

'I don't think so.' He smiled as he replaced the bottle. 'A little less uptight, perhaps,' he added, proffering another strawberry.

She had plenty to be uptight about, Kate thought, taking a distracted bite and watching him transfer the rest to his own mouth.

Somehow, imperceptibly, as they talked, he'd been moving closer to her. Now, his knee was almost brushing hers, and his arm was along the back of the sofa behind her. She could even catch the faint, expensive fragrance of the cologne he used, reminding her, all too potently, of the brief giddy moments she'd spent in his arms.

She felt his hand on her shoulder, gently stroking its curve, and jumped, splashing champagne on to her skirt.

Michael clicked his tongue reprovingly, and leaned forward, brushing the drops from the fabric, his fingers lingering on her stockinged knee.

He said softly, 'I do not think the mark will be permanent.'

But he was so wrong, Kate thought, her pulses leaping frantically. Because she could be scarred for life.

He kissed her cheek, his lips exploring the hollow beneath the high bone, then dropped a fugitive caress at the very corner of her mouth. He traced the line of her jaw with tiny kisses, before allowing his tongue to tease the delicate whorls inside her ear.

As her head sank, helpless, on to his shoulder, his lips brushed her temples, her forehead, her half-closed eyes.

Everywhere he touched her, her skin bloomed, irradiated with a delight—an urgency she had never known before. Her whole body was melting, liquid with desire.

But he didn't kiss her mouth, as she needed him to do so badly, and his hand only caressed her shoulder and arm through the thin wool, and not her eager breasts.

And she was longing to feel his hands—his mouth on her body. To know him naked against her.

How was it possible, she wondered dazedly, for him to touch her so little, yet make her want him so much?

'Michael.' Her voice was husky suddenly, pleading. 'This—isn't fair.'

She felt him smile against her hair. 'Are you speaking of love—or war, *matia mou*?'

'But you said you wouldn't...'

'I came a long way to see you, *agapi mou*. Do you grudge me this small taste of you?' He tugged at her earlobe gently with his teeth. 'After all, I am torturing no one but myself.'

'You know,' she whispered. 'You know that isn't true.'

She turned, pressing her mouth almost frantically to his, begging him wordlessly for the response she craved.

But he moved back a little, framing her face between his hands.

He said, 'I think, Katharina, it would be wise if I took you somewhere for dinner now. We need other people round us.'

'Why?' She stared at him.

'Because if we stay here, you may have too much champagne and I—I may succumb to temptation.' He got to his feet in one swift lithe movement, pulling her up with him.

His voice sank to a whisper, 'So let us behave well, *pedhi mou*—for tonight at least.'

As they rode down in the lift, she said, 'I'm not really dressed for going out to dinner. Can it be somewhere not too smart?'

'Of course. No problem.'

'Oh,' Kate said. 'You've just reminded me of something.'

'What is it.'

She frowned, trying to remember. 'That night on Zycos, you were in my room talking to another man. Something about problems—solving them or causing them. I can't quite recall…'

There was an odd silence, then he shrugged. 'You must have been dreaming again, *pedhi mou*.'

'But it seemed so real,' she protested.

'So did the other dreams you had that night,' he reminded her drily, sending warm colour into her face. He paused, his mouth hardening and his eyes suddenly remote. 'But always reality is waiting.'

She felt as if a cold hand had touched her. She said his name questioningly, and he looked back at her, his face relaxing.

'Come, my beautiful one.' He took her hand. 'Let us enjoy our own dream a little longer.'

He was warning me, Kate thought, tears running down her face in the darkness. Because that's all it ever was—all it ever could be—a dream, and I was a fool to believe in it. To believe in him.

But I did, and now I have to live with the consequences. And the memories. And I don't know if I can bear it...

Lack of sleep left her feeling jaded, and aware of a slight headache the following morning. Although that was probably the least of her troubles, she reminded herself wearily.

And her day proved just as tricky as she'd expected. The French youngsters hadn't the slightest interest in the Tower of London and, clearly, would have preferred playing computer games in some arcade. But, in a way, Kate was glad of the challenge. Because it stopped her from thinking.

But when she'd bidden a final '*au revoir*' to her reluctant charges and their harassed supervisors, she was once again alone, with a decision to make, and nowhere to hide.

She would have to agree, she thought wearily, as she let herself into the flat. Let him see that no sacrifice was too great in her determination to end their marriage.

But first a hot shower, to remove the kinks of the day, she thought, peeling off her clothes and reaching for her gingham robe. And also to give her time to think how to phrase her acceptance of his outrageous terms in a way that would leave her a modicum of dignity.

Not easy, she told herself wryly, as she adjusted the temperature control of the water.

She was just unfastening her robe when her front door buzzer sounded. For a moment she stood still, staring into space, her mouth drying as she realised the probable identity of her visitor.

Michael couldn't wait for her answer, of course. Oh, no, he had to apply the pressure, she thought bitterly.

She could always pretend to be out, she told herself, then remembered that her living room light was on and clearly visible from the street. On the other hand, she didn't have to let him in.

She tightened the sash round her waist, then walked to the intercom panel by the door.

'Yes?' Her tone was curt.

'Darling,' Grant said. 'I need to see you. Please let me in.' It was almost, but not quite, a relief to hear him.

She said, 'It's not really convenient…'

'Katie,' he interrupted firmly. 'This is important. We have to talk.'

Sighing, Kate released the front entrance button, and walked to her own door.

'I've been worried about you,' he said, as he came in. 'You haven't returned any of my calls.'

She sighed again, under her breath. 'Grant, when I came back from Greece you were very kind, and I'll always appreciate it, but we can't live in each other's pockets. But as I've tried to tell you, we both need to move on.'

'Darling, you need time. I understand that. But as for moving on…' He handed her the newspaper he was carrying. 'Have you seen this?'

It was a picture of Michael, leaving the airport, smiling, and a caption.

Millionaire tycoon Michael Theodakis flew in yesterday to finalise the acquisition of the ailing Royal Empress group for his Regina Hotel chain. He is also planning a romantic re-union with his English bride of eight months, Katharine, who has been spending a few weeks in London.

'Oh, God.' Kate's throat tightened uncontrollably, as she threw the paper to the floor. 'I don't believe this.'

'Talk to your lawyer,' Grant advised authoritatively. 'Get an injunction.'

She wrapped her arms round her shaking body. 'It's a little late for that. I've already seen him.'

Grant stared at her. 'But when you came back, you said it was over. That you were never going to see him again.'

'Mick has other ideas.' Kate drew a steadying breath. 'In fact, he's asked me to go back to Kefalonia with him for a family wedding. But it's no romantic reunion,' she added wearily, as Grant's mouth opened in protest. 'It's a *quid pro quo* arrangement. I do him this favour. He gives me a quick divorce.'

'Kate, for God's sake.' Grant's voice rose. 'Don't tell me you're actually considering this preposterous deal.'

'Oh, but she is,' Mick said softly from the doorway. 'If it is any concern of yours.'

He was leaning against the doorframe, apparently at his ease, but his eyes were like obsidian, and there was a small, cold smile playing about his mouth.

Kate swallowed. 'How—how did you get in?'

'Your obliging neighbour again.' His icy gaze scanned the gingham robe, then turned inimically on Grant. 'She did not realise you were already—entertaining.'

'I'm not,' Kate said angrily aware that her face had warmed. But what the hell did she have to feel guilty about? Mick was the one who'd betrayed her. Who'd destroyed their marriage.

She bent and retrieved the newspaper. 'Grant just came to bring me a message. He's—just leaving.'

'Kate,' Grant gasped.

She didn't look at him. 'Just go—please.'

'Very well.' He gave Mick a fulminating look as he stalked past him. 'But I shall be back.'

'No,' Mick said, his eyes flicking him with cool disdain. 'You will not.'

For a moment they faced each other, then Grant, his face working, turned away, and Kate heard him going down the stairs.

Mick walked forward into the room, and kicked the door

shut behind him. He said, 'Your guard dog lacks teeth, *pedhi mou.*'

'Grant is a friend, nothing more.' Kate faced him defiantly.

'You once thought you were in love with him,' he said. 'And now I find you here with him, half-naked.'

'I'm perfectly decent,' she flung at him. 'I was about to have a shower when he arrived.'

Mick took off his jacket and flung it across a chair. 'Did you plan to share it with him, as you used to do with me?' His voice was low and dangerous.

'And what if I did?' Her voice shook, not just with anger but pain. 'You have no right to question me—not with your track record, you—appalling hypocrite.'

'You think not? Maybe it is time I reminded you, *agapi mou*, that you are still my wife.'

He reached her in one stride. His hands grasped her arms, pulling her forward, and his mouth descended crushingly on hers. At first she fought him in sheer outrage, but he was too strong, and too determined, his fingers tangling in her hair, as his lips forced hers apart.

She couldn't breathe—she couldn't think. She could only—endure, as his hand swept her from breast to thigh in one stark act of possession. Reminding her with terrifying emphasis that her body's needs had only been suppressed. Not extinguished.

When at last he let her go, she took a shaky step backwards, stumbling over the hem of her robe in her haste, and pressing a hand to her reddened mouth.

'You bastard,' she choked. 'You bloody barbarian.'

'I am what I always was,' Mick retorted curtly. 'And I have warned you before not to make me angry.'

'You have no right to be angry. Or to accuse me when you—you…'

The words stuck in her throat. She couldn't speak them. Couldn't face him with his betrayal. Not then. Not now. It hurt too much, and always had. Besides, she might cry in front of him—the great agonised sobs which had torn her apart night after night when she'd first fled from Kefalonia. And she couldn't let him see what he had done to her—how close he'd brought her to the edge of despair and heartbreak.

By remaining silent, she could perhaps hang on to some element of her pride.

He shrugged. 'I'm a man, Katharina, not some plaster saint on an altar. I made no secret of it, yet you still married me.' His tone was dry.

'And very soon lived to regret it,' she flashed.

'Even with all that money to sweeten my barbaric ways,' he mocked her. 'You are hard to please, my Kate.'

She said in a low voice, 'I am not—your Kate.'

'The law says otherwise.'

'Until I get my decree.'

'For which you need my goodwill,' he said softly.

'I think the price may be too high.' She steadied herself, and looked back at him. 'I want it understood that my return to Kefalonia does not give you the right to—maul me whenever the whim takes you.'

'Not a touch, *agapi mou*?' His drawl mocked her. 'Not a kiss?'

'Nothing,' she said. 'Otherwise the deal's off—however long it takes me to be rid of you.'

'I'll settle for a pretence of affection, and some common civility, *matia mou*.' There was a harsh note in his voice. 'I'm told when you worked on Zycos, you were a model of diplomacy. Bring some of your professional skills to bear.'

Kate bit her lip. 'When exactly am I expected to begin this—charade?'

'At once.' He pointed to the crumpled newspaper she was still clutching. 'As you see, your tabloids have discovered that we are both in London, but not together. That must be remedied at once. I do not choose to have my private life examined by the gutter press.'

Kate stiffened. 'In what way—remedied?'

'By packing what you need, and coming with me to the hotel tonight. Making the resumption of our marriage public.'

'But we're getting a divorce,' she objected. 'You can hardly keep that a secret.'

'Let us deal with one problem at a time. Tonight, I require you to accompany me to the Royal Empress.'

'The Royal Empress.' The breath caught in her throat. 'No—I won't do it. I agreed to attend Ismene's wedding, but nothing was said about—cohabiting with you here in London.'

He said coldly, 'That is not for you to choose. Nor is it what I intended, or wished,' he added with cutting emphasis. 'However, it is—necessary, and that must be enough.' He paused. 'But I am using the penthouse suite—one that holds no memories for either of us.'

She looked down at the floor, swift colour rising in her face, angry that he should have read her thoughts so accurately. Angry, too, that she'd let him see she was still vulnerable to the past.

'It is larger too,' he went on. 'With luck, *matia mou*, we may never be obliged to meet. And certainly not—cohabit.'

Kate bit her lip. 'Very well,' she agreed, her voice constricted. She hesitated. 'I—I'll get my stuff together. Perhaps you'd send the car for me—in an hour.'

Mick sat down in her armchair, stretching long legs in front of him. He said, 'I can wait.'

'But I've got things to do,' she protested. 'I told you—I was going to have a shower.'

'Then do so.'

'There's no need to stay on guard,' she said. 'You surely don't think I'm going to do a runner?'

His mouth curled slightly. 'It would not be the first time, my dear wife. I am not prepared to take the risk again. Now, go and take your shower.'

Kate gave him a mutinous look, then went into her bedroom, and closed the door. She looked over the small stock of clothing in her wardrobe, most of it cheap casual stuff bearing no resemblance to the collection of expensive designer wear that she'd abandoned on Kefalonia.

But, then, she was no longer the same girl, she reminded herself.

She put underwear, a couple of cotton nightdresses and some simple pants and tops in to her travel bag. After her bath, her housecoat and toiletries would join them.

She collected fresh briefs and bra, and picked a knee-length denim skirt and a plain white shirt from her remaining selection of garments. Practical, she thought, but the opposite end of the spectrum from glamorous.

Carrying them over her arm, she trailed self-consciously from the bedroom to the bathroom.

Mick was reading her discarded newspaper.

'I hope you've forgotten nothing,' he said courteously, without raising his eyes.

'I hope so too.' Damn him, she thought. He never missed a trick.

And she didn't need him to point out, however obliquely, the contrast between the warm joyous intimacy of their early married life where no doors were ever closed, and the embarrassed bitter awkwardness of their present relationship. She was already well aware—and hurting.

'Would you like me to wash your back?' His voice followed her. It held faint amusement, and another intonation that sent a ripple of awareness shivering down her spine.

'No,' she said curtly and slammed the door on him, and the memories the question had evoked. She shot the bolt for good measure, although it was too flimsy to debar anyone who really wanted to come in.

She swallowed, firmly closing her mind against that possibility.

The warm water was comforting but she was not disposed to linger. Besides, commonsense told her that it would not be wise to keep Mick waiting too long, she thought wryly, as she dried herself swiftly and put on her clothes.

Armouring herself, she realised, as she brushed back her hair, and confined it at the nape of her neck with a silver clip. And if Mick didn't like it, he could lump it, because she was going to need every scrap of defence she could conjure up.

Drawing a deep breath, she slid back the bolt and emerged.

She said, 'I'm ready.'

He was shrugging on his jacket, but he paused, looking her over with narrowed eyes in a lengthening silence.

'Are you making some kind of statement, Katharina?' His voice was gentle, but cold.

'I dress to please myself now.' Kate straightened her shoulders. 'I'm sorry if I don't meet your exacting standards.'

Mick sighed. 'Tomorrow, *pedhi mou*, I think you must pay a visit to Bond Street.'

She lifted her chin. 'No. And you can't make me.'

He gave her a thoughtful glance. 'Is this what you wear at your work?'

'Of course not. The company supplies a uniform.'

'But now you are working for me,' he said softly. 'In a different capacity. Which also requires a uniform. So, tomorrow you will go shopping. You understand?'

Looking down at the floor, she gave a reluctant nod.

'And you will also wear this.' He walked across to her, reaching into an inside pocket, and produced her wedding ring.

'Oh, no.' Instinctively, she put both hands behind her back. His name was engraved inside it, she thought wildly, and the words 'For ever.' She couldn't wear it. It was too cruel. Too potent a reminder of all her pitiful hopes and dreams.

She said, 'I—I can't. Please…'

'But you must.' He paused, his gaze absorbing her flushed cheeks and strained eyes, then moving down to the sudden hurry of her breasts under the thin shirt, his dark eyes narrowed, and oddly intent.

He lifted his hand and ran his thumb gently along the swell of her lower lip. He said in a low voice, 'I could always— persuade you, *agapi mou*. Is that what you want?'

A shiver tingled its way through her body. 'No.'

'Then give me your hand.'

Reluctantly, she yielded it. Watched, as he touched the gold circlet to his lips, then placed it on her finger. Just as he had done on their wedding day, she thought, as pain slashed at her. And if he smiled down into her eyes—reached for her to kiss her, she might well be lost.

But he stepped back, and there was the reassurance of space between them.

And, building inside her, anger at his hypocrisy—his betrayal.

She whispered, 'I hate you.'

There was a sudden stillness, then he gave a short laugh.

'Hate as much as you want, Katharina *mou*,' he said harshly. 'But you are still my wife, and will remain so until I choose to let you go. Perhaps you should remember that.'

As if, Kate thought, turning blindly away, as if I could ever forget.

CHAPTER SIX

THE journey to the hotel was a silent one. Kate sat huddled in her corner of the limousine, staring rigidly through the window, feigning an interest in the shop-lined streets, the busy bars and restaurants they were passing.

Anything, she thought shakily, that would reduce her awareness of the man beside her. And the unbridgeable gulf between them.

As the driver pulled up in front of the Royal Empress, she heard Mick swear softly under his breath.

He said quietly, 'Not a word, *matia mou*—do you hear me?'

Then, suddenly, shockingly, she was being jerked towards him. She felt the silver clip snapped from her hair, found herself crushed against him, breast to breast, held helplessly in his arms while his mouth took hers, hard, experienced and terrifyingly thorough.

Then the car door was open, and she was free, emerging dazedly on to the pavement, standing for a moment as cameras flashed, then walking pinned to Mick's side, his hand on her hip, to the hotel entrance.

'Quietly, my red-haired angel.' She heard the thread of laughter in the voice that whispered against her ear. 'Scream at me when we're alone.'

People were greeting her. She saw welcoming, deferential smiles, and heard herself respond, her voice husky and breathless.

The manager rode up in the lift with them, clearly anxious that his arrangements should be approved by his new employer.

It was a beautiful suite. Even anger and outrage couldn't

blind Kate to that. There was the usual big, luxuriously furnished sitting room, flanked on either side by two bedrooms, each with its own bathroom.

There were flowers everywhere, she saw, plus bowls of fruit, dishes of handmade chocolates, and the inevitable champagne on ice. By the window was a table, covered in an immaculate white cloth, and set with silverware and candles for a dinner *à deux*.

All the trappings, Kate thought, her heart missing a beat, of a second honeymoon…

Someone was carrying her single bag into one of the bedrooms with as much care as if it was a matching set of Louis Vuitton, and she followed, hands clenched in the pockets of her navy linen jacket.

One of the walls was almost all mirror and she caught a glimpse of herself, her hair loose and tousled on her shoulders, her mouth pink and swollen from kissing, even a couple of buttons open on her shirt.

She looked like a woman, she thought dazedly, whose man couldn't keep his hands off her.

'We are alone.' Mick was standing in the doorway behind her, his dark face challenging. 'So, you may shout as much as you wish, *pedhi mou.*

She took a deep, breath. 'What the *hell* was all that about?' Her voice shook.

He shrugged. 'I saw the cameras waiting for us. They wanted proof that our marriage was solid. It seemed wise to give it to them. I have my reasons,' he added coolly.

'Reasons?' she echoed incredulously. 'What possible reason could there be?' She tried to thrust her buttons back into their holes with trembling fingers. 'You made it look as if we'd been having sex in the back of the car.'

'No,' he said. 'The prelude to sex perhaps.'

'There's such a big difference.' Her voice radiated scorn.

He had the nerve to grin at her. 'Why, yes, *matia mou.* If

you remember, I prefer comfort—and privacy. I find the presence of a third person—inhibiting.'

But there was always someone else there, she thought in sudden agony, although I didn't realise it then. Every time we touched—made love, Victorine was there—Victorine...

She lifted her chin. 'I hope you haven't arranged any more—photo opportunities. Because I won't guarantee to co-operate.'

'Is that what you were doing in the car—co-operating?' Mick asked sardonically. 'I would never have guessed.'

She glared at him. 'I never pretended I could act.'

He said courteously, 'You do yourself less than justice, *pedhi mou*.' He glanced at his watch. 'At what time do you wish them to serve dinner?'

'I'm not hungry.'

Mick sighed. 'Would your appetite improve if I said that you were dining alone?' he asked wearily.

'Oh.' She was taken aback. 'You're going out?'

He shrugged. 'Why not?'

She bit her lip. 'I'll order something later—a club sandwich maybe.'

'The chef will be disappointed—but the choice is yours.'

She unfastened her travel bag. 'I think we both know that isn't true,' she said tautly. 'Or I wouldn't be here.'

She extracted her uniform dress and jacket, and moved towards the fitted wardrobes.

'What are those?' His tone sharpened.

'My work clothes.' Kate paused, hanger in hand.

'Why have you brought them?'

'Because I have a job to go to in the morning,' she said. 'But perhaps it's a trick question.'

'You had a job,' Mick corrected, the dark brows drawing together haughtily. 'If you write out your resignation, I will see it is delivered.'

Kate gasped. 'I can't do that. And I won't,' she added

stormily. 'When this—farce is over, I'm going to need a career.'

'But the farce has still a long time to run,' Mick said with steely softness. 'And in the meantime, Katharina *mou*, my wife does not work.'

'And how long does this embargo last?' Her voice shook. 'Until after the divorce?'

'Forever,' he said curtly. 'Married or divorced, I shall continue to support you financially. As I am sure your lawyer has made clear,' he added with a certain grimness.

'Yes,' Kate said raggedly. 'And I want nothing from you—except my freedom. You don't have to buy me off, *kyrie*, or pay for my silence, either.' She took a deep breath. 'Our marriage—should never have happened, but I won't dish the dirt on it—sell the unhappy details to the newspapers. And I'll sign any confidentiality clause that your legal team can dream up.'

He was very still. He said slowly, '"Unhappy details" *matia mou*? Is that—truly—all you remember?'

For a moment, her mind was a kaleidoscope throwing up image after image. Mick walking hand in hand with her through the snow in Central Park—teaching her to skate, both of them helpless with laughter—fetching paracetamol and rubbing her back when she had curse pains.

And holding her as she slept each night.

That above all, she thought with agony. The closeness of it. The feeling of total safety. Of what I thought was love...

She looked stonily back at him. She said, 'What else was there?'

He said with immense weariness, 'Then there is nothing more to be said.'

As he turned away, she said swiftly, 'Before you go—may I have my hairclip, please.'

'I'm sorry.' Face expressionless, he gave a brief shrug. 'I must have dropped it in the car—or in the street, perhaps. Is it important?'

'No,' she said slowly. 'It doesn't really matter.'

And watched him walk out, closing the door behind him.

'Nothing matters,' she whispered, when she was alone. 'Nor ever will again.' And felt tears, hot and thick in her throat.

She walked over to the wide bed, and sat down on its edge, burying her face in her hands.

Who was the first person, she wondered, to state that love was blind?

Because she'd realised that she'd fallen in love with Michael Theodakis before they'd even sat down to their first dinner together, loved him, and longed for him during the weeks that followed.

Every night that he'd been in London, and he seemed to be there a great deal, his car was waiting for her when she left work.

He took her to wonderful restaurants, to cinemas, theatres and to concerts. He took her for drives in the country, and walks in the park.

He did not, however, take her to bed.

His lovemaking was gentle, almost decorous. There were kisses and caresses, but the cool, clever hands that explored her body aroused, but never satisfied. He always drew back before the brink was reached, courteously, even ruefully, but with finality.

Leaving her stranded in some limbo of need and frustration, her senses screaming for fulfilment.

She was on wires, her eyes as big as a cat's, her face all cheekbones.

Only Sandy knew her well enough to be concerned—and to probe.

'Do you know what you're doing?' she asked abruptly one day, when Kate was trying on the little black dress she was planning to borrow from her.

'What do you mean?' Kate's tone was defensive.

Sandy sighed. 'You're swimming with a shark, love.' She sat down on the edge of the bed.

'I thought you liked Mick.' Kate stared at her distressed.

'I do like him. He's seriously good-looking, too charming for his own good, and filthy rich. What's not to like?'

Kate forced a smile. 'And I'm none of those things, so why is he bothering with me? Is that it?'

Sandy spread her hands. 'Kate, I'm in love with Gavin, and going to be married, but when Mick Theodakis does that smiling-with-his-eyes thing, I become a melted blob on the carpet. I can understand why you're seeing him.'

She paused. 'But honey, he's seen a lot of women. He's been on some ''eligible bachelors of the world'' list since he was in his teens.''

She shook her head. 'You know who he used to date? That supermodel who became an actress—Victorine. One of the girls on the social page told me that they were a real item. He was supposed to be crazy about her—talking marriage—the whole bit. Now, he's back on the market, and she's gone to ground somewhere, and no one's heard of her for over a year.'

She got to her feet. 'The thing is, he may not believe in long-term commitment, Katie, and I don't want you to break your heart.'

I think, Kate told herself wryly, that it may be a little late for that.

The following day Mick flew to New York and was there for about a week. He called several times, but, just the same, she missed him almost desperately.

On the day of his return, she flew out of the office, only to find a complete stranger waiting for her.

'Kyria Dennison?' He was a stocky man, with dark shrewd eyes, and a heavy black moustache, and she recognised him as one of the men sitting with Mick in the nightclub the night they met. 'I am Iorgos Vasso. Kyrios Michalis sends his apologies, and asks me to escort you to the hotel.'

'Is he ill?' Kate questioned anxiously.

The dark eyes twinkled. 'He is jet lagged, *kyria*. Sometimes it affects him more badly than others.'

'Oh,' Kate said slowly. 'Well—maybe I should leave him to rest.'

'Jet lag is bad,' Iorgos Vasso said solemnly. 'But disappointment would be far worse. Let me take you to him.'

'Your voice sounds familiar,' Kate said, frowning a little, as the car inched its way through the traffic. She paused. 'Didn't I hear you talking with Mr Theodakis in my room that night on Zycos—about solving a problem?'

He shrugged, his smile polite and regretful. 'Perhaps, *kyria*. I really don't remember.'

She sighed. 'It doesn't matter.'

Mick was waiting for her impatiently in the suite. He looked rough, but his smile made her heart sing. He pulled her into his arms and held her for a long time.

'This week has been hell,' he told her quietly. 'Next time, I take you with me.'

They dined quietly in the sitting room, but he only toyed with his food.

'I'm, exhausted, *pedhi mou*,' he told her frankly, when the meal had been cleared away. 'Would you mind if I took a nap for half an hour? I will try to be better company afterwards.'

'You're sure you don't want me to go—give you some peace?'

'No.' He kissed her. 'Wait for me—please.'

He went into the bedroom, and shut the door. When he still hadn't reappeared nearly two hours later, Kate went across and tapped on the door.

There was no reply, so, she turned the handle gently and peeped in. One shaded lamp burned in the room and Mick was lying on top of the bed, sound asleep, his shoes and jacket discarded.

Kate walked to the bed, and stood looking down at him.

She had never seen him sleeping before and, with his long eyelashes curling on his cheek, he looked much younger. Almost vulnerable.

He's not going to wake up, she thought. I could simply kiss him goodnight, and leave.

Instead, she found herself kicking off her own shoes, and lying down beside him on the satin coverlet.

She wasn't planning on sleeping herself. She just wanted to lie quietly for a while, and watch him, and listen to his soft, regular breathing.

But the room was warm, and the bed soft and comfortable, its crisp linen faintly scented with lavender and, in spite of herself, Kate found her eyelids drooping.

She thought, 'I ought to go home…' And then she stopped thinking altogether.

She awoke suddenly with a start, and looked around, momentarily disorientated, wondering where she was. Then she saw Mick, propped on one elbow, studying her, his face grave, his dark eyes hooded.

She said, a little breathlessly, 'I must have—fallen asleep. What time is it?'

'The middle of the night.' His brows lifted. 'You should be more careful, *matia mou*. Has no one told you it is dangerous to tempt a hungry man with crumbs?'

She said, with a catch in her voice, 'Perhaps I'm starving too.'

He smiled into her eyes, as he smoothed the dishevelled hair back from her face, and ran his finger gently across her parted lips.

He said softly, 'I hope it is true, yet you may still change your mind—if you wish.' He paused. 'But if you allow me to touch you, it will be too late.'

'I'm here because I want to be,' she whispered. 'Because I can't help myself.'

She sat up, and pulled off her black sweater, tossing it to the floor.

Mick drew a sharp breath, then took her into his arms, kissing her slowly and very deeply.

His hands were unhurried, too, as they removed the rest of her clothes, his lips paying sensuous homage to every curve and hollow that he uncovered.

When she was naked, he looked at her for a long moment. He said huskily. 'How beautiful you are.'

Shy colour burned in her face, but she met his gaze. 'You've seen me before.'

'But then you were angry.' His hand cupped her breast, his fingers teasing her nipple, making it stand proudly erect. 'You were not like this. So sweet—so willing.'

But when she tried to unbutton his shirt, to undress him in turn, he stopped her, his hands closing over hers.

'Not yet.' He kissed her again, his mouth warm and beguiling, then bent his head to her breast, his tongue flickering against the taut rosy peak. 'First, *agapi mou*,' he murmured, 'I need to pleasure you.'

It was a long, languorous journey into arousal. Kate found herself drifting almost mindlessly, aware only of the message of her senses in response to the whisper of his hands and mouth on her body. Conscious of the slow, irresistible heat building within her that demanded to be assuaged. Somehow.

When his hand parted her thighs, she heard herself make a small sound in her throat, pleading, almost animal.

'Yes.' His low voice seemed to reach her from some vast distance. 'Soon—my dove, my angel, I promise.'

His fingers explored her gently, making her gasp and writhe against his touch. Almost immediately it changed, his fingers still stroking her delicately, but creating a new, insistent rhythm as they did so. Gliding on her. Circling. Focusing on one small, exquisite point of pleasure.

Her body moved restlessly, searching, seeking, as her awakened senses whispered of a goal to be attained.

As his fingers strummed the tiny moist pinnacle of heated

flesh, his mouth enclosed her breast, caressing the sensitised peak with his tongue.

Delight lanced through her as she arched towards him in wordless demand.

It was difficult to breathe. Impossible to think. She could only—feel.

Then, deep inside her, she experienced the first sweet burning tremors that signalled her release. Felt them ripple outwards. Intensify. Heard herself sob aloud as the last vestiges of control fell away, and her entire being was consumed—ravished by pulsations so strong she thought she would be torn apart.

The storm of feeling lifted her, held her in a scalding limbo, then let her drift in a dizzying spiral back to earth.

She lay, dazed, trying to regulate her ragged breathing.

She was vaguely aware that Mick had moved slightly, shifting away from her, and she tried to murmur a protest from her dry throat.

He said softly, 'Rest a little, *pedhi mou.*' And she felt him draw the sheet over her damp body.

She floated, rocked by some deep and tideless sea, her body still tingling from the force of its enrapturement.

She realised that Mick had returned to lie beside her. She reached out a drowsy hand and encountered bare skin.

Her eyes opened. 'Oh.'

'Oh?' There was a smile in his voice, but his face was serious and very intent. He took the welcoming hand and guided it down his body. 'Touch me,' he whispered. 'Hold me.'

At first her compliance was tentative, but she gradually became more confident, encouraged by his small groans of pleasure as she caressed him.

He kissed her hotly, his tongue gliding against hers. His fingers stroked her breasts, moulding them, coaxing them to renewed delight.

His hands strayed the length of her body, delineating the

long supple back, the slender curves of her hips, and thighs. Where they lingered.

Kate was trembling suddenly, aware that the same delicious excitement was overtaking her again. Beginning, incredibly, to build inside her.

She was lying facing him, and Mick's hands slid under her flanks, raising her slightly towards him. He kissed her mouth gently.

He said, 'Take me—please, my dove. My beautiful girl.'

She brought him into her slowly, the breath catching in her throat as she realised how simple it really was—how right. And just how much she had wanted to feel all that silken strength and potency inside her. To possess, and be possessed.

'Do I hurt you?' His whisper was urgent.

'No.' Her answer was a sigh. 'Ah, no.'

His movements were gentle at first, and smoothly, rhythmically controlled. And all the time he was watching her, she realised. Looking into her eyes. Observing the play of colour in her face. Listening for any change in her breathing.

And she smiled at him, her eyes luminous.

He hesitated, then moved away from her.

'What's the matter?' She stared at him in shocked bewilderment. 'Did—did I do something wrong?'

'No, *matia mou*.' He stroked her cheek reassuringly. 'I need to protect you, that is all.'

When he turned back, he lifted himself over her, entering her in one strong, fluid movement. She wound her arms round his neck, and, instinctively, lifted her legs to clasp him closer.

The rhythm he was imposing was more powerful now, and she joined it, moving with him in breathless unison.

She could feel the first, elusive blossoming of pleasure, and clung to him, striving for it. Demanding it.

The next moment, her whole being was convulsed in a fierce and scalding rapture. She cried out in ecstatic surprise, and heard Michael answer her as his own body shuddered into climax.

When she could speak, she said, 'Is it always like that?'

'Always with you, *agapi mou*.' He smoothed the hair back from her damp forehead, then wrapped her in his arms. She curled against him, sated and languid, and felt his cheek rest against her hair.

There was a silence, then he spoke, his voice barely a whisper. 'Marry me.'

She turned her head, and stared at him, her eyes wide, and her lips parted. 'You don't mean that.'

'I am perfectly serious,' he told her. 'I am asking you to be my wife, Katharina *mou*.'

'But you can't,' she said, almost wildly. 'It's ridiculous. I—I don't belong to your world.'

'We have just made our own world, *agapi mou*. I want no other.'

'But your family,' she protested. 'They'll expect you to marry some heiress.'

'My father lives his life.' His voice was oddly harsh. 'And I live mine. I wish to spend it with you.' He paused. 'But perhaps you don't want me?'

She said, 'I think I've wanted you since that first night on Zycos. And, yes, I'll marry you, Kyrios Michalis.'

He framed her face in his hands, and kissed her deeply, almost reverently.

He said, 'We should celebrate. I'll call room service and tell them to bring champagne.'

She smiled up at him. 'And strawberries?'

'You remember that, hmm?' He threw the covering sheet aside and got out of bed, stretching unselfconsciously.

Watching him, Kate felt her mouth go dry, and her throat tighten.

She said, 'Of course. But I couldn't understand why you didn't just—seduce me, there and then.'

Mick picked up a red silk robe from a chair and slipped it

on. He said softly, 'But I have been seducing you, *agapi mou*, every moment we have spent together since I first saw you. Don't you know that.'

He blew her a teasing kiss and walked away into the sitting room.

Two weeks later they were married in a quiet registry office ceremony with Sandy and Iorgos Vasso as witnesses.

They spent a brief honeymoon on Bali, then flew back to New York where Mick was supervising the completion of the latest Regina hotel.

'Does he usually take so personal an interest?' Kate asked Iorgos, who had soon become a friend.

'This is particularly important to him,' Iorgos admitted. 'There are elements on the board who have always been opposed to any expansion outside the Mediterranean, or indeed to any kind of change,' he added drily. 'It is no longer a foregone conclusion that he will succeed his father as chairman of the board when Ari eventually retires. So, Michalis needs a proven success to overcome the doubters.'

'I see.' Kate paused. 'Is his father one of the doubters?'

'That is something you should ask your husband, *kyria*.'

'I have.' Kate sighed. 'I asked him, too, when we'd be going to Greece so that I could meet his family, and he just changed the subject.'

She shook her head. 'He never talks about family things. Why, I didn't even know his mother had been a native New Yorker until I discovered we were living in her old home.'

'Does it make a difference?'

'No, but I'd like to have been told. And I wish he'd discuss this estrangement with his father, because I know it exists.'

He said gently, 'You are a very new wife, *kyria*. Maybe Mick feels you have enough adjustments to make for now. Enjoy the happiness you find in each other, and leave any problems for another day.'

And with that, she had to be content.

The apartment, in an exclusive district, was a sumptuous,

gracious place, all high ceilings, and rich wood panelling, and Kate had loved it on sight.

Mick gave her *carte blanche* to change anything she wanted but, in the end, she altered very little, replacing some carpets and curtains, and introducing a lighter colour scheme for their bedroom.

'I'm saving my energies for the nursery,' she told him happily.

'Well, there is no hurry for that.' He kissed her. 'Unless I am not enough for you,' he added softly.

The hotel was completed by Easter, and Kate, smiling confidently to conceal her inner trepidation, cut the ribbon which declared the New York Regina open for business.

It was barely a week later when she returned from a shopping trip to find a full-scale row in progress, with Mick pacing the drawing room, his face set and thunderous, while Iorgos tried unavailingly to calm him.

'What's happened?' Kate put down her packages, alarmed.

'We have been sent for,' Mick flung at her.

'Mr Theodakis has requested Michael to bring you to Kefalonia,' Iorgos explained more temperately.

'Is that such a bad thing?' Kate felt her way cautiously, keeping a wary eye on her husband's angry face. 'After all, we were bound to pay a visit eventually—weren't we?'

Mick snorted in exasperation, and stalked over to the window.

'It would not be wise to refuse,' Iorgos said quietly. 'Consider that, Michalis.'

'I have,' Mick said curtly, without looking round. 'And I know it must be done.'

For the first time in their marriage, he did not come to bed that night. Kate, disturbed, found him in the drawing room, slumped on a sofa with a decanter of whisky for company.

She had never seen him like this, she thought, as she knelt beside him. 'Darling, what's wrong? Talk to me, please.'

He looked at her, his eyes weary, and frighteningly distant.

'The reality I once spoke of, *pedhi mou*. It has found us. Now leave me. I need to be on my own—to think.'

And she had turned and gone back to their room, alone and suddenly scared.

CHAPTER SEVEN

KATE'S first glimpse of Kefalonia had been from the company private jet.

In spite of the uneasiness of the previous week, she couldn't repress a tingle of anticipation as she looked down on the rocky landscape beneath her.

Maybe, she thought, things will change now we're here. Go back to the way they were.

Because, ever since his father's summons, there'd been a strange new tension between Mick and herself which she seemed powerless to dispel, however much she tried.

Now, when he made love to her, he seemed remote, almost clinical in the ways in which he gave her pleasure. The warmth, the teasing, the laughter that had made their intimacy so precious was suddenly missing.

For the first time it was almost a relief that Mick still insisted on using protection during lovemaking, because she didn't want their baby to be conceived in an atmosphere like this.

She'd been surprised too when Mick told her to pack summer clothes and swimwear.

'But it's only April.' She stared at him. 'How long will we be staying on Kefalonia?'

'I am Greek, Katharina.' His voice was cold. 'The Villa Dionysius is my home.'

She said quietly, 'I'm sorry. I thought your home was with me. But I'll pack for an indefinite stay if that's what you want.'

His smile was brief and wintry. 'Thank you.'

She'd read as much as she could about the island and its history, prior to setting out, and knew that, because of the devastation caused by the earthquake which had struck in 1953, most of its buildings were comparatively modern.

But the Theodakis family home, the Villa Dionysius, had somehow survived. And soon she would be there.

Again she was aware of an odd prickle of nervousness, but told herself she was being ridiculous. Mick and his father might have been at odds in the past, but now a reconciliation was clearly indicated, and maybe her marriage was going to be the means of bringing that about. Which had to be a good thing—didn't it?

When they reached the villa, her spirits rose. It was a large rambling single-storied house, white-walled, with a faded terracotta roof. Flowering vines and climbing shrubs hung in festoons over the door and windows, and the garden was already bright with colour.

The whole place, she thought, had an air of timelessness about it, as if it had grown out of the headland on which it stood amid its encircling pine trees.

As she got out of the car, Kate could smell the resin, and hear the rasp of cicadas in the sunlit, windy air. Through the trees, she could see the turquoise sea far below, dancing with foam-capped waves.

She thought, 'I was crazy to worry. This is paradise.'

As she turned to look at the villa, the big door swung open, and a woman stood, dramatically framed in the doorway. She was tall and slim, with black hair that hung like a shining curtain down her back. Her skin was magnolia pale, and her almond-shaped eyes were tilted slightly at the corners. Her smiling mouth was painted a deep, sexy crimson, and in her figure-hugging white dress, she looked like some exotic, tropical flower.

Kate's throat tightened in instant, shocked recognition. She was aware of Mick standing rigidly beside her, his face like stone.

For a moment the newcomer stayed where she was, as if allowing them to fully appreciate the picture she made.

'Welcome home, *cher*.' Her voice was low-pitched and throaty. 'You shouldn't have stayed away so long.'

She walked to where Mick was standing, twining her arms round his neck, and kissing him on the lips.

'Mmm,' she murmured as she stood back. 'You taste so good—but then you always did.'

She looked at Kate. 'And this is your new wife.' Her eyes flickered over the suit in dark-green silk with a matching camisole that Kate had worn for the journey, and her smile widened. 'Won't you introduce me?'

'I already know who you are,' Kate said steadily. 'You're—Victorine.'

Not gone to ground, as Sandy had said, she thought, her heart pounding sickly, but here on Kefalonia, living in Mick's home...

But how? Why?

'I'm flattered.' Victorine laughed. 'On the other hand, you, *chère*, came as a complete surprise to—all of us.' She looked at Mick, pouting in reproof. 'Your father wasn't very pleased with you.'

Mick said harshly, 'When was he ever?' He paused. 'Where is he?'

Victorine shrugged. 'Waiting in the *saloni*. It's quite a family gathering. But you must promise me not to quarrel with him again. Though I'm sure you'll be on your best behaviour—now that you are married.'

Kate said, coolly and clearly, 'It was a long flight. I think I'd like to take a shower and change before any more introductions.'

'But of course.' Victorine turned to Mick. 'You have your usual suite in the West wing, *cher*.' She paused. 'Is there any particular room you would like Katherine to have?'

Mick said coldly, 'My wife sleeps with me.'

The slanting brows lifted. 'How sweet—and domestic.' She smiled at Katherine. 'You have managed to tame him, *chère*. I congratulate you.' She lowered her voice confidentially. 'Michael used to hate to share his bed for the whole night with anyone.'

Kate smiled back at her. 'Well,' she said lightly. 'That proves I'm not just—anyone.'

She walked sedately beside Mick through the wide passages, but under her calm exterior she was seething with a mixture of emotions. Anger was paramount, with bewilderment a close second.

At the end of one corridor were wide double doors, heavily carved. Mick opened them silently, and ushered her through. Kate found herself in an airy spacious sitting room, furnished in dramatic earth colours, with low sofas clustering round a table in heavy glass cut in the shape of a hexagon.

Beyond it was the bedroom, its vast bed draped in a coverlet the colour of green olives, which matched the long curtains at the windows.

Mick strode across the room, and opened another door. He said, 'The bathroom is here. You will find everything you need.'

'Including honesty?' Her voice shook. 'And some straight talking?'

Mick took off his jacket and tossed it across a chair.

He said shortly, 'Katharina—we are both jetlagged and out of temper, and I am shortly to have a difficult interview with my father. Oblige me by postponing this discussion.'

She said, 'No, I think I deserve an explanation now.' She began to wriggle out of her suit.

His mouth tightened. 'What do you wish to know?'

She stared at him. 'You and Victorine—you were lovers. You—you don't deny that.'

'No,' he said coldly. 'I do not. And isn't it a little late to start making my past an issue?'

'Yet now I find her—here—in your home.' She spread her hands. 'Why?'

'She is my father's mistress.' His tone was harsh. 'Does that satisfy your curiosity?'

Kate shook her head. 'You mean you passed her on—when you had finished with her?'

'No,' he said. 'I do not mean that. Victorine makes her own choices. And so does my father.'

'Did you—love her?'

His brows lifted mockingly. 'You have seen her, *agapi mou*,' he drawled. 'It must be clear what I felt for her.'

'And—now?'

'Now, I am with you, *pedhi mou*.'

She stared at him. Her voice was almost a whisper. 'Why did you marry me?'

He said, 'For a whole number of reasons.' He looked her over, standing in front of him, wearing only a few scraps of silk and lace, and his mouth twisted. 'And this is only one of them.'

Two strides brought him to her. Before she could resist, he picked her up in his arms and carried her to the bed.

She was beating at his chest with her fists. 'Put me down,' she ordered breathlessly. 'Do you hear.'

'Willingly.' Mick tossed her on to the mattress, following her down with total purpose, deftly unfastening his clothing.

'No.' Kate struggled, trying ineffectively to push him away. 'Don't you dare. I won't...'

'No, my Kate?' The dark eyes challenged her, laughter dancing outrageously in their depths. 'And how are you going to stop me?'

He bent to her, pushing the lacy cup away from her breast with his lips, and allowing his tongue to tease her uncovered nipple, while his hand slid under the silken rim of her briefs.

She said his name on a little sob, and her arms went round her neck, her body opening in heated, moist surrender as he entered her.

When the storm was over, Kate lay beneath him, drained and boneless.

'What happened?' Her voice was a shadow.

'My new cure for jet lag, *agapi mou*.' He kissed the tip of
her nose. 'I may patent it.'

'You'll make another fortune,' she said weakly. 'I don't
think I'll ever move again.'

'Unfortunately, you must. We have a shower to take, and
my father to meet.' He sat up, raking the sweat-dampened
hair back from his forehead. 'He will not appreciate waiting
much longer,' he added with a touch of grimness.

'Yes,' she said. 'Of course.' She watched him disappear
into the bathroom and gave a happy sigh, stretching languidly.

Then paused. Because, in reality, she thought frowning,
she was no wiser about Victorine—or Mick's relationship
with her, past or present.

Her concerns had been smothered by the most passionate
lovemaking she'd experienced for days, but they hadn't been
answered.

And I need answers, she thought, and shivered.

Aristotle Theodakis was standing by the window of the *saloni* as they came in, a dark figure against the sunlit vista of
the sea outside. He turned to regard them frowningly, his
whole stance radiating power and a certain aggression.

He was not as tall as his son, Kate saw, but more ruggedly
built. His thick hair was silver, and his eyes were brilliant
and piercing beneath their heavy brows.

He was undoubtedly a handsome, charismatic man, Kate
thought, as she walked across the room towards him, her
hand clasped firmly in Mick's. But she was still amazed that
Victorine could have abandoned the son for the father.

She glanced around her, trying to assimilate something of
her surroundings. The *saloni* was a vast room, but furnished
with comfort rather than overt luxury. The colours were cool,
and clear, and the walls and surfaces uncluttered. One of the
few embellishments was a large portrait of a dark-haired
woman with a serene face positioned above the huge, empty

fireplace, which Kate assumed was the late Regina Theodakis.

She was aware of other people in the room too—a tall fair-haired woman standing quietly beside the fireplace, and, at her side, a much younger girl, with dark hair and eyes, her vibrantly pretty face spoiled by a sullen expression.

Mick halted a couple of yards from his father and inclined his head, coolly and unsmilingly. 'Papa.'

Aristotle Theodakis did not even glance at Kate. He said in his own language, 'I have spent months trying to prevent my daughter from making a fool of herself over some penniless nobody. Now, my son does the same thing. I had other plans for you, Michalis.'

Before Mick could reply, Kate said in her clear, careful Greek, 'Perhaps your children are old enough to decide their own fates, *kyrie*.'

His head turned abruptly towards her, and she waited to be blasted out of existence. Instead, he said slowly, '*Po, po po*. So, you speak our tongue?'

'Not very well. But Michael has been teaching me.'

'Hmm.' He looked her over, slowly, as if something puzzled him, taking in the simple cream dress she'd changed into. 'Perhaps he is not as stupid as I thought.'

He stepped forward, opening his arms imperatively and, after a brief hesitation, Mick returned his embrace.

'Sit down.' He waved Kate towards one of the wide, deeply cushioned sofas which flanked a low table. 'Ismene will pour you some iced tea. And for the sake of your wife and Linda, we will speak English, Michalis.'

He indicated the fair woman. 'Katharina—this is my late wife's cousin, Linda Howell. She used to be my daughter's companion.'

'And she still could be,' Ismene said petulantly, pouring the tea into tall glasses. 'Why can't I go and live in her house at Sami?'

'Because she would be too soft with you,' her father

growled. 'You would be running off to meet Petros Alessou all the time, and she would do nothing to stop you.'

'It's hard to object to Ismene meeting with a young man she's known since childhood.' Linda's voice was quiet, with a slight American drawl. She gave Kate a rueful look as she came to sit beside her. 'I'm afraid you've walked into an ongoing problem.'

'There is no problem,' Ari Theodakis scowled. 'Ismene does not see the Alessou boy, and that is final.' He snorted. 'A newly qualified doctor, with only his ideals in the bank. A fine match for my daughter. And the problems it has caused with his father.' He threw up his hands. 'I haven't had a decent game of backgammon in weeks.'

He looked at Kate. 'Do you play?'

'No,' lied Kate who had seen the speed and ferocity that the Greeks brought to the game, and didn't fancy her chances.

'Then Michalis can teach you that too—in the evenings while you are waiting for my grandson to be born.'

There was a sudden devastating silence. Kate gasped. 'Mr Theodakis—there isn't—I'm not…' She paused, aware her cheeks were burning, and turned to Mick whose expression was like stone.

'Of course not,' Linda said soothingly. 'Ari—you're impossible,' she added sternly. 'Why, the children are still on honeymoon.'

His shrug was unrepentant. 'Then why the hasty marriage?'

'Because there was no reason to wait.' Mick's tone was silky, but there was danger in it too. 'And I thought, Papa, that you wished me to be married—settled in life. You—and your supporters on the Theodakis board.'

'I did. I do.' Ari Theodakis frowned. 'But a man needs children to give him real stability.'

'Yes,' Mick said quietly. 'But in our own good time—not yours.'

'Well, it's just not fair,' Ismene burst out. 'I'm not allowed to see Petros, yet Michalis has married someone without money, and Papa did not interfere.'

Mick's face relaxed slightly. 'Only because I did not give him the opportunity, little sister.'

'So you can marry a penniless nobody, and I am expected to take Spiros Georgiou just because his family is rich. A man who wears glasses and has damp hands, besides being shorter than I am.'

There was real unhappiness mingled with the outrage in Ismene's voice and Kate bit back her involuntary smile.

'And you will mind your tongue, my girl,' her father cautioned sternly. 'Or go to your room.'

Ismene set down the jug with a crash. 'It will be a pleasure,' she retorted, and flounced from the room.

Kate heard Linda Howell sigh softly.

She said, 'Katherine, shall we take our tea out on the terrace and leave the men to talk?'

Kate forced a smile. 'That would be good.'

The terrace was wide and bordered by an elaborate balustrade. Kate leaned on the sun-warmed stone and took a deep breath, as she looked down through the clustering pines to the ripple of the sea. 'It's beautiful.'

Linda smiled. 'It's also a minefield,' she said wryly. 'As you must have noticed.'

'Yes.' Kate bit her lip. 'Has there—always been friction between Mick and his father.'

'Not when Regina was alive, although I know she could foresee problems when Mick became fully adult and challenged Ari's authority.

'Is that her portrait over the fireplace?'

'Yes.' Linda's mouth tightened. 'I'm surprised it's still there. Each time I visit, which isn't often these days, I expect to find it's been consigned to some cellar.'

'You and Regina were close?'

'We were raised together. My father was a career diplomat,

and always on the move, so I stayed in New York with my aunt and uncle. Regina and I were more like sisters than cousins. When she married Ari, the villa became a second home for me. After she died so suddenly, it seemed natural to stay on and care for Ismene.' Her blue eyes were sad. 'And apart from that Ari and I could help each other grieve.'

'How did she die?'

'She had this heart weakness. It was incredible because she was the strongest person I knew—she was a marvellous rider, and she sailed and played tennis like a champion. But she had a really hard time when Michael was born, and the doctors warned her against any more pregnancies. But she and Ari had always wanted a daughter, so she decided to take the risk.' She shook her head. 'She was never really well afterwards and one day—she just went.'

She pursed her lips ruefully. 'I wish, for her sake, I'd done a better job with Ismene, but each time I tried to impose rules, Ari would undermine them. He wanted Ismene to be a free spirit like her mother. What he didn't grasp was that Regina's freedom came from self-discipline. Now he's trying to close the dam, and it could be too late.'

'Because of this Petros?' Kate drank some of her tea. 'You think they should be allowed to marry?'

'He's a great guy, and she's known him for ever. I always guessed that one day she'd stop looking on him as just another big brother, and she could have made so many worse choices.' She sighed. 'But she approached it the wrong way. She should have let Ari think it was all his idea. Just before you arrived, she demanded that Petros come to tonight's family dinner as her future husband.' Linda pulled a wry face. 'I tried to talk her out of it. The Theodakis men do not respond well to ultimatums.'

'I'd noticed.' Kate set her glass down on the balustrade. 'Mick's been in an odd mood ever since his father sent for us.' She paused. 'Of course there could be another reason for that,' she added carefully.

'Ah,' Linda said. 'So you've met Ari's other house guest?'

'Yes.' Kate stared hard at the view.

Linda sighed. 'If you want me to give an explanation, I can't. She was with Mick, now she's with Ari. End of story.'

Kate caught a sudden glimpse of pain on the calm face, and realised she'd stumbled on a different story altogether.

'But whatever happened,' Linda went on after a pause. 'Mick married you, and not the dynastic heiress his father would have chosen.' She gave Kate a swift smile. 'Maybe we'd better check on them—see there's no blood on the floor.'

'Is there really that much friction?' Kate asked, troubled.

'It's natural.' Linda shrugged. 'Mick's the heir apparent, and he has a lot of support in the company, but Ari's still king, and he's not ready to abdicate—not by a mile. They'll work it out.' She paused. 'And if things get too heavy, you can always retreat to the beach house.'

She pointed downwards through the trees to a splash of terracotta. 'Ari had it built for when there was an extra influx of guests, but Regina really made it her own place. He was away a lot, and she found the villa big and lonely without him. It has its own pool, and this wonderful platform overlooking the sea where she used to sit and paint.'

She glanced at her watch, and uttered a faint exclamation. 'Hey, I must be off.'

'Aren't you staying for dinner?' Dismayed, Kate took the hand she was offered.

'No, I was asked to meet you, which I've done, and now I'm going home.' She smiled at Kate. 'I hope you'll come and visit at Sami. Get Ismene to bring you over. You didn't see her best side today, but she has a lot going for her. And she could do with a friend.'

'Perhaps,' Kate thought as she watched her go. 'Ismene isn't the only one.'

She turned back to look down at the beach house. It sounded as if it could become a sanctuary. Tomorrow, she decided, she would find her way down there. Ask Ismene to show her the way perhaps.

She heard the sound of voices, and Mick and his father emerged from the *saloni* and came to join her.

'Has Linda gone?' Mick put his arm round her, resting his hand casually on her hip.

'Yes, you've just missed her.'

'I asked her to stay for dinner.' There was a touch of defensiveness in Ari's tone. 'But she said she had plans.'

'Well, perhaps she did.' Mick shrugged. 'I hope so. She's a very beautiful woman.'

There was a silence, then Ari turned to Kate. 'Well, *pedhi mou*. Do you think you will be happy here?'

'I'm happy to be wherever Michael is,' she returned quietly.

'Good—good.' He smiled. 'I am glad my son is proving an attentive husband.'

The colour deepened in Kate's cheeks, but she returned his gaze without wavering. 'I have no major complaints, *kyrie*.'

Mick looked at her, his mouth relaxing into a faint smile. He said softly, 'You will suffer for that tonight, my girl.'

'Well restrain your ardour until after dinner,' Ari said with sudden joviality. 'Androula is preparing her special lemon chicken and she will not forgive if you are late.'

He clapped Mick on the shoulder. 'It will be like old times, *ne*?'

Mick looked at the sea, his face expressionless. 'As you say.'

They're like a pair of dogs, Kate thought uneasily, circling each other, getting in the odd nip. But the main event is still to come.

'I thought tomorrow I would ask your sister to show me around,' she said later, when she was alone with Mick in their bedroom, changing for dinner. 'Get to know her.'

'A word of advice,' Mick said, adjusting his black tie.

'Don't get drawn into Ismene's intrigues. They always end in tears.'

'I'm not,' Kate protested. She was sitting at the dressing table in bra and briefs putting the finishing touches to her makeup. 'But your father's choice of a husband for her doesn't sound very appealing.'

'Don't worry about it. There will be no enforced marriage.' He paused. 'Your hair looks beautiful.'

'Someone called Soula did it.' Kate touched the artfully careless topknot with a self-conscious hand. 'Apparently your father sent her to look after me. She did all our unpacking, too, and would have helped me dress if I'd let her.'

'Then I'm glad you sent her away,' Mick said softly. 'I wish to retain some privileges.' He went into the adjoining dressing room, and emerged a moment later with a length of black silk draped over his arm. 'Wear this tonight, *agapi mou*.'

'Really?' Kate's brows lifted doubtfully. It was an elegant bias-cut dress with a low neck and shoestring straps that he'd bought her in New York. 'Isn't that a little much for a family dinner. I—I can't wear a bra with it.'

'I know.' He undid the tiny clip, and slipped off the scrap of lace. 'So—have this in its place.'

It was a diamond, cut in a classic tear-drop shape, and glowing like captured fire against her skin. Kate gasped in disbelief, as Mick fastened the fine gold chain round her neck. Her voice shook. 'It's—beautiful.'

His eyes met hers in the mirror. 'But the setting,' he told her gently, 'is even more exquisite.' And for a tingling moment, his hands grazed the tips of her bare breasts. 'A jewel,' he whispered. 'For my jewel.'

He dropped a kiss on her shoulder and straightened. 'Stand up, *matia mou*.'

She obeyed, and he dropped the black dress deftly over her head, without disturbing a strand of hair, and zipped it up.

She said unsteadily, 'You are—almost too good at that.'

Laughing, he took her hand. 'You inspire me, my Kate.'

Then why don't you tell me you love me? she wondered fiercely. Because you never have. Not once in all these months.

When she entered the *saloni* on Mick's arm, she found it deserted apart from Ismene who was glancing through a fashion magazine beside the log fire which had been kindled to fight the evening chill. The younger girl looked up. 'Michalis, Papa wishes you to go to him in his study. There has been a fax you should see.'

'Very well,' Mick said. 'But look after Katharina for me. Get her a drink—and call her no names,' he added grimly.

Ismene came over to her with an ouzo, looking subdued.

'I wish to apologise, sister. I was rude when I called you a penniless nobody. Although Papa said it first,' she added, her brow darkening.

Kate laughed. 'Let's forget it and begin again, shall we?'

'I would like that. But I cannot help being jealous, because Michalis has married whom he wishes, and I may not.' She gave Kate a speculative look. 'You are not like his other women,' she offered.

Kate's smile held constraint. 'I've noticed.'

Ismene giggled. 'So you have met her. I wish I had been there. How she must hate you.'

Kate said slowly, 'But—that's all in the past now—surely?'

'Is it?' The pretty face was suddenly cynical. 'Maybe. Who knows?'

Kate struggled with herself and lost. 'How did Victorine come to be with your father?'

Ismene shrugged. 'It is a mystery. We thought at first that she had come to wait for Michalis—to be with him when he returned. We could not believe that Papa had invited her—and that she was his *eromeni* instead.'

She shook her head. 'And when Michalis did come, he was so angry—like a crazy man. We could hear him with Papa, shouting at each other.' She shuddered. 'Terrible things were said.'

'Did he care about her so much?' Kate concentrated fiercely on her drink.

Ismene shrugged. 'Naturally. She was the ultimate trophy woman, and Papa took her from him.

She brightened. 'But now you and Mick are married, he need not stay away any more. Because he cannot still be in love with Victorine, and Papa need not be jealous.'

'No.' Kate said quietly, her throat tightening. 'It's all— worked out very well.'

'I wish life could be as good for me. Do you know that Papa will not even allow my Petros to come to the house any more.' She tossed her head. 'But it makes no difference, because we are still engaged to each other.'

Kate picked her words carefully. 'Perhaps your father feels you're still young to be making such an important decision.'

Ismene snorted disrespectfully. 'I am the same age as Mama when Papa married her. And I would not be too young if I agreed to marry that horrid Spiro. Although I would rather die.'

Kate's face relaxed into a grin. 'I'd say you had a point,' she conceded.

Ismene looked at her hopefully. 'Perhaps Mick would speak to Papa for me. Talk him round?'

Kate gave a constrained smile, but did not answer because at that moment Victorine entered the *saloni*. She was wearing another clinging dress in fuchsia pink, its low-cut bodice glittering with crystals.

She helped herself to a drink, then came across to Kate, her eyes fixed on the diamond pendant.

'A new necklace, *chère*?' She ignored Ismene. Her mouth smiled, but her eyes were venomous. 'Men usually buy their wives expensive gifts because they feel guilty about something. I wonder what Mick has on his conscience?'

'Bitch,' Ismene whispered succinctly as Victorine moved off towards the fire, using the distinctive swaying walk which had graced so many catwalks. 'Don't let her wind you up.'

Easier said than done, Kate thought wryly.

Ari gave her the place of honour beside him at dinner, and talked to her kindly, but she had the feeling she was being screened, so it wasn't the most comfortable meal she'd ever had.

It was undoubtedly one of the most delicious though, and she said so as she finished the famous chicken, fragrant with lemon.

'I'm glad you liked it.' He gave her an approving smile. 'From tomorrow, it will be for you to order the meals, *pedhi mou*, and run the household. I have instructed Androula, and Yannis my majordomo, to come to you for your orders each day.'

Kate stared at him. 'But I've never...'

'Then you must begin.' His tone demolished further protest, and alerted the attention of everyone round the table to Kate's embarrassment. 'You are the wife of my son, and you take your rightful place in his home.'

He gave Mick a fierce look, and received an unsmiling nod in reply.

'And don't keep me waiting too long for my grandson,' he added, more jovially, turning back to Kate, who looked down at her plate, blushing furiously, aware that Victorine was watching her.

It was a long meal and, afterwards, there was coffee in the *saloni*, and another hissed diatribe from Ismene about her father's injustice, and the general misery of her life.

In fact, meeting Linda had probably been the highlight of a rather fraught day, Kate thought, as she prepared for bed that night.

When she emerged from the bathroom, Mick was standing

by the window in his dressing gown, staring into the darkness.

She slid her arms round his waist. 'Coming to bed?'

'Presently.'

She rested her cheek against his chest. She said softly, a smile in her voice, 'Well, we have our instructions. Your father wants a grandchild.'

He detached himself from her embrace. He said coldly, 'Understand this, Katharina. I give orders. I do not take them. And now I intend to sleep.'

He took off his robe and tossed it over a chair, then walked, naked, to the bed, and got in, turning on his side so that his back was towards her for the first time in the marriage.

Leaving her standing there, shocked, bewildered and suddenly totally isolated. With Mick's diamond burning like ice between her breasts.

CHAPTER EIGHT

I BELIEVED, Kate thought flatly, that it wasn't possible to be more unhappy—more alone than I was that night. But what did I know?

She looked round the impersonal luxury of the hotel room she now occupied alone, and shivered.

She should have realised, she thought. Made the connection there and then. Seen that her brief marriage had begun to collapse—and faced the reason.

Yet, on that following morning, when she'd woken to find herself in his arms, and heard him whisper, 'I'm sorry, *agapi mou*. Forgive me...' she'd been able to tell herself it was just a temporary glitch. That he'd had a difficult day too.

And she'd drawn him down to her, her lips parting willingly under his kiss.

Of course, Kate thought flatly, as the memories stung at her mind, I didn't realise just how much there was to forgive.

Because I was never a real wife—just a red herring, intended to draw his father away from the truth about his relationship with Victorine. The solution to a problem, just as I heard him discussing with Iorgos that night on Zycos.

And Mick didn't want us to have a child because he knew the marriage wasn't going to last. At least he didn't pretend about that.

And that, too, is why he never said he loved me. It was as near as he could get to honesty.

She heard herself moan, softly and painfully. She got up from the bed and began to pace restlessly round the room, then paused, and took a deep breath.

She shouldn't be doing this to herself, and she knew it. It was all still too new. Too raw.

After all, less than two months ago, she'd still been living in her fool's paradise.

And soon now she would be back on Kefalonia, and all the old wounds would be open and bleeding again.

She would have to stand in the village church, and watch Ismene make her marriage vows to the man she loved, and see Petros' rather serious face alight with tenderness as he looked at her.

And she would have to see Mick and Victorine together, exchanging their secret lovers' glances. Become part of the betrayal she had run from. Until Mick chose to let her go.

I can't do it, she thought, nausea acrid in her throat. No one should be expected to play a part like that. Pretend...

But no matter how battered she felt—how emotionally bruised—she couldn't deny the magic of those first weeks she'd spent on Kefalonia.

Beginning at breakfast that first morning when Ismene, eyes dancing, told her that Victorine was no longer at the villa.

'She's on her way to Paris to do some shopping,' she confided. 'To buy a bigger diamond than yours, Katharina *mou*,' she added naughtily.

Kate tried to look reproving. 'Has your father gone with her?'

'No, no.' Ismene looked shocked. 'Because there will be meetings soon with some of the other directors of our companies. Last time Victorine was *so* bored.' She rolled her eyes. 'She likes the money, you understand, but she is not interested in how it is made. Maybe this is why Papa encouraged her to go,' she went on. 'Or perhaps he is still not quite sure...' She stopped, guiltily, her eyes flying to Kate's suddenly frozen face. 'But no—that is silly.'

'Yes,' Kate agreed quietly. 'Very silly.'

'And, of course, you will be Papa's hostess—to prove to everyone that he and Mick are friends again.' Ismene went on eagerly. 'There has been much anxiety, you understand,

and people have taken sides, which is not good. But everything will be better now.'

'I hope so.' Kate forced a smile. 'Perhaps Victorine won't come back.'

'But she will.' Ismene pulled a face. 'Unless she finds a richer man than Papa.'

Whatever the reasons for it, Kate couldn't be sorry about Victorine's absence, especially when days lengthened into weeks with no sign of her return.

Not that she had time to brood about anything. Her new responsibilities had not been exaggerated, she discovered from the moment Yannis and Androula took her on the promised tour of the house.

The Villa Dionysius was much larger than even her first impression had suggested—a positive labyrinth of passages, courtyards and rooms, and Kate saw all of it, down to the cellars, the food stores and the linen cupboards.

'Each generation has added to the house,' Yannis told her proudly. 'And you and Kyrios Michalis will do the same—when the children come.'

Kate bit back a smile. It was ridiculous, she thought, the way everyone was trying to prompt them into parenthood. And what a pity she couldn't share the joke with Mick.

She couldn't help being nervous as the first of the promised guests began to arrive, but was able to draw on her training as a courier to give each of them a composed and smiling welcome, and make sure their comfort was catered for in every way.

It was not an easy time. Not all the meetings went smoothly, and she was aware of tensions and undercurrents as people came and went. Both Mick and his father were grim and thoughtful at times.

But at last, all the visitors departed, and Kate, their compliments still ringing in her ears, was able to draw breath.

'You have done well, *pedhi mou*,' Ari told her. He gave a satisfied smile. 'In fact, it has all been most successful.' He darted a glance at Mick. 'And I am not quite ready for Yeronitsia, *ne*?'

'Yeronitsia?' Kate repeated puzzled.

'A high rock near Ayios Thomas,' Mick supplied unsmilingly. 'From which, legend says, the old and useless used to be thrown. My father,' he added, 'likes to joke.'

But Kate couldn't feel it had been a joke. And a few days later, when Linda took her on a tour of the island, she mentioned it, while they were sitting drinking coffee on the waterfront at Fiscardo.

Linda sighed. 'You're right, it's not funny, but I guess it was inevitable. Ari was so pleased and proud when Mick joined the company, but less so as he began to find his own voice—formulate his own ideas.'

She shrugged. 'You can understand it. Ari was proud of what he'd achieved, and was wary of change—especially the kind of expansion Mick was advocating. Also,' her smile was wry, 'he was beginning to feel his age, and he resented this. He began to say that Mick was too young—too wild to step into his shoes. That the Theodakis corporation should not go to someone with such a high-profile social life. And for a time there, Mick supplied him with all the ammunition he needed,' she added ruefully.

'And, Ari likes to play games—to hint at his retirement in private, then deny it in public. But there've been signs that the board is getting restive—that support for Michael is growing. I—I hope Ari goes with dignity before he's forced out. It would have broken Regina's heart to know how far things had deteriorated between them,' she added huskily.

She didn't speak Victorine's name, but then she didn't have to, Kate thought with a sudden chill.

And one day soon the beautiful Creole would return.

But, in the meantime, Kate could relax and enjoy herself. Already the Villa Dionysius was beginning to feel like home. The staff were so well-trained that the house almost ran itself, and this gave her the opportunity to explore the rest of the island, sometimes with Linda, but usually and joyfully in Mick's company, making the most of its many beauties before the influx of tourists arrived.

She loved hearing him talk about Kefalonia's sometimes stormy history, and share his knowledge of the archaeological discoveries that had taken place over the years.

She was thrilled by the various underground caves with their dark and secret lakes that he showed her, but shivered away from the village of Markopoulo after Mick told her that the Church of Our Lady there was visited each August by crowds of small snakes.

'They crawl up to her icon,' Mick said, amused at her horrified expression. 'We look on them as good luck, especially as they stayed away during the last war, and in the earthquake year.'

'I prefer miracles that don't wriggle,' Kate said with dignity. 'I think I shall arrange to be somewhere else in August.'

Remembering those lightly spoken words now, Kate bit her lip until she tasted blood. Perhaps she shouldn't have been so flippant about the island's luck. Because hers had begun to run out not long afterwards.

Ismene's feud with her father over her wish to marry Petros had shown no signs of abating. Although she had been forbidden to see him, she continued to meet him in secret and, on several occasions, Kate had been her unwilling accomplice, driving her into Argostoli, the island's capital, on vague shopping expeditions.

Ismene had insisted on introducing them, and Kate had to admit that, apart from his lack of worldly goods, she couldn't fault him. He was more serious in his manner than Ismene, but blessed with a quiet sense of humour. He was also good looking, and intelligent.

'Papa says he is not good for me,' Ismene said soberly as they drove home. 'But, in truth, Katharina, he is much too good, and I know it. All the same, I will be a good and loving wife to him.'

Kate found herself unexpectedly touched to the heart by this little speech. But when she mentioned it to Mick, he was angry.

'I told you not to get involved,' he reminded her coldly. 'Now you are joining her in her deceit.'

They almost had a row about it, and matters did not improve when Ismene mounted another tearful and highly vocal campaign to get her father to approve her engagement.

Kate had not been altogether sorry when Mick had insisted on the move down to the peace of the beach house. It had already become one of her favourite places, and she had taken to swimming in the pool there every day anyway, now that the real summer heat had begun, but the sea was still cold.

It was much smaller than the villa, with just two bedrooms, a large living room, as well as a kitchen and bathroom, but it was furnished with exquisite comfort, and it had the great advantage of seclusion. And the big platform at the front that Linda had mentioned was perfect for sunbathing.

'A second honeymoon,' Kate said dreamily on their first evening alone there.

Mick raised his eyebrows. 'And less chance for you to become embroiled in Ismene's mischief, *matia mou*,' he told her, pulling her into his arms.

She was disappointed when she discovered that he was about to depart on visits to the Regina hotels on Corfu, Crete and Rhodes, and that she would not be going with him.

'It's pure routine. You'd be bored.' He'd kissed her swiftly as he left for the airport. 'Try not to let Ismene and Papa kill each other, and I'll be back before you know it.'

But she felt restless, edgy without him. The days were long, but the nights were longer, and his daily phone calls were only part consolation.

She had to put up with sulks from Ismene too, when the younger girl discovered that Kate was not going to drive her to any more secret rendezvous.

She began to spend more time at the beach house. Quite often she was joined there by Linda, and Ismene too when she regained her good humour, and Kate enjoyed preparing poolside lunches for them.

Regina Theodakis had clearly been keen on reading as well as painting, and a large, crammed bookcase was one of the features of the living room. Kate found herself making new discoveries every day, as well as renewing her acquaintance with some old favourites.

Mick had been gone almost two weeks, when Victorine returned. As soon as Kate walked into the villa she was aware of a subtle shift in the atmosphere. She didn't really need Ismene's whispered, 'She's back,' to know what had happened.

'And she's in a really good mood—all smiles,' Ismene went on disparagingly. 'You should see the luggage she's brought back. She must have bought the world. And she's given me a present.'

She extracted a silky top with shoestring straps and exquisite beading from a bag emblazoned with the name of a boutique from the exclusive Kolonaki Square in Athens, and held it up. 'See?'

Kate's brows rose. 'Very nice,' she commented drily. 'Perhaps she's going on a charm offensive.'

But her optimism was short-lived.

'The sun has given you some colour, *chère*.' Victorine was stretched out on a lounger on the terrace, wearing a miniscule string bikini, the expression in her eyes concealed behind designer sunglasses. 'That shade of hair can make a woman look so washed out,' she added disparagingly.

'And good morning to you, too,' Kate said coolly, pouring herself some fruit juice.

'So you are not pregnant yet.' Victorine began to apply a fresh layer of sun lotion to her arms. 'Ari is very disappointed. It might be wise not to keep him waiting too long, or he might begin to wonder about this marriage of yours.

Especially as Michalis has apparently become—restless again, and left you all alone here.'

'Mick's on a business trip,' Kate said, resisting the urge to throw the fruit juice over her antagonist. 'We don't have to be joined at the hip every moment of the day.'

'Or the night either.' Smilingly, Victorine recapped the bottle. 'You are very understanding to allow him these little diversions, *chère*. I hope your trust is rewarded. Michalis can be so wicked when he gets bored.'

'Well, you should know,' Kate said blandly, returning her glass to the tray, and walking off.

But even the pleasure of having the last word couldn't sweeten the little exchange for her.

'I'll keep out of the way,' she thought, thanking her stars that she had a sanctuary, but, to her dismay, Ari made it clear that he expected her to be present at dinner that evening, and perform her usual duties, so she reluctantly obeyed.

Victorine was in her element at dinner, her behaviour to Ari seductively possessive, as she regaled them with the latest film-world gossip, hinting at the lucrative contracts that were still being offered her.

'But how could I be away for months at a time, *cher*, when even a few weeks is too much.' Lips pouting, she put a caressing hand on Ari's arm.

Kate was just wondering what excuse she could make to avoid coffee in the *saloni* when the door of the dining room opened, and Mick walked in.

Amid the exclamations of astonishment and welcome, Kate got shakily to her feet.

'Why didn't you tell me?' she whispered, as he reached her.

'I wanted to surprise you, *agapi mou*.' His arms went round her, drawing her to him. His mouth was warm on hers. 'Have I succeeded?'

'Shall I tell Androula to bring you some food, boy?' Ari barked.

'I had an early dinner in Athens with Iorgos. Now I just want to wash off the city grime, and relax a little.' He smiled at Kate. 'Come and run a bath for me, *matia mou*,' he invited softly.

As Kate went with him, blushing, to the door, she was suddenly aware of Victorine watching her, her eyes cold with derision, and something oddly like pity...

'Was it a successful trip?' Kate lay in the circle of Mick's arms, as the scented water lapped round them.

'The homecoming is better.' He wound a long strand of her damp hair round his fingers and kissed it. 'Maybe, I should go away more often.'

'I disagree.' She touched his face gently with her hand, then paused. 'I didn't know you were going to Athens.'

'Nor did I, but it was unavoidable. A last-minute thing.' He picked up the sponge and squeezed warm water over her shoulders. 'So, what has been happening here? Has Ismene been behaving herself?'

'I try not to ask.' She bit her lip. 'Victorine came back this morning.'

'Leaving a trail of devastation in every design salon in Europe, no doubt.'

Had she imagined the fractional hesitation before his dismissive reply.

'She was shopping in Athens too,' she ventured.

'It's a big city, *agapi mou*.' He kissed the side of her neck. 'Now, let's dry ourselves. Our bed is waiting, and you can show me all over again how glad you are to see me.'

And Kate forgot everything—even that strange, niggling doubt—in the passionate bliss of their reunion.

But, with hindsight, she could have no doubt that Mick had been with Victorine in Athens. He'd brushed aside her tentative query, but he hadn't denied it.

And, however much she'd longed for his return, she

couldn't pretend it was all honey and roses in the days that followed.

Within twenty-four hours, it was evident that relations between Ari and himself were strained, and Mick seemed to retire into a tight-lipped, preoccupied world of his own.

More visiting executives came and went, and there was another endless stream of meetings. Kate struggled to fulfil her role as hostess, but found her smile beginning to crack after a while. She felt as if she was living on the edge of a volcano, but, when she tried to question Mick about what was going on, she found herself blocked.

'But I want to help,' she protested.

'You are helping.' He kissed the top of her head. 'Be content.'

But that was easier said than done.

Even when they made love, Kate had the feeling that he'd retreated emotionally behind some barrier, and she had to search for him, reach out to him, in the joining of their bodies.

But at least in the early afternoons she had him all to herself. They had gone down to the cove to swim at first, but then had found Victorine there, sunbathing in nothing but a thong. Mick ignored her stonily, but, when he found Ismene emulating her, he gave his sister a telling-off in cold, fierce Greek which reduced her to tears.

After that, they had stayed up at the beach house, and Mick had given strict orders that their privacy there was not to be disturbed by anyone. Even Ismene did not dare to intrude on them.

One hot and windless day, lying in the shelter of a poolside umbrella, Kate put down her book, and said, 'When are we going to have a baby?'

He was glancing frowningly through some papers. 'Has my father been asking again?'

'No,' she said. 'This time it's all my own idea. Michael—can we at least talk about it—please?'

His mouth tightened. 'This is not a good time for me, *pedhi mou*.' His voice was gentle but inflexible.

She swallowed. 'Then when can we have a discussion about our marriage—our future?'

He was silent for a moment. 'When I get back from America. We'll talk then.'

She sat up, staring at him. 'You're going to New York? When?'

'Next week. I shall be gone about ten days—perhaps less.'

She said breathlessly, 'Take me with you.'

'It's a business trip, Katharina,' he said. 'I shall be in meetings twelve hours a day. We would never see each other.'

'Mick—please. This is important to me.'

'And you are important here,' he said drily. 'I gather the household can't function without you.'

'That's nonsense, and you know it.' Her voice rose. 'The house runs like clockwork.'

'But you, *agapi mou*, wind the clock. My father is pleased with you.'

She said huskily, 'Is that why you're abandoning me here—to keep him sweet? He already has someone to fill that role.'

His tone was curt. 'Be careful what you say.'

'Michael.' Her voice appealed. 'I'm your wife. I want to be with you. Can't you understand that?'

'But you would not be with me,' he said. 'Because I should always be with other people.' He picked up his papers again. 'And I will soon be back.'

She said raggedly, 'This is why your mother used to stay here, isn't it? Not because it had wonderful views she could paint, but because the villa was too big and too lonely, and your father was always away on business as well. Maybe she even persuaded herself she didn't mind. But I do mind, Michael. I mind like hell.'

'Is it really such a penance to stay here?' He got to his

feet angrily. 'You live in comfort. The servants adore you. Ismene loves you as a sister in blood.'

'And your ex-mistress thinks I'm a bad joke.'

'Ah, Victorine,' he said softly. 'Somehow I knew the conversation would come round to her.'

'You can't pretend it's a normal situation.'

'But one we have to accept—for now, at least.' There was finality in his tone.

'Can you accept it?' She was frightened now, but she pushed herself on. Letting her darkest thoughts out into the harsh sunlight. 'Is that why we live down here, Michael—because you can't bear to see her—to think of her with your father? Tell me—tell me the truth.'

In spite of the intense heat, his glance chilled her. Silenced her. Made her heart flutter in panic.

'You are being absurd, Katharina. Unless you wish to make me angry, do not speak of this again.' He picked up his watch, and fastened it on to his wrist. 'I am going to shower, and drive into Argostoli. At the risk of being accused of abandonment,' he added cuttingly, 'I am not going to invite you to come with me.'

When he'd gone, she retrieved her book, and tried to read, but the words blurred and danced in front of her eyes. Her throat tightened painfully, and she thought, 'Oh, God, what have I said? What have I done.'

He returned while she was dressing for dinner—several scared, aching hours later. She'd put on the black dress he liked, and hung his diamond at her throat.

'Mick.' Her voice shook. 'I'm sorry. I didn't know what I was saying.'

He put his hands on her shoulders. In the mirror, she met his gaze, hooded, enigmatic.

He said, 'Perhaps we both have some thinking to do, Katharina. And my trip will give us the necessary space, *ne*?'

No, she thought. We don't need that. There's too much space between us already. I can't reach you any more.

But she smiled steadily, and said, 'I expect you're right.' And knew she was weeping inside.

Kate put her hands up to her face, wiping away the tears she did not have to hide any more.

Why did she have this total recall, she asked herself desperately, when amnesia would have been so much more merciful?

She thought I can't go on—torturing myself like this. I can't...

She went into the bathroom and washed her face, trying to conceal the signs of distress.

Then she went out into the sitting room. She would have to confront Michael once and for all. Tell him she'd changed her mind. That even if their divorce took for ever, she would not go back to Kefalonia and be made to relive any more of her humiliation and betrayal.

She was halfway across the room when his bedroom door opened and he came out. He was wearing dark, close-fitting pants, and a white shirt, with a silk tie knotted loosely round his throat. He was carrying a light cashmere jacket in a fine check over one arm, and fastening his cuff-links with his free hand as he walked.

He halted, his brows lifting. 'You should have stayed in your sanctuary a little longer, *matia mou*.' His tone was sardonic. 'Then you would have been spared the sight of me.'

'You're going out?'

'Evidently.'

'Where are you going?'

'Be careful. Katharina *mou*,' he said softly. 'You are beginning to sound like a wife. Although I am sure you do not wish to be treated as one.'

She flushed, biting her lip. 'It's just that—I need to talk to you.'

'But I am not in the mood for conversation. I am going

out to find some congenial company.' His eyes raked her dismissively. 'God knows it will not be difficult.'

She flinched inwardly. 'Please listen to me.'

'No, Katharina. We have already said everything that is necessary to each other.'

She lifted her chin. 'I've changed my mind.'

He was very still. 'In what way?'

'I can't go back with you,' she said rapidly. 'I won't.'

'Your rebellion is too late, *matia mou*. I shall not permit you to back out now.'

'You can't make me.' The words were uttered before she had time to think. And they were a mistake. She knew that even before she saw him smile.

'You don't think so? I say you are wrong, my wife.' He tossed his jacket on to a sofa. Took a step towards her.

'Perhaps I shall stay here after all, and show you that I can—persuade you to do anything I want. That I can take from you anything I desire, and you will let me. Because— still—you cannot help yourself. And you know it.'

He paused, letting the words sink in. 'Or would you prefer to stick to the bargain we have made after all—and spend your nights alone?'

'Yes,' she said. She kept her voice level, even though she was shaking inside. 'Yes, I would—prefer that.'

'You are wise.' His voice was mocking, as he retrieved his coat and shrugged it on. The dark eyes were hard. 'It has been a long time since I touched you, *agapi mou*, and almost certainly I would not have been gentle.'

He watched the colour drain from her face and nodded. He added courteously, 'I wish you a pleasant evening,' and went.

CHAPTER NINE

As THE plane began its descent to Kefalonia airport, Kate broke the silence she'd maintained throughout the flight.

'The divorce.' Her voice was constricted. 'Have you really told—no one? Not even Iorgos Vasso?'

He would not have to tell Victorine, she thought. Because she already knew...

'No one.' Mick's tone was uncompromising, his eyes cold as he turned to look at her. 'And I intend it to remain a private matter between us, for the present, anyway. I do not wish to spoil a happy time for my sister.'

She bit her lip. 'You're all heart.'

He sighed. 'However if that is your attitude, we will deceive no one. And you will have reneged on our bargain.'

'God forbid,' Kate said bitterly. 'Don't worry, *kyrie*, I'll play the dutiful wife—in public at least.'

He said, 'It will also be necessary for us to exchange a few remarks from time to time—in public at least,' he added drily.

She lifted her chin. 'I'll do that too—if I must.'

'A small price to pay for freedom, surely?'

Oh, no, she thought, pain closing her throat. It's going to cost me everything.

The days they'd spent together in London had been almost more than she could bear. Not that they'd been together in any real sense, she reminded herself. Mick had been scrupulous about keeping his distance. During the daytime, he'd been in meetings, and she tried not to think where he could be spending his evenings and the greater part of each night. Clearly fidelity, even to Victorine, had never been on his agenda.

They deserve each other, she thought wrenchingly.

Yet, at the same time, all she knew was that she lay alone in the darkness, unable to sleep, straining her ears for the sound of his return.

And that, of course, was madness.

She had little to fill her days either. Iorgos Vasso had dealt with her employers, agreeing an extended and unpaid leave of absence, rather than the notice that Mick had advocated. He'd also arranged with an astonished Mrs Thursgood to have Kate's flat kept an eye on, and her mail forwarded.

The life she'd begun laboriously to assemble was being smoothly erased, she realised helplessly, and when she came back from Kefalonia, finally alone, she would have to rebuild it all over again.

Although that, at least, would give her something to think about, which she suspected she might need.

In accordance with Mick's instructions, she'd trawled reluctantly round Bond Street and Knightsbridge and bought some new clothes, more in keeping with her role as Mrs Theodakis, but she'd kept her expenditure to an absolute minimum.

And she would bring none of them back with her when she left. Her Kate Dennison gear was safely stowed in the bottom of one of her cases, waiting for this nightmare to be over.

The drive to the villa seemed to take no time at all. She had wanted time to compose herself for the ordeal ahead—to resist the ache of familiarity in the landmarks they were passing. To fight to the death the sense of homecoming that had assailed her as soon as the plane touched down.

The staff were clearly delighted to have her back. She was greeted with beaming smiles on all sides, and conducted ceremoniously indoors.

I feel a traitor, she thought angrily.

Her father-in-law was in the *saloni* glancing through some

papers, but he rose as Kate walked in and welcomed her with a swift, formal embrace.

'It is good to see you.' He stepped back, and looked at her critically. 'But you are thinner. This will not do.' He glanced at Mick. 'You will have to take better care of her, my son.'

'I intend to,' Mick returned, unsmilingly.

'I was worried when you went without saying goodbye.' Ari indicated that Kate should sit beside him. 'But Michalis told me it was an emergency. That you had been called away urgently.' He paused, eyeing her shrewdly. 'I hope it is all resolved now.'

She mustered a taut smile. 'Well—nearly, I think.'

'Perhaps we could have helped,' Ari suggested. 'We have teams of lawyers—accountants—business advisers—all with too little to do. Did Michalis not explain this?'

Kate bit her lip. 'It was a—private matter. I didn't want to trouble anyone else.'

'You are a Theodakis now, Katharina.' Ari patted her hand. 'Your problems are ours. But, you will be tired after the flight. Michalis, take her down to the beach house, and see that she rests.'

Kate's heart was thumping as she walked beside Mick down the track through the pine woods. How many times had she taken this same path with him, she wondered, knowing their bed and his arms awaited her?

And now she was on her way to pain, betrayal and deception. Just as she had been only a few short weeks before.

She stumbled on a loose stone, and he caught her arm, steadying her.

She wrenched herself free, glaring at him. 'Don't touch me. Don't dare.'

There was a shocked pause, then he said bleakly, 'You would rather fall than have me catch you. I understand.'

For a moment there was an odd expression on his face—bewildered. Almost—lost.

He still can't believe he isn't irresistible, Kate thought, lashing herself into fresh anger.

The house was just as she remembered it, with its faded terracotta tiles, and white walls festooned with flowering plants.

There were flowers inside, too, she discovered dazedly. In the master bedroom, every surface was covered by bowls full of blossoms. Like some bridal bower, she thought, checking in the doorway, faint nausea rising within her, as she looked across at the bed and remembered...

Saw her luggage standing in the corner.

She turned on Mick, standing silently behind her, her voice was harsh, strained. 'No—not this room. I won't stay here. Please have my things put in the other bedroom.'

His brows snapped together. 'I have been using that myself.'

'Then you'll have to change,' she flung at him.

You sleep in here. You live with the memories. Because I won't. I can't.

'If not, I'm leaving,' she went on recklessly. 'Going back to England, and to hell with our deal. To hell with everything. And if it blows your whole scheme out of the water—tough. But there's no way I'm going to sleep in that bed ever again.'

His face looked grey. He said hoarsely, 'Katharina—how in the name of God did we come to this?'

'Ask yourself that, *kyrie*.' Her voice was like stone. 'I'm just passing through.'

She went past him and walked the few yards down the passage to the second bedroom. The queen-size bed had clearly been freshly made up with clean sheets, and she sank down on its edge aware that her legs were shaking.

Mick followed. He said quietly, 'I have left a few things in the closet. I'll take them.'

'Yes,' she said. 'Then I can do my own unpacking.'

'Soula will do that, as usual.' He paused. 'And your clothes will stay in the other room—with me.'

'No.' Kate got to her feet. 'You can't do that.'

'You came here to preserve the illusion that we still have a marriage.' His voice bit. 'Most couples share a room—a bed. I ask you only to share a wardrobe. You may sleep where you please, *pedhi mou*. The night brings its own privacy.'

She bit her lip. 'Very well. Then I'll try and choose everything I need for the day each morning. At other times, I— I'll keep out of your way.'

There was silence, then he said very softly, 'I do not know if I can bear this.' And went.

Kate stood in the middle of the room, her arms wrapped round her body, until she stopped shaking. She felt bone-weary, but she knew that if she lay down, she would not be able to relax.

But it was still very warm for late September, so perhaps she would sit by the pool—or even go for a swim.

Her bathing suits were all in the master bedroom, she realised without pleasure. She went quietly along the passage, and knocked on the half-open door, but Mick was nowhere to be seen, so she went in.

The scent of the flowers was almost overwhelming as she searched for her black bikini.

As she retrieved it, and the pretty black and white overshirt that accompanied it, she heard swift footsteps approaching, and, a moment later, Ismene flung herself at her.

'Kate *mou*, at last. Oh, I am so happy you have come. I was so afraid you would not.' She pulled a face. 'Michalis made me send you the invitation. He said only when you saw it in black and white would you believe Papa had agreed.'

'What made him change his mind?' Kate shook her head. 'He seemed so adamant.'

Ismene shrugged, her expression puzzled. 'I do not know. He talked very strangely to me. Said how few people found the one person in the world who could make them happy, and what right had he to deny me when Michalis had you, and he himself had loved Mama so much.'

She lowered her voice confidentially. 'Do you think he is growing tired of Victorine, perhaps? Wouldn't it be wonderful if he sent her away?'

Kate forced a smile. 'I—wouldn't count on it.'

'Anyway, what of you, sister?' Ismene went on, after a pause. 'Why did you leave like that—without even saying goodbye, *po, po, po*?'

'It was an emergency,' Kate said steadily, falling back on the agreed story. 'A family thing. I—I can't really discuss it.'

'But all is well now, and you will be staying here?'

Kate forced a smile. 'Nothing is certain in this uncertain world,' she said. 'But I'll definitely be here to see you married.'

'My dress is wonderful,' Ismene confided. 'Silk organza, and the veil my mother wore. Petros and I will marry in the morning at our village church, and then there will be a celebration in the square. And at night there will be a party here with dancing.' She sighed. 'But I shall miss most of that because I shall be on my honeymoon.'

Kate laughed in spite of herself. 'A honeymoon is far better than any party, believe me.'

Ismene eyed her speculatively. 'You and Michalis—did you do it *every* night?'

Kate gasped, feeling a wave of heat swamp her face, as she searched vainly for a reply.

Mick said from the doorway, 'That is none of your business, Ismene *mou*.' He strolled into the room, his face expressionless as he surveyed his wife's embarrassment. 'And if you make my Kate blush again, I shall tell Petros to beat you.'

She sent him a mischievous look. 'Perhaps I should enjoy that. But I can tell when I am no longer wanted,' she added with a giggle. 'I will see you later, Katharina.'

And she flew off again, leaving husband and wife facing each other.

Kate's face was still burning. She said, 'I—I thought I'd sit by the pool.'

He glanced at the bikini, dangling from her hand, and his mouth curled. 'Then I will use the beach.'

She looked at the floor. 'Isn't that rather going to extremes?' she asked in a low voice. 'Surely we don't have to avoid each other to that extent.'

'Ah, but we do,' he said. 'I promise you, *agapi mou*. You see, I still find the sight of you wearing next to nothing too disturbing to risk.' He began casually to unbutton his shirt. 'I am sure you understand.'

Kate sank her teeth into her lower lip. 'Yes,' she said. 'Yes, of course.' She remembered suddenly that the beach was Victorine's favourite haunt. 'But I'm sure you'll find an even more appealing view,' she added hastily, regretting it at once.

Mick tossed his shirt on the bed, and gave her a narrow-eyed look. 'What is that supposed to mean?'

She shrugged. 'Nothing. After all, you were the one who told me Kefalonia was a beautiful island.'

'But clearly not beautiful enough to tempt you to stay in our marriage.'

She stared at him in disbelief. 'You dare say that to me?' Her voice shook. 'When it was you—you...'

'You knew what I was when you met me.' Mick unbuckled his belt and unzipped his trousers. 'I never pretended that I could give you my undivided attention.'

'Am I supposed to admire your honesty?' Kate asked bitterly.

'I would have settled for acceptance.' He slipped his discarded trousers on to a hanger, put them in the closet, then walked over to her. 'Have you forgotten all the happy hours we spent in this room, *matia mou*.' His voice sank huskily. 'Is my sin really so impossible to forgive?'

It occurred to her suddenly that he was wearing nothing but a pair of his favourite silk shorts. Her throat tightened, and, flurried, she took a step backwards.

'Don't run away, Katharina *mou*.' He spoke softly, seductively. 'And don't you fight me any more. Stay with me now. Let me make amends to you. Show you how much I need you.'

His hands were gentle on her shoulders, drawing her close.

For a crazy moment, she found herself remembering how long it was since she'd really touched him. Since she'd let her fingers stray over his naked skin, tracing the steel of bone and muscle. Since her lips had adored the planes and angles of his lean, responsive body.

She wanted to run her fingers along the line of his shoulder, and kiss the heated pulse in his throat. She was hungry—frantic to feel the maleness of him lifting gloriously to her caress.

And then as if a light clicked on in her head, she remembered, and pulled herself free.

'Don't touch me,' she said between her teeth. 'Oh God, I should have known I couldn't trust you.'

Something flickered momentarily in his eyes, then he laughed curtly. 'You have a short memory, dear wife. This is my room—you were quite insistent about it. And I did not invite you here. You came of your own free will. You watched me undress.' He shrugged, his mouth twisting. 'It could be thought you were sending me a signal.'

'Then think again,' Kate flashed stormily. 'Do you seriously think that an—afternoon romp with you could repair the damage between us? And in this of all places.' She drew a harsh shuddering breath. 'Oh, God, I despise you. I hate you.'

He said quietly, 'I am beginning to understand that. I confess that I thought a—romp could be a start for us. A new beginning. But I see now that there is no hope.'

He paused. 'I will tell Soula to take all your clothing and

belongings to your own room after all. Then you need never set foot in here again.' He turned away. 'Now go.'

All Kate really wanted to do was crawl into her room, and hide in some dark corner while she licked her wounds.

But that was impossible. Even though she was dying inside, she had to salvage her pride—to pretend she didn't care. That Michael no longer had the power to hurt her.

She'd said she was going to spend some time by the pool, and that she would do, she resolved, straightening shoulders that ached with tension. Even if it killed her.

She stripped, and put on her bikini. The golden tan which she'd acquired earlier in the summer still lingered, she thought, subjecting herself to a critical scrutiny in the long wall mirror.

But, she was still losing weight. When she'd married Michael, her figure had been nicely rounded in all the right places. Now she could count the bones in her ribcage.

But, even at her best, she'd never come near Victorine's sinuously voluptuous quality, she thought, biting into her lower lip.

And her performance in bed would never match the sultry Creole's either.

That was a painful truth she could not avoid.

She was married to a passionate, experienced man, who had taken her for his own reasons. And, for him, the gift of her loving heart would never have been enough.

He wanted more, she thought. The kind of sophisticated playmate he'd been accustomed to in the past. Something she could never be.

Of course, he'd been endlessly patient with her in those first months, but, however willing the pupil, it was probably inevitable that he'd become bored with being the teacher. And the novelty had worn off for him long ago.

But that didn't mean she would ever accede to his cynical suggestion that she go along with this smokescreen marriage she'd been tricked into. Turn a blind eye to his amours for the prestige of being Mrs Michael Theodakis.

She felt tears prick at her eyelids, and fought them back.

This might be the norm for marriage in the circles Michael Theodakis moved in, but it would never do for her. She cared too much, which no doubt rendered her doubly unfashionable. And no amount of money or luxury was going to change a thing.

Sighing, she trailed out into the sunshine.

It might be the day from hell, she thought, unhappily, as she adjusted the umbrella over her lounger and stretched out on the cushions, but there was still the evening, with the inevitable family dinner to endure somehow.

And Victorine…

There hadn't been a glimpse of her so far, or a mention, but Kate knew the other woman would simply be biding her time, waiting for the most destructive moment. She shivered. The sun was still warm, but the memory of that other hot, golden day hung over her like a shadow, impossible to dispel.

She'd run down through the pines that day with wings on her feet, on fire to see Mick—to throw herself into his arms and resolve the differences that had caused them to part in anger.

She'd been stupid to make the matter of her travelling with him into an issue. She should have been persuasive rather than confrontational. But when she realised that he meant what he said, and she was not going with him to New York, she'd simply lost her temper.

'I'm not some submissive wife,' she'd hurled at him. 'You can't just dump me in any convenient backwater while you go off roaming the world.'

'My work involves travel,' Mick snapped back. 'You know this. You have always known it, so why the fuss?'

'Because we're married, and I want to be with you—not spending my life alone in some different part of the universe.

I'm your partner, Mick, not your housekeeper. Or your mother,' she added recklessly.

And because we were happy in New York, she thought. Because we were by ourselves with no family around—or memories of the past...

His face closed. 'We will leave my mother out of the discussion, if you please. She was content with her life.'

'Was she?' Kate asked bitterly. 'I'd like to have her ruling on that. Just because she knew her place, it doesn't follow she was happy with it.'

The dark brows drew together. 'You go too far, my girl. And you would be alone anyway on this trip. I have already told you I would have no time to give you, or your reproaches, when you tell me that you're bored,' he added bitingly.

'I presume you'd be coming home to sleep at some point?' Kate glared at him. 'I'd be with you then. Or is that the problem?' she went on recklessly. 'Are you not planning to spend all your nights in the same bed, *kyrie*? Is that why you don't want me with you—because I might cramp your style?'

His face was like stone. 'Now you are being ridiculous,' he said harshly. 'And insulting. I have given you my reasons. Let that be the end of it.'

She said shakily, 'Don't tempt me...'

Her words dropped like stones into the taut silence.

Mick sighed. 'Katharina *mou*, I swear I will be back before you know it.'

'Oh, please.' Her voice radiated scorn. 'Don't hurry back on my account.'

That night, when he tried to take her in his arms, she'd turned away from him. 'I have a headache.'

There was a silence, then he said coldly, 'That is a lie, and we both know it. But let it be as you wish. I will not plead.'

And when she'd woken the next morning, he'd gone.

'Kyrios Michalis told us that you were unwell, *kyria*,'

Soula said, her forehead wrinkled with concern. 'And that we were to let you sleep.'

She said quietly, 'That was—considerate of him.'

But she couldn't fool herself. Not for a minute. For the first time, she and Mick had parted in anger and silence, and it hurt.

Nor was it any consolation to remind herself that it wasn't just a tiff, but a matter of principle.

I didn't handle it well, she told herself ruefully. And the headache thing was just stupid. All I've done is deprive myself of some beautiful memories to help me through his absence.

She sighed.

She'd have to make sure his welcome home was just perfect, which shouldn't be too difficult—especially if he was missing her as much as she was already longing for him.

As soon as he calls, she thought, I'll tell him so. Put things right between us.

But the first time he telephoned, she was visiting Linda.

'He was sorry to have missed you, *pedhi mou*,' Ari told her, and Kate made a secret resolve to stay round the villa and await his next call, however long it took.

But this plan misfired too, for, a few evenings later, her father-in-law informed her that Mick had telephoned during the afternoon.

'Why did no one ring me at the beach house?' she protested. 'I've been there all day.'

'It was only a brief call,' Ari said soothingly. 'And I thought also you had gone to Argostoli.'

She caught a glimpse of Victorine's catlike smile, and knew exactly who had sown that little piece of misinformation.

She managed a casual, smiling shrug. 'Ah well, better luck next time.'

But she wouldn't trust to luck, she decided grimly. Not with a joker like Victorine in the pack. She would phone their New York apartment herself. But her calls were fruit-less, because, as he'd predicted, he was never there.

And in spite of herself, she could not help wondering where he was—and who he might be with...

'You're looking a little ragged round the edges, honey,' Linda told her critically one day.

'Is that all?' Kate forced a smile. 'According to Victorine, I've lost what few looks I ever possessed. Not a day goes by without some snide remark,' she added smoulderingly.

Linda sighed. 'The woman is poison. Men can be so damned blind sometimes...' She paused. 'Anyway, Mick wouldn't want you to mope.'

Kate sighed. 'I'm not sure I know what Mick wants any more.'

'Theodakis men are never predictable.' Linda's tone was wry. 'It's part of their charm.'

She was silent for a moment. 'I'm going across to Ithaca tomorrow to collect some pots a friend of mine has made for me. Come with me.' Her eyes twinkled suddenly. 'After all, Ithaca's the island where Penelope waited all those years for Odysseus to come back. Maybe it'll put things in perspective for you.'

Kate smiled reluctantly. 'Not if I remember correctly some of the things Odysseus got up to on his travels. But I'd love to come.'

It would be good to get right away from the villa for a few hours, she thought. Ismene had relapsed into a slough of simmering discontent which made the atmosphere disagree-able enough without the addition of Victorine's softly-spoken jibes.

Much as she liked her father-in-law, he was no judge of women, she thought. Then paused, her heart thudding, as she remembered that Mick had been equally culpable in that par-ticular respect.

After all, he chose her first, she thought, biting her lip.

'Come to the beach with me?' Ismene pleaded in an undertone at breakfast the next day. 'I need to talk to you, sister. To ask your advice.'

'I can't, Ismene. I'm going to Ithaca with Linda.' Kate said. She was faintly ashamed of her relief that she had a get-out. Besides, she reminded herself, she had already given Ismene the best possible advice many times—to be patient, and to try not to antagonise her father any more.

She turned to Ari. 'I hope that's all right. I'll be back for dinner.'

He waved an expansive hand. 'Enjoy your day, *pedhi mou*. I shall not be here either. An old friend of mine is staying near Skala, and we are going fishing together.' He looked at Victorine who was crumbling a bread roll and looking exquisitely bored. 'Are you sure you will not come with us, *chrisaphi mou*.'

Victorine shuddered elaborately. 'I'm sorry, *cher*, but I can think of nothing worse. Except, perhaps, a trip to Ithaca,' she added, flicking a derisive glance at Kate.

'Then it's fortunate we didn't invite you,' Kate said sweetly, as she rose to her feet.

But, in the hallway, she was waylaid by Yannis. 'The telephone for you, *kyria*.'

Could it be Mick? Kate wondered, her heart lurching in sudden excitement. She glanced at her watch, trying to work out the time difference as she lifted the receiver, but it was Linda's voice that reached her.

'Kate, honey, we're going to have to take a rain check on the Ithaca thing. I'm starting a migraine, so I'll be out of things for at least two days.'

'Oh, Linda, I'm so sorry. Is there anything I can do?'

'Not a thing.' Linda gave a weak chuckle. 'I just need to lie down in the usual darkened room, and take my medication. I'll be in touch when I'm better.'

Kate replaced the receiver and stood irresolute for a moment. She could always stay at home, she supposed, but then she was bound to be buttonholed by Ismene with another list of complaints about her father's tyranny, and she wasn't sure she could cope.

I have my own problems, she thought sighing.

And it might also be difficult to avoid Victorine, and the constant pinpricks she liked to inflict on Kate's already sensitised skin.

So she would use her day of freedom to go for a drive, she decided. To revisit some of the places Mick had shown her in happier times. And, to try and get her head together.

The holiday season was in full swing now, so she avoided the usual tourist spots, and drove up into the Mount Enos national park. She left her car near the tourist pavilion, and walked up through the dark firs to the summit. There was no mist today, and she could see the neighbouring island of Zakynthos rising majestically out of the turquoise and azure sea, and, further to the east, the mountains of the Peleponnese.

The air was like spring water from a crystal glass. It was very still. No voices—just the faint sigh of the breeze in the clustering trees, and the distant drone of an aircraft making its descent.

She looked, up, shading her eyes, to track its progress, and suddenly Mick was there with her, his image so strong that she could have put out a hand and touched him.

The clustering islands blurred, and the iridescent glitter of the sea broke into tiny fragments as the tears came.

She whispered brokenly, 'Michalis *mou*.'

She knew in that moment that whatever their differences, however great the apparent difficulties, she would do anything to make her marriage work.

Mick would never fit some Identikit New Man pattern of the ideal husband. In spite of his cosmopolitan background, he was too fiercely Greek for that. But, if he beckoned, she would walk through fire for him, and that was all that really mattered.

There would have to be adjustments, and these would need to be mutual, because she was no doormat, but she felt more at peace, and more hopeful than she had done for weeks.

She drove down with care to the main road, and turned north. She had a leisurely stroll along the beautiful Myrtos beach, then drove on to Assos for a seafood lunch.

When she got back to the villa, she decided as she drank her coffee, she would get on the phone to New York, and stay on it until she'd spoken to Mick, and told him she loved him. She'd call the apartment, the office—even his favourite restaurant if she had to, but she'd find him.

Or, she would take the first flight she could get to America and tell him in person.

I'll get Yannis to call the airline, she thought in sudden excitement. He can make me a reservation. And I'll do it now.

There was a telephone in the taverna, but, before she could tell Yannis what she was planning, he had burst into excited speech. 'Kyria Katharina, it is so good that you have rung. Because Kyrios Michalis is here. He returned two hours ago. He asked for you, and I told him you had gone to Ithaca.'

'That didn't happen, Yannis. I'm at Assos instead, and I'm coming straight back. But please don't tell him. I want to surprise him.'

'You are coming back from Assos, and you wish to make it a surprise, *kyria*,' he repeated, and she knew he was smiling. 'I understand. I will say nothing.'

As she drove back, she remembered the aircraft she'd heard on the mountain—the certainty that Mick was with her.

I must have sensed that was his plane, she thought wonderingly.

She'd been in such a hurry to see Mick, she'd left the keys in the car, hurtling recklessly down the track to the beach house.

She was breathless, laughing as she'd opened the bedroom door. And seen, in one frozen, devastating moment, the end of her marriage, and the ruin of her happiness. The death of faith and trust. The total destruction of every cherished hope and dream she'd ever had.

Or ever would have.

Because until she could stop loving Mick, cut him out of her heart and mind forever, she would be unable to move on.

And she knew now, with a terrible certainty, that, in spite of what he'd done, it wasn't over yet.

Because nothing had changed, she thought despairingly. This was the truth she had to face.

That, God help her, she was doomed to love him for all eternity.

CHAPTER TEN

KATE wrapped her arms round her body, stifling the involuntary moan of pain forcing its way to her lips as she remembered Victorine's mocking smile, and the way she'd allowed the encircling towel to slip down from her bare breasts.

How she'd glanced at the bed, where Mick lay face down, his naked body totally relaxed in sexual exhaustion, as if to silently emphasise the totality of the betrayal.

Of course, I was supposed to be on Ithaca, Kate thought. And Ari was out on his friend's boat. They must have thought they were safe—that it was the perfect opportunity.

But how many times before that? How many snatched hours had there been?

There was Athens, of course. Victorine had practically flaunted that red flag in front of her.

So many signs. So many signals that she'd been too naïve—too trusting—too damned stupid to pick up.

She bit into her lip. The earthquake of realisation might be over, but the aftershock still lingered. The agony of accepting that her marriage had only ever been a cynical charade to conceal Mick's secret passion for his father's woman—the flamboyant, sensual beauty he had never ceased to want.

There was no one she thought bitterly, whom he would not betray in his pursuit of Victorine.

But he would not consider that he'd short-changed his convenient wife in any way. After all, she'd had his name, his money, and sex on demand—she would no longer call it love-making—so what more could she possibly want?

I wanted love, she thought achingly. The one thing he never offered.

Had it never occurred to either of them that she might carry her pain and shock to Aristotle Theodakis? That this reckless, forbidden passion might have robbed Mick of his other major ambition—to rule the Theodakis empire?

Or had he counted on Kate's innate sense of decency to keep him safe? The knowledge that she would not willingly involve anyone else in her suffering—especially the father-in-law who had treated her with such unfailing kindness?

But then Mick liked to take chances—in his business as well as his personal life. For him, that would have been just one more justified risk.

Like bringing her back here...

Her throat was dry and aching. She got up from the lounger, and trailed wearily into the house. She needed a cool drink.

In the kitchen refrigerator she found a tall jug of fresh lemonade, and she filled a tumbler, and added ice cubes.

She'd just taken a long, grateful swallow, when she heard footsteps approaching quickly along the tiled hallway and Victorine appeared in the doorway. She was wearing a brief white skirt, and a low-cut silk top in her favourite deep pink.

'So.' Her voice had a metallic ring. 'You came back. I did not think it possible.'

'Well, don't worry.' Kate replaced her glass with care on the counter top, aware that her hand was shaking. But she kept her voice steady, and her glance level. 'It's only a short visit. I'll be gone soon—permanently.'

Victorine hunched a shoulder, her gaze inimical. 'What have I to worry me? I am merely astonished you have so little pride that you return here.'

'I came for Ismene's sake, and at her invitation. No other reason.' Kate lifted her chin. 'But there is one thing. While I am here, you will not set foot in this house again. You and Michael must find some other corner to pursue your sordid little affair. Do I make myself clear?'

Victorine shrugged gracefully. 'As crystal, *chère*. But it

makes little difference.' She gave Kate a cat-like smile. 'We can wait. Anticipation can be—most exciting, don't you find?'

'Why yes,' Kate said calmly. 'For instance, I can hardly wait to get out of here, and leave this whole squalid situation behind me.'

Victorine laughed, her eyes hard. 'You are being very sensible. No scenes. No whining. Be sure that Michalis will pay generously for your discretion.'

No, thought Kate. I'm the one who'll pay. For the rest of my life.

Her voice was cool and clipped. 'Kindly go now, Victorine, and stay away from me. Or I might change my mind, and blow the whole thing out of the water.'

She retrieved her glass, and moved towards the window, deliberately turning her back on her adversary and, after a moment, she heard the receding click of her heels as the other woman retreated.

She leaned against the wall, her shoulders sagging wearily, sudden tears thick in her throat. She'd won the encounter, but it was a hollow victory.

But, if self-interest prompted the Creole girl to keep her distance, it might make Kate's enforced stay on Kefalonia marginally more bearable.

Certainly, it was the best she could hope for.

She glimpsed her reflection in the window, the white strained face, the over-bright eyes, and trembling mouth.

And thought, 'You fool. Oh, God, you pathetic fool.'

She took a long, warm bath, then lay on her bed, with the shutters closed, and tried to sleep. To stop her brain treading the same unhappy paths all over again.

Selective amnesia, she thought, staring into the shadows. That was what she needed. The events of the past year painlessly removed from the memory banks.

And if she'd only obeyed her instincts and not gone to the

Zycos Regina with Lisa that night, she would never have met Mick, and none of this would have happened.

When she eventually dozed, she was assailed by brief troublous dreams, which left her tense and unrefreshed.

But she had no real reason to feel relaxed, she reminded herself ironically. She had the evening's family dinner to get through.

She pulled a straight skirt in sapphire-blue silk jersey from the wardrobe, and found the matching top, long-sleeved, and scooped neck.

She was brushing her hair, and trying to decide whether to sweep it up into a loose knot, or leave it unconfined on her shoulders, when there was a swift tap on the door and Mick walked in.

She swung round defensively. 'I didn't say "Come in."'

His smile did not reach his eyes. 'But I'm sure the words were hovering on your lips, *agapi mou*,' he drawled.

He placed a velvet covered case on the dressing table, and put a small Tiffany's box beside it.

'Your pendant,' he said. 'I would like you to wear it tonight.'

'And your orders naturally must be obeyed.'

He said quietly, 'I'd hoped you would look on it as a request, Katharina—but, so be it.'

She touched the other box. 'And this?'

'Some earrings to match it.' He paused. 'I brought them back from New York some weeks ago, but you were not here to receive them.'

Kate stiffened. 'Another attempt to salve your guilty conscience?' Her voice bit.

He was silent for a moment. 'What do you wish to hear? That I am not particularly proud of myself? I admit it.'

'Big of you to say so,' she said huskily. 'Only, it doesn't matter any more.'

'It matters to me.' He pushed the little box towards her. 'Please open your gift.'

'I prefer to regard it as an unwanted loan.' She had to stifle a gasp when the blue fire of the exquisite drops flared up at her from their velvet bed.

'Put them on,' Mick directed softly. Standing behind her, he buried both hands in the silky mass of her hair, and lifted it away from her ears, watching as Kate, summoning every scrap of self-control she possessed, fastened the tiny gold clips into her lobes.

'Beautiful.' He bent his head, letting his lips graze the smooth curve between throat and shoulder, his hand gently stroking the nape of her neck.

She felt a shiver run through her nerve-endings at his touch. Experienced the shock of need deep within her.

She looked down at her hands, clenched together in her lap, refusing to meet the compulsion of his dark gaze in the mirror.

She said in a stifled voice. 'Don't—touch me.'

There was a silence, then he straightened, moving unhurriedly, away from her.

He said mockingly, 'You have a saying, *matia mou*—that old habits die hard. I suspect it may be true for us both.'

A moment later, she heard the door close.

But when she emerged from her room, he was waiting for her.

'I regret the necessity.' He spoke curtly. 'But it will look better if we arrive together.'

'And we must never forget appearances.' She fiddled with the thin wool wrap she was wearing round her shoulders.

'But, of course not. Isn't that why you're here?'

And there was no answer to that, she reflected bitterly, as she walked up through the tall sighing pines, at his side.

The evening was not, however, as bad as she'd expected. Petros was there, with his parents whom she had never met before. Dr Alessou was a squarely built, grizzled man, and his wife was tall with a shy smile, and Kate liked them both immediately. It was a pleasure to stand and talk to them, as well as a lifeline.

Linda was also present.

'Hi, stranger.' She gave Kate a swift hug. 'It's good to have you back.'

'Thank you.' Kate's smile was constrained, and Linda's brows drew together as she studied her.

'Come to lunch tomorrow,' she said. 'If Mick can bear to let you out of his sight.'

Kate straightened her shoulders determinedly. 'That's—not a problem.'

'Really?' Linda queried drily. 'I'll expect you at twelve.'

The only awkward moment came halfway through the meal, when Ismene, who was on bubbling form, spotted Kate's earrings.

'Are they to welcome you back?' she demanded breathlessly. 'How much he must have missed you, *po, po, po.*' She sent a laughing look at her silent brother. 'If I were Katharina, I would go away again and again. What will you bribe her home with next time, Michalis—a ring, perhaps, with a stone like a quail's egg?'

He was leaning back in his chair, out of the candlelight, so Kate could not see his expression. But his voice was cool even with a note of faint amusement. 'I am saving that, *pedhi mou,* until our first child is born.'

'What is this?' Ari barked jovially from the head of the table. 'Have you some news for us, my girl?'

'No.' Kate was burning from head to foot. Suddenly she was the focus of everyone's attention—genial, interested, excited—and, in one case, poisonous. She just wanted to get up from the table and run. 'No, of course not.'

'They are both young.' Dr Alessou looked at her kindly. 'There is plenty of time. Ari, my friend.'

'But times are changing.' Ari Theodakis looked round the table commandingly. 'I have reached a decision. At the next full meeting of the board, I shall officially announce my retirement as chairman of the International Corporation. It is time I made way for new blood.'

He inclined his head towards Mick. 'I leave my companies in your safe hands, my son.'

There was an astonished silence.

'But what are you going to do, Papa?' Ismene was wide-eyed.

He smiled benignly. 'I have my plans. My friend Basilis Ionides has just completed the purchase of his property, which as you know includes the old Gianoli vineyard. We are going to restore its fortunes—make wine together. And I shall tend my olives, go fishing, and sit in the sunlight. And play with my grandchildren.' He grinned at Dr Alessou. 'I may also find time for the occasional game of *tavli*, eh, my friend?'

Kate still struggling to regain her composure saw Victorine's face turn to stone, indicating that Ari's announcement was news to her. She saw, too, the lightning glance that the other woman darted at Mick.

He's got what he wanted, she thought. And now he can have her too. Once he's officially chairman, there'll be nothing to stop him.

And Victorine likes the high life. She wants a millionaire not a Kefalonian farmer. Vines and olive groves will never be enough for her. Surely Ari must realise that.

But there won't be a thing he can do about it, once he's given up the reins. So, there'll be a ghastly scandal, the press will have a field day, and the family feud will break out all over again.

She looked down at the golden gleam of her wedding ring. And she would be bound to be dragged into it too—splashed across the newspapers as the wronged wife. Made to relive every bitter moment all over again. A far cry from the quiet divorce she'd planned.

But no one could hope to escape unscathed from this kind of situation, she reminded herself wretchedly. It was only astonishing that no enterprising journalist had managed to dig out the facts about this sordid little love triangle a long time ago.

Or was it just proof of the influence the Theodakis family were able to wield, and the privacy their money had always succeeded in buying for them?

But it wasn't her problem. Not any longer. And in a few months she'd be free of it all, she told herself, sinking her teeth into her bottom lip. And her transient encounter with the rich and mighty would be eventually forgotten.

Although, not by her. That was too much to hope for.

She was sitting in her own little cocoon of silence amid the welter of laughter and surprised comment around the rest of the table when a slight prickle of awareness made her look up.

Mick was watching her across the table. He was frowning faintly, his face taut, the dark eyes concerned, and questioning.

Oh, please don't worry, she assured him silently, and bitterly. I won't rock the boat. Not at this juncture.

I'll run away again, as soon as Ismene's wedding is over, and you can tell your father I couldn't cope with the prospect of being the chairman's lady. That I simply wasn't up to it. The truth can wait for a more convenient moment—after the official announcement that you're the new chairman.

She drank some wine from her glass, then turned determinedly to Dr Alessou, an authority on island history, to ask a bread and butter question about St Gerassimos, who was Kefalonia's patron, and to whom the village church was dedicated.

He launched himself into his subject with enthusiasm, and when Kate next dared steal a glance under her lashes at Mick, she found he was talking with smiling courtesy to the doctor's wife.

*   *   *

The evening seemed endless, and wore the air of an occasion, thwarting any hopes Kate might have had of making an unobtrusive exit.

Especially when Yannis entered ceremoniously with champagne.

'A double celebration,' Ari explained. 'My retirement, and your return to us, *pedhi mou*.'

Kate smiled, and felt like Judas.

But at last the Alessous took their leave, and Kate felt free to escape too.

She said a general 'Goodnight,' but she had only gone a few yards down the moonlit track to the beach house, when Mick caught up with her.

'What do you want?' She faced him defensively.

'It's our first night here together,' he said. 'It would be thought odd if I did not accompany you.'

'It must be a relief to know that you won't have to keep up appearances for much longer.'

'So it seems.' His tone was wry. 'It came as quite a bombshell.'

'The first of many, I'm sure,' Kate said crisply, and set off down the track, shoulders rigid.

'And for that very reason, we need to talk, my Kate.'

She said unevenly, 'Don't call me that. And there's nothing more to discuss. We established the terms for my return in London. Nothing has changed.'

'You were very angry in London. I have been waiting— hoping that, perhaps, your temper had begun to cool.'

'I'm not angry, *kyrie*. I'd just like to get on with the rest of my life.' She paused, wrapping her arms defensively round her body, not looking at him. 'After all, you've just achieved your heart's desire.'

He said slowly, 'If you think that, *agapi mou*, then our marriage has taught you nothing.'

'Then it's as well it's over,' Kate returned curtly, and walked on.

He caught her arm, and spun her round, making her face

him in the moonlight. He said quietly, 'I do not—cannot believe you mean that, Kate. Not in your heart.'

'Fortunately I've started using my brain instead, *kyrie*. Something our marriage *has* taught me.' She tried to tug herself free. 'Now let go of me.'

'How easy you make that sound.' Mick's voice was bitter. 'But perhaps I am not ready to give up on us so easily, *matia mou*.'

She took a step backwards. 'You can say that.' Her voice shook. 'You *dare* to say that.'

'Katharina.' He sounded almost pleading. 'I know what I did was wrong, but is my fault really so unforgivable? Could we not—negotiate some new terms?'

What do you want from me? she cried silently. To go on with this charade—pretend we have a marriage? Enjoy the money and the prestige and turn a blind eye to your other pleasures? Because I can't. I can't...

She said tautly, 'That's impossible, and you know it.'

'I know nothing any more.' Mick's voice was harsh. 'Except that, for one stupid act, my life with you has been destroyed.'

'I was the stupid one,' Kate said bleakly. 'Thinking I could ever be content with the kind of half-life you had to offer.'

'*Agapi mou*.' There was real anguish in his tone. 'Believe me, I never meant to hurt you like this.'

No, she thought. Because I was never meant to find out. I was expected to stay the naïve innocent until you decided otherwise.

'Oh, my Kate.' His voice sank to a whisper. 'Even now, couldn't you find it in your heart to forgive me? Offer me another chance? We could be happy again...'

'No.' She began to walk down the track again. 'I'm not the same person. Not the blind idiot you married.'

She knew that note in his voice. It had always been the prelude to lovemaking. And she had always responded to it.

He was still holding her arm, as he walked beside her, and

she felt his touch through the silky sleeve, scorching her flesh, burning her to the bone. She was falling to pieces, suddenly, blind and shaking. Her reason fragmenting.

And soon—all too soon—they would reach the house where the lamps would have been lit in their absence, and the wide bed in the main bedroom turned down in readiness, just as always.

That room, where the pale drapes shimmered in the breeze through the shutters, and the moonlight dappled the floor.

Where she heard her name whispered in the darkness and opened her arms to him in joy and welcome.

That was how it had been only a few short weeks before.

And how it could never be again.

That was the truth—the rock she had to cling to as emotion and stark need threatened to overwhelm her.

'I've changed too, *agapi mou*.' His voice reached her softly, pleadingly. 'Surely—surely that could be a start—a way for us to find each other again.'

'You said you wouldn't do this,' Kate accused raggedly. 'Oh, why the hell did I come back here? Why did I ever trust you?'

'Did you really believe I would just let you walk away?' Mick followed her into the dimly lit hallway. 'And I said I would allow you to sleep alone—not that I wouldn't fight to get you back.'

'Well the battle's over, *kyrie*.' She wrenched herself free from his detaining hand. 'And you lost.'

'Are you so sure?' he asked quietly. His eyes went over her, registering the widening eyes, the tremulous parted lips, and the uncontrollable hurry of her breathing.

He moved towards her, and she took a swift step backwards only to find further retreat blocked by the wall behind her.

Slowly and deliberately, he rested his hands against the wall on either side of her, holding himself at arm's length, not touching her in any way, but keeping her trapped there just the same.

Over his shoulder, she could see the half open door of his bedroom. All the flowers had been removed, but their scent still seemed to hang in the air, sweet and evocative.

'Shall I show you that there are no certainties between a man and a woman, *matia mou*—just an infinite range of possibilities?' There was a note of shaken laughter in his voice. 'Won't you let me make amends for the past?'

Kate lifted her chin, making herself meet the power—the unconcealed hunger of his dark gaze with white-faced defiance.

'What are you suggesting, *kyrie*—that we should solve everything by having sex?'

His brows lifted 'It might at least provide a beginning—a way back. And I had hoped that we would make love to each other,' he added with cool emphasis.

Kate shrugged. 'Dress it up however you want. It comes to the same thing in the end.'

'No,' he said with sudden bitterness. 'It does not, my innocent wife.' He looked down at her, his mouth tightening harshly. 'Do you wish me to demonstrate.'

'No.' Her voice was a thread.

He sighed. 'Don't fight me any more, Kate *mou*.' His voice gentled. 'Because I could—make you want me, and you know that.'

'Not any more.' She crossed her arms defensively over her breasts—a gesture that was not lost on him. 'Understand this, Michael. Whatever you did to me, whatever you called it, it would be nothing more than rape. And I'm sure you don't want that on what passes for your conscience.'

His head went back as if she had struck him across the face.

He said hoarsely, 'Kate—you do not—you cannot mean this. In the name of God, you are my wife.'

'Only in the eyes of the law,' Kate said. 'And even that will change soon.' She swallowed. 'Now let me go.'

There was a long, tingling silence. She saw the incredulity in his eyes fade and become replaced by something infinitely more disturbing—even calculating. A look that sent a shiver curling through her body.

Then Mick straightened slowly, almost insolently, his arms dropping to his sides.

So that technically she was free. And all she had to do was turn and walk away. Only she couldn't seem to move— leave the support of the wall, or the ice-cold compulsion of his gaze.

He said too softly, 'So—what are you waiting for. To be wished a restful night, or, perhaps—this?'

There was not even time for a heartbeat. Suddenly, Kate was in his arms, crushed without gentleness against his lean body, her parted trembling lips being plundered by his.

There was no tenderness in the kiss he subjected her to. Just a ruthless, almost cold-blooded sensuality that bordered on punishment.

Her first faint moan of protest was smothered by the bruising pressure of his mouth. After that, she was incapable of speech or even thought. Even to breathe was a difficulty. But there was no mercy in the arms that held her, or the hard lips that moved on hers with almost brutal insistence.

Behind her closed eyelids, fireflies swirled in a frantic, mocking dance.

In spite of herself, her starved body was awakening to stinging, passionate life under the searing shock of his kiss. The scent, the taste of him filled her nose and mouth with a frightening familiarity. The awareness that he was strongly starkly aroused sent swift heat coursing through her veins, and awoke memories as potent as they were unwelcome.

Her head was reeling. Her legs were shaking under her. She was going to faint. She might even die. But nothing mattered except the urgent, agonised necessity of feeling the burning strength of him inside her, filling her.

She pressed herself against him, letting the wild current of feeling carry her away to recklessness.

Later, she would be ashamed. Would hate herself.

But tonight, for a few brief hours, he would belong to her alone. An encounter to treasure in the loneliness ahead.

And in that instant she found herself free, her release as sudden and startling as a blow. Mick stepped backwards, away from her, studying her through narrowed eyes, as he fought his own ragged breathing.

Kate sagged back against the wall, staring back at him, her wide eyes clouded with desire, a hand pressed to her swollen mouth as she waited.

Waited for him to lift her into his arms, and carry her to bed. Waited to feel his mouth on hers again, demanding the response she longed to give.

He was close enough to touch, yet the distance between them had suddenly become a vast and echoing space, impossible to bridge.

And his smile, she saw, was cold, and faintly mocking.

Swift dread invaded her, like a sliver of ice penetrating her heart.

'*Kalinichta, matia mou,*' he drawled. 'Goodnight—and I wish you sweet dreams. As sweet as that night on Zycos, perhaps.'

She watched him walk away from her across the passage, and heard the finality of his door closing.

Shutting her out. Leaving her in a limbo of her own making, composed of shame and regret.

CHAPTER ELEVEN

IT WAS a long time before Kate could move. Before she could find the strength to walk, stumbling a little, the few yards to her own room.

She closed the door with infinite care, then trod across the room to the bed. She sat on its edge, hands clenched in her lap in a vain attempt to stop them shaking.

She'd made him angry. That was the only logical explanation for the last shattering minutes. She'd refused to be manipulated. To allow herself to be used.

Because that was all it was, she told herself. He couldn't risk a rendezvous with his mistress, and he needed a woman. So, why not amuse himself by seducing his gullible wife all over again?

Kate winced as her teeth grazed the tender fullness of her lower lip.

Perhaps he'd thought again about the public resumption of his liaison with Victorine, recognising it as the kind of conduct the Theodakis board would condemn.

Or maybe he'd decided he needed the surface respectability of his current marriage after all, no matter what might happen in private.

The cynicism of it nauseated her.

But, that being the case, why hadn't she walked away from him, while she had the chance? What had induced her to stay, and provoke him into that storm of devastation that he'd unleashed on her.

It was madness—and, bitter as the acknowledgment might be, she only had herself to blame.

And why hadn't she fought him? she asked herself wildly.

She could have struggled—kicked—bitten. But she'd done none of those things.

She slipped off her shoes, and lay back on the bed in a small, defensive curve.

Because she hadn't wanted to, she thought. That was the next unpalatable truth she had to deal with.

However much her reason might condemn Mick, and affirm that she could not go on living with him after such a betrayal, her physical responses were operating on a different planet.

At his lightest touch, her body seemed to open, like a flower, creating that deep, molten ache which only he could heal. Even the thought of him could make her whole body clench in hunger and need.

None of the hurt, the anger and bitterness had managed to cure her of wanting him, and she was going to have to live with that.

But, which was far worse, Mick was totally aware of the war going on between her mind, and her too-eager senses, because he knew her better than she knew herself.

He'd pinpointed her weakness with mind-numbing brutality, leaving her without a hiding place, or even an excuse. And he'd done it quite deliberately.

He was also the one who had, in the end, walked away.

And, somehow, she had to survive the despair and humiliation of that knowledge, and go on.

When all she really wanted to was run ignominiously away.

Except that would be pointless, Kate thought, burying her face in the pillow. There could be no escape, because Mick had her on the end of some invisible chain, and all he had to do was tug, and she would be drawn back inexorably. And no amount of time or distance would change a thing.

And how was she going to live with that?

She cried for a while, then, silently, achingly. When there

were no more tears left, she sat up wearily, pushing back her hair from her face.

She took the diamonds from her ears and around her throat, and put them back in their cases, then undressed, and donned her simple white cotton nightshirt.

She had known from the beginning, she thought, as she lay in the darkness listening to the whisper of the sea, that she and Mick came from two different worlds. Yet in truth they were light years apart.

How could he regard such a transgression, such a complete betrayal, so lightly? she asked herself wretchedly. Unless he felt he was powerful enough to ignore the normal rules of morality.

He'd clearly expected her to shrug and smile, and take him back when he asked for forgiveness. Presumably that was how other wives of his acquaintance reacted to their husbands' passing adulteries.

But this was no trivial, transient affair, she reminded herself unhappily. No moment of weakness to be instantly regretted.

Because Victorine had clearly got into his blood. A habit he was unable to break. Maybe even a necessity…

Her mind closed at the thought.

Perhaps he even hoped that I'd be docile—besotted enough to accept some kind of *ménage à trois*, she thought bitterly.

She shivered, and turned over, trying to compose herself for sleep, but it would not come. Her mind was wide awake, endlessly turning on the treadmill of their last encounter.

Or perhaps she was just scared to sleep. Frightened in case the dreams that Mick had ironically wished for her might indeed be waiting to enclose her in their dark thrall, and draw her down to her own private hell.

It was nearly dawn when she at last closed her eyes, and only a few hours later when the sun woke her again, pouring through the slats in the shutters.

For a moment, she was tempted to stay where she was. To

pull the sheet over her head, and lie still, like a hunted animal gone to ground. Or even to feign illness.

But Ismene wanted her to talk about the wedding arrangements, she remembered, and she was also having lunch with Linda. Life was waiting for her, and could not be avoided.

It won't be for much longer, she told herself, as she bathed and dressed in her denim skirt and a simple white vest top. She hung small gold hoops in her ears, and used concealer to cover the shadows under her eyes, and blusher to soften her pallor.

She could hear the clash of crockery in the kitchen, and a woman's voice singing softly in Greek as she went through the living room, and out on to the terrace by the pool.

A table had been laid there, now littered with the remains of breakfast, and Mick was seated beside it, engrossed in some papers.

He was wearing shorts and a thin cotton shirt, open to the waist, and his hair was damp, indicating that he'd been swimming.

Kate paused, slipping her hands into the pockets of her skirt, and feeling them ball nervously into fists.

He glanced up at her hesitant approach, his gaze cool, almost dispassionate, with none of the mockery she'd feared.

He said, '*Kalimera*,' and pushed a small silver bell across the table towards her, as she took her seat. 'If you ring, Maria will bring you some fresh coffee and hot rolls.'

'Is that who was in the kitchen?' Kate frowned. 'Why is she here?'

'I decided it would be better if one of the servants was here to look after us.' His tone was expressionless.

'But I've always done that.' The words were out before she could stop herself.

'Ah, yes,' he said. 'But that was then. This is now.' His brief smile did not reach his eyes. 'And I have resolved, *matia mou*, to spare you *all* your wifely duties.'

She was aware that warm colour was staining her face, but kept her voice steady. 'I see.'

'But, of course, there are also the nights,' he went on. 'When Maria will not be here.' He paused. 'So, a man is coming from Argostoli this afternoon to put a lock on your bedroom door—in case my animal instincts should suddenly overwhelm me, you understand.'

'Please—don't...' Her voice was husky.

'Why not?' Mick shrugged. 'I am merely trying to simplify matters. To make your final days here as trouble free—and as safe—as I can. I thought you would be grateful.'

'Yes,' she said. 'You're—very considerate.'

'Thank you.' His mouth twisted. 'Perhaps we can maintain the normal courtesies, if nothing else.' He rose, stretching casually, causing Kate to avert her gaze rapidly from the long, tanned legs and the silken ripple of muscles across his bare chest and diaphragm.

'Now ring for your breakfast,' he added, putting his papers together. He offered her a quick, taut smile. 'I will not stay here to spoil your appetite.'

She wasn't hungry, but she made herself eat some of the rolls, honey and fresh fruit that Maria brought.

She might be sick at heart, she thought, but there was no point in making herself physically ill as well.

After all, the last thing she wanted was to look as if she was fading away under Victorine's gloating gaze.

'You do not look as if Michalis allowed you much sleep last night, sister,' was Ismene's exuberant greeting, when Kate joined her up at the villa. She gave her a wide smile. 'Life is good, *ne*?'

'Very good,' Kate returned, mentally crossing her fingers for the lie. And so much for cosmetic cover-ups, she added silently.

It was a relief to escape from her own problems into Ismene's joyful plans for her marriage.

Rather to Kate's surprise, the wedding was not to be some

glittering international event packed with the rich and famous.

The Theodakis clan was a vast one, and Petros also came from a large and widespread family. After that the guest list seemed restricted to old friends.

Most of the arrangements were already in place, largely thanks to Linda, Kate gathered. Her own task was largely one of room allocation at the villa, and booking accommodation in local hotels for the overflow.

As she'd suspected, Victorine's sole contribution had been a series of snide remarks about Ismene's marrying beneath her.

'But I told her that would never be her problem,' Ismene said with undisguised satisfaction. 'As there is no way down from the gutter.'

Kate choked back a laugh. 'Ismene—you could get into real trouble.'

'I thought so too,' Ismene admitted. 'But although she told Papa and he was stern with me, I do not believe he was really angry.' She gave Kate a hopeful look. 'Do you think he is becoming tired of her, Katharina? I could not bear it if she became my step-mother. And nor could Michalis.'

'No.' Kate's throat tightened. 'I—I'm sure he couldn't.' She hesitated. 'I think maybe we need to leave them to—work things out for themselves.'

But, perhaps, in the end, everyone would get what they wanted without scandal or an explosive rupture between Mick and his father, she thought later, as she drove down to Sami.

If Ari no longer wanted Victorine, he might not care too much if she was ultimately reunited with Mick. Father and son seemed to share a cynical view of women as commodities to be traded.

If only she herself could have been excluded from this sexual merry-go-round.

Yet, she knew in her heart that, in spite of betrayal and

heartbreak, she would not have missed the heady delights of those first months with Mick for anything in the world.

Although that was small consolation when she contemplated the empty desolation that awaited her.

'I thought we'd have lunch in the garden,' Linda said briskly, leading the way to her sheltered courtyard. 'While we still can. The weather's going to change,' she added, directing a critical look at the sky.

'How do you know?' Kate asked baffled.

'Live here for long enough, and you get the feeling for it.' Linda smiled at her. 'I bet Mick would tell you the same.'

'Yes.' Kate returned the smile with determination. 'Can you forecast whether we'll have a fine day for the wedding?'

'I can guarantee it.' Linda poured wine. 'The sun always shines on the Theodakis family. Haven't you noticed?' She paused as her maid brought bread and salad, and a platter of *crasato*—pork simmered in wine. So Kate was not forced to reply.

'Well,' Linda said when they were alone, and eating. 'What's the problem?'

Kate dabbed at her lips with the linen napkin. 'I don't know what you mean.'

Linda sighed. 'Honey—who are you kidding? You do not have the look of a girl in the throes of a blissful reunion with her man. And Mick looks as if he's strung up on wires, too. So, what's happening.'

Kate stabbed at her pork. 'I can't tell you. Not yet.'

Linda whistled, her face concerned. 'That bad, huh?' She was silent for a moment. 'I admit I wondered when you just disappeared like that. I planned to talk to Mick about it, if he'd let me, but he was never around long enough. Always working like a demon, rarely touching base. Which should have told me something, too,' she added thoughtfully.

'But when I heard he was bringing you back, I hoped that meant you'd managed to resolve your differences. God knows, there were bound to be plenty. You're both strong characters. But so were Ari and Regina, and they rode out their storms. In fact, they thrived on them. I thought you'd be the same.'

Kate smiled over-brightly. 'I think that would rather depend on the storm.' She took some more salad. 'This food is delicious. And what herb has Hara used in the potatoes?'

Linda picked up the cue, and the conversation turned to food, and, from there, to the wedding.

'Have you decided what you're going to wear?' Linda asked.

Kate wrinkled her nose. 'Not really. I have this pale-green dress that Mi...that I bought back in New York. That's a possibility. But Ismene is talking of going to Athens shopping for a couple of days with Mrs Alessou,' she added. 'I could always go with them and find something there.'

They were just drinking their coffee, when they heard footsteps and Ari came round the corner of the house. He halted, brows lifting when he saw Kate.

'*Me sinhorite*. I beg your pardon, Linda. I did not realise you had a visitor. I should have knocked at your door and not taken it for granted that you could receive me.'

'Old friends never intrude,' Linda assured him, her face faintly flushed. 'Sit down, Ari, and have some coffee with us.'

'No, no, I was just passing, and I thought...' He sounded awkward. 'The vineyard I mentioned last night. I am going there now, and I wondered if you would care to come with me. But I see it is not possible. Another time, perhaps.'

'It's perfectly possible,' Kate said firmly, concealing her surprise. She pushed back her chair, and stood up. 'I was about to go, anyway. I have an ocean of things to do this afternoon.'

'You could always come with us, *pedhi mou*,' Ari suggested, with what Kate felt was real nobility.

She smiled and shook her head. 'Not today. Three's a

crowd, and always will be.' As I know only too well, she added under her breath, wincing.

'So,' she said mischievously, as Linda accompanied her out to her car. 'How long has this been going on?'

Linda's flush deepened. 'There's nothing "going on",' she responded with dignity. 'Just as I said, we are old friends. And he dropped by a couple of times while you were away to ask my advice about Ismene. That's all.'

Kate kissed her lightly. 'And now he wants to consult your expertise on winemaking. Fine.'

She was smiling to herself as she drove away. Maybe one good thing was going to emerge out of this unholy mess after all, she thought wistfully.

Although it would also mean that Mick was totally free to reclaim Victorine for himself. His trophy woman, she thought, as an aching sigh escaped her.

Within a few days, the countdown to the wedding had begun in earnest, leaving Kate little time for unhappy introspection. But, though her days might be full, her nights were another matter. Behind her locked door, she tossed and turned, searching vainly for peace and tranquillity.

Sharing the beach house with Mick was not easy, although she couldn't fault his behaviour. He was working hard, constantly away on short trips. But, when he was at home, he kept out of her way as much as possible, and, when they did meet, treated her with cool civility. Which, she supposed, was as much as she could hope for.

The weather had changed as prophesied, and rain fell from grey skies accompanied by a swirling wind. Without her usual escape routes through the pine woods, and to the beach, Kate began to feel almost claustrophobic, especially as nervous pressure began to build up at the villa with Ismene complaining that the village party would be ruined.

Even when money was no object, weddings were still tricky to arrange, Kate realised, as she dealt with temperamental caterers, and found a replacement for the folk-dance troupe whose leading male dancer had broken his leg.

The shopping trip to Athens was a welcome break, with Ismene making heroic and endearing efforts to keep her spending within bounds, so as not to shock her future mother-in-law.

Kate had no need to set herself any such limits. She had been stunned to discover how much money was waiting in her personal account. It seemed that Mick had continued to pay her allowance during their separation. She couldn't fault his generosity in that regard, she thought, biting her lip.

And yet, in the end, she spent hardly anything. She trawled the boutiques and designer salons around Kolonaki Square with almost feverish energy, and tried on an astonishing array of garments to try and find an outfit for the wedding, but there was nothing that aroused more than a lukewarm interest in her.

In the past, when she'd gone clothes shopping, Mick had usually accompanied her. It had been fun to emerge from the changing room and parade breathlessly in front of him, waiting for him to signal approval or negation as he lounged in one of those spindly gilt chairs.

A nod was generally enough but, sometimes, she saw his attention sharpen, brows lifting, and mouth slanting in a smile as his eyes met hers, making her dizzyingly aware that he was anticipating the pleasure of taking off whatever expensive piece of nonsense she was wearing.

Now, it no longer mattered what she wore, she thought.

And she had the pale-green dress in reserve, she reminded herself. It was simple and elegant, and not overtly sexy, so it was suitable for a wedding, and, hopefully, would enable her to fade into the background during the day-long celebration.

But her restraint had not passed unnoticed.

'She tried on every dress in Athens,' Ismene reported teasingly on the evening of their return, when the family had assembled in the *saloni* before dinner. 'And bought none of them. What do you think of that, Michalis?'

'Only that, for once, my prayers have been answered,' he returned wryly. Above the laughter, he added, 'And, anyway, I have my own ideas about what Kate should wear to your wedding, *pedhi mou*.'

'*Po, po, po.*' Ismene turned to Kate. 'What is he planning, do you suppose?'

'Who knows.' Kate made herself speak lightly. 'Your brother is good at surprises—and secrets.'

Her glance met his in unspoken challenge.

He said softly, 'And for that, *matia mou*, I shall make you wait until the day itself.'

As they went into the dining room, Kate found Victorine beside her.

'Your thrift is admirable, *chère*, and also wise.' The crimson mouth was smiling, as she whispered in Kate's ear. 'After all, one's financial circumstances can change so quickly, *n'est ce pas*? It is good to be prepared.'

Kate drew a sharp breath. 'I am more than ready, believe me,' she said icily, and turned away.

In spite of Ismene's gloomy forebodings, the clouds rolled away the day before the wedding, and a mellow sun appeared, bringing the island to life in shades of green and gold.

In twenty-four hours it will all be over, Kate thought bleakly. Ismene will be a wife—and I shall cease to be one.

A top hair stylist had come from Athens to attend to the bride, on the morning of the wedding, but Kate had declined his services. She already planned to wear her hair loose, with a small spray of cream roses instead of a hat.

But she still hadn't the least idea what dress Mick wished her to wear. The subject had not been referred to during any of their fleeting encounters, and she was damned if she was going to ask.

Let him be mysterious, she told herself, lifting her chin.

What difference does it make? It's just one more thing to endure on one more day from the rest of my life.

She had a leisurely bath, applied her favourite body lotion, and put on bra and briefs in ivory silk and lace, smoothing gossamer tights over her slim legs.

Holding her robe round her, she walked back into her bedroom, and checked, her lips parting in a little cry of shocked negation.

Lying across her bed was a slender slip of a dress in cream silk, cut on the bias so it would swirl around her as she moved, and beside it, its matching collarless jacket, the front panels embroidered with a delicate tracery of gold and silver flowers.

Her own wedding dress—worn only once before on that December day in London when all the happiness she'd ever dreamed of seemed to be within her grasp.

The last time she'd seen the dress, it had been hanging in her closet in the New York apartment.

He'd brought it back with him specially, she realised numbly. But why?

How could he hurt her like this? Why provide such a potent reminder of how things had once been between them, when they both knew their marriage was over? And that he was about to discard her forever?

She snatched up the folds of silk from the bed, and stormed down the passage to his room, rapping sharply at the closed door.

He called, '*Peraste*,' and Kate opened the door and marched in.

He was standing at the dressing table fastening his tie, but turned, brows raised, his gaze flicking her robed figure, and the dress hanging over her arm.

He said coolly, 'Is there a problem? Do you need help with your zipper perhaps?'

'No problem. I simply came to return this.' Kate confronted him, chin lifted, allowing anger to mask her hurt and bewilderment. 'I won't wear it. You can't expect me to.'

He turned back to the mirror, making minute adjustments to the elegant knot at his throat.

'But I do expect it, Katharina *mou*,' he told her quietly. 'None of my family were at our wedding, so they have never seen you in that dress, or known how beautiful you looked. An omission I intend to rectify today.'

He paused. 'Besides, I told them last night what I was planning, so you cannot disappoint them. Such a romantic gesture to convince them all that we are the picture of marital harmony,' he added icily. 'Remember our bargain, and that you still have your part to play in it.' His smile was hard. 'Look on it as your costume for the last act, if you prefer. That might make it easier to bear.'

She said unevenly, 'I never thought you could be so cruel. Don't my feelings matter in all this?'

'Did you consider mine when you ran back to England?' he shot back at her. 'Without giving me a chance to explain—to apologise? Forcing me to invent stories to explain your absence.'

She said shakily, 'What you did was beyond apology. It would have been more honourable to have accepted responsibility and told the truth. But of course that might have jeopardised your ultimate ambition.'

'We are preparing for my sister's wedding,' Mick said flatly. 'Shall we discuss my ambitions at a more convenient moment?' He turned and confronted her, hands on lean hips, long legs sheathed in elegant charcoal pants, his crisp white shirt dazzling against his olive skin.

'Now go, and change,' he directed. 'Unless you wish me to dress you with my own hands,' he added significantly.

She took a step backwards. 'You wouldn't dare.'

'Don't tempt me, *agapi mou*.' His voice slowed to a drawl, blatantly sexy, almost amused. 'Or we might miss the wedding altogether. Now go.'

She gave him a fulminating glance, then turned and went out of his room back to her own, trying not to run.

She closed her door and leaned against it. Her reflection in the mirror opposite showed spots of colour burning in her pale face, and an almost feral glitter in her eyes.

Further protest was futile, and she knew it. Even if she locked herself in, and refused to go to the wedding, she couldn't win. Because no lock would be strong enough to keep him out, if he decided to impose his will on her, and she knew it.

'Damn him,' she said raggedly. 'Oh—damn him...'

CHAPTER TWELVE

KATE learned to smile that day. To smile at the aunts, uncles and cousins who embraced her and welcomed her so warmly to the family.

To smile at Ari when he said slowly, 'But what a vision, *pedhi mou*. A bride again yourself. Your husband is indeed a fortunate man.'

To smile as she stood beside Mick in the small incense-filled church, brilliant with candlelight and glittering with icons, and he took her hand in his. And the female members of both families sighed sentimentally, because they thought it was a gesture of love and he was remembering his own wedding day. Because they didn't know the truth—that it was all a pretence.

And to smile, at last, with genuine mistiness at Ismene, as she appeared, amid gasps and sighs from the onlookers, in her shimmering gown, her veil floating around her, to join her bridegroom.

It was a beautiful ceremony full of symbolism and ritual, and Ismene's voice was tremulous as she took her vows in front of the tall bearded priest. Petros was looking at her as if she was some goddess come to earth, and Kate felt tears prick her eyelids as she scattered handfuls of rice over the newly married pair at the conclusion of the marriage.

Afterwards musicians conducted Ismene and Petros to the square outside. It was festive in the sunlight, draped with bunting, and wreaths of flowers. Long tables had been set up, with platters of fish and chicken, bowls of salad and hummous, and still-warm loaves of bread. There was lamb roasting on spits, and tall jugs of local wine. The whole village seemed to be in attendance, and there was a carnival atmosphere as they jostled for seats.

Kate realised that Mick was taking her to the top table, where the bride and groom were already ensconced. Victorine had not attended the church ceremony, but she was there now in a vivid yellow dress and a matching picture hat, fussing over where to sit.

Kate hung back. 'Please, I—I'd rather sit somewhere else.'

He said quietly, 'Kate, you are my wife, and you will take your proper place.'

'Well, my son,' Ari came up to them. 'Are you asking Katharina's forgiveness for having cheated her?'

There was a sudden roaring in her ears. She said faintly, 'What—did you say?'

But he'd turned back to Mick. 'Your wedding should have been like this. Not in some cold London office,' he chided jovially. 'But I was thinking, as I watched the children just now, that we should ask the good father to perform a blessing on your marriage, in the church with all of us to see. Kate would like that, *ne*?'

Kate murmured something faintly, and let Mick lead her away. She stole a glance at him, and saw that his face was grim, his mouth hard and set.

She said, with a catch in her voice, 'We can't go on like this. You must—say something.'

He said brusquely, 'I intend to.'

She saw an empty chair and took it, finding herself wedged between Dr Alessou and an elderly aunt, with a fierce stare and a diamond brooch like a sunburst.

She applauded as Petros and Ismene walked round the square, handing out sugared almonds from decorated baskets, and pretended to eat when the food was served. And she did not once look at Mick who was sitting further down the table, with Victorine beside him.

Was it intended as some kind of public declaration? she wondered. Had it begun?

It was good when the dancing started, and she had something she could focus on. The dancers wore traditional costume, the men in waistcoats and baggy breeches, with broad sashes and striped stockings, and the girls, their heads covered by scarves, in long skirts under flowered aprons, but there was no doubting the sheer athleticism of their performance.

And when they'd finished their exhibition, it was everyone else's turn. The dancers began to weave their way round the square, between the tables, pulling people up to join them in a long chain.

Kate saw Linda seized, laughing a protest as she went.

Then they reached her, and a plump woman in a red dress grabbed her hand, tugging her up in turn.

At first Kate felt clumsy—a fish out of water—as she tried to copy the intricate pattern of steps they were repeating over and over again, but the women holding her hands on either side were loud in their encouragement, and gradually the rhythm took over, and she was able to follow them with mounting confidence.

I used to do this kind of thing all the time when I was a rep, she thought. I'm just out of practice.

As the chain twisted and wove past the top table again, she saw Ari clapping enthusiastically, and Ismene and Petros beaming at her. And she saw Mick, his expression unreadable. And his companion, her beautiful face a mask of contempt.

To hell with her, Kate thought with sudden passion. To hell with both of them.

The sun was on her face, and the throb of the music had found an echo in her veins. In spite of herself, she was caught up in the sheer exuberance of the moment. The unexpected pleasure of belonging.

The rhythm changed, and she found herself dancing with a man from the village, linked to him by the coloured handkerchief he ceremoniously offered her.

She was breathless when the music eventually paused, and excused herself smilingly, amid protests.

She sank into her seat, grateful for the water that Dr Alessou poured for her.

'Why did he do that?' she asked, as she put down the empty glass. 'With the handkerchief, I mean? The other men are holding the women's hands.'

The doctor smiled at her. 'Because you are still a new wife, *kyria*, and it is believed that your hand should touch no other man's but your husband's.'

'Oh,' Kate said, and hastily poured herself some wine.

At sunset, the cars arrived to take the guests back to the villa, and the private evening party, but the celebrations in the village would clearly go on well into the night.

The *saloni* had been cleared for dancing, and there was more food laid out in the dining room.

Petros and Ismene opened the dancing, moving slowly to the music in each other's arms. Champagne was drunk, then Ari made a speech formally welcoming Petros to his family, and then the bride and groom were free to get changed and leave on their honeymoon.

Kate was at the back of the laughing throng that watched them depart, and she turned back with a sigh, wondering if it would be noticed if she too slipped away.

The music had resumed in the *saloni*, the small band playing something soft and dreamy, and people were heading back there. Kate went along with them, ostensibly part of the group, but separate, making her private plans.

She'd go out on the terrace as if she needed air, then take the steps at the end to get to the beach house. Where she would pack. She wouldn't be able to get off the island tonight, but she would leave first thing in the morning, and Mick would be free to do whatever he wanted. And she would not have to watch.

She began to move round the edge of the room, looking

down to avoid eye contact. Trying to be as unobtrusive as possible.

Only someone was barring the way. She raised unwilling eyes and saw Mick regarding her gravely.

He said quietly, 'Dance with me, *matia mou*.'

'In order to keep up appearances?' Kate lifted her chin. 'I think I'll sit this one out.'

'No,' he said. 'You will not. You have danced with everyone else today. Now it is my turn.' He took her hand and drew her on to the floor.

His arms enfolded her, holding her intimately against him, as they began to move to the music.

For a moment, Kate was rigid in his embrace. Her reason, the sudden clamour of her outraged senses were all telling her that this was a pretence too far. That she should not permit him to take this advantage.

Then, almost imperceptibly, she began to relax. To move with the flow, and go where the music and her husband's arms took her.

She felt the touch of his cheek against her hair. The swift brush of his mouth on her temple.

Even with that briefest of contacts, she felt her heartbeat hurry into madness. She felt the warm blood mantling her face. Was aware that her nipples had hardened in sweet, excruciating need against the silk that covered them.

And as if in response to some secret signal, Mick's arms tightened around her, his hand feathering across her spine, and his lips grazing the curve of her cheek, the corner of her trembling mouth.

With a little sigh of capitulation, Kate slid her arms up around his neck and buried her face in his shoulder.

She was no longer a separate entity, she realised, but part of him. Indivisibly. Unequivocally. Bound to him in some mysterious region of the senses where logic, commonsense— even decency—counted for nothing.

Where the only truth was that he was her man, and she

was his woman, and she would burn for him until the end of eternity.

She could count every day, every moment, every second that they had been apart. Recall every night when her imagination had brought him hauntingly back to her.

She could think of nothing—remember nothing—anticipate nothing but the glide of his hands on her naked skin delighting every pulse, every nerve. The lingering arousal of his mouth. The moment when her starved body would open to receive him.

She was dimly aware that the music had stopped—had been replaced by another sound.

As she raised her head uncertainly she realised with shock that she and Mick now had the floor to themselves, and the sound she could hear was applause from the other guests, clustering round to watch them in laughing, vociferous approval.

Bringing her back with a bump to sudden, stark reality.

Kate's face flamed in horrified embarrassment, and she tried to tug free, bent on flight, but Mick was holding her too firmly.

'Smile, *agapi mou*,' he murmured, acknowledging the plaudits with mocking self-deprecation.

She said between her teeth, as she obeyed, 'You'll stop at nothing, will you?'

'At very little, certainly.' He spun her round, away from him, then pulled her close, his lips taking hers in a brief hard kiss. 'And before tonight is over, you will be glad of it, my wife,' he added softly. 'This nonsense between us is over, and you are coming back to my bed where you belong.'

He released her, and she walked away from him, trying not to run. At the edge of the floor, she nearly collided with someone. She glanced up, her lips shaping an apology, and saw it was Victorine, her eyes glittering with malice and derision.

She held Kate's arms above the elbow, and leaned forward as if to embrace her.

'That was good, *chère*,' she breathed in her ear. 'What a pity Michalis has to run the Theodakis corporation. He would have made such a wonderful actor.'

Kate shook her off, uncaring who might see, and pushed past. She had to fight her way out of the room. Everyone wanted to speak to her, it seemed, and shake hands. But, at last, she won free, and found a quiet corner where she could recover her equilibrium a little.

She asked a passing waiter to bring her some fruit juice, and stood, sipping it, relishing its coolness against her parched throat, as Mick's parting words ran mad circles in her brain.

It was some new game he was playing. It had to be. He wasn't serious. He couldn't be. Because they had a deal. A bargain.

But all the same, she wouldn't waste any time getting away. Not the airport this time, but one of the ferries. It didn't matter which. Nothing mattered very much. Not any more.

And because of that, she could go back into the *saloni* this one last time, and act as the hostess. She could talk to people, and dance with anyone who asked her. And she would not— *not* let herself think of Mick's arms, and the familiar strength and urgency of his body.

No, she thought. She would never think of that again. And one day, her mind would have ground the image of him into such tiny particles that she would actually be able to forget him, and start to live again.

It was dawn before the party ended, and the last stalwarts made their way to their rooms, or were driven to the nearby hotels.

She saw Mick go into the study with his father, laughing, their arms round each other's shoulders, and drew a deep breath. She would never have a better opportunity.

She slid out of the house, and went down through the quiet pines to the beach house.

There was a chill in the air, heralding an autumn she would never see. And a chill in her heart that no sun could ever warm.

Once in her room, she drew a steadying breath. It was time to go.

She took Mick's diamonds from her ears and throat, and replaced them in their cases, then removed her wedding dress, and hung it back in the closet.

She would take with her only what she had brought, she decided, slipping on her robe, and fastening its sash.

She found her smallest travel bag, and began to fill it with underwear and shoes. She still had money left over from the Athens trip, and her car keys.

But not her passport, she realised with sudden dismay. Mick had that. She could remember him slipping it into the inside pocket of the jacket he'd been wearing.

Oh, let it still be there, she thought with panic. Don't let him have locked it in the desk up at the villa.

She trod barefoot down the passage, and went into his room, trying unsuccessfully to remember which coat it had been. Well, she would simply have to look in all of them, she thought sighing. Starting with the one hanging on the back of the chair.

'Tidying up for me, *agapi mou*?' His voice from the doorway behind her made her jump, and she whirled, holding his jacket against her like a shield. 'Maria will complain.'

He came further into the room, and kicked the door shut behind him. He was in his shirt sleeves, his tie hanging loose, his coat slung over one shoulder. And he was smiling.

He said softly, 'So you are here at last.'

'No,' she said. 'You—you're mistaken. I came to look for something.'

'And so did I.' He tossed his jacket and tie on to the empty chair, and began to unbutton his shirt, his eyes never leaving hers.

'What are you doing?' Her voice sounded high, unnatural.

'Taking off my clothes. I usually do before I go to bed. And then, *matia mou*, I shall undress you.'

Kate backed away. 'Don't come near me,' she said hoarsely.

'But that wouldn't work.' He dropped his shirt to the floor, and unzipped his pants. 'For what I intend, my Kate, we need to be gloriously, intimately close. As we used to be, such a short time ago. Before I made you angry and you decided you hated me.'

She said passionately, 'But I do hate you. And I am not— *not* going to allow you to do this.'

He sighed. 'Kate, I was your lover for six exquisite months. I know your body as well as I know my own. I can feel your response when I touch you, and while we were dancing tonight, you wanted me.'

'No.' She wanted the denial to be fierce, but instead it sounded as if she was pleading. 'You can't do this.'

'I must,' he said almost gently. 'Because without you, *agapi mou*, I am dying inside. I need you to heal me. To make me whole again.'

He took her in his arms, the naked heat of his body permeating her thin robe.

He said softly, 'Don't fight me, Kate. I am so very tired of fighting.' And then he kissed her.

His lips were a seduction in themselves, moving warmly and persuasively on hers, coaxing them apart, while his hands untied her sash, and pushed the concealing robe from her shoulders. Her eyes closed and she surrendered, allowing him the access he desired to the sweet moisture of her mouth.

Then he lifted her, and carried her to the bed, lying beside her as his long supple fingers began to rediscover her. And the scraps of silk and lace she was wearing were no barrier at all.

When he kissed her again, she responded swiftly, ardently, making her own feverish demands.

The tips of her bared breasts grazed his chest. Her hands sought him. Enclosed him.

And she felt, in her turn, the shiver of his touch on her thighs, and heard herself moan softly in need.

He whispered, 'No, *agapi mou*. You take me.'

And he turned on to his back, lifting her above him. Over him.

Her possession of him was slow and sweet, her body closing round him like the petals of a flower as she filled herself with him deeply, gloriously.

And he lay watching her, the breath catching in his throat as he caressed her, his fingertips brushing subtly across her flesh, making the pink nipples pucker and lift.

His hands stroked the length of her body from her shoulders to her flanks, and back again, tracing the vulnerable curve of her spine so that her body arched in sudden delight.

She began to move on him slowly, savouring every distinct, separate sensation, then increased the rhythm, hearing his breathing change as she did so.

She controlled him like a moon with a tidal sea, using her body like an instrument to bring him pleasure.

And then, before she was even prepared for it, all control was gone, and their locked bodies were straining frantically together seeking a consummation.

She heard him gasp her name, and answered him wordlessly as they took each other over the edge, and down into the abyss.

Afterwards, he slept in her arms, and she held him, as the slow tears edged out from under her lashes, and scalded her face.

Then quietly, inch by inch, she eased herself away from him, towards the edge of the bed. She found her robe, and put it on, then retrieved her underwear.

Moving gingerly, she opened the closet door, and began to search through his clothes for her passport.

It was nearly ten minutes before she found it. Ten precious moments of early morning turning into broad daylight, and increasing the risk of discovery.

She took one last look at Mick's sleeping figure.

She thought, 'Goodbye, my love' and knew that her heart was weeping. Then she slipped quietly out of the door, and back to her room.

She collected fresh undies, and a straight cream skirt with a black short-sleeved top, then went into the bathroom to shower and dress, and collect her toiletries.

The house was still quiet, and there was no sign of Maria. Maybe everyone was sleeping late today. So far, so good, thought Kate and went quickly and cautiously across the passage and into her room.

Mick was standing by the window. He'd dressed in denim pants and a polo shirt, and his arms were folded across his chest.

She halted, her throat closing in panic. She said huskily, 'I thought you were asleep.'

'I missed you beside me,' he said. 'And it woke me.'

He looked from her to the hastily packed travel bag, his mouth curling.

He said quietly, 'Were you planning to leave me another note, Katharina? What would this one have said, I wonder?'

'The same as the last one.' She flung back her head. 'That our marriage was a mistake, and I can't stay with you.'

'Nor can you leave,' he said. 'Not now. Because a little while ago, we may have given our child life.'

She stared at him. 'No.' Her voice shook. 'That's—not possible.'

He sighed. 'You cannot be that naïve. But the point is this. I want to make a baby with you, if not now, then in the future. And I intend our child to grow up with both parents.'

She said slowly, 'You want a child? But why now—of all

times? You've always refused to consider it before.' She paused. 'Oh, I understand. I suppose my replacement doesn't want to be pregnant. Doesn't want to spoil her wonderful figure. So, you'll just use me instead.' She gave a small, hysterical laugh. 'My God, I should have seen that coming.'

He said impatiently, 'You're talking like a crazy woman. What replacement in the name of God?' He didn't wait for an answer. 'But if you want to know why I hesitated over a baby, it was because I was scared.'

'You—scared?' Kate stared up at him in patent unbelief. 'Oh what, pray?'

He said roughly, 'Of losing you, *pedhi mou*, as I lost my mother. If she had not given birth to Ismene and myself, she could have been alive today. But the strain of it weakened her heart.'

'And you thought that might happen to me? That's absurd.' She lifted her chin. 'I prefer my own version. That you want a child, and you know Victorine won't give you one.'

'Victorine?' he repeated. 'What does she have to do with all this.'

'She's your mistress.' At last she'd made herself say the word. 'And she's going to be your wife, once you've got rid of me and taken over the company. So there's no room for me. And if I am having a baby, I'm damned if I'll surrender it to you to bring up—with her. The stepmother from hell.'

Mick said slowly, 'Why, in the name of God, should I marry Victorine? Yes, we were involved—once. You knew that. But it is long over. And will never be resumed.'

She said, 'That isn't true. Because you were here with her—on the day you came back from the States. When you thought I was in Ithaca. I *found* you together, both of you naked. In—that other room. In that bed—where we...' She couldn't finish the sentence.

He stared at her. 'You—found us having sex?'

'No,' Kate said. 'It was just the aftermath, but it had the same kind of punch. You were asleep on the bed, and she'd been having a shower. Neither of you were wearing any clothes.' Her voice shook. 'She—suggested I should—knock in future.'

He was very still. 'So, possessing this indisputable evidence, maybe you would prefer it if I left, and took Victorine with me.'

'I don't think she'd go.'

'No?' His smile chilled her. 'Well, let us see.'

He took Kate by the wrist, and marched her to the door. She struggled a little.

'Let me go. Where are you taking me?'

'We're going up to the villa,' he said. 'To ask her.'

CHAPTER THIRTEEN

'MICK, you can't do this.' Kate stumbled in his wake as he strode up the track towards the villa. 'You'll ruin everything for yourself. Lose everything you've worked for.'

'You speak as if that matters,' he threw over his shoulder at her. 'There are worse losses.'

'But think what it will do to your father,' she panted. 'Even if he did take her away from you, he doesn't deserve that kind of humiliation.'

'Now there we differ. A man who does that deserves everything he gets.' He walked into the villa's hallway, pulling Kate behind him, and paused. 'I presume they will still be in their suite at this time.'

'Yes,' she said. 'But please stop and think before you go in there.'

'What is there to think about?' Mick swung round, his eyes blazing. 'According to you, my passion for Victorine has corrupted my mind—my sense of honour. Therefore, I no longer have to consider the consequences of my actions.'

Kate said shakily, 'In that case, I'd rather stay here.'

'But you cannot,' he said. 'Because this is the moment when all your reasons for leaving me will be totally confirmed. When your condemnation of me for a liar and an adulterer will be completely justified.

'So, you should be there, *agapi mou*. It is not something you can afford to miss. Come.'

Kate went with him because she had no choice. She was trembling as he knocked imperatively at his father's door, and heard him call, 'Enter.'

They found Ari lying on the sofa, in dressing gown and

pyjamas, reading a newspaper, with a pot of coffee beside him.

He put down his book and studied them frowning slightly. 'Is this not a little early for social calls? All our guests are still asleep.'

'I am aware of that,' Mick said brusquely. 'But I have a matter to deal with which will not wait. I need to speak to Victorine urgently.'

Ari's frown deepened. 'She is also sleeping. Perhaps I can give her a message for you—at some more reasonable time?'

'No,' Mick said. 'I need to talk to her. We have been having a passionate affair behind your back, you understand, and I have decided to ask her to go away with me.'

Kate folded her arms across her body, feeling suddenly sick. She waited for the explosion, but it didn't come.

Instead, Ari said composedly, 'I see now why this cannot wait. I will fetch her.'

He rose and went into the bedroom and, a few minutes later, Victorine emerged. She was wearing a black lace nightgown with a matching peignoir clutched round her.

Her hair was a mess and Kate noticed with pleasure that her eyes were puffy.

'What is this, *cher*?' She seated herself on the sofa, disposing her draperies with conscious elegance. She was smiling, but her eyes were wary. 'Ari says you want me.'

'More than life itself, it seems,' Mick said. 'So much so, that I have wrecked my marriage for you. And now I am here to put an end to all this hidden passion and deceit, and admit our love openly.'

Victorine stiffened. She said. 'What are you talking about? Have you gone mad?'

'I have simply decided that nothing matters more than our love.' Mick shrugged. 'Naturally, I shall have to resign from the Theodakis Corporation, when the press learn the truth. But that will simply give me more time to devote to you, my dear Victorine, and your career. It is fortunate that you have an alternative source of income. I have become used to certain standards.'

He smiled blandly at her. 'So, if you will pack your things, we can be leaving.'

She said hoarsely, '*Tu es fou*. You are crazy—or drunk. What nonsense is this?'

'No nonsense, my sweet. Have you forgotten that Kate found us enjoying an illicit afternoon of love together? I think—I really think you should have mentioned to me that she saw us. It explains so much.'

Victorine looked at Kate, her face ugly. 'She is lying,' she said. 'She is trying to make trouble for me.' She turned to Ari, who was standing beside her, his face expressionless. '*Cher*, you do not believe this ridiculous story?'

'You were in our bedroom,' Kate said steadily. 'Mick was asleep, and you were combing your hair. You had a towel on, and nothing else. And you told me to knock in future.'

'No.' Victorine's voice rose. 'None of this is true. You are making it up—to blacken me in Ari's eyes. But it will not work.'

'Are you telling me you have forgotten it all?' Mick asked reproachfully. 'The passion we shared? The promises we made to each other?'

Victorine transferred her glare to him. 'I am saying it did not happen,' she returned shrilly.

'It was the day Mick came back from New York,' Kate continued. An immense calm seemed to have settled on her. 'I was supposed to go to Ithaca, and Mick's father had gone fishing with a friend. But my trip was cancelled, and when I rang home, Yannis told me that Mick was here. So, I came rushing back to the beach house to see him. Only, I found you as well.' For the first time there was a break in her voice.

'A terrible betrayal.' Ari's tone was meditative. 'We have both been deceived, Katharina.' He paused. 'Is this why you went back to England so suddenly, *pedhi mou*?'

'Yes.' Kate bit her lip.

'Without speaking of what you had seen—or demanding an explanation from my son?'

'I couldn't say anything. It was too painful. And there was no reason for anyone else to be hurt,' she added with difficulty. 'Besides, the evidence was there. I know what I saw.'

'So, you decided to spare my feelings at the expense of your own.' Ari nodded thoughtfully. 'That was kind, my child, but unnecessary. I have long known the truth.'

He looked at Mick. 'What happened that afternoon, my son?'

'I wish I knew.' Mick shrugged. 'I returned from New York earlier than planned, but when I arrived Yannis told me Kate had gone out for the day.

He frowned. 'I went down to the house to change. The jet lag had hit me hard, so I tried taking a shower. In the end, I decided to have a brief nap. I remember nothing more.'

He looked at Kate. 'Except that at some point you touched me, and said my name. I suppose you were trying to wake me. And I said "I love you."'

Kate's eyes widened, and her hand went to her throat.

'But when I eventually awoke,' he went on almost conversationally. 'It was to find you had left me—with a note simply stating our marriage was over.'

His mouth twisted. 'I assumed that you were still angry about my refusal to take you to New York—and that other disagreement we'd had.

'But I couldn't believe you'd gone without giving me a chance to put things right between us, and so I got angry too.

'But, of course, I didn't realise you'd discovered my flagrant infidelity,' he added reflectively. 'Little wonder that you did not wish to remain with me.'

'Ari,' Victorine spoke desperately. 'Don't listen to them. This is all nonsense. You heard—their marriage is in deep trouble, and because of that they are trying to destroy our relationship too.'

'What I see,' Ari said, 'Is that something happened that afternoon that was sufficient to put Katharina to flight. To make her wish to end her marriage to my son. And that is serious.

'Or perhaps not,' he added meditatively. 'Maybe it was intended as a joke—only it misfired a little.' He looked at Victorine. 'Is that how it was, *kougla mou*?'

His voice was gentle, but there was a note in it that sent a shiver down Kate's spine.

There was a long taut silence, then Victorine said sullenly, 'A joke, yes. But she was too stupid to realise she was being teased,' she added with a venomous look at Kate.

'I see.' Ari nodded. 'But why did you not explain this good joke as soon as you saw that it had gone wrong? That it had caused real hurt? Because you must have realised this very quickly.'

There was another silence, then Victorine shrugged defensively. 'They were—neither of them here. Michalis was working, and the girl was in London.'

'The girl?' Mick's voice bit. 'You will speak of my wife with respect.'

'What is there to respect?' Victorine spat back at him, her face twisted, ugly with dislike. 'She has nothing—is nothing—that pale-faced English bitch. What has she to offer any man? And you—you could have had me.'

There was another telling silence, then Mick said gently, 'There was never any question of marriage between us, Victorine, and I made that clear to you from the first. If you believed that might change, I am sorry.'

'Sorry.' She threw back her head and laughed harshly, the creamy skin tinged with an unhealthy flush. 'Yes, you have been sorry, Kyrios Theodakis, as you deserve. Because no man ever finishes with me. I am the one who leaves—always. Always—do you hear me?'

'Is that what this was all about?' Mick closed his eyes for a second. 'Dear God, it is unbelievable.'

'And then your wife left you,' Victorine went on gloatingly. 'So you found out what it was like. Oh, that made me happy.' And she laughed again.

'Please.' Kate's voice was barely audible. 'I don't think I can bear any more of this.'

'You do not have to, *pedhi mou*. None of us do.' There was a cold harshness in Ari's voice. He looked at Mick, 'Go with your wife, my son. Make things right between you.'

He paused. 'But first be good enough to ask Iorgos Vasso to come here. There are arrangements to be made. And send Androula also,' he added. 'Victorine will need help with her packing.'

'You are telling me to go?' Victorine's voice cracked.

'*Ne,*' he said. 'As I should have done long ago.' He gave a bitter sigh. 'I was wrong to bring you here, and I knew it. It was an act of stupidity and vindictiveness by a man who had quarrelled with his son.' He looked at Mick. 'You made me feel old, Michalis, and I did not wish that. I wanted my youth back again—my strength. But I have learned my lesson.'

'You can send me away—after all we have been to each other?' Victorine's tone was pleading.

'You are a beautiful woman, Victorine. And I am a rich fool. It is not a very admirable combination. But, let us not waste time in recrimination,' he added more briskly. 'Iorgos will arrange to have you flown anywhere you wish to go.'

She stumbled to her feet. 'Yes,' she said thickly. 'You are a fool—to think that I could ever want you. It was Michalis—always. Can't you see that? I thought if I came here, I could make him want me again.'

'Yes,' Ari said quietly. 'He saw that, but I would not, and we quarrelled again. But now it is all over. And you, *kougla mou*, will have to find another rich fool.'

'But then he brought *her*,' Victorine went on as if he had not spoken. 'And I saw the way he looked at her, and spoke. I knew that he loved her, and I wished to destroy that. I was there when Yannis took her call, so I went down to the beach house and found Michalis asleep.' She gave a throaty giggle. 'It was perfect. All I had to do was undress also—and wait.'

Kate pressed her knuckles against her mouth. 'Oh, God.'

Mick's arm was round her, holding her as she swayed. 'Come, *agapi mou*. You don't need to hear any more. Let us go back to the house.'

'Look after her,' Ari called after them. 'But do not forget that we have guests. I need Katharina to preside at the breakfast table.'

'Then you will be disappointed, Papa,' Michael tossed back at him. 'Do not expect either of us until dinner.'

In the hallway, he said, 'I must find Iorgos, and Androula. Will you wait for me?'

'Yes,' she said. 'I'll wait.'

He framed her face with his hands, looking into her eyes. 'And you won't run away from me again?'

Her lips trembled into a smile. 'Not this time. I'll be on the terrace.'

Outside, the wind was fresh and clean. Kate leaned on the balustrade, looking down at the foam-capped waves through the trees.

He came to stand beside her. 'What are you thinking?'

She said, with a shiver, 'That was—horrible.'

'Perhaps.' He shrugged. 'But also effective.'

'I almost feel sorry for her.'

'Save your compassion, my Kate. She showed no pity for you.'

Kate hesitated. 'Whatever she's done, she *is* very beautiful. Were you ever in love with her?'

'No,' he said quietly. 'I found her amusing at first, but I soon realised that her loveliness was only skin deep. I ended the relationship without regret.'

'How on earth did your father get involved with her?'

'To spite me,' he said wryly. 'You heard what he said, *matia mou*. They met at a party, not by chance, I am sure, and somehow she convinced him that she had ditched me, not the other way around, and that she found younger men boring.'

He grimaced. 'At the time, it was what he wanted to hear. He was very lonely when my mother died, and Linda had become, perhaps, too much part of the household. A companion for Ismene rather than himself.'

He sighed. 'I knew what she was, and tried to warn him. But that was a disaster. He said that I was jealous because she'd found him the better man. I could have dealt with that, but then Victorine started to make him jealous by coming on to me.' He shook his head. 'It was a nightmare.'

She said neutrally, 'So—you needed a wife. An answer to your problem.'

'If you remember,' he said softly. 'I said you would create more problems than you would solve. And how right I was.' He tutted reprovingly. 'Fighting with me. Refusing to be demure and obedient like a good Greek wife.'

'Is that what you wanted?'

'I wanted you, *agapi mou*.' He put his arm round her, as they walked down the steps to the track. 'From that first moment. Did you think it was a coincidence I turned up in London?' He shook his head. 'It was not. I came to find you.'

He gave her a swift, sidelong glance. 'If I am honest, I am not sure I intended marriage, not at first. But long before we made love, I knew that I could not live without you.'

'And yet you went to New York on your own.'

'Yes,' he said. 'And missed you like hell at every moment. Is that what you wanted to hear? That's why I came back early—to tell you that I was all kinds of a fool, and ask you to forgive me. And promise that I would never go anywhere without you again.'

He was silent for a moment. 'I also knew that I had to tell you why I'd been reluctant for us to have a baby. That it wasn't fair to hide my fears from you. Only, I wasn't used to having to explain myself—or to being married.'

'You will have to make allowances for me, *agapi mou*,' he added ruefully.

'When I awoke and found you gone, I felt as if someone had ripped out my heart. I wanted to come after you right away, but I told myself I should give you a chance to cool down—to miss me a little.'

'And instead, I asked for a divorce.'

'That,' he said quietly, 'was the worst day of my life. I kept asking myself how this could have happened? How I could have lost you. And began to come up with answers I did not want.'

'What sort of answers?'

He sighed. 'A friend of mine on Corfu met a girl on holiday,' he said reluctantly. 'The marriage lasted a year, then she went back to England, and took their child. She told him she had never loved him, and never wished to live in Greece. It was only his money she wanted. The divorce settlement.'

Kate gasped. 'And you thought that I—I was the same?' She tried to pull away from him. 'Oh, how could you?'

But he held her firmly. 'When you are hurt and angry, anything seems possible,' he told her levelly. 'And after all, my Kate, you had never once told me you loved me.'

She said breathlessly, 'But you knew how I felt. You must have done.'

'I knew you liked being in bed with me.' His tone was wry. 'But I needed more. I wanted you to speak the words.'

'Well, you didn't say them either,' Kate pointed out. 'Or not until that dreadful afternoon—and even then I thought you'd mistaken me for Victorine.'

'However deeply asleep I was, I would always hear your voice, *agapi mou*. Know your touch, and no other. Every soul in this world could see that I was crazy for you—even Victorine,' he added soberly.

She shivered. 'And she nearly destroyed us. Oh, Mick, happiness is such a fragile thing.'

'Together, we will make it strong.' He lifted her up into his arms and carried her over the threshold of the beach house.

'Our marriage begins again here,' he told her softly. 'I love you so much, my Kate.'

'Yes.' She smiled up at him, her eyes luminous. 'And I love you, Michalis *mou*. Now and for ever.'

'For ever,' he whispered. And kissed her.

HIS FORBIDDEN
BRIDE

CHAPTER ONE

'I'VE been giving matters a lot of thought,' said George. 'And I feel very strongly that you and I should get married.'

Zoe Lambert, who had just taken a mouthful of Chardonnay, managed by a superhuman effort not to choke to death.

If anyone else had made a similarly preposterous suggestion, she would have laughed them to scorn. But she couldn't do that to George, sitting across from her at the table in the wine bar, with his untidy brown hair, and crooked tie.

George was her friend, one of the few she had at Bishop Cross Sixth Form College, where he was a member of the maths department, and after the weekly staff meeting they usually went for a drink together, but they'd never had a date as such. Nor was there the slightest spark of attraction between them. And even if she'd ever been marginally tempted to fall in love with George, the thought of his mother would have stopped her dead in her tracks.

George's mother was a frail widow with a tungsten core, and she took no prisoners in her bid to keep her son safely at home with her, an obedient and enslaved bachelor. None of George's sporadic romantic interests had ever thrived under the frost of her pale blue gaze, and she planned that none of them ever would. And those steely eyes would narrow to slits if she found out that her only son was in the town's one and only wine bar with Zoe Lambert of all people, let alone proposing marriage.

She took a deep breath. 'George,' she said gently. 'I don't think…'

'After all,' George went on, unheedingly, warming to his

5

theme. 'You're going to find things difficult now that you're—alone. You were so brave all the time your mother was—ill. Now I'd like to look after you. I don't want you to worry any more about anything.'

Except your mother poisoning my food, thought Zoe. Urged on, no doubt, by her best friend, my aunt Megan.

She winced inwardly as she recalled her aunt's chilling demeanour at the funeral two weeks earlier. Megan Arnold had curtly accepted the commiserations from her late sister's friends and neighbours, but had barely addressed a word to the niece who was now her only living relative.

Back at the cottage, after the service, she had refused all offers of food and drink, staring instead, in silent and narrow-eyed appraisal, at her surroundings.

'Never mind, dearie,' Mrs Gibb, who'd cleaned the cottage each week for Gina Lambert over the past ten years, whispered consolingly as she went past a mute and bewildered Zoe with a plate of sandwiches. 'Grief takes some people in funny ways.'

But Zoe could see no evidence of grieving in her aunt's stony face. Megan Arnold had stayed aloof during her younger sister's months of illness. And if she was mourning now, she kept it well hidden. And there'd been no sign of her since the funeral either.

Zoe shook away these unpleasant and uneasy reflections, pushed a strand of dark blonde hair back from her face, and looked steadily at her unexpected suitor with clear grey eyes.

'Are you saying that you've fallen in love with me, George?' she asked mildly.

'Well—I'm very fond of you, Zoe.' He played with the stem of his glass, looking embarrassed. 'And I have the most tremendous respect for you. You must know that. But I don't think I'm the type for this head-over-heels stuff,' he added awkwardly. 'And I suspect you aren't either. I really think it's more important for people to be—friends.'

'Yes,' she said. 'I can understand that. And you could

be right.' *But not about me,* she thought. *Oh, please God, not about me.*

She swallowed. 'George, you're terribly kind, and I do appreciate everything you've said, but I'm not going to make any immediate decisions about the future.' She paused. 'Losing my mother is still too raw, and I'm not seeing things altogether clearly yet.'

'Well, I realise that, naturally.' He reached across the table and patted her hand, swiftly and nervously. 'And I won't put any pressure on you, I swear. I'd just like you to—think about what I've said. Will you do that?'

'Yes,' Zoe told him, mentally crossing her fingers. 'Of course I will.'

My first marriage proposal, she thought. How utterly bizarre.

He was silent for a moment. 'If you did think you could marry me at some point,' he said hesitantly, 'I wouldn't want to—rush you into anything, afterwards. I'd be prepared to wait—as long as you wanted.'

Zoe bit her lip as she looked back at the kind, anxious face. 'George,' she said. 'I truly do not deserve you.' And meant it.

It was hard to think about anything else as the local bus jolted its way through the lanes half an hour later, but she knew she had to try. Because George's extraordinary proposal was only one of her current problems. And possibly the least pressing, bless him.

She had come to Astencombe to share her mother's cottage three years ago when she had left university, and not long before Gina Lambert's condition had first been diagnosed. But the property was only rented. It had belonged to Aunt Megan's late husband, Peter Arnold, and he had agreed the original lease with his sister-in-law.

Zoe suspected this had always been a bone of contention with his wife, and, since his death, Aunt Megan had raised the rent slowly and steadily each year, although as a wealthy and childless widow she could not possibly need the money. She had also insisted that maintenance and repairs were the responsibility of her tenant.

Gina, also a widow, had eked out her husband's meagre company pension with her skill as a landscape artist, but it had been a precarious living, and Zoe's salary as an English teacher had been a welcome addition to the household budget. Particularly when the time had come when her mother had no longer been able to paint.

Finding a local job and living at home was not what she'd planned to do originally, of course. At university she'd met Mick, who'd intended, after graduation, to travel round the world for a year, taking what work he could find to earn his living on the way. He'd wanted her to go with him, and she'd been sorely tempted.

In fact, she'd gone home for the weekend to tell her mother what she meant to do, but had arrived to find Gina oddly quiet, and frail-looking. She had stoutly denied there was anything the matter, but Zoe had soon learned through the village grapevine that Aunt Megan had made one of her periodic descents the day before, and, as Adele who lived next door had put it, 'There'd been words.'

Zoe had spent the whole weekend trying to tell her mother about her plans, and failing. Instead, obeying an instinct she barely understood, she had found herself informing Mick that she'd changed her mind about the trip. She'd hoped against hope that he loved her enough not to want to go without her, but she'd been rudely disappointed.

Mick, she realised with shocked hurt, was not about to change his mind—just his choice of travelling companion. And the love she'd blithely thought was hers for ever had proved a very transient affair instead. Within days she'd been comprehensively replaced in his bed and affections.

But it had taught her a valuable lesson about men, she thought wryly, and maybe it was better to be dumped in England than the middle of the Hindu Kush. Since Mick, she'd had no serious involvement with anyone. And now she'd been proposed to by George, who did not love her either. History, it seemed, was repeating itself.

If I'm not careful, I shall get a complex, she told herself.

Looking back, however, she had no regrets about sacrificing her independence. The job and the village might have their limitations, but she was so thankful that she'd been there for her mother through the initial tests, the hospital treatments, and subsequent brief remission. And through her mercifully short final illness. Even at the last Gina's warmth and optimism had not deserted her, and Zoe had many memories to treasure in spite of her sadness.

But the fact remained that she'd reached the end of a chapter in her life. And she didn't see the rest of her life being devoted to Bishops Cross college. She had the contents of the cottage, and a little money to come from her mother's will as soon as it was proved. Maybe this was her chance to move on, and make a new life for herself.

One thing was certain. Aunt Megan would not be sorry to see the back of her.

How could two sisters be so totally unalike? she wondered sadly. True, her aunt was the elder by twelve years, but there had never seemed to be any sibling feeling between them.

'I think Megan liked being an only child,' Gina had explained ruefully when Zoe had questioned her once on the subject. 'And my arrival was a total embarrassment to her.'

'Did she never want a baby of her own?' Zoe asked.

Gina looked past her, her face oddly frozen. 'At one time, perhaps,' she said. 'But it just—didn't happen for her.' She sighed briefly. 'Poor Megan.'

Megan was taller, too, thinner and darker than her younger sister, with a face that seemed permanently set in lines of resentment. There was no glimpse in her of the underlying joy in living that had characterised Gina, underpinning the occasional moments when she'd seemed to withdraw into herself, trapped in some private and painful world. Her 'quiet times' as she'd called them wryly.

Zoe had wondered sometimes what could possibly prompt them. She could only assume it was memories of her father. Maybe their quiet, apparently uneventful marriage had concealed an intense passion that her mother still mourned.

Her aunt was a very different matter. On the face of it Mrs Arnold seemed to have so much to content her. She'd never had to worry about money in her life, and her husband had been a kind, ebullient man, immensely popular in the locality. The attraction of opposites, Zoe had often thought. There could be no other explanation for such an ill-assorted pairing.

In addition, her aunt had a lovely Georgian house, enclosed behind a high brick wall, from which she emerged mainly to preside over most of the organisations in the area, in a one-woman reign of terror. But not even that seemed to have the power to make her happy.

And her dislike of her younger sister seemed to have passed seamlessly to her only niece. Even the fact that Megan Arnold had once taught English herself had failed to provide a common meeting ground. Zoe couldn't pretend to be happy about her aunt's determined hostility, but she'd learned to offer politeness when they met, and expect nothing in return.

She got off the bus at the crossroads, and began to walk down the lane. It was still a warm, windy day, bringing wafts of hedgerow scents, and Zoe gave a brief sigh of satisfaction as she breathed the fragrant air. Public examinations always made this a difficult term at college, and she might unwind by doing a little work in the garden tonight, she thought as she turned the slight corner that led to home. She'd always found weeding and dead-heading therapeutic, so while she worked she could consider the future as well. Review her options.

And stopped dead, her brows snapping together, as she saw that the front garden of the cottage had acquired a new and unexpected addition. A 'For Sale' board, she registered with a kind of helpless disbelief, with the logo of a local estate agency, had been erected just inside the white picket fence.

It must be a mistake, she thought, covering the last few yards at a run. I'll have to call them.

As she reached the gate, Adele appeared in the neighbouring doorway, her youngest child, limpet-like, on her hip.

'Did you know about that?' she inquired, nodding at the sign. And as Zoe speechlessly shook her head she sighed. 'I thought not. When they came this morning, I queried it, but they said they were acting on the owner's instructions.' She jerked her head towards the cottage. 'She's there now, waiting for you. Just opened the door with her own key and marched in.'

'Oh, hell,' Zoe muttered. 'That's all I need.'

She pulled a ferocious face as she lifted the latch and let herself into the cottage.

She found Megan Arnold in the sitting room, standing in front of the empty fireplace, staring fixedly at the picture that hung above the mantelpiece.

Zoe hesitated in the doorway, watching her, puzzled. It was an unusual painting, quite unlike Gina Lambert's usual choice of subject. It seemed to be a Mediterranean scene— a short flight of white marble steps, scattered with the faded petals of some pink flower, flanked on one side by a plain white wall, and leading up to a terrace with a balustrade. And on the edge of the balustrade, against a background of vivid blue sky and azure sea, a large ornamental urn bright with pelargoniums in pink, crimson and white.

What made it all the more curious was that the Lamberts had always taken their holidays at home, usually in Cornwall, or the Yorkshire Dales. As far as Zoe was aware, the Mediterranean was an unknown quantity to her mother. And it was the only time she'd ever attempted such a subject.

Her aunt suddenly seemed to sense Zoe's scrutiny, and turned, her face hard and oddly set.

'So here you are.' Her greeting was abrupt. 'You're very late.'

'There was a staff meeting,' Zoe returned with equal brevity. 'You should have let me know you were coming, Aunt Megan.' She paused. 'Would you like some tea?'

'No, this isn't a social call.' The older woman seated herself in the high-backed armchair beside the empty fireplace.

My mother's chair, Zoe thought with a pang, trying not to feel resentful. It was, after all, her aunt's house, but it was small wonder there'd been friction in the past if she made a habit of walking in whenever the whim took her.

Megan Arnold was dressed as usual in a pleated navy skirt with a matching hand-knitted jacket over a tailored pale blue blouse, and her greying hair was drawn back from her thin face in a severe knot.

'As you can see I've placed the house on the market,' she went on. 'I've instructed the agents to commence showing the property at once, so you'll have to remove all this clutter.' She waved a hand at the books and ornaments that filled the shelves on either side of the fireplace. Then paused. 'I'd be obliged if you'd remove yourself, too, by the end of the month.'

Zoe gasped helplessly. 'Just like that?'

'What did you expect?' Megan Arnold's mouth was a hard line. 'My husband allowed your mother to have this property for *her* lifetime only. The arrangement did not mention you. You surely weren't expecting to stay on here,' she added sharply.

'I wasn't expecting anything,' Zoe said, with equal crispness. 'But I did think I'd be allowed some kind of breathing space.'

'I feel you've had plenty of time.' The other woman was unmoved. 'And in the eyes of the law, you're merely squatting here.' She paused. 'You should have no difficulty in finding a bedsitting room in Bishops Cross itself. Somewhere convenient for your work.'

'A bedsit would hardly be adequate,' Zoe said, keeping tight hold on her control. George must have known about this, she thought with shock. His mother must have told him what her aunt was planning. Or he heard them talking one day at the house. And that's why he asked me to marry him. Because he knew I was going to be virtually homeless almost at once.

She shivered. Oh, George, why didn't you warn me instead of trying to play Sir Galahad? she thought desperately.

She drew a deep, steadying breath. Did her best to speak normally. 'Not all the furniture came with the cottage. Some of it belonged to Mother, and I'll want to take it with me, as well as her books and pictures.'

She saw Megan Arnold's gaze go back to the painting above the mantelpiece, and decided, however belatedly, to try an overture. To heal a breach that had never been of her making. 'Maybe you'd like to have one of them yourself, as a keepsake,' she suggested. 'That one, perhaps.'

Her aunt almost recoiled. 'Wretched daub.' Her voice shook. 'I wouldn't have it in the house.'

Zoe stared at her, appalled at the anger, the bitterness in her tone. She said slowly, 'Aunt Megan—why—why do you hate her so much?'

'What are you talking about? I—hate Gina—the perfect sister?' Her sudden laugh was shrill. 'What nonsense. No one was allowed to hate her. Not ever. Whatever she did, however great the sin, she was loved and forgiven always. By everyone.'

'She's dead, Aunt Megan.' Against her will, Zoe's voice broke. 'If she ever hurt you, I'm sure it wasn't intentional. And, anyway, she can't do so again.'

'You're wrong.' Mrs Arnold lifted her chin coldly. 'She never had the power to affect me in any way. Because I always saw her for what she was. That innocent, butter-wouldn't-melt façade never fooled me for a minute. And how right I was.'

She stopped abruptly. 'But that's all in the past, and the future is what matters. Selling this cottage for a start.' She stood up. 'I suggest you hire a skip for all this rubbish—or take it to a car-boot sale. Whatever you decide, I want it cleared before the first viewers arrive. Starting with this.'

She reached up and lugged the Mediterranean painting off its hook, tossing it contemptuously down onto the rug in front of the hearth. There was an ominous cracking sound.

'The frame,' Zoe whispered. She went down on one knee, almost protectively. 'You've broken it.' She looked up, shaking her head. 'How could you?'

Her aunt shrugged, a touch defensively. 'It was loose anyway. Cheap wood, and poorly made.'

'Whatever.' Zoe was almost choking. 'You had no right—no right to *touch* it.'

'This is my property. I shall do what I wish.' Her aunt reached for her bag. 'And I want the rest removed, and all the holes in the plaster made good,' she added. 'I shall be back at the end of the week to make sure my instructions are being followed. Or I shall arrange a house clearance myself.'

She swept out, and a moment later Zoe, still kneeling on the rug, heard the front door slam.

To be followed almost immediately by the back door opening, and Adele calling to her.

'Jeff's looking after the kids,' she announced as she came in. 'I saw Madam leaving, and came to make sure you're all right.'

Zoe shook her head. 'I feel as if I've been hit by a train,' she admitted. She swallowed. 'God, she was vile. I—I can't believe it.'

'I'll put the kettle on,' said Adele. She paused. 'What happened to the picture?'

'She threw it on the floor. It was completely crazy. I

mean, I don't think it's necessarily the best thing my mother ever did, and it spent most of its life up in the attic until she moved here, but...' She paused, lost for words.

'Well, I've always liked it,' Adele said. 'Greece, isn't it? My sister gets concessionary rates, so we went to Crete last year, and Corfu the year before.'

Zoe shrugged. 'It's somewhere in that region, I guess.' She gave it a doubtful look, then got to her feet, holding the damaged frame carefully, and placed the picture on the sofa. 'Only we've never been there. My father didn't like very hot weather.'

'Well, perhaps she copied a postcard or something that someone sent her,' Adele suggested as she filled the kettle in the kitchen.

'Maybe.' Zoe frowned. 'It was one of those things I always meant to ask about, but never did.'

'So, when are you being evicted?' Adele asked as they sat at the kitchen table, drinking their tea.

'I have to be out by the end of the month,' Zoe admitted. 'And she means it.'

'Hmm.' Adele was thoughtful for a moment. 'Do you think she really is crazy?'

'Not certifiably,' Zoe said wryly. 'Just totally irrational where my mother is concerned.'

'Well, maybe that's not entirely her fault,' Adele said meditatively. 'My gran remembers her as a child, and she said she was a nice-looking kid, and the apple of her parents' eye. Then your sister came along, as an afterthought, and immediately she was the favourite. And ''the pretty one'', too.'

She shrugged. 'That can't have been very nice. And not easy for any kid to handle. So, maybe it's just common or garden jealousy.'

'From Queen of the Castle to the Queen in *Snow White*?' Zoe pondered. 'Well, you could be right, but I have the feeling there's more to it than that.'

'And it won't help that you're the image of your mum

at the same age.' Adele poured more tea into her mug.
'Though they weren't always bad friends—according to
Gran, anyway,' she added thoughtfully. 'There was a time
when they did things together—even went away on holiday. Although even then your aunt behaved more as if she
was her mother than her sister by all accounts.' She pursed
her lips. 'Maybe that's what caused the trouble.'

She paused. 'So what are you going to do? How are you
going to manage, if she's turning you out?'

Zoe grimaced. 'I'm going to have to find a flat—unfur-
nished.'

'Or even a small house. You'll miss the garden.'

'Yes.' Zoe's lip quivered suddenly. 'Among so many
other things.' She forced herself to smile. 'Maybe Aunt
Megan's doing me a favour. I'd just been thinking that my
life could do with a whole new direction. This could be
exactly the impetus I need. I might even move right away
from here.'

'Some place where the wicked Queen can't barge in,
using her own key,' Adele agreed. 'Although I'd miss you.'

'Well, I won't be going immediately.' Zoe wrinkled her
nose. 'My contract stipulates one full term's notice. But I
can be looking—and planning.'

'You don't think some prince on a white horse is going
to gallop up and rescue you?' Adele asked, deadpan.

One already tried, thought Zoe, but he drives a Metro,
and always stays inside the speed limit. And, anyway, I'm
not sure who'd be rescuing whom...

'Not in Bishops Cross,' she returned, also straight-faced.
'White horses can't cope with the one-way traffic system.'

She finished her tea, and put the mug in the sink. 'I'd
better arrange to have my mother's things taken out and
stored in the short term,' she mused aloud. 'Aunt Megan
mentioned a skip,' she added with a touch of grimness.
'And I'd put nothing past her.'

'Not after that picture,' said Adele. 'Pity about that. Nice
and bright, I always thought.'

'It's not terminally damaged—just needs a new frame. I'll take it in with me tomorrow.'

'It'll be awkward on the bus. And there's a framing shop a couple of doors from where Jeff works. Why don't I ask him to drop it off for you on his way to work? Then you can pop round in your lunch break and choose another frame. Just tie a bit of paper and string round it, and I'll take it with me now.'

'Oh, Adele, that would be kind.'

Adele had always been a good neighbour, Zoe reflected as she hunted for the string. And, after Aunt Megan, her cheerful practicality was balm to the spirit.

'She's made a real mess of it,' Adele commented grimly as Zoe went back into the sitting room. 'Even the backing's torn away.' She tried to smooth it back into place, and paused. 'Just a minute. There's something down inside it. Look.' She delved into the back of the picture, and came up with a bulky and clearly elderly manilla envelope.

She handed it to Zoe who stood, weighing it in her hands, staring down at it with an odd feeling of unease.

'Well, aren't you going to open it?' Adele prompted after a moment. She laughed. 'If it was me, I couldn't wait.'

'Yes,' Zoe said, slowly. 'I—I suppose so. But the fact is, it has been waiting—for a pretty long time, by the look of it. And, as my mother must have put it there, I'm wondering why she didn't tell me about it—if she wanted me to find it, that is.'

Adele shrugged. 'I expect she forgot about it.'

'How could she? It's been hanging there over the mantelpiece ever since she moved here—a constant reminder.' Zoe shook her head. 'It's something she wanted to keep secret, Adele, when I didn't think we had any secrets between us.' She tried to smile. 'And that's come as a bit of a shock.'

Adele patted her on the shoulder. 'It's been quite a day for them. Why don't I leave you in peace while you decide what to do? You can bring the picture round later on, if you still want it re-framing.'

Left to herself, Zoe sank down on the sofa. There was no message on the envelope, she realised. No 'For my daughter' or 'To be opened in the event of my death'.

This was something that had remained hidden and private in Gina Lambert's life. And if Aunt Megan hadn't totally lost it, and thrown the picture on the floor, it would probably have stayed that way.

Maybe that was how it should be left. Maybe she should respect her mother's tacit wish, and put it in the bin unopened.

Yet if I do that, Zoe thought, I shall always wonder...

With sudden resolution, she tore open the envelope and extracted the contents. There was quite an assortment, ranging from a bulky legal-looking document to some photographs.

She unfolded the document first, her brows snapping together as she realised it was written in a foreign language. Greek, she thought in bewilderment as she studied the unfamiliar alphabet. It's in Greek, of all things. Why on earth would Mother have such a thing?

She put it down, and began to examine the photographs. Most of them seemed to be local scenes—a village street lined with white houses—a market, its stalls groaning with fruit—an old woman in black, leading a donkey laden with firewood.

One, however, was completely different. A garden guarded by tall cypresses, and a man, casually dressed in shorts and a shirt, standing beneath one of the trees. His face was in shadow, but some instinct told her that he was not English, and that he was looking back at whoever was holding the camera, and smiling.

And she knew, without question, that he was smiling at her mother.

She turned her head and studied the framed photograph of her father that occupied pride of place on the side table beside her mother's chair. But she knew already that the shadow man was not John Lambert. The shape was all wrong, she thought. He'd been taller, for one thing, and thinner, and the man in the snapshot seemed, in some strange way and even at this distance in time and place, to exude a kind of raw energy that her father had not possessed.

Zoe swallowed. I don't understand any of this, she thought. And I'm not sure I want to.

She felt very much as if she'd opened Pandora's box, and was not convinced that Hope would be waiting for her at the end.

She turned the snapshot over, hoping to find some clue— a name, perhaps, scribbled on the back. But there was nothing. Slowly and carefully, she put it aside with the rest, and turned to the other papers.

There were several thin sheets stapled together, and when she unfolded them she realised, with sudden excitement, that this must be a translation of the Greek legal document that had so puzzled her.

She read them through eagerly, then paused, and went back to the beginning again, her brain whirling. Because the stilted, formal language was telling her that this was a deed of gift, assigning to her mother the Villa Danae, near a place called Livassi, on the island of Thania.

Zoe felt stunned, not merely by the discovery, but by its implications.

This was a gift that Gina Lambert had never mentioned, and certainly never used. And that she'd clearly not wanted known. That she'd hidden in the back of a picture, which itself suddenly assumed a whole new significance.

Was it the recapturing of a cherished, but secret memory? Certainly that was how it seemed, particularly when she recalled how it had never been on show during John Lambert's lifetime.

She read the translation through a third time. The name of the gift's donor was not mentioned, she noticed, although she guessed it would be in the original. And there were no restrictions on the villa's ownership either. It was Gina's to pass on to her heirs, or sell, as she wished.

Yet there was nothing in the few remaining papers, consisting of a few tourist leaflets, a bill from a Hotel Stavros, and a ferry ticket, to indicate that she'd disposed of the Villa Danae.

And she left me everything, thought Zoe, swallowing. So, unlikely as it seems, I now own a villa in Greece.

She realised she was shaking uncontrollably, her heart thudding like a trip-hammer. She made herself stand and walk over to the cupboard where her mother's precious bottle of Napoleon brandy still resided, and poured herself a generous measure. Emergency tactics, she told herself.

When she was calmer, she fetched the atlas, and looked to see where Thania was. It was a small island in the Ionian sea, and Livassi seemed to be its capital, and only large town.

Not very revealing, Zoe thought, wrinkling her nose.

But Adele's sister works in a travel agency, she reminded herself. She'd be able to tell me all about it—and how to get there.

Because she had to go to Thania, there was no question about that. She had to see the Villa Danae for herself—if it was still standing. After all, it had belonged to an absentee owner for a long time, and might be in a state of real neglect and disrepair. But I have to know, she thought, taking another swift swig of her brandy as her pulses began to gallop again. And I have some money saved, and the whole summer vacation in front of me. There'll never be a better opportunity.

She wouldn't keep the house, of course. If it was habitable, she'd put it on the market. If it was falling down, she would just have to walk away—as her mother, apparently, had done before her.

But I'm not just going to see the villa, she thought. I want to find the answers to some questions as well. I need the truth, however painful, before I move on—start my new life.

She picked up the photo of the shadow man, and stood, staring down at him, wondering, and a little scared at the same time. Asking herself who he could be, and what his part in this mystery might be.

She sighed abruptly, and hid him back in the envelope with the rest of the paperwork.

I'll find you, too, she thought. Somewhere. Somehow. And whatever the cost.

And tried to ignore the involuntary little shiver of misgiving that tingled down her spine.

CHAPTER TWO

THE rail of the boat was hot under Zoe's bare arm. Ahead of her, the craggy outline of Thania rose from the shimmer of the sea.

Even now, with her target in sight, Zoe could still hardly believe she was doing this. The tension inside her was like a knot, endlessly being pulled more tightly.

She had told no one the real purpose of her visit to the island, not even Adele. She'd pretended that the envelope had merely contained souvenirs of what had been, clearly, a holiday her mother had once enjoyed, but memorable to no one but herself, and consequently not worth mentioning.

'I need a break, so why don't I try and discover what she found so entrancing?' she'd laughed.

'Well, don't be too entranced,' Adele warned. 'And don't let any local Adonis chat you on board his boat,' she added severely. 'We don't want you doing a Shirley Valentine. You have to come back.'

I'm my mother's daughter, Zoe thought wryly. And she came back, whatever the incentive to stay.

Aloud, she said lightly, 'No danger.'

She'd told the same story of her mother's favourite island to Adele's sister Vanessa when she made the booking at the travel agency. Notwithstanding, Vanessa had tried hard to talk her into going somewhere larger and livelier.

'Thania's never been a typical tourist resort,' she'd protested. 'A number of rich Athenians have homes there, and they like to keep the hordes at bay. The hotels are small, and the beaches are mostly private. It's all low-key and the nightlife barely exists. The ferry runs just twice a day from Kefalonia.'

She brightened. 'Why don't you stay on Kefalonia instead? See all the places where they filmed *Captain Corelli's Mandolin*. There's plenty to do there, and you could always go on a day trip to Thania if you really want to see it.'

Zoe shook her head, keeping her face solemn. 'Nicholas Cage went back to America a long time ago, so I think I'll pass on Kefalonia this time around. Besides, somewhere small and peaceful is exactly what I want.' She paused, then tried to sound casual. 'I believe there's a Hotel Stavros in Livassi. Maybe you could book me in there.'

Vanessa stabbed frowningly at her computer keys, then nodded with a touch of resignation. 'Argonaut Holidays go there, one of the few companies that do, and they have vacancies, surprise, surprise.' She stabbed again. 'Bath, balcony, sea view?'

Terrace, thought Zoe, with steps leading up to it, and the sea beyond…

She smiled. 'Ideal.'

She'd met with downright disapproval from George, who was still plainly disappointed that she'd gently but firmly turned down his proposal. 'But you never go abroad on holiday.' He sounded injured.

'No, George,' she said, still gently but firmly. 'I never have in the past, that's all.'

'But if you'd mentioned it sooner, we could have gone somewhere together,' he protested. 'My mother did a tour a couple of years back—"The Treasures of Italy". She enjoyed it, and the hotels were of a high standard. We could have done the same thing.' He paused awkwardly. 'I understand Greek plumbing is—rather eccentric.'

'I know,' she said. 'They told me all about it at the travel agency, and it's not a problem.' She gave him a steady look. 'Besides, George, your mother would never have let you go on holiday with me—even if we'd been married.'

He flushed uncomfortably. 'You're wrong, Zoe. She's

always telling people how happy she'd be to have me off her hands—to have grandchildren.'

Certainly, thought Zoe, if it could be done by divine intervention, without having an all too human daughter-in-law in the equation.

'So where exactly are you going?' he asked.

Zoe shrugged, trying not to look shifty. 'I thought I'd do some island hopping—never too long in one place. See what appeals,' she told him airily.

She hated fibbing to George, but she knew his mother would have her destination out of him before his supper was on the table, and Aunt Megan would be next in line for the information. And, given her aunt's extreme reaction to the picture, this would be bad news.

What a pity, she thought, that I can't go to her. Ask her about it. Because she must know. I'm sure of that.

She hadn't seen Mrs Arnold since that day, not even when she'd taken the cottage keys round to the house and dropped them through the letterbox. Her aunt had probably been at home, but there had seemed little point in another confrontation, whatever its purpose.

And she'd been frantically busy. In addition to the usual end of term workload, she'd managed to find herself temporary accommodation in a top-floor flat in an old Victorian house within walking distance of the college. It was furnished and the rent was reasonable, enabling her to put her mother's cherished pieces in store for the future.

Which was something else she hadn't mentioned to George—the fact that she'd given in her notice at the college and would be leaving at Christmas. Finding another job in a different area. A challenge that awaited her when she got back from Greece.

'Ah, well, "sufficient unto the day",' she told herself silently.

She took a bottle of water from her shoulder bag, and drank thirstily. As she replaced the bottle she heard the crackle of paper, reminding her of the purpose of her visit.

She'd brought the Greek deed of gift, together with the translation, and the photographs. But she had no intention of barging in and making a claim straight away.

First, she told herself, I need to find out how the land lies. For all I know, the villa's original owner may have had second thoughts and revoked the gift years ago.

So I'll find the house, and see who's living there now. And if it's obvious that giving it away was just a temporary aberration on someone's part a long time ago, then I'll just enjoy my holiday, and no harm done.

After all, it is a little bit too much like a fairy tale.

The Villa Danae, she thought. She'd checked in a book of Greek myths and discovered that Danae had been one of the many loved by Zeus, who had visited her in a stream of golden light. She'd subsequently given birth to Perseus and been set adrift on the ocean with her baby in a locked chest, but they'd both survived and Perseus had gone on to cut off the head of the Gorgon Medusa, and win the hand of Andromeda.

This is my own quest, she thought. My private odyssey. And decapitation will probably not be involved.

The harbour at Thania was only small, and occupied mainly by caiques rather than expensive yachts. The town itself was built on the side of a steep hill, with serried ranks of red-roofed houses looking as if they might tumble forward into the sea. On the quayside ahead, Zoe could see the striped awnings of tavernas, and among them a larger building, three storeys high, its white paint gleaming in the sunlight, which she knew from the picture in the Argonaut brochure was the Hotel Stavros.

It was mid-afternoon, by this time, and the heat was intense. Zoe had dressed for coolness in white cut-off trousers, and a sleeveless navy top, knotted at the midriff. She'd covered her exposed skin in high-factor sunblock, and braided her hair into one thick plait, cramming over it a wide-brimmed linen hat.

Ready for anything, she thought, briskly swinging up her travel bag as the ferry moved into its allotted place on the dock. There were few other passengers, and those, she guessed, were locals rather than tourists.

Zoe was aware she was being surveyed with friendly interest, and as she went ashore, treading gingerly down the rickety gangplank, the captain gave her a gap-toothed smile and a hoarse grunt of appreciation.

No point trying to hide herself in the crowd, then, she decided, amused.

She made straight for the hotel, climbing two steps to the terrace with its tables and chairs, and tubs planted cheerfully with pelargoniums. Inside the double glass doors, the tiled reception area was apparently deserted, but Zoe was glad to stand and catch her breath for a moment, in its air-conditioned coolness.

And, as if on cue, the fringed curtain at the rear of the desk stirred, and a girl, plump, red-haired and smiling, emerged to meet her.

'Hi,' she greeted Zoe casually. 'You must be Miss Lambert. I'm Sherry.'

'And you're British.' Zoe shook hands with her, smiling back. 'I didn't expect that.'

'And I didn't expect to meet and marry a Greek hotel owner two years ago,' the other girl admitted candidly. 'So, it's a bit of a novelty for me, too.' She handed Zoe a registration card and a pen.

'I'll show you your room,' she went on, taking down a key from a rack on the wall behind her. 'Leave your bag, and Stavros will bring it up in a minute.'

'The Stavros for whom the hotel was named?' Zoe asked, trying to do mental sums about his possible age.

Sherry shook her head, leading the way up a marble staircase. 'That was his uncle—a real character. Great eye for the ladies even now. Never married because he thought it would cramp his style,' she added with a rich chuckle. 'My Stavros took over the hotel when he decided to retire a few years ago. Now he sits under the trees in the square, playing lethal games of backgammon.'

'Sounds a marvellous life,' Zoe said, committing all this information to memory.

'Here we are.' Sherry threw open a door, allowing Zoe to precede her into a cool, shadowy room, its shutters closed against the glare of the sun. Sherry pulled back the thin drapes and unlatched the shutters, revealing spotless cream walls to match the tiled floor. There was a cupboard built into one wall with a hanging rail, and a modest chest of drawers beside the low bed, with its crisp, snowy linen, and terracotta coverlet folded back across the foot.

'It's lovely,' Zoe said with total sincerity.

'If you need a blanket, which I doubt, just ask.' Sherry opened another door. 'And this is your shower room. It's pretty basic—you sit on that little wooden bench to wash, and all the water goes down that drain in the middle, as you see—but you can generally have a warm shower when you want one.' She paused. 'I'll leave you to look round. Can I get you a drink—a cold beer, maybe—or some lemon tea?'

'Tea would be wonderful,' Zoe accepted gratefully. Left to herself, she stepped out onto the balcony, finding to her pleasure that her room overlooked the harbour.

She could quite see why her mother had loved it here, no matter what might or might not have befallen her.

A tap on the door, signalling the arrival of her luggage, brought her back into the room.

Stavros was dark and swarthy, with a quiet, courteous manner. 'My wife wishes to know if you would like your tea in your room, *kyria*, or downstairs in our courtyard?'

'Oh, downstairs, I think. I only need a few minutes to unpack.'

The courtyard was at the rear of the hotel, shaded by a massive vine. Zoe sat at a corner, sipping her tea and considering her immediate options. At some point she would have to seek out Uncle Stavros of the roving eye, she thought, and see if, by some remote chance, he remembered her mother. Any information she could glean would be welcome, she acknowledged with a faint sigh.

A large hairy dog, resembling a moving hearthrug, came sauntering out of the hotel and ambled up to her, panting amiably, and clearly waiting to have his head scratched and his floppy ears gently pulled.

'You're a good boy,' Zoe told him softly as she complied. She would have a dog, she thought, when she found a place of her own to live. Her mother had wanted one at the cottage, but Aunt Megan had instantly vetoed the idea.

'Don't let Archimedes be a nuisance,' Sherry warned when she came to collect the tray.

'Why on earth did you call him that?' Zoe asked, intrigued.

'Because he once climbed in the bath with Stavros and nearly flooded the place.' Sherry stroked the untidy head. 'He's now barred for life from all bathrooms.'

'While we're on the subject of water,' Zoe said, laughing, 'where's the best place to swim from?'

Sherry considered. 'There's the town beach,' she said. 'Turn left out of the hotel, and keep walking. It's not bad, but it can get pretty crowded. There are some good beaches on the other side of the island, but you can only reach them by boat, and Stavros sometimes gets up a trip for guests if enough are interested.

'Apart from that...' She pulled a face, and took a swift look round. 'Not all the villa owners are here the whole time, and we occasionally take advantage of that, and use their beaches when they're away. What the eye don't see,' she added cheerfully. 'But don't tell Stavros I said so, because he gets twitchy.'

She lowered her voice confidentially. 'As a matter of fact, one villa overlooks a really pretty cove, but it's not used because the place has never been lived in. I go down there sometimes, although Stavros isn't very happy about it. He has a real thing about privacy, and upsetting the owners.'

Zoe swallowed. 'But if it's not used, it sounds ideal,' she said huskily. 'Maybe you could give me directions.' She paused. 'Does it have a name—this house?'

'Mmm.' Sherry nodded as she prepared to depart. 'The Villa Danae. You could walk there,' she added over her shoulder.

I not only could, Zoe thought exultantly, when she was alone. I will. Tomorrow.

Half-buried in long grass, the small wooden board was shaped like an arrow and pointed down a narrow dusty track. The faded words 'Villa Danae' were only just legible, as Sherry had quietly warned her as Zoe had eaten her breakfast of warm rolls, flower-scented honey, and thick, creamy yoghurt.

Now she paused, hitching the cream canvas bag that held her towel, sun lotion and paperback novel into a more comfortable position on her shoulder.

Even though she'd been waiting for this moment, she was sorely tempted to walk on. To let the past rest in peace. To go with the flow, and let herself be absorbed effortlessly into Thania's languorous charm. To simply have a much-needed vacation.

But that would not quell the wondering, she told herself. And when she got back, and saw Gina's picture newly framed and hanging in her bedroom, she might kick herself for wasting a golden opportunity.

She turned with renewed determination, and plunged down the rutted track. It led down through a grove of olive trees, and, although it was still comparatively early in the day, she was grateful for their silvery shade. The air was very still, and the cloudless sky had a faintly misty look that promised soaring temperatures to come.

She was wearing a thin, floating sundress, sleeveless and

scoop-necked, in gentian-blue, over a matching bikini, and her hair was piled up in a loose knot on top of her head.

She rounded a steep bend in the track, and saw, beyond the shelter of the olive grove, the more vivid green of grass and colourful splashes of flowers. Not the desolate wilderness she'd half expected. And a little further on, set like a jewel in the encircling garden, was the house, all immaculate white walls and terracotta roof.

Zoe paused, her hand tightening unconsciously round the strap of her bag. Immediately in front of her was the turquoise gleam of a swimming pool, from which a flight of broad, shallow steps led up to sliding glass doors. Behind these was a low, pillared room like an atrium, cool with marble and towering green plants, and furnished with comfortable white chairs and loungers.

Trying not to feel too much like an intruder, Zoe skirted the pool, climbed the steps and tried the doors, but they were securely locked.

It's like looking into a showcase, she thought as she walked on. You can admire, but not touch.

And halted abruptly, her heart jolting as she reached the foot of another flight of steps, so immediately familiar she could have climbed them in her sleep. Pale steps, she recognised breathlessly, dusty with the faded blossoms of the bougainvillea that cascaded down the side of the house. Steps that led up to a terrace, its balustrade supporting a large stone urn, heavy with clustering flowers. As she'd known there would be. And beyond that the dreamy azure of the sea.

She steadied herself, then, quietly and cautiously, she climbed up to the terrace. She found herself standing on a broad sweep of creamy marble that ran the entire length of the house. Stone troughs massed with more flowers marked the length of the waist-high balustrade, while below it, from a gated opening, another curved flight of steps led down through cypress trees standing like sentries to a perfect horseshoe of pale sand, and the vivid blue ripple of the sea.

Behind her, shuttered glass doors masked the ground floor rooms completely. But what had she expected? The place laid open for her inspection, and a welcome mat waiting?

I should have gone to see a lawyer, she told herself restively, walking along the terrace. Had the whole legal situation checked out. Approaches made.

She found the main entrance round the corner, a solid wooden door, heavily carved, and growing beside it, in festoons of blooms that softened the dark wood and white walls, an exquisite climbing rose, its petals shading from creamy yellow to deep gold.

Zoe found herself thinking of the shower of radiance in which Zeus had come to Danae in the legend, then told herself she was being fanciful. Whoever had planted the garden had simply loved roses, that was all. The troughs and urns along the terrace had been fragrant with them, and she could see even more in the beds that bordered the lawn. And sexual predators in Greek mythology had nothing to do with it.

Without knowing why, she stretched out a hand and touched one of the heavy golden heads, almost as if it were a lucky charm. Then she reached for the heavy iron door handle and tried it.

To her amazement, it yielded, and the door opened silently on well-oiled hinges. The Villa Danae was welcoming her, after all.

She stepped inside and closed the door behind her, standing for a moment, listening intently for a footfall, a door closing, a cough. The sound of a human presence to explain the unlocked door. But there was nothing.

She found herself in a wide hall, confronted by a sweep of staircase leading up to a galleried landing. On one side of it was the glass wall of the atrium. On the other were more conventional doors leading to a long living room, where chairs and sofas were grouped round an empty fireplace. A deep alcove at the far end of the room contained a dining table and chairs.

Everything was in pristine condition. No one had ever lounged on those cushions, she thought, or lit a fire in that hearth, or eaten a meal at the table.

On the atrium side, she found a tiled and fully fitted kitchen, with a walk-in food store, and a laundry room leading off it, all of them bare as if they'd been somehow frozen in time, and were waiting for the spell to be broken.

Taking a deep breath, Zoe went upstairs, annoyed to find she was tiptoeing.

The first room she came to was the master bedroom, dim and cool behind its shutters. She trod across the floor, unlatched the heavy wooden slats and pulled them open, then turned, catching her breath.

It was a vast and luxurious room, with apricot walls and an ivory tiled floor. The silk bed covering was ivory, too, as were the voile drapes that hung at the windows.

There was a bathroom with a screened-off shower cubicle, and a sunken bath with taps like smiling dolphins, and a dressing room as well. There were toiletries on the tiled surfaces, and fluffy towels on the rails. Everything in its place—an enchanted palace waiting for its princess. But for how long?

Zoe walked slowly back to the window, and slid it open with care, then stepped out onto the balcony, lifting her face to the slight breeze. Before her were the misty shapes of other islands rising out of the unruffled blue of the Ionian sea.

More roses here, too, she saw, spilling over the balcony rail from their pottery tubs in a cascade of cream and gold. Their scent reached her softly, and she breathed it in, feeling herself become part of the enchantment.

She thought, Can this really be mine?

And in the same heartbeat, realised she was not alone after all. That there was someone below her on the terrace.

She froze, then peered with infinite caution over the balcony rail.

A man, she registered, with his back to her, moving unhurriedly along the terrace, removing the dead heads from the blossoms in the stone troughs.

The gardener, she thought with relief. Only the gardener. One of the support team employed to keep Villa Danae in this immaculate condition.

He was tall, with a mane of curling black hair that gleamed like silk in the sunlight, his skin like burnished bronze against the brief pair of elderly white shorts that were all he was wearing. She saw broad shoulders, and a muscular back, narrowing to lean hips, and long, sinewy legs.

The kind of Adonis, she thought, with a faint catch of the breath, that Adele had warned her about.

Of course, she could only see his back view, so he might well have a squint, a crooked nose, and dribble. But somehow she didn't think so.

And anyway, his looks were not her concern. What she needed to do was get out of here before he looked up and saw her.

With infinite caution, she backed away into the room. She dragged at the windows, tugging them together. They came with a whisper, but, to Zoe's overwrought imagination, it seemed like a rumble of thunder in the stillness of the morning. She waited for a shout from below. The sound of an alarm being given, but there was nothing, and, biting her lip, she closed the shutters, too. So far, so good, she thought with a tiny sigh of relief.

His work seemed to be taking him to the far end of the terrace, away from the main door, so if she was quick she could be out of the villa and back into the shelter of the olive grove before she ran any real risk of discovery.

And she would content herself with just this one visit, she promised herself silently as she let herself out of the bedroom and closed the door quietly behind her. After all, she had seen everything she needed to see.

From now on she would stick firmly to the town beach, and let her lawyer investigate whether or not the Villa Danae was her inheritance.

Well, she thought, smiling. I can dream, I suppose.

She had taken three steps down the stairs before she realised she was not alone. And just who was standing at the bottom of the flight, leaning casually on the polished rail, watching her—waiting for her, a faint grim smile playing round his mouth.

She checked with a gasp, turned to stone at the sight of him. Her instinct was to turn and run back the way she'd come, but common sense prevented her. This staircase was the only way out, and the last thing she wanted was to find herself trapped in a bedroom with this half-naked stranger in pursuit.

She was frightened, but at the same time—incredibly— her senses were registering other things. Telling her that the man confronting her with such cool arrogance was as seriously attractive as her instinct had suggested. Not conventionally handsome, maybe. His high-bridged nose was too thin, and his mouth and chin too hard for that. And his eyes were darkness. Meeting his gaze was like staring into impenetrable night, she thought, tension tautening her throat.

But, at the same time, she knew instinctively that there wasn't a woman in the world who would take one glance and not want to look again—and again. Because he was totally and compellingly male.

He said quietly, '*Kalimera.*'

Maybe, she thought breathlessly. Maybe there was a way she could bluff her way out of this.

She spread her hands. Tried an apologetic laugh. 'I'm sorry—I don't understand. I don't speak Greek.'

He shrugged. 'Then we will speak in English. It's not a

problem,' he added drily as her face fell. 'Tell me what you are doing here.'

She said swiftly, 'I'm not a thief.'

'No,' he agreed thoughtfully. 'Because there is nothing here that you could conveniently steal.' The dark glance swept her, assessing the flimsy blue dress, the canvas beach bag. 'Or hide,' he added.

He looked her over again, more searchingly. 'So, I ask again—what is your reason for being here?'

'Someone mentioned there was a house for sale round here,' Zoe improvised swiftly. 'I thought it might be this one, as it's obviously empty.'

'No,' he said. 'It is not this house.' He paused, his gaze steady and ironic. 'And no one would have told you that it was.' His voice was low-pitched but crisp.

'You don't think the owner might have put it on the market and not told you?' she parried.

'No,' he said. 'That would not happen either.'

'Well, it's still a fabulous house.' Zoe lifted her chin. 'Maybe the owner would be prepared to rent it out.'

His brows rose. 'You have nowhere to stay?'

'Yes,' she said. 'Of course I have. But this is such a lovely island. Perhaps I could come back—stay longer.'

'You arrived—when?' His mouth twisted. 'Yesterday?'

'It doesn't take long,' she said. 'To find something—beautiful. And decide you want more.'

The dark eyes looked her up and down again with mockery in their depths—and something infinitely more disturbing. 'Well, we agree on something at least,' he drawled, and laughed as the sudden colour drenched her skin.

She was suddenly stingingly aware of all that tanned bare skin, so negligently displayed, and also how little she herself was wearing. And how this had not escaped him for a minute.

She wished with all her heart that she were sitting at her table under the vine leaves, finishing breakfast, and contemplating nothing more risky than a day on the town beach.

Because she was in danger. Every nerve in her body was telling her so.

Just let me get out of here, relatively unscathed, she prayed silently and wildly.

'Now let me tell you how I see the situation,' he went on, almost casually. 'I think you are staying at the Hotel Stavros. That Stavros' wife has told you the cove that belongs to the house is good to bathe from, and that she comes here herself—not often but enough, and thinks that no one knows. And that once here, because you are a woman, you could not control your curiosity. So, you found an open door, and came in.'

She hated herself for blushing. Hated him more for having made her do it. She said coldly, 'You're right, up to a point. But I was intrigued to hear the house was empty, because I might actually be interested in—acquiring it.'

'And I have told you,' he said. 'It is not for sale.'

'Really?' She shrugged a shoulder. 'Well, that's not something I choose to discuss with the hired help.' She paused to allow that to sink in, and was annoyed to see his smile widen. 'Is the owner on Thania at present?'

'No,' he said. 'Athens.'

She wanted to say, That's what you think, and wave the deed of gift in his face, yet caution prevailed.

But, there will come a time, she promised herself. And anticipation will make it all the sweeter. Because the first Greek phrase I shall learn is 'You're fired'.

She allowed herself a slight frown. Regaining lost ground, she told herself. Deliberately establishing a formal distance between them. Someone with business to transact dealing with a minor member of staff. That was how to handle things.

'That's a pity,' she said. 'But I suppose there's someone on the island who can tell me how I could contact him.'

'Why, yes, *thespinis*. You could always ask me.' His face was solemn, but his voice quivered with amusement, leaving her with the uneasy feeling that he knew exactly what she was doing.

She lifted her chin. 'I hardly think I should approach him through his gardener,' she said sharply.

'But I am not merely the gardener,' he said, softly. 'I take care of a great many things for him. But if you wish to speak to him directly, he will soon be here on Thania. Within a week, I believe.'

'And staying here?'

'No,' he said, after a pause. 'He never stays here. He has a villa of his own quite near.'

'That's such a shame,' Zoe said, and meant it. 'It's a wonderful house, but it's bound to deteriorate if it isn't lived in—and loved.'

'You are wrong, *thespinis*,' he said. 'One thing this house has never lacked is love. It was built into every wall—every beam—every stone. Love is the reason it exists.'

She was shaken by the sudden passion in his voice—and by the odd raw note of anger, too.

She said, with a touch of uncertainty, 'I'll wait, then— and speak to him. When he arrives.' She paused. 'And now I'd better go.'

'And where will you go?' That strange, harsh moment had passed and he was smiling again, the dark eyes speculative as they studied her. 'Down to the cove as you intended?'

Zoe bit her lip. 'No—that was a bad idea, and I'm sorry.'

'Why?' he said. 'The sea is warm, and the sand inviting. And you will not be disturbed.'

She was already disturbed, she thought. Stirred in every fibre of her being, and it was not a sensation she relished, or even wished to admit.

Turned on by a good-looking Greek, she derided herself. How shameful—and how pathetic.

She shrugged, attempted a smile of her own. 'All the same...'

'You like his house,' he said. 'I am sure my employer would wish you also to enjoy his beach. There is a way down from the terrace. I will show you.'

'I really don't think…'

'Is that why you came to Thania—to think?' He straightened in a leisurely manner, moving back a little. Offering her, she realised, free passage past him. 'Then stop thinking, *thespinis*. Learn to relax. Begin—to feel.'

'Perhaps, then,' she said. Adding primly, 'But I don't want to take you away from your work.'

'You will not,' he said. 'But my work, alas, will take me away from you. So, you see,' he added gently, 'there is nothing to fear.'

Zoe stiffened. 'I'm not in the least afraid,' she told him curtly. 'I can't believe your employer lists harassing tourists among your duties.'

'Ah.' He sent her a glance that glinted with amusement. 'But I am not always on duty.' There was a tingling pause, then he turned, and walked to the main door. 'Make your decision, *thespinis*,' he added briskly. 'I am waiting to lock up.'

Biting her lip, she followed him out of the house, and round the terrace to the gate she'd noticed earlier, which he courteously unlatched for her.

'I suggest you come back this way,' he said. 'The track that Stavros' wife uses is rather too steep.'

'Thank you,' Zoe said coldly.

'*Parakalo.*' He grinned at her. 'It has been my pleasure.'

As she descended the steps she was conscious of his gaze following her. Knew the exact moment he turned away, as if a wire joining them had suddenly snapped.

A few minutes later, she heard the sound of a Jeep starting up, and driving away.

Alone at last, she thought. And was shocked to discover her relief tinged by something very like regret.

CHAPTER THREE

I'M MAKING altogether too much of this, Zoe told herself determinedly. He's gone. And it's time I pulled myself together, and forgot about him.

She'd had a wonderful swim, and now, having applied sun lotion to every exposed portion of her skin, she was stretched out on her towel with her book. But she could not concentrate on the printed words. They seemed to dance away out of reach, leaving her to focus almost helplessly on a dark face, with eyes that smiled, looking up at her from the foot of a marble staircase.

In a way it was understandable that he should be imprinted so firmly on her mind. After all, he'd caught her in the act of having a humiliating snoop on private property. He could have handed her over to the police, or even exacted a very different form of retribution, she thought, swallowing.

But she had to put all that behind her now, and plan her next move instead.

I'm here for a purpose, she told herself strongly. And I'm certainly not a lonely heart tourist looking for a holiday romance with some Greek version of Casanova.

Or even a mild flirtation, she made the hasty addendum. Although, to someone like him, it would probably be as natural as breathing. See a woman. Chat her up. Tell her that she's beautiful and desirable. Make her day.

Well, it hasn't made my day, she thought, broodingly.

She sat up, rummaging in her bag for her bottle of water. There wasn't a great deal left, she realised with a frown. She would have to ration herself.

She tossed her book aside, and turned onto her front,

undoing the clasp of her bikini top. A little serious sun-bathing, she decided, and then she would go back to the hotel, and sit in the shade with a cold drink.

She pillowed her head on her folded arms, and closed her eyes. The murmur of the sea seemed to fill her head, soothing away the doubts and alarms of the day.

It's just so perfect here, she thought drowsily as everything slid away. It seemed that she was standing in front of Gina's picture, stepping into it like Alice, and entering its world. Retracing her steps in slow motion through every room. Taking a dream-like possession.

She did not fall deeply asleep. She was aware of sand under her fingers, the texture of the towel beneath her bare breasts, and the strength of the sun on her back, like the caress of warm hands. She sighed a little, wriggling her shoulders slowly and pleasurably, then let herself drift again.

Until she found herself once more at the top of the stairs—looking down. Meeting his gaze. And, this time, watching him walk up the steps towards her...

She came back to reality with a sudden jolt, heart thudding. She propped herself up on an elbow, staring around her in sudden, inexplicable alarm, but the rest of the beach was deserted.

She sank back onto the towel with a little groan of relief, then paused, her brows snapping together. Because the bottle of sun lotion that she'd replaced in her bag after use was there in front of her on the sand, propped against an insulated cool-box, which had appeared from nowhere.

Both of them telling her quite clearly that, although she might be alone now, she'd had company quite recently. While she'd been asleep, in fact, and vulnerable.

Her throat tightened as she smelt the distinctive scent of freshly applied lotion on her skin, and remembered the vivid sensation of stroking hands on her bare back. And her drowsy, sensuous reaction...

Oh, God, she thought, he'd been here—touching her.

Seeing her next door to naked. And making no secret of it either. Feverishly, she snatched up her bikini top, and fastened it round her with shaking hands. Locking the stable door, she realised, after the horse was long gone.

He'd said he was leaving, she thought numbly. She'd heard him drive off. And now he'd come sneaking back. All Adele's warnings returned in Technicolor to haunt her. To tell her to get out while the going was good.

She grabbed her bag, and pushed her book and the sun lotion into it. He'd mentioned another way off the beach that Sherry used, and she didn't care how steep or stony it was. It would certainly be safer than going up to the villa, and encountering him again.

Then as she reached for her dress she saw him coming down the steps, a sun umbrella under one arm, and a bottle of water in his other hand. And a towel, she noted, draped round his shoulders.

Too late to run now, she thought, cursing under her breath. She got to her feet, and watched him approach, hands on her hips.

She said glacially, 'I thought you had other duties elsewhere.'

'I also have a lunch break.' He indicated the cool-box, apparently oblivious to the hostility in her tone. 'I thought you might like to share some food with me.'

'Then you thought wrong.' She gave him the full glare that worked so well with stroppy teenagers, both eyes like lasers.

'As you wish.' His own tone was equable. 'But at least drink some of this water I have brought for you. It is dangerous to become dehydrated, and your own supply has nearly gone.'

He pushed the tip of the umbrella he was carrying deep into the sand, and adjusted it, so the shade fell across her towel.

'You dared to go through my things...'

He shrugged. 'I was looking for the lotion to put on your

back. You were in danger of burning. I saw then how little water you had.'

Oh, God, he made it all sound so bloody *reasonable*, she raged inwardly. As if his motives were of the purest.

She said stiffly, 'I'm sure you meant to be kind...'

'Is that what I intended?' He grinned at her. 'Well, maybe. A little. Or, perhaps, I was thinking how angry my employer would be if he found you were in the clinic with first-degree burns or heatstroke, and unable to talk business with him.' He held the bottle of water out to her. 'Now drink some of this.'

'That won't be necessary,' she denied swiftly. 'I'm going back to the hotel. I can get a drink there.'

'I see.' He was quiet for a meditative moment. 'Have you been to Greece many times before?'

'No,' she said. 'This is actually my first visit, but...'

'But it is wiser to rest in the heat of the day,' he supplied decisively. 'And not go walking when there is no necessity.' He put the bottle down on her towel, and paused. 'Don't you like the beach?'

'It's perfect,' Zoe said shortly.

'Until I came to spoil it for you,' he added drily. 'You have a very eloquent face, *thespinis*.'

'Yet you seem determined to stay, all the same.' She observed him spreading his towel on the sand with misgiving.

'I come every day at this time,' he said. 'Whereas you, *thespinis*, are here only at my invitation.' He allowed that to sink in. 'And the beach is surely big enough for us to share for a short while.'

'I'm not sure your employer would agree,' she said tautly. 'Does he know this is how you spend your time?'

'He would certainly consider it one of my duties to offer hospitality to his guest.'

'I am not,' she said. 'His guest. Officially. And you have a very strange idea of hospitality.'

'Why?' His brows lifted. 'I have brought you food, drink

and shelter.' He stood, hands on hips, and looked her up and down slowly, and with unconcealed appreciation, his eyes lingering on the smooth rise of her breasts above the flimsy cups of her bikini. 'But if there is any requirement I have not supplied, you have only to tell me,' he added silkily.

'Thank you,' Zoe said through gritted teeth. 'You've already done more than enough.'

He laughed. 'Then shall we declare a truce, *thespinis*? It is too beautiful a day to fight. And if you won't eat with me, at least drink some water.'

Zoe gave him a mutinous look, then knelt, and carefully decanted some of the water he'd brought into her own container. 'Thank you.' Stonily, she placed the bottle on the outermost corner of the towel, where he had now stretched himself, very much at his ease.

'Efharisto,' he corrected, lazily. 'If you are going to stay on the island for any length of time, you need to learn a little Greek.'

'I have a phrase book,' she said. 'So I don't need personal tutoring—thanks.'

His brows drew together. 'You also have attitude,' he told her drily. 'Maybe you could learn, instead, a little *philoxenia*—the Greek warmth towards strangers. Because others may not understand.'

'Perhaps,' Zoe said, lifting her chin coolly, 'this is not a situation where warmth is advisable.'

He propped himself up on one elbow and looked at her measuringly. 'What makes you so nervous?' he asked. 'You think that I intend, maybe, to force myself upon you?' He shook his head. 'No, *thespinis*. In the first place, it is far too hot. In the second, rape has no appeal for me.'

He lay back, looking up at the cloudless sky, lacing his fingers behind his head, his voice meditative.

'I prefer a cool room, with the shutters drawn, a comfortable bed, a bottle of good wine, and a girl who wishes to be with me as much as I want her.'

He turned his head, sending her a faint smile. 'And nothing less will do. So, you see, you are quite safe.'

Her face warmed. She said huskily, 'You paint—a vivid picture.'

'And, I hope, a reassuring one.'

'Yes,' she said. 'Oh, yes.' And tried to subdue the betraying quiver deep inside her.

'Enough to tell me your name?'

She hesitated. 'It's—Zoe.'

'A Greek name,' he approved softly. 'And I am Andreas.' He paused. 'So now that we are properly acquainted, will you share some lunch with me?'

There seemed no good reason to refuse. And perhaps it would be sensible to be a little conciliatory to someone who might be in a position to help her.

So she gave a constrained smile, and murmured, 'That would be—nice.'

The cool-box contained cold chicken, a bag of salad leaves, black olives, tomatoes, feta cheese and some fresh bread. There was also, she noted, a plastic box containing dark grapes and peaches, as well as two chilled bottles of beer, two glasses wrapped in napkins, paper plates, and some cutlery.

This had never been planned as a solitary meal, she thought. And her agreement, it seemed, had been taken for granted. But then he probably didn't get many refusals, she thought, with an inward grimace. And at least he'd brought beer, and not the bottle of good wine he'd mentioned earlier. So attempted seduction did not appear to be on the menu.

It was also clear that she was expected to set out the plates, and divide the food between them. Woman's work, she supposed with irony. And found herself wondering who had assembled the picnic in the first place.

Yet, in spite of her reservations, she enjoyed the meal. The chicken was succulent and the olives and tomatoes had a superb tangy flavour that made those in the supermarket at home seem pallid by comparison.

'Would you like a peach?' He peeled it for her deftly, and she watched his hands, observing the long fingers and well-kept nails. Pretty fastidious for a gardener, she thought. And although his deep voice with its husky timbre was faintly accented, his English seemed faultless.

Andreas, she thought, and wondered...

The fruit was marvellous, too, ripe and sweet, although she was embarrassed to find the juice running down her chin, and into the cleft between her breasts. Something that was not lost on him, she realised with vexation, trying to mop herself discreetly with her napkin.

To deflect his attention, she said, 'Do you like gardening?'

'I enjoy seeing the results,' he said. 'Why? Are you thinking of hiring my services when you come to live at the house?'

She dried her fingers. 'I haven't given it a thought,' she fibbed.

He shrugged a shoulder. 'Then think of it now.'

'Are you so much in demand?'

'Of course,' he said promptly. 'But I could be persuaded to make time for you in my busy schedule.'

He either had the biggest ego in the western world, Zoe told herself seething, or it was a wind-up, and she was sure it was the latter.

But whichever it was, it remained light years away from the taciturn attitude of Mr Harbutt, who wore heavy boots and corduroy trousers summer and winter, and smelled faintly of compost, and who'd done the heavy digging at the cottage for her mother.

She said coolly, 'I think you could prove too expensive for me.'

'You devastate me,' Andreas said lightly. 'Perhaps we could work out a deal together—some kind of reciprocal arrangement.' He watched her stiffen, then went on silkily,

'Much of the island's economy is conducted on the barter system. If you are to live here you will have to accustom yourself.' He paused. 'Tell me, Zoe *mou*, what do you do for a living?'

'I teach,' she said shortly. 'English.'

'Then there is no problem,' he said. 'I will look after your garden. You can give me English lessons.'

Zoe sent him a fulminating look. 'I think your English is quite good enough already.'

His own eyes danced. There were, she noticed unwillingly, tiny gold flecks in their dark depths. 'Thank you,' he said. 'I think.' He sighed elaborately. 'Then we will just have to come up with something else.'

'Or I could simply find another gardener.' She paused. 'But perhaps your boss will refuse to rent the house to me.'

'I do not see how he could resist you, Zoe *mou*. Particularly when I shall give you my strongest endorsement.'

'You think mowing grass and removing weeds gives you special insight into character?' Her brows lifted. 'How fascinating. And your boss will listen to you?'

'He trusts my judgement,' Andreas said slowly. 'When I tell him which plants will grow and thrive, and those that are weak and not worth the trouble. I find human nature is much the same.'

Aghast, she heard herself say, 'And which am I?'

There was a sudden hard edge to his smile. 'When I have come to a decision, Zoe *mou*, I will tell you.'

He collected up the debris from their meal and put it back in the cool-box. Then he stood up, unzipped his shorts unhurriedly, and stepped out of them, revealing brief black swimming trunks, and walked off down the beach.

She felt her mouth dry as she watched him go. He had a miraculous body, she thought, lean, hard and perfectly proportioned. And a long, lithe stride like the prowl of some great cat.

And while the predator was away, the mouse would be wise to make a dash for it, she told herself, swiftly pulling herself together as he plunged into the water and began to swim away, out to sea, with a strong, clean stroke.

She put on her dress, shook out her towel, grabbed her bag and made for the steps. With every yard, she expected to hear him shout after her, or even to feel his hand, damp and salty, on her shoulder halting her. Turning her towards him.

At the top of the steps, Zoe risked one swift look back. His dark head was perfectly visible, his lean body cutting effortlessly through the water. A man in his physical prime enjoying the challenge of tough exercise, and, thankfully, oblivious to her departure.

All the same, once she reached the shade of the olive trees she began to run, pausing only when she reached the road, a hand pressed to her side.

I think, she told herself, her flurried breath hoarse in her throat, that's what they call a lucky escape.

She was hot and sticky by the time she reached the hotel. She collected her key from the hook and went up to her room, guiltily glad that Sherry wasn't around to ask about her day.

By the time she sat down for dinner, she would hopefully be feeling more composed, with some bland comment about Thania's undeniable charm carefully lined up.

Something on the lines of 'Nice island, shame about the natives'? Well, perhaps not, she thought, her mouth twisting.

Or maybe she could make a joke of it all. 'Up at the villa, I ran into the gardener from hell. Who does that guy think he is?' And perhaps Sherry would know, and tell her.

But why did she even want to know?

Because this is a very small island, she thought. And although she intended to avoid the Villa Danae until its supposed owner returned from Athens, she was bound to run into Andreas at some future point, so needed some plan to respond to the situation.

She sighed impatiently. Don't fool yourself, she muttered under her breath. He won't waste any more time on you. You can't be the only female tourist under twenty-five on Thania, and he wants someone warm and willing. He told you so himself.

In the shower, she turned the water to cool, letting it run through her hair and cascade down her overheated body.

It was annoying to contemplate how easily Andreas had been able to get under her skin.

Face it, she thought. You've been out of the mating game too long to know how to deal with someone like that. If you ever knew at all, that is. Dear old George with his bumbling proposal is more your mark, my dear. Not someone who's clearly been sex on legs since the day he was born.

She towelled herself dry, and put on her thin silk wrap, then helped herself to a can of lemonade from the mini-fridge in the corner, and took it out onto the balcony with the papers for the Villa Danae.

What she needed was someone to verify the translation of the original document gifting the villa to her mother. She supposed she could ask Stavros, but the gift was clearly the action of a rich man, and she remembered what Sherry had said about her husband not wishing to offend any of the influential residents on Thania.

She also had to find out the identity of Andreas' employer in Athens. If she hadn't been caught totally on the wrong foot, she would have asked. But being caught in the villa had thrown her mental processes into turmoil.

And her emotions had followed, she thought, biting savagely at her lower lip.

Andreas had knocked her sideways, in a way that was completely foreign to her nature, and it was pointless to deny it. Thank God her instinct for self-preservation had still been working, she thought, shifting restlessly in the cushioned chair.

And anyway, she'd had enough sun for one day. Against

the concealing silk, her skin felt warm, but not burning. And for that, she supposed, moving her shoulders experimentally, she had to thank Andreas' ministrations with the sun lotion.

She could still feel the glide of his hands on her back, and yet with Mick, who'd been her only lover to date, she could not remember a single detail of their intimacy.

I shouldn't be able to remember Andreas' touch like this, she thought almost frantically. I was asleep, for God's sake.

But if you hadn't gone on sleeping, said a small, sly voice in her head. If you'd woken, what would you have done? Would you have lain still, pretending? Or would you have turned over, offering your bare breasts? Drawing him down to you, because you could not help yourself?

She felt her throat tighten uncontrollably. Her breathing quicken.

This, she told herself forcefully, is not good. Don't even go there.

Nothing had happened. Nothing was going to happen. But she would have to watch every step she took from now on.

I had no idea, she thought drearily, fanning herself with the papers, that I could be so susceptible.

The ferry was just leaving, and for a moment she almost wished she were on it.

I really shouldn't have come here, she thought, frowning. Not without knowing the score in advance. And I certainly shouldn't have betrayed my interest in the house so soon. But what real choice did I have between that, and being hauled off by the local police for trespass?

She sighed again, ruefully. It was all just an unfortunate combination of circumstances.

But from now, I'll cool it, she told herself. Sherry is bound to know when Andreas' boss returns from Athens, and I'll make sure I keep any questions casual and discreet.

And if I happen to meet Andreas again in the meantime, I'll let him think that I was simply winding him up in turn.

Trying to get myself out of a tight spot with a few well-chosen fibs.

That was the best—the only way to handle things. For all kinds of reasons, she thought, of which her own peace of mind was only one.

'Did you find the beach all right?' Sherry asked that evening, setting a dish of taramasalata on Zoe's table.

'Oh, yes.' Zoe allowed herself a wry smile and a shrug. 'Only it wasn't quite as deserted as you said.'

'Oh, heck.' Sherry wrinkled her nose. 'Is Steve Dragos back? I hadn't realised. I thought he was still wrapped in cotton wool in Athens after his heart attack.'

'I don't think the guy I met is a candidate for heart trouble,' Zoe said. Although he might cause his fair share of it, she added silently. 'He seemed to be some sort of gardener-caretaker.'

'Really?' Sherry looked surprised. 'I didn't know there was one. Maybe he's some relation to Hara who looks after the house. What's his name?'

'I'm not sure he mentioned it,' Zoe said untruthfully, filling her glass with water. It had occurred to her suddenly that she didn't want to have all her prejudices about Andreas confirmed. To be told by Sherry that his bed was collapsing from all the notches in its post. Or even to be teased about her encounter with him. 'So,' she went on. 'Who is this Steve Dragos?'

'Oh your usual multimillionaire.' Sherry shrugged. 'Runs fleets of tankers and freight carriers round the world. And somehow, in between it all, found the time to build the Villa Danae.'

'Heavens,' said Zoe, rather faintly. 'I—see.' She paused. 'Yet he doesn't live there.'

'Oh, no. He has an even more palatial villa just up the coast.' Sherry gave her an anxious look as she unloaded from her tray the small carafe of white house wine that Zoe had ordered. 'I hope you didn't get into trouble for being there,' she added quietly.

'No, it was fine,' Zoe assured her. She lowered her voice in turn. 'But they know you use the beach sometimes.'

'Hell,' Sherry said gloomily. 'Steve Dragos must have a spy camera up on some satellite. Thank God I'm not into skinny-dipping.' And she went off to take the order from a German family at an adjoining table.

Zoe had a lot to think about as she ate her grilled swordfish, and its accompanying salad. Was the man in the photograph this Steve Dragos—and had he given the Villa Danae to her mother? And, if so—why?

What on earth had Gina Lambert been doing mixing in that kind of super-wealthy society? It made no sense. Family life had been comfortable, but there was little money to spare. And certainly no indication from her mother that she'd once moved with the jet set.

She had the uneasy feeling that she was getting into deep water, but she couldn't back off now. She needed desperately to know everything.

Her sense of disquiet was also heightened to simmering point by the expectation of seeing Andreas walk into the courtyard at any moment. After all, he knew where she was staying, and she'd been secretly convinced he would come to find her, if only to make some edged remark about her ignominious retreat. On the other hand, maybe he'd decided to shrug her off as the one that got away. Because that had been her intention—hadn't it?

All the same, every new arrival sent her heart thumping, but there was no tall, arrogant figure scanning the tables with narrowed dark eyes.

Her hasty departure seemed to have had the desired effect, she thought. She should be grateful for that, and she knew it.

Every glance, every smile he'd sent her had revealed the practised womaniser, she told herself. And his relationships would be just as fragile and ephemeral as any of the butterflies with wings like chocolate velvet that she'd seen in the garden at the villa. Which was the last thing she needed.

She ate her dessert of fresh apricots, and lingered over the coffee and Metaxa that rounded off the meal.

'That was wonderful,' she sighed when Sherry came to clear the table. 'My compliments to the chef.'

'That's my mother-in-law,' Sherry told her cheerfully. 'The most unflappable woman in the universe. And a great dancer, too. You'll see her in action tomorrow night when we have live music.'

All the other diners were leaving, most of them to walk along the harbourside and find a taverna for a final nightcap. Zoe supposed she could do the same, but instead she found herself going back to her room.

It's been quite a day, she thought, and a comparatively early night will do me no harm at all.

Besides, it was unexpectedly lonely being on one's own in a foreign country, where other people all seemed to be couples or family groups.

Had Gina been lonely, too, and tempted, as a result, away from the normal pattern of her existence? Was that what this was all about—a holiday fling with a man, who turned out to be rich enough to give houses as farewell presents instead of the conventional piece of jewellery?

It wasn't a very palatable possibility, she thought, opening her door. But it made sense.

As she switched on the light, she glimpsed herself in the wall-mirror, a girl with pale hair and wide, expectant eyes in a black slip of a dress cut low across her breasts. A dress to please a man, she thought with sudden self-contempt. In spite of everything she'd told herself that afternoon.

Maybe this was how it had begun for her mother, too. Perhaps Gina had stood in a room like this one, feeling the stir of sheer physical attraction along her senses. Finding it irresistible.

Had she stayed here, and fought for her self-respect, or had she gone back, flitting like a slender ghost, to where he'd been waiting for her in the shadow of the cypress trees?

But Andreas was not waiting anywhere for her, she reminded herself. His work was over for the day, and he was probably at home in some small white house in Livassi, with a wife and brood of children.

She made a sound in her throat, muffled, painful.

I walked away, she thought. I behaved well. I did the right thing. The only thing.

So why do I feel as if I lost?

CHAPTER FOUR

Zoe slept badly, and was wide awake in time to see the sun rise in a flawless sky, promising another intensely hot day.

She'd had time, during the night, to decide her next move, so she showered and dressed in a knee-length black linen skirt, with a matching vest top over her bikini. Her hair she twisted into a loose knot on top of her head secured by a silver clasp.

'Not going back to the cove?' Sherry asked, pouring breakfast coffee into her cup.

'I think that would be pushing my luck an inch too far,' Zoe admitted with utter truth, at the same time stifling a pang of totally unsuitable regret. 'I thought I'd do some sightseeing instead, before it gets too warm. Discover what Livassi has to offer.' *And, maybe, meet Uncle Stavros...*

'Well, don't blink,' Sherry advised. 'Or you might miss it.' Then, relenting, 'Actually, Livassi's really pretty, and the church is lovely with some terrific frescos. But they like you to cover your shoulders if you plan to visit.'

'I've got a shirt to put on.' Zoe delved into her bag, and produced it, checked in black and white, with long sleeves and voluminous enough to wear as a beach cover-up later.

'And watch out for the icon,' Sherry added as she turned away. 'It's supposed to help women get pregnant so you might want to give it a wide berth.'

'That's OK.' Zoe tried a nonchalant shrug. 'I'm totally celibate.'

'That's what they all say,' said Sherry darkly.

And that, thought Zoe, is what I have to believe, and keep to. At all costs.

The hill up to the main square was steep, and narrow enough to force her to leap into doorways as cars and scooters roared heedlessly past.

By the time she reached the top, she was hot and breathless, but she had to admit that the square with its Venetian-style colonnade and small Byzantine church was well worth the effort.

There were tables in the middle of the square under the trees, and benches, but, as yet, they were unoccupied. Perhaps the games of backgammon didn't take place at weekends, she reflected, disappointed. Well, there would be other days.

She took some photographs, then, pulling on her shirt, went into the cool, incense-laden atmosphere of the church. A bearded priest in dark robes replacing candles in tall holders gave her a lightning glance, then made her a slight bow of unsmiling approval.

She trod round slowly, her sandals noiseless on the stone flags, looking at the murals that depicted scenes from the life of Christ, which she recognised, and various angular, wistful-eyed saints, which she didn't.

There were numerous icons in niches round the walls, all of them apparently venerated, so she had no idea which one to avoid.

In any case, she thought, her mouth twisting, it was a real man she needed to shun, not a gilded representation painted on wood.

The heat was like a blow from a clenched fist as she emerged into the sunlight. She ordered an iced drink made from fresh lemons at a *kafeneion* under the colonnade, and settled down under its striped awning to look around her.

One of the tables under the trees was occupied now by a group of elderly men hunched round a board, their hands moving with incredible speed as they threw dice and moved counters. But which of them, if any, was Uncle Stavros? And she could hardly interrupt their concentration in order to ask, she decided wryly.

She retrieved from her bag the small guide book she'd bought on her way up the hill, and began to flick through it.

But apart from extolling the wondrous peace and quiet of the island, and the fact that it was used as a retreat by some of the rich and famous, there was not a great deal the author could say.

There was a bay where Odysseus might or might not have paused for breath on the last leg of his epic journey back to Ithaca, and which bore his name on the off chance. There was a ruined monastery, and a couple of tiny fishing villages with wonderful views over the Ionian Sea. There were any number of walks, none of which would take more than a few hours to complete, including one up the steep slopes of Mount Edira, with even more breathtaking views.

And there were the Silver Caves. These, she read, were situated on the other side of the island, and led to a small subterranean lake. Some mineral in the rock gave it a metallic sheen, and affected the colour of the water, too, hence the name. Boats could be hired to row across the lake, and at night, when moonlight penetrated a fissure in the roof, visitors would feel they were enclosed in a precious silver casket.

Not for the claustrophobic then, Zoe thought drily, but she had to admit it sounded appealing.

There was also an echo in the caves, which had been used for generations on the island by lovers to test the fidelity of their chosen partners. If you called the loved one's name, and it echoed back, then you had nothing to fear. But if there was silence...

Hideous embarrassment all round, thought Zoe, entertained.

As she closed the book she was suddenly aware that she was being watched.

She glanced up and met the frowning gaze of a newcomer to the backgammon game. He was solidly built, with a mass of silver hair under a rakish peaked cap, his once handsome face heavily lined. His hands were clasped in front of him on top of a walking stick.

Even when Zoe met his eye, he did not look away, but went on staring at her curiously, almost fiercely, as if he knew her, but was cursing the fact that he could not place her.

But I bet I know who you are, Zoe told herself silently. *Kalimera*, Uncle Stavros.

She had half risen from her chair with the intention of going over to speak to him when he rose and moved away, walking quickly for a man leaning heavily on a stick.

Zoe sank back, feeling oddly deflated. She knew from photographs how closely she resembled her mother at the same age.

It was clear he'd picked up the family resemblance, she thought flatly, but he hadn't wanted to renew the acquaintance. Nor had he wished to be questioned about it.

Well, this is only the third day of my vacation, she thought. There's plenty of time ahead for his curiosity to get the better of him. And I'm sure it will.

If not, I'll make the first approach myself.

She looked rather defensively at the backgammon players, but they were totally absorbed in their game. None of them had a second glance to spare for her.

Ah, well—investigation over for today, she thought, leaving the money on the table for the waiter. And back to being a tourist again.

But all the way down the hill she found herself remembering that concentrated, almost worried stare, and wondering...

Sherry, reflected Zoe, had not been joking about the town beach getting busy. She was beginning to know how a sardine had to feel as the tin closed round it, and it wasn't even noon yet, she thought, groaning.

It seemed the entire population of Livassi had turned out to sun themselves, and bathe in the shallow water. Or play something like volleyball without the net, she thought without pleasure as a large beach ball thudded down beside her, yet again, spraying her with fine sand.

The young Greek who ran over to retrieve it gave her a flashing smile that bordered on a leer, while his friends shouted something that might have been encouragement.

'Hey, pretty girl, you want to play?' he demanded.

'No, thank you,' Zoe returned austerely, adding a muted glare, then transferred her attention ostentatiously back to the book she was reading.

There were four of them altogether, and they'd been a nuisance ever since they arrived. And because she was a girl on her own, they seemed to have singled her out for special attention, she realised with growing annoyance. The ball was being deliberately batted in her direction, so that they could come rushing over in turn, strutting their stuff, bending far too close, and making grinning remarks that she was grateful not to understand. Until now, when they'd worked out that she was English rather than German or Swedish as they'd probably assumed.

For the first time, she regretted being alone, realising that it made her conspicuous, and a sitting target for the local Romeos.

She looked surreptitiously around, hoping to see one of the families who were also staying at the hotel, but everyone around her seemed to be Greek. And, anyway, she was probably fussing too much about a bit of innocent horseplay, she told herself, and eventually, when she didn't respond, they'd get bored and stop.

But ten minutes later, when she was still being regularly spattered with sand, she decided to cut her losses, and go.

It wasn't really such a hardship, she told herself. It was lunchtime, and she could try the fish taverna she'd passed on the harbourside. Perhaps by the time she came back they would either have moved on, or found some other female to pester.

She slipped her check shirt over her bikini, fastening the

middle buttons, then collected her things and stood up.
She'd hoped they were too immersed in their game to notice, but by the time she reached the stony track bordering
the beach that led back to the harbour, she realised to her
alarm that two of them were following her.

She quickened her pace, stumbling a little as the loose
pebbles on the track rolled under her sandalled feet, and
the stocky one who had spoken to her in English caught
up with her effortlessly, putting a hand on her arm.

'You come—have drink in my brother's bar?' He
grinned at her, his eyes insolent, as he looked her up and
down.

'No, thank you.' Zoe's response was cold and unsmiling.
She tried to tug herself free, but to no avail. His hand closed
on her more firmly.

'We want you to be friendly.' His companion came to
her other side, so that she was effectively trapped between
them. 'I work on Zakynthos last year.' He rolled his eyes
lasciviously. 'All English girls very friendly.'

'You have apartment?' the first one asked. 'We go
there—have drink maybe, *kougla mou*. Is quieter—more
private.' He pushed up her sleeve, stroking the skin on the
inside of her arm with hot, damp fingers.

Zoe's anger began to give way to something like fear.
But she dared not show it.

She said furiously, 'Let go of me. Let go at once.'

The second youth laughed, showing a broken tooth. 'Be
nice, honey girl, and we show you a good time.'

'And I,' said Zoe, 'will show you the inside of a jail
cell.'

With a strength she'd not known she possessed, she
wrenched herself loose and set off, running. But before
she'd gone more than a few yards she cannoned into someone who was standing, blocking her way, and recoiled with
a scream.

'Hush, *pedhi mou*.' It was Andreas' voice. His hands

descended firmly on her shoulders, holding her. 'All is well. You are safe.'

He looked past her to her assailants, speaking softly in his own language.

Zoe saw with disbelief that all the macho bluster and posturing had suddenly gone out of them, just as if someone had thrown a switch. They were staring at the ground, muttering and shrugging, looking hangdog, and almost embarrassed. Then, as Andreas spoke more sharply, they turned and slouched away back to the beach.

'My God.' Her voice was shaky. 'They didn't put up much of a fight.'

His brows lifted. 'You would like me to call them back, perhaps.'

'No—oh, no.' She paused. 'What did you say to them to make them—disappear like that? Do they know you?'

'Of course,' he said. 'Thania is a very small island. And, among other things, I reminded them that we all work for the same man, who would not be pleased to find them accused of sexually harassing a tourist. Although I have to tell you that they are both more stupid than dangerous.'

'Not,' Zoe said, 'from where I was sitting.' She took a deliberate step away from him, releasing herself from his grasp, and gave him a frowning look. He was wearing denim trousers, and his thin white shirt was unbuttoned, revealing, once again, more smooth brown skin than she wished to see. She hurried into speech. 'Is that all you said to them?'

'There were embellishments,' he said. 'But I will not trouble you with those.'

'Oh.' She digested that, then looked at him with renewed suspicion. 'Anyway, what are you doing here?'

'I thought—rescuing you from annoyance.'

She brushed that aside impatiently. 'I mean—how did you happen to be here just in the nick of time? Isn't that rather a strange coincidence?'

'Ah,' Andreas said softly. 'A conspiracy theory. But

there is no need for paranoia, *pedhi mou*. Or to imagine that I hired those idiots to annoy you, so that I could play the part of some knight in shining armour,' he added. 'You needed help, and I happened to come along. That is all.'

'You just *happened* to be here?'

He shrugged. 'This is a public path, leading to a public beach,' he countered. 'Why should I not be here?' He paused. 'Although I admit I was coming to look for you.'

Her already flustered heartbeat began to pound to a different rhythm. 'Why should you do that?'

And why did I ask that, she wondered despairingly, when I don't want to hear the answer?

'Because the beach at the house seemed quiet without you.' He smiled at her. 'And yesterday you left without saying goodbye.'

Zoe stared down at the dusty track. 'I felt embarrassed,' she said in a low voice. 'An intruder. I—I had no real right to be there, and I knew it.'

'Even though I had made it clear you were a welcome guest?'

'Well, it was hardly your place to do that,' she returned. 'However strict he is about hassling women tourists, your boss might not appreciate your entertaining visitors in his absence.'

'I promise you he would feel honoured.'

She hunched a shoulder. 'All the same, I think it would be better to keep my distance from now on.'

He frowned slightly. 'So the house no longer interests you?' he queried. 'You have changed your mind about wishing to live there.'

'I didn't say that.'

'Good,' he said. 'Because I have told my employer of your interest, and he is looking forward to meeting you.'

She drew a swift, astonished breath. She hadn't expected that. She'd intended to make her own enquiries—stay in control of the situation, yet now it seemed to be taken out of her hands.

'Isn't that a little premature?' It was her turn to frown
'I gather he's been very ill.'

'He is on the mend. Also bored. He needs entertainment—a new interest, which you could provide.'

'I want to discuss business with him,' Zoe said shortly
'I'm not a cabaret act.'

'No,' he said, silkily. 'They tend to smile more.'

She bit her lip. 'I'm—sorry. I'm still rather stressed, I
think.'

'You need food,' he said. 'And a glass of wine. So, have
lunch with me, and over the meal you can express your
gratitude to me for coming to your aid, as I am sure you
wish to do.'

Zoe felt her jaw begin to drop, and restored it hurriedly
to its correct position. Somehow, he'd wrong-footed her
again. How on earth did he do that?

Not that it altered a thing. She wasn't prepared to venture
on another meal *à deux* with him, even if there was a table
between them, and loads of other people around this time.
It was too dangerous. Her reaction to him was too extreme.
As it was, she was shaking inside.

She managed a small cool smile. 'I already have plans
for lunch,' she said. 'So I'd better say thanks here and now.
You saved me from a—nasty situation, and I am grateful.
Truly.' She contemplated offering to shake hands with him,
and decided against it. 'So, thank you again and—see you
around.'

She walked away, trying not to hurry, and certainly not
risking even a glance over her shoulder to see how he had
taken his rejection. Surely by now he'd have got the message, she argued with herself. Besides, remembering the
prices she'd checked on the menus displayed outside the
fish taverna earlier, she'd be doing him a favour. He
couldn't afford them on a gardener's wage.

The taverna was crowded, nearly all the tables being occupied, and Zoe was hesitating at the entrance, wondering
whether to return another day instead, when a smiling

waiter materialised beside her. 'You want good fish. Come, please. I have a nice table for you.'

He whisked her under the green awning to a secluded spot in the corner, shaded by a flowering vine growing up a trellis.

Nice, thought Zoe, sinking into her chair with an inner sigh of contentment, was not the word.

She reached out a hand and touched the petals on the small jar of golden rosebuds occupying the centre of the snowy cloth, then paused as a swift glance around her revealed that hers was the only table with such a decoration.

The waiter came bustling back, bringing chilled water and a basket containing crusty bread and, she realised with growing unease, two sets of cutlery.

She began, 'Excuse me...' but he was off, weaving his way among the tables to return a moment later with an ice bucket and a bottle of white wine.

This time, Zoe pushed back her chair with determination. 'I'm sorry,' she said. 'There's obviously been some mistake.'

'No,' Andreas said. 'No mistake at all.' And he slid almost casually into the chair opposite and smiled at her. 'I hope you are hungry. Kostas has lobster for us.'

She sat, frozen in fury, staring at him, while the waiter filled their glasses. As soon as he'd departed, she leaned forward. 'Let's get one thing straight,' she said in an icy undertone. 'There is no "us".'

'No?' His brows lifted mockingly. 'Yet all it takes is for two people to be together—and we are certainly that.'

'And just how did this togetherness come about?' Zoe demanded. 'How did you know where I was planning to eat? Or did you book tables in every taverna in town?'

He shrugged. 'Sooner or later, everyone comes to eat at Kostas' taverna. I thought you would like it here, and took a chance.'

'Well, it hasn't paid off,' she flung at him. 'I'm going.'

'You don't like lobster?'

'This has nothing to do with food.' She rose. 'I don't like being second-guessed and manipulated. Particularly when I'd made it clear I was lunching alone.'

He said meditatively, 'That word "alone" again.' He paused. 'Tell me, *pedhi mou*, do you know what "Zoe" means in Greek?'

'No,' she denied curtly.

The dark eyes met hers, held them. 'It means life,' he said. 'So—how can you be so afraid to live?'

Colour rushed into her face. 'That's a vile thing to say. And totally untrue.'

The dark eyes raked her harshly. 'Then why do you reject friendship when it is offered?'

'Friendship?' she asked bitterly. 'Is that what your colleagues had in mind just now?'

'You believe that I am like them?' His tone was incredulous.

She looked down at the table. 'How do I know?' Her voice was muffled. 'How can I possibly tell? We only met yesterday. We're barely acquaintances.'

'That is something I am trying to change,' he said. 'But not with any great success. Sit down, Zoe *mou*, and I will tell you anything you wish to know.'

'Besides,' he added gently as she hesitated, 'Kostas will be sad if we waste his wonderful lobster.'

Mutinously, Zoe resumed her seat. 'I don't know why I'm doing this,' she muttered.

'Because you're hungry,' Andreas said promptly. 'Also thirsty.' He lifted his glass. 'To your eyes, *agapi mou*.'

Startled by the intimacy of the toast, and conscious that she was blushing, Zoe reluctantly touched her glass to his. 'Cheers,' she said awkwardly.

The waiter reappeared with dishes of houmous and tzatziki, a bowl of black olives and a platter of mixed salad.

'You like Greek food?' Andreas proffered the bread.

'Everything I've had so far has been wonderful.'

'That is just as well,' he said drily. 'On Thania, you will

find little else. No fast food or English pubs,' he added with a touch of grimness.

'Aren't they a fact of life in holiday resorts?'

'On other islands, perhaps.' He sounded quietly certain. 'But not here. We do not wish to go down that road. Thania belongs to its islanders. They fish, and grow their olives and make their wine, and are content with that.'

'And sometimes they garden for rich men,' Zoe said. She tore off a piece of bread and dipped it into the tzatziki. 'Will that make you happy for the rest of your life?'

'Probably not,' he said. 'But gardening is only part of my duties, as I told you, Zoe *mou*.' He smiled at her. 'And I enjoy variety.'

'I bet,' Zoe said under her breath.

His smile widened into a grin, leaving her with the uncomfortable feeling that he knew exactly what she was thinking. 'And what of you, *pedhi mou*? Do you plan to teach English for ever?'

She shrugged a touch defensively. 'Probably.'

He said softly, 'But what a waste. You are not tempted to marry—have children of your own?'

She was assailed by a sudden memory of George doggedly proposing to her in the wine bar, and bit down a giggle.

She met his gaze squarely. 'Not in the slightest. I have a very fulfilling career.'

His brows lifted. 'So, it also keeps you warm in bed at night?'

She flushed again. 'I don't think that's any of your damned business. And I thought the point of this lunch was for me to find out about *you*.'

'Ask what you want,' he said. 'I am ready to answer.'

'Well, your second name might be a start.' She tried to sound casual, not easy when her nerves seemed to be stretched on wires.

Oh, what's the matter with me? she wondered savagely. Any other single girl on holiday would relish being chatted up by someone with half his attraction and sheer charisma. And any of my students would make a better fist of responding than I'm doing. Why can't I just—go with the flow?

'My second name is Stephanos,' he said. 'Andreas Stephanos.' He paused. 'What next, Zoe *mou*? My age—weight—height?'

She bit her lip. 'I hardly think that's necessary.'

Besides, she thought, she already knew what there was to know in that area. Every quivering sense she possessed had made sure of that. He had to be in his early thirties, at least six foot, if not more, and she would bet good money that he wasn't carrying a surplus pound.

'Then what else?' He leaned back in his chair, watching her with amusement. 'My star sign—my income?'

She shrugged again. 'For the first, I'd say Scorpio. The second doesn't concern me.'

He sent her an ironic look. 'Then you must be a very unusual woman.'

'I think so.' She paused. 'Was I right about your birthday?'

His mouth twisted wryly. 'As it happens—yes.' He poured some more wine into her glass. 'So, why don't you ask another question?'

'Because I can't think of one,' she said baldly.

'No? You don't want to know if I'm married?'

She helped herself to more houmous while she considered how to reply. At last she said, 'I'm not sure I should get a truthful answer.'

'What point would there be in lying?' Andreas asked flatly. 'On an island this size, someone would soon tell you if I had a wife.' He grimaced. 'Probably the wife herself—using her fingernails.' He was silent for a moment. 'And what of yourself, Zoe *mou*. You wear no ring, but that means little in this present world. Is there a man longing for your return? Unable to sleep because you are not in his arms?'

'Oh, there's a whole string of them,' she told him airily. 'I'm the original party girl. Never a dull moment with me around.'

'Now that I can believe,' he said, drily. 'But not the rest.'

She drew a pattern on the tablecloth with the tip of her finger. 'I haven't had much time for relationships lately. My mother became very ill, you see, and I went to live with her.'

'I am sorry.' He hesitated. 'She's better now, I hope?'

Zoe went on looking down at the tablecloth, tracing meaningless circles. She gave a silent and desolate shake of her head.

'Ah, *pedhi mou*,' he said, and his voice was gentle. 'Then that is something we share—the loss of our mothers.'

'Oh.' She glanced up quickly, meeting his gaze. 'I—I'm sorry. Did it happen recently?'

'Ten years ago. And she had been in poor health for a very long time before that.' He paused. 'But when it happens, it is still no easy thing, *ne*?'

'Not easy at all.' She gave a small sigh. 'Do you still have your father?'

'Yes.' His mouth curved faintly. 'Very much so.' He gave her a searching look. 'But not you, I think.'

'No,' she said in a stifled tone. 'So now I have to make another life for myself. And this holiday is just its beginning.'

He put a hand over hers, stilling the restless movement. 'Is this why you wish to be alone?' he asked quietly. 'Because you think that if you shut everyone out of this new life of yours, then you will suffer no more pain?' He shook his head. 'It does not work like that, I promise you. Sooner or later, someone will come into your world, and whether they bring heaven or hell, you will not be able to deny yourself.'

She looked down at the long brown fingers covering hers. And felt her whole body clench in sudden yearning.

Hastily, she withdrew her hand, making a business of taking more bread, filling her plate with salad and olives.

She said lightly, 'You make it sound rather frightening— and I've had enough scares for one day.'

'Well, they are over now,' he said. 'And no one else on Thania will make you afraid. I guarantee that.'

Zoe gave him a sceptical look. 'You really have such influence?' She kept her tone light.

'I am known as a man who keeps his word.' He sounded equally casual but she believed him.

'Then it's lucky I ran into you,' she said.

'Not luck, *matia mou*,' Andreas said softly. 'Fate. And here comes our lunch,' he added prosaically as Zoe stared at him, the breath suddenly catching in her throat.

The lobsters were wonderful, served plain grilled, with a dish of melted butter, and another containing a rich pink sauce made from the coral.

And it was impossible, Zoe found, to stay aloof, as she knew she needed to do, during such an informal, messy meal, with Andreas showing her, laughing, how to crack even the tiniest claws and extract every last delicious scrap of meat.

Afterwards, there was a platter of cherries, their creamy skins just flushed with red, and tiny cups of thick Greek coffee served with brandy.

'I don't think I can move,' Zoe confessed.

Andreas smiled at her lazily. 'Then don't do so, *pedhi mou*,' he advised. 'There is no hurry.'

One glance around her told her that he was right. After the earlier buzz, an air of somnolence had settled over the taverna. Most of the customers seemed content to settle back in the shade and let the afternoon pass. Even the voices were hushed. Those drifting away were mostly couples, she realised, and she found herself remembering, with a shiver of awareness, what Andreas had said to her about cool shuttered rooms in the heat of the afternoon. And wondered if he was remembering, too.

'I—I suppose not,' she said, trying to maintain her composure. 'But I'm sure you have places to go, and things to do.' *And people to see...*

He had said he wasn't married, she thought, but there could still be a woman or several in his life. He'd probably been fighting them off, but not too hard, since puberty.

He shrugged. 'They can also wait.' His half smile was wry. 'Unless you want to be rid of me.'

'Of course not.' Well, it was partly true, she thought. Common sense and recklessness were fighting it out in her head. 'And you've been very kind,' she added hastily. 'It's just that I feel I've taken up quite enough of your time.'

He gave her a slow, heavy-lidded glance. 'You think I am merely being kind, Zoe *mou*?' he drawled. 'Are you really so naive?'

'I'm not naive at all,' Zoe said jerkily. 'I was actually giving you the benefit of the doubt. But I see I was wrong.' She reached for her bag. 'And I'd like to pay for my own lunch.'

'You are wasting your time,' Andreas told her, unruffled. 'Kostas will not take your money.'

She lifted her chin. 'Why not?'

He leaned forward, looking into her eyes. He had amazing eyelashes, she found herself thinking inconsequentially, long, thick and curling. Astonishing on someone so completely and disturbingly male.

'For the same reason that you may pursue your quest for solitude on the town beach this afternoon, if you wish,' he told her softly. 'Because you have been with me, and, by this time, it will be known. Which makes you safe from all annoyance.'

Zoe pushed back her chair and rose. She was trembling again, but this time with anger at his sheer presumption.

'Except yours, I assume.' Her voice bit. 'And that's hardly reassuring. But I don't choose to be patronised, and I certainly shan't be going back to the town beach. There must be a corner of this island where your reputation doesn't carry, and I intend to find it, and spend the rest of my holiday in peace.'

'Peace?' he echoed derisively, getting to his feet in turn. 'You forfeited all hope of that when you came to the villa yesterday. And you know that as well as I do, my girl, so don't look at me with those innocent, injured eyes.'

Zoe drew herself up. 'Given the choice,' she said with icy clarity, 'I won't be looking at you at all.'

And she turned and walked out of the taverna, and along the harbourside to the questionable sanctuary of the hotel.

CHAPTER FIVE

'A LUCKY escape.' That's what Zoe kept telling herself, over and over again, as she lay on the bed staring up at the ceiling. And that was what she had to think. Because anything else was impossible.

Having lunch with Andreas Stephanos had been one of the biggest mistakes of her life, and she was ashamed to think how spinelessly she'd succumbed to his invitation.

And also, she realised, wincing, how much she'd enjoyed herself.

But the worst thing of all, she thought broodingly, was the way she'd found herself watching the lurking smile in his dark eyes, and the sensuous curve of the firm mouth. Feeling, as she did so, the muscles of her throat tighten in unfamiliar excitement.

There was no denying that Andreas Stephanos was a dangerously attractive man, and it was only his shameless suggestion that everyone on the island now regarded her as his personal property that had brought her to her senses at last. Before it was too late.

What she could not understand was how he'd managed to acquire such power over his fellow islanders. Was it the influence he seemed to possess with his rich boss, or sheer force of personality? Probably a combination of both, she thought.

Whatever, he was someone she seriously needed to avoid.

She'd been hot and breathless when she got back to the hotel, her legs shaking under her. Her first act had been to take a cool shower, but it had not had the calming effect she'd hoped for.

The thin wrap she was wearing seemed to grate unbearably against her sensitised skin, and there was a deep trembling ache inside her that she found she was unable to dispel.

'Ridiculous,' she told herself forcefully. 'Ludicrous, in fact.'

She'd always regarded herself as being reasonably level-headed. So how could she explain this totally overheated reaction to a man she'd met twice, and in whose company she'd spent little more than a couple of brief hours?

I just don't do things like this, Zoe thought fretfully, turning over and burying her face in the flat, hard pillow. And, anyway, it's not what I'm here for. I have a serious purpose, and I won't allow myself to forget it.

But the Villa Danae would have to be forbidden territory from now on, or at least until she had the chance to talk to the unknown Steve Dragos, and find out what possible connection he'd had with her mother. And, even then, because of his recent ill health, she would need to tread carefully.

Or she could simply let sleeping dogs lie, she thought restively. Abandon the whole thing, and get her holiday company to book her an earlier return flight. Let the past keep its secrets, and concentrate on the future. In many ways that was a much more appealing alternative.

Except that Gina Lambert's painting would still be there waiting for her—a constant reminder that there was a mystery still unsolved. And that she'd let a golden opportunity slip by. Besides, running away wasn't her style, whatever the provocation.

No, it was better to stay here, she decided with renewed determination. Get things sorted once and for all, whatever the outcome.

And let Andreas Stephanos see that she was one tourist who was immune to the undoubted lure of his physicality.

But if that was the case, asked a sly voice in her brain, why didn't she simply exclude him from the equation altogether? Relegate him to some mental and emotional dumpbin as she'd done with Mick, and poor George?

Because it's not as simple as that, she thought forlornly. And no amount of wishing will make it so.

And the implications of that kept her tossing restlessly until it was time to put on her silky slip of a black dress, do her face and hair, and go down for dinner.

'So, how was the grand tour of Livassi?' Sherry asked as she poured Zoe a retsina.

'I thought it was delightful,' Zoe said with sincerity. 'Even down to the backgammon players.'

Sherry's eyes twinkled. 'Did you meet Uncle Stavros?'

Zoe paused, weighing her words. 'I think he was just leaving as I got there,' she said neutrally. No need to mention, she thought, that her arrival seemed to have driven him to instant retreat.

'Not like him to miss out on an attractive blonde,' Sherry commented cheerfully. 'He must be feeling his age at last.'

Zoe shrugged with a smile. 'Perhaps,' she said, and reached down a foot from her stool in the small tiled bar area to scratch gently an ecstatic Archimedes who was sprawling beside her.

Other guests began to drift in and Sherry went off to serve them.

Zoe sipped her wine, enjoying its distinctive resinated flavour. Sherry's comment about old Stavros seemed to confirm her own impression, she thought. But she wasn't just any blonde. She was her mother's daughter, and he'd picked up on the resemblance, and been disturbed by it. Well, she'd go back to the square tomorrow, and if he tried to disappear again she would follow, and ask a few pertinent questions. Find out what he knew about Gina, and her time on Thania. Because there had to be something.

From the courtyard, she could hear the sound of musicians tuning up, and remembered that Sherry had said there would be dancing.

Time to stop pondering, and start enjoying instead, she told herself. She had a leisurely dinner of lamb, baked in the oven with tomatoes and herbs, accompanied by fried potatoes, green beans, and a full-bodied red wine, and savoured every mouthful.

There were extra tables and chairs tonight, she noticed, and these were rapidly being filled up by local people. Clearly, the Saturday dance at the Hotel Stavros was a real social event, but attended, she saw with relief, mainly by large family groups.

It began with a short display by two young couples in traditional local dress, who began threading their way between the tables, encouraging the hotel guests to join them in a long chain. When they reached Zoe, she shook her head with a smile. She'd never been much of a dancer, she thought wryly, and she was frankly deterred, anyway, by the intricacy of the steps.

It was pleasant to sit in her corner, drinking wine, and listening to the faintly oriental sound of the bouzouki players. She was clapping to the rhythm, her attention concentrated on the dancers, now moving in a wide circle, when she felt a sudden sharp prickle of awareness, bordering almost on fright. Realised that the music was dying, and an odd silence had fallen.

Her hands stopped, and balled into sudden fists, which she buried in her lap. She turned her head to look at the courtyard's lamplit entrance, with a mixture of excitement and dread, knowing all too well as she did so exactly who would be there.

Andreas was standing in the archway, one hand negligently on his hip, the other holding a jacket slung carelessly over one shoulder. His eyes were fixed on her, a faint smile playing about his mouth. He was wearing close-fitting black trousers, and an immaculate white shirt, with the cuffs turned back to reveal tanned forearms. He was seriously clean-shaven tonight, and the thick, curling dark hair was brushed back from his face. Zoe could see at his throat the gleam of a heavy gold chain.

He looked, she thought, with a swift inward shiver, quite incredible.

As her gaze met his he inclined his head briefly and gravely in silent acknowledgement.

Zoe felt the breath catch starkly in her throat. She thought, When he comes over—what am I going to say— what am I going to do?

Then watched, astonished, as he turned away and walked to a table on the other side of the courtyard. Its occupants rose to receive him, offering an uproarious welcome, and, Zoe saw, several pretty girls were already jockeying for position.

Her heart felt suddenly like a stone in her chest. She thought blankly, Well—that's that, then.

She didn't have to worry about what to say, because he didn't want to hear it.

But what else could she have expected? He'd probably spent everything he possessed on that lunch, and then watched her walk out on him. Little wonder he was seeking more congenial company.

And that meant she was free. Which was exactly what she wanted. Well—wasn't it? So, she'd done exactly the right thing.

She picked up her wineglass and took a hasty gulp, angrily aware that a war between her rational self and some dreaming, emotional creature that she'd barely known existed had suddenly begun raging inside her, and for no good reason.

I must have a crush on him, she thought. And at my age, too. The kind of thing I never bothered with when I was a schoolgirl. Oh, God, sad or what?

And, of course, she couldn't simply get up and walk out, because that would look as if his actions had the power to hurt her. As if it mattered that he hadn't sought her. No, she would have to sit for at least another half-hour, if not more, and tough it out.

Or even more than that, she told herself wretchedly. She would have to look as if she was really enjoying the music, and supremely indifferent to his presence at the same time. Rather like crossing a tightrope above a pit full of wolves. Especially when all she really wanted to do was go up to her room, bury her face in the pillow, and put her fingers in her ears. And pretend that this ache inside her did not exist.

She shivered, and drank some more wine. She didn't want to look across at him, but found her eyes straying in that direction just the same. He was bending his head, listening to the girl triumphantly occupying the seat next to him, a sloe-eyed creature with a sulky, sexy mouth, now all smiles and chatter.

Her hand was on his sleeve, Zoe noted, and her head was practically on his shoulder. No expertise needed to read that body language. In fact, the lady might as well be wearing a sign round her neck, saying 'Take me—I'm yours.' Except that he'd probably already done so on a number of occasions, she thought, biting her lip.

She was thankful when the folk dancers returned, and provided an alternative focus for her rapt attention.

But her small carafe of wine was almost empty, and there was a limit on how long she could sit, looking bright and fascinated, and anywhere but at him.

Yet she must have been doing it well, because this time she had no inkling of his approach until his voice said softly in her ear, 'Dance with me.'

She jumped, her hand catching the wineglass and sending the last remaining drops cascading across the cloth.

'Look what you've made me do.' She sounded more breathless than cross.

'I think you will be forgiven. Now, come.'

She rose, but hung back. 'I don't know any of the steps.'

'Then I shall teach you.' He walked behind her, close

but not touching, to the space that had been cleared for dancing. Evasion was impossible. She could feel the stares trained on her like searchlights from around the room, and heat invaded her face. Glimpsed Sherry looking as if she'd been poleaxed.

She whispered urgently, 'Andreas—I can't...'

'Yes,' he said quietly. 'Zoe *mou*, you can.' He produced a snowy handkerchief from his pocket, and shook it out, offering her a corner to hold. 'You see?' His smile was ironic. 'We do not even have to touch.' He paused. 'Now, there is a pattern of steps to be repeated. Watch what Soula does, and follow.'

Zoe obeyed mutely, staring down at the other girl's feet in their white stockings and flat-heeled black shoes. Stumbling a little at first, she began to copy what she was doing, listening to the insistent beat of the music—so much steadier than the thudding of her own heart—and gradually relaxing into it. Laughing as she found herself twirled one way, and then another. Gasping as the lead male dancer leapt high into the air before performing a series of amazing high kicks and even somersaults.

But, all the time, conscious of the man beside her holding the other end of the handkerchief. Joined to her, yet at a distance.

She was almost sorry when the music ended and the smiling, breathless line dispersed.

Somehow, she found herself back at her table. The stained cloth had already been cleared, she saw incredulously, and more wine had appeared, with clean glasses, and tiny cups of thick black coffee, very strong and sweet. And Andreas was sitting beside her. As, she thought shakily, he'd undoubtedly planned all along...

'So, *matia mou*,' he said softly. 'You have been lying to me.'

'Lying?' Her heart skipped a beat. He knew, she thought, who she was, and why she had come to Thania. And she wasn't prepared for this kind of confrontation—at least, not with him. 'I—I don't understand.'

'You told me you could not dance.'

'Oh,' she said. 'Oh—that.'

'Yes—*that*.' There was a note of faint mockery in his voice. 'What else could it be?' He paused. 'A little more practice, and you will be perfect.'

At dancing, she wondered, or lying?

She tried for a cool note. 'Is it necessary that I should be?'

'Why, yes,' he said. 'If you still plan to live at the Villa Danae. Or have you had second thoughts, perhaps?'

She shrugged. 'It will all depend on how negotiations go with your employer.' She paused. 'Tell me about him—this Steve Dragos.'

He drank some coffee, his expression meditative. 'What do you wish to know?'

She hesitated. 'Well—how old is he, for one thing?' *And did he ever know a girl called Gina who came here once, for another?*

'He is no longer young,' Andreas said. He gave a soft laugh. 'Although he would not thank me for saying so. And he is still of an age to be susceptible to a smile from a beautiful girl, if that is what you want to know,' he added drily.

Zoe flushed. 'It's not what I meant at all,' she disclaimed hastily. 'You—you seem very fond of him.'

It was his turn to shrug. 'He has been good to me over the years—in his way.'

'So he's bought your loyalty.' And for a lot of money, she thought. Because as well as the beautifully worked gold chain at his throat, he was wearing a watch that looked like a Rolex, except that it couldn't be. More likely, she told herself, it was one of those cheap imitations—wasn't it?

Andreas had straightened, the dark eyes sparking at her, his mouth suddenly hardening into coldness. 'You think, perhaps, that I am for sale?' His tone was quiet—dangerous. 'Then, you are quite wrong. I belong to no one but myself.'

Zoe lifted her chin. 'You take his money,' she pointed out.

'I earn what I am paid,' he said softly. 'Do not doubt it, Zoe *mou*.'

'And is scaring people witless one of your duties?' she asked baldly.

For a moment his brows snapped together, then his face relaxed into a grin. 'Who am I supposed to have frightened?' he asked lightly. 'You, *pedhi mou*? Surely not.'

'I saw the effect you had on those stupid boys today,' she said. 'And when you walked in tonight, everyone—stopped.'

'Did they, *matia mou*?' he said, with a touch of mockery. 'I did not notice. I could see only you.'

She swallowed. 'That—is so not true.'

'Yet here I am,' he said. 'With you, and no other.'

'Why?' Her breathing had quickened uncontrollably. 'Because I walked away from you today, and you needed to re-establish your ascendancy? In case word got round and you—lost face?'

He gave her a long, steady look, making her meet his gaze. 'Is that truly what you think, Zoe *mou*—that I have something to prove?'

She bit her lip. 'No,' she admitted reluctantly, at last. 'No, I don't. But I still don't understand why people seem so in awe of you.'

He was still watching her, his expression unreadable. 'Perhaps I simply benefit from the respect they give my employer.'

'Is he really so powerful—even from a distance?'

'You must judge that for yourself, *pedhi mou*, when you meet him.'

'Yes,' Zoe said without enthusiasm. 'I suppose so.' She glanced at him under her lashes. 'Do you know yet when that will be?'

'As soon as his doctors permit.' He was silent for a moment. 'If you are so impatient, *matia mou*, maybe I should introduce you to my friend Dimitrios. He deals in real estate, and could find you another property which would suit you just as well.'

'Oh, no,' Zoe said too quickly, and his brows drew together.

'You mean it must be the Villa Danae, or nothing? Why?'

She was on dangerous ground, but she managed to summon up a careless smile. 'Oh, we have a saying in the UK about property buying—location, location, location. And the Villa Danae is just perfect in that respect. I would never find anywhere that measured up to it.'

She paused. 'And it's never been lived in—allowed to achieve its full potential. I find that—tragic.'

'Ah,' he said softly. 'But even a paradise like Thania can have its share of tragedies, Zoe *mou*. And perhaps it is unwise to fix your heart on this particular house. My—boss has agreed to see you, nothing more.'

For a moment, she was tempted to confide in him—to tell him why she had come to Thania and ask for his help.

Then common sense reasserted itself, telling her to do no such stupid thing. Andreas was Steve Dragos' man. He'd made that perfectly clear. So, was it likely that he'd get involved in anything that might be contrary to the interests of such a powerful employer?

He'd get in touch with him immediately, she thought. Warn him. Because the potential loss of such an expensive and beautiful house was bound to matter.

Whatever might have happened in the past—whatever promises could have been made, time had moved on, and there was no guarantee that Mr Dragos would let Villa Danae go without a struggle.

And, no matter how many legal-sounding documents she could produce, he'd be able to hire any number of high-powered international lawyers to range against her.

Besides, instinct told her that any help she might acquire from Andreas Stephanos might well cost her more than she could afford to give.

It was better by far to keep her own counsel, she thought, swallowing, and catch Steve Dragos off guard. If that was possible.

She smiled at him, drank some wine. 'Well,' she said. 'I'll just have to keep my fingers crossed.'

'And if that doesn't work—if you don't get the house—you will leave?'

She hunched a shoulder. 'That's the plan.'

He leaned back in his chair, watching her through half-closed eyes. Paying lingering attention, she realised, to her blonde hair, piled in a loose knot on top of her head. To the low neckline of the black dress and the way it skimmed the top of her breasts. Dwelling meditatively on her mouth.

Making her know simply by a glance what it would be like to be touched—to be kissed by him, she thought in shaken bewilderment.

He smiled, as if he was perfectly aware what was on her mind.

'Then I shall have to find some way to persuade you to change your mind, *agapi mou*,' he drawled.

'Ah,' she said, snatching at her control. 'But perhaps I'm like you.'

'Like me?' He frowned slightly.

'You said you belonged to no-one,' she reminded him coolly. 'Well, neither do I. And I do just as I please.'

'But there may come a time,' he suggested softly, 'when you may also wish to—please me.'

There was a swift, taut silence, then Zoe shrugged. 'It seems to me that there are quite enough people doing that already,' she told him lightly. She managed, somehow, not to glance at the table across the room, and the sullen looks being directed at them by the Greek beauty.

His mouth twisted in wry acknowledgement. 'Maybe you have been sent to Thania to teach me the error of my ways.'

'I think that would take far more time than I have to spare,' she dismissed.

'And I think you are right, *agapi mou*.' He grinned lazily at her. 'It would probably take a lifetime. And in the meantime, I shall teach you to dance. A much easier thing.' He got to his feet. 'Come.'

Well, it was one thing she could agree to, Zoe thought with an inward sigh as she rose and followed him. Probably the only thing. And she sighed again.

It was an unforgettable evening, a breathless, exhilarating whirl of sound and rhythm, allowing her no time to think, or question the wisdom of her actions. Her head was spinning. She felt as if she were flying.

And Andreas was at her side throughout, joined to her always by that square of white linen, whispering encouragement, the dark eyes intent on her flushed, happy face.

'No more,' she protested laughingly, at last, leaning against one of the wooden posts that supported the overhead vine, a hand pressed to her side.

'But the night is only just beginning.'

Zoe shook her head. 'Not for me,' she said. 'I need to get some rest. As it is, I probably shan't be able to walk in the morning. My feet will be too sore.'

'Then ride instead.' His voice was quiet, but insistent. 'I will bring the Jeep to the hotel at ten o' clock, and show you my island.'

Zoe hesitated. Dancing with him, surrounded by a crowd of other people, was one thing. Spending a whole day together on their own was a different matter entirely.

Her throat tightened. She said, uncertainly, 'Andreas…'

'Zoe *mou*,' he returned softly. He studied her for a moment. 'Are you truly so scared to be alone with me?'

'No,' she said. 'Of course not.'

He grinned at her. 'Little liar.' He paused, his face becoming serious again. 'But I swear you have nothing to fear. You honour me with your company, nothing more.'

He added softly, 'Besides, I shall never ask anything of you, *agapi mou*, that you do not wish to give.' He put one hand under her chin, tilting up her face, making her look at him. 'Now will you come with me?'

She heard herself say, 'Why not?' And could immediately think of a thousand sane and sensible reasons to refuse. But she'd committed herself now, and she would not go back on her word. Her pride would not allow it.

She felt his thumb stroke the line of her jaw, gentle as a feather from the breast of a dove, and smothered an instinctive gasp as she felt her nipples harden instinctively against the soft fabric of her dress.

She took a hasty step backwards, jerking her chin away, and the abrupt movement proved the last straw for her already dishevelled hair, which came tumbling down onto her shoulders.

'Damn.' She made a dive for the clasp which had fallen to the floor, but Andreas was too quick for her, straightening with the worked silver clip in his hand.

'Leave it,' he advised, the dark eyes warm and slumbrous as they observed her. 'Your hair is better like that. Beautiful. And it will soon be spread across a pillow anyway,' he added softly.

Heat rose in her face. The image was too personal—too intimate, and she needed to distance herself, and fast before, dear God, that too-knowledgeable gaze of his observed her state of arousal.

She held out her hand. 'May I have my clip back, please?'

'Tomorrow,' he said, and slipped it into his trouser pocket. 'After you have seen Thania with me.'

Zoe bit her lip. She said, coldly, 'Perhaps I'll decide it isn't worth the trouble, after all.'

'Then it will stay with me,' he said, unabashed. 'A cherished memento of you, Zoe *mou*.'

'You have an answer for everything, don't you?' she said bitterly.

'Not yet,' he said. 'But I live in hope.' He allowed her to digest that, then inclined his head, coolly and courteously. '*Kalinichta, agapi mou.* Until tomorrow.'

She said in a stifled voice, 'Goodnight,' and walked away, threading her way between the tables, hardly aware any more of the curious and speculative glances coming her way.

Once in her room, she kicked off her sandals and fell, face down, across the bed, burying her face on her folded arms.

And I'm going to spend the day with him tomorrow, she groaned inwardly. I must be crazy.

She tried to comfort herself with the reflection that it would give her the opportunity to explore Thania with someone who knew the island and loved it. But it was still a high-risk situation, and she knew it.

But he promised I'd be safe, she argued with herself, defensively.

No, came the uncompromising reply. He said he'd take nothing that you didn't wish to give. That's entirely different.

And, as a guarantee, it was totally meaningless. Because he knew that she wanted him, she realised, shocked. And he was confident that, with a little time and patience, she'd be his. And of her own free will, too.

Zoe sat up slowly, pushing her hair back from her face. That's why he didn't make any move on me tonight, she told herself, bleakly. He knew I'd be expecting him to escort me to my door—to try to kiss me goodnight at the very least.

Yet he didn't. In fact, he hardly touched me.

Except once, she reminded herself, and she could still feel the marks of his fingers against her jaw as if she'd been branded there.

But during the dancing they'd always been divided by that silly handkerchief. No real physical contact at all.

This was clearly a game, she thought, for which he'd

invented his own rules a long time ago. And this worried her.

It was disturbing, too, to realise how little she still knew about him. True, it hadn't been an evening for the exchange of confidences, but he seemed to be becoming more of an enigma with every hour that passed.

But if he's a gardener, she thought, I'm Helen of Troy.

She could hear the faint sound of the music floating up to her. No doubt he'd rejoined his Greek girl, and coaxed her back to smiles by now. Maybe she'd even persuade him to spend tomorrow with her instead.

After all, they both live here, she told herself, whereas I—well, I could just be passing through.

She undressed and put on her wrap, then cleaned off the small amount of make-up she was wearing, and brushed her hair. It was thick and silky, she thought, shaking it back from her face, but it didn't make her a beauty. Nothing could, although she supposed she was on the attractive side of ordinary.

Just remember that, she told herself caustically, and take the sweet talk with a large pinch of salt.

If Andreas kept her hair clasp, she'd have to find another, she thought as she put down the brush. But there'd been a shop selling crafts and jewellery in copper and pewter as well as silver on the way up to the square. She could look there.

If Andreas didn't come tomorrow…

She was tired, she wanted to sleep, but she couldn't switch off the constant images passing and re-passing through her mind. The room felt stifling, too, and the sheets seemed to graze her like sandpaper.

Eventually, she got up, put on her wrap again, and went out onto the balcony. She sat lifting her face to the faint breeze from the harbour, listening to the lap of the sea, and the creaking of the timber caiques at anchor. There were no other sounds. The hotel lights were extinguished, and the dancers had dispersed. Andreas too would be—somewhere. Not alone, perhaps.

It shocked her to discover how much that possibility hurt. And how hard she had to fight to block the image of Andreas, his naked skin dark against the sheets of some woman's bed, his body arched above her in the act of love.

She even found herself wondering what kind of a lover he would be. Demanding or patient? Fierce or gentle? Or, maybe, all of them, she thought, and was horrified to recognise her own mounting excitement.

This was what he'd sensed, of course, from that first moment of their meeting. This was why he could take his time with her, not touching or kissing, because it would simply intensify the yearning. Make her want him more with every passing moment.

Until, inevitably, she could bear no more, and turned to him, offering herself.

Zoe shivered. It can't matter, she told herself desperately. *He* can't matter. I mustn't allow this to happen.

Yet already it seemed to be beyond her control, and she knew it.

Knew, too, that wherever Andreas had spent the night, he would be waiting for her outside the hotel in the morning, as he'd promised.

In just a few hours from now, she thought, staring blindly at the starlit sea. And I'll go with him this time—this one last time. Then, never again. Because it's too dangerous, and I can't afford to take that kind of risk.

And found, suddenly, the lonely, bitter taste of tears in her throat.

CHAPTER SIX

IT TOOK for ever next morning to decide what to wear. Zoe found herself trying and discarding almost every piece of clothing she'd brought with her.

Eventually, she picked what she would have worn had she been spending the day on her own—as, of course, she still might be, she swiftly reminded herself—putting on her blue bikini topped by a pair of white cut-off trousers, and a pretty overshirt in shades of blue and gold.

Her hair she wore deliberately pulled back from her face, and confined at the nape of her neck with a rubber band.

A glance at her watch told her it was nine-thirty, and she still had time for breakfast. Maybe food would calm the nervous churnings in her stomach, although she doubted it. But at least it would give her an occupation. Stop her prowling up and down her room, endlessly packing and repacking her canvas bag.

Sherry was quick and efficient with the rolls and coffee, but Zoe couldn't help noticing that she seemed to lack her usual ebullience.

'Hangover?' she teased as she poured herself some orange juice.

'I didn't have time to get one,' Sherry said, putting down small pots of cherry jam and honey.

'It was a terrific night,' Zoe agreed. 'But how do you stand the pace?'

'Each Sunday, I ask myself the same thing,' Sherry said wryly. She forced a shadow of her normal grin. 'Ignore me. I'm suffering from a touch of the ex-pats this morning.'

'Then you don't recommend life on Thania?'

'On the contrary, it's wonderful—with the right person,' Sherry said with bite.

'Ouch.' Zoe gave her a surprised look. 'What's Stavros done to upset you?'

'A slight difference of opinion, that's all.' Sherry paused. 'So what have you got planned for today?'

'I'm doing the island tour,' Zoe said. She hesitated. 'Actually, with Andreas—the man I was dancing with last night.'

'I noticed.' There was an odd note in Sherry's voice. 'How did you two happen to meet?'

'I told you—he's the gardener at the Villa Danae.' Zoe spread honey on a roll and took a bite. 'But judging by the way everyone jumps when he's around, I think he runs a protection racket on the side.'

Sherry's laugh rang hollow. 'Did he tell you his other name?'

'Stephanos,' Zoe said, stirring her coffee. 'Andreas Stephanos. But you must know him, surely?'

'I've seen him around, but he doesn't often come to our dance nights. I think his boss keeps him too busy.' Sherry hesitated. 'And you're seeing him today?'

'Yes.' Zoe nodded. She gave Sherry a frowning look. 'Don't you approve?'

'It's really none of my business.' There was constraint in Sherry's voice. 'Just—look after yourself, that's all.'

Zoe smiled at her. 'I intend to,' she said. 'You really don't have to worry.'

'It's just that I'm not sure if you know what you're getting into,' Sherry began, only to be halted by Stavros suddenly appearing beside her.

'Darling.' His smile did not reach his eyes. 'Some guests are asking about a packed lunch. Will you deal with it?'

Sherry bit her lip. 'Yes—I'll be right there.'

Zoe watched them go, surprised. Their usual cheerful, jokey relationship was clearly suffering from a bump in the road this morning. And when she walked through the reception area a little later, she could hear the sound of a low-voiced but furious argument coming from the office.

Zoe grimaced inwardly. She'd got to like them both, and, whatever the problem, she hoped it would blow over soon.

Then she saw that the Jeep was parked right in front of the hotel, and Andreas was lounging at the wheel, lean and casual in denim shorts and a short-sleeved blue cotton shirt, his eyes masked by sunglasses, and all other considerations were swept from her mind.

He raised a hand in greeting as she halted uncertainly at the top of the steps, and leapt out to take her shoulder bag and open the passenger door for her.

'*Kalimera,*' he greeted her. 'Did you sleep well?'

'Not really.' Pointless trying to pretend the shadows under her eyes didn't exist. 'It was so hot. There seemed to be no air.' *And there was the thought of you, burning in my brain, refusing to let go.*

He frowned swiftly. 'I will tell Stavros to have a fan taken to your room.'

'Oh,' Zoe said as the Jeep started off. 'Is Stavros under your thumb, too? That could explain something.'

He shot her a sideways look as the Jeep swung up the hill towards the square. 'What might it explain?'

Zoe looked coolly back at him. 'I don't think Sherry, his wife, approves of me spending too much time with you, and I'm awfully afraid they've been having a row about it.'

'I am sorry to hear it.' His tone was dry. 'But marital quarrels are part of life, and no doubt they will enjoy the eventual reconciliation.' He paused. 'Did Stavros' wife indicate a reason for her disapproval?'

'Not as such. She probably thinks you've acted as island guide for too many other women tourists.'

'Then she is wrong.' There was a faint snap in his tone. 'You are the first, Zoe *mou.*'

'Well, please don't be cross about it.' Zoe suddenly realised she'd said too much and could have bitten off her tongue. Andreas, she thought, alarmed, would be formidable if angered. 'I think she was just—anxious about me,' she added in an effort to smooth things over.

His smile was wintry. 'A concern I share with her, *pedhi mou*. So she need have no fears. You are safe in my care.'

The Jeep turned into the square, and slowed to allow a small boy leading a puppy on a long piece of string to cross in front of it.

Andreas turned to look at her, his face softening. He said, 'You believe that, don't you, *agapi mou*?'

'Yes.' Zoe swallowed. 'Yes, I—I do.' And it was true, she thought, although she could not explain her own certainty. On the other hand, perhaps she was just being appallingly naive, and would live to regret it.

He took her hand and carried it swiftly to his lips. 'Then our day begins here,' he told her softly.

She could feel herself blushing, and glanced hurriedly round the square instead. The backgammon players were out in force already, she noticed with amusement.

And among them Uncle Stavros, on his feet, staring at her and then at her companion, eyes fixed, mouth parted in shock as if he'd seen a ghost.

Zoe tensed, feeling the force of his gaze like a slap across the face. And as the Jeep moved off again she saw him take a step forward, his stick raised, his face distorted by a thunderous frown.

'Is something wrong?' Andreas was alerted by her sudden intake of breath.

'No, not a thing.' She was making no more trouble for Stavros' family. But, all the same, what the hell was the matter with everyone today? she asked herself in bewilderment.

She hurried into speech, trying to regain her equilibrium, which had been jolted by the nasty little incident. 'The church is beautiful, isn't it? I visited it yesterday.'

He grinned at her. 'Did you see the icon of the Virgin of the Cave?'

She looked back at him, demurely. 'Not after Sherry had warned me about it.'

'I doubt that the icon by itself could do much,' Andreas returned pensively. 'Although, naturally, I have never tested its powers,' he added silkily.

'Of course not.' Zoe tried to keep a straight face, and failed abysmally.

'That's better,' he approved as she began to shake with laughter. 'Sometimes you seem to have all the cares of the world on your shoulders, *pedhi mou.*'

'Perhaps I'm just not used to having holidays.' *Or meeting someone like you.*

'Then I shall do my best to make this one special for you,' Andreas told her quietly. He paused. 'I am glad to see you are wearing shoes you can walk in. I thought we would go first to Mount Edira before it becomes too hot.'

Zoe thought privately that it was pretty warm already, but she said nothing.

The Jeep sped on. Livassi was far behind them now, and they were climbing on a road little better than a cart-track, which wound its way upwards through groves of olive trees, their silver leaves glittering in the sun. Craning her neck, Zoe could see nets spread on the ground beneath, waiting to catch the coming harvest.

'I can see the road-surfacing scheme has been a great success,' she commented breathlessly, nearly jolted out of her seat by one pothole.

'Most of the traffic has four legs,' Andreas returned. 'They manage just fine.'

The track became steeper and the olives yielded to pine trees. The air was cooler here in their shade and faintly scented with resin. Zoe sniffed pleasurably, then took it deep into her lungs.

Andreas swung the Jeep off the track, and parked on a rare level stretch under the trees.

'From here, we walk,' he said. He gave her a wry grin. 'If you are not too bruised.'

She said lightly, 'I'm tougher than I look. Lead the way.'

She had half expected him to take her hand, but he did not, and in places it was something of a scramble to follow his long, sure stride. But when they reached the small concrete viewing platform that had been constructed near the summit, allowing an all-round view, she forgot everything else, drawing a breath of sheer wonder.

Her voice shook a little. 'Oh, God, it's just—so beautiful.'

'Yes,' he said. 'Each time I come here, I cannot believe that I spend time anywhere else.'

Below them was the green of the island itself, dotted with a patchwork of tiny coloured roofs, edged by faint strips of silvery sand. And beyond was the sea, stretching to the misty horizon in shades of turquoise and azure, broken only by the craggy amethyst shapes of the neighbouring islands.

'There is Zakynthos.' Andreas pointed. 'And that is Kefalonia.'

'They look almost close enough to touch.' Zoe shook her head.

'I advise a more conventional approach,' he said lazily. 'We could sail there one day, if you would like.' When she did not reply immediately, he went on smoothly, 'And the tiny one near Kefalonia is Ithaca, the place that Odysseus struggled to return to for so many years.'

'Hmm.' Zoe wrinkled her nose consideringly. 'According to the version I read, he didn't struggle that hard. In fact, he was constantly allowing himself to be diverted—generally by beautiful girls.'

Andreas tutted in amused reproof. 'Also by monsters, storms, and the malice of the old gods, Zoe *mou*. And his wife waited for him, faithfully and patiently through many long years, so he cannot have been all bad if he could inspire such devotion.

'Besides, not all the women he met were well disposed towards him,' he added. 'After all, Circe turned his men into animals.'

Zoe gave him a limpid look. 'Someone once suggested that Circe was the first feminist.'

'*Po, po, po,*' he said softly. 'And do you share her view, *agapi mou*, and believe that all men are beasts?'

'No, of course not.' She hesitated. 'Although the pair I encountered yesterday made me wonder.'

'They have spent too much time away from Thania,' he said, with faint contempt. 'Working in bars and clubs where foreign girls get drunk, and strip off their clothes, and encourage men to do the same. So, to their limited reason, all foreign girls must be like that. But that is not an excuse,' he added levelly.

'No,' Zoe said. She paused awkwardly. 'Andreas—I didn't thank you properly yesterday for rescuing me, and I want to apologise for that.'

'It's not a problem.' He shrugged. 'You were upset.' He pointed again. 'Do you see that little bay? That is where legend says Odysseus rested before the gods allowed him to return at last to his home. I thought maybe we could swim there this afternoon. That is, of course, if you have brought your swimming costume.'

'And if I haven't?'

He smiled at her. 'Then we shall still swim, *matia mou*,' he said softly. 'But I shall keep my eyes closed.' He paused. 'However, I would bet good money that it will not be necessary. That you are wearing a bikini under those charming clothes.'

Zoe bit her quivering lip. 'You see altogether too much, Mr Stephanos.'

He shrugged again. 'Perhaps because I like to look. And to look at you, Zoe *mou*, is a pleasure.' His smile widened. 'And what of you?' he questioned gently. 'Have you seen enough?'

If he meant himself, Zoe thought with a pang, then she would never see enough. She could go on filling her eyes with him for the rest of her life. Not a realisation to give her much pleasure or peace of mind.

Hurriedly, she swung round, shading her eyes. 'Can we see the Villa Danae from here?'

'Yes, if you have the eyes of a hawk.' His hands descended on her shoulders, turning her slightly, forcing her to control an involuntary quiver of response. 'There is the beach, and that little spot of colour is the roof. You see?'

Zoe peered down. 'And your own home—where is that?'

His brows lifted. 'Are you planning to pay me a visit?'

'No,' she denied quickly. 'Just—curious.'

'It is not easy to distinguish from this height,' Andreas said after a pause. 'The roof tiles are green and a little faded. But one day, soon, I will show you—if you wish.'

She said haltingly, 'Well—perhaps.' Then, 'Shall we go down, now?'

If the climb up had been something of a struggle, the descent was even more difficult. Even in her flat canvas shoes, Zoe found she was constantly slipping on the loose earth and pine needles.

And once she lost her footing altogether and cried out as she began to slide downhill. Andreas, walking ahead, immediately spun round and grabbed her, holding her against him to steady her. And for a few heart-stopping seconds she felt the strength of him, and the heat penetrating her thin layer of clothing as if it did not exist. She was aware of his breath on her face, drank in the warm scent of his skin with shaking voracity. As his clasp tightened she thought, He's going to kiss me, and her whole body tingled with longing and delight.

Then, with abrupt suddenness, she was free. Set at a brief but definite distance. She could have wept with the disappointment of it. And with the shock of what, she realised, was a rejection.

Her face burned, and she could not meet his gaze. 'I'm sorry,' she mumbled. 'That was clumsy of me.'

'No, *agapi mou*,' he said. 'The fault is mine. After all, I promised to take care of you.'

He took her hand firmly in his for the rest of the way.

helping her over the steepest sections of the track. But if he'd been a paid guide, his touch could hardly have been more impersonal.

By the time they got back to the Jeep, Zoe's heart was thumping like a trip-hammer, but it had nothing to do with the gradient. Because she knew that her feelings and desires back there on the mountain must have been shamingly transparent. He could not have missed the blatant signals she'd been giving out as her body had been pressed to his. So, why had he chosen to ignore them?

He knew I wanted him, she thought, humiliated. *He must have known. I did everything but put my arms round his neck and draw him down to me.*

I shall never ask anything of you, agapi mou, *that you do not wish to give.* His own words, still teasing at her mind—even stinging a little.

But she had wanted to give, she thought wretchedly. She'd needed his arms to hold her, and his mouth to find hers, and he had turned away—kindly, courteously, but definitely.

Because, presumably, he was regretting his pursuit of her. He was tired of the game he'd been playing, and decided to end it.

And now, somehow, she had to deal with her own regrets.

'Are you all right, *pedhi mou*?' He had shut the passenger door of the Jeep, and was regarding her with a faint frown.

Make it mundane, she thought. Bring the situation back to basics, as if a few moments ago had never happened.

'I'm a little thirsty,' she admitted, sounding half amused, half apologetic. 'Because things were a bit fraught at the hotel, I forgot to bring any water.'

'I have some in a cool-bag,' he said. He paused. 'But I also have a better idea, if you can wait for a minute or two.'

'Whatever you say.' She achieved a smile. Kept it cool and friendly. 'You're in charge, after all.'

She'd expected to be driven to a village with a *kafeneion* but at the foot of the track he turned the Jeep onto a path between the olive trees until they came to a small, single storey house, painted white, and almost fiercely neat in spite of the chickens pecking in the dust outside the only door.

A small woman emerged from the house, dressed in black, her hair covered by a scarf, her broad smile revealing gaps in her teeth. As Andreas climbed out of the Jeep to greet her she burst into a flood of shrill Greek, reaching up to pat him on the shoulder.

Then she snatched up a pitcher like a flower vase from a rickety table outside the door, and trotted off round the house with it.

'Come down, *agapi mou*, and meet Androula,' Andreas invited, walking round to the passenger side. 'She is an old friend, and she has gone to fetch us some water from her own spring, which comes straight from the mountain—the nearest we have to nectar.'

Zoe got out of the Jeep. 'Are you sure about this?' She glanced around her. 'Certain we're not imposing on her?'

'She loves company,' he said. 'And she will be delighted that I have brought you to her.'

'Does she live alone here?' Zoe asked doubtfully. 'It's very isolated.'

'No, she lives with Spiros, her husband, but he will be off attending to his melon patch.'

Androula was back, almost at once, her pitcher brimming. Nodding and smiling, she offered it to Zoe first.

The water was crystal clear, and so cold that it made her gasp. Zoe drank deeply, thirstily relishing its chill against the burn of her throat.

'Good?' Andreas asked as she lowered the pitcher at last.

'Better than that.'

To her surprise, he took the pitcher from her, and drank

in turn while Androula smiled widely, nodding her approval.

Zoe wasn't sure how she felt about it. In a way, sharing the container was almost as intimate as a kiss. But perhaps Androula was simply short of glasses, she told herself. And, anyway, it was no big deal. She could not allow it to be.

Androula put a small brown hand on her arm, gesturing towards the house with the other.

'She wishes you to go in, and sample her honey cakes,' Andreas explained. 'A mark of great favour,' he added.

She said lightly, 'Then how can I resist?'

Inside, the house seemed to consist of one spotlessly clean room. Curtained alcoves built into the thick walls contained beds, and there was also a fireplace, a stove for cooking, a table and some hard-looking chairs. On the top of a chest of drawers was an icon of the Virgin and Child, with a votive light burning beside it.

One wall lit up the rest of the rather gloomy interior, covered as it was from top to bottom in vivid picture postcards from every corner of the world.

'From their son,' Andreas said, seeing her looking at them, while Androula bustled around. 'He was a merchant seaman, and travelled everywhere. And, unlike Odysseus, always he sent cards home so that they would know where he was, and that he was safe.'

'And is he still safe?'

'Very much so,' Andreas said drily. 'He met an Australian girl, and now he lives in Queensland. Every six months he sends his parents the money for their airfares, so that they can visit him, and they put it in the bank instead, so it will be there for him if disaster should strike.'

'What a shame,' Zoe said softly. 'Do you think they will ever go?'

'I doubt it. I think he will have to bring his wife and child to them instead. And then, of course, he will stay. Or so Androula believes.'

'She thinks he'll give up the good life in Australia for Thania? Why?'

'Because of the water from the spring,' he said after a pause. 'There is an old superstition that anyone who drinks it will always return here.'

In the deafening silence that followed, Zoe heard herself swallow. She said huskily, 'Then it's a good thing I'm no superstitious.'

Andreas smiled at her. 'And neither am I, *matia mou*, he said softly. 'Neither am I.'

The honey cakes were delicious and Zoe could praise them without reserve, while Andreas translated for her.

When it was time to leave, Zoe found her hands clasped between Androula's gnarled ones, while the older woman spoke to her softly and earnestly.

'What did she say?' Zoe asked as they emerged into the sunlight. 'I feel such an idiot not to be able to understand.'

His voice was expressionless. 'That she will pray to the Virgin of the Cave to send you tall sons.'

She kept her smile in place as if it had been nailed there 'Wonderful,' she said, lightly. 'My entire future mapped out on the strength of one drink of water. Maybe I should stick to the bottled Loutraki brand from now on.'

Andreas made no reply, simply revved the engine and started off, sending dust and pebbles flying.

Back on the road, they travelled a mile, perhaps two, in a silence that Zoe was the first to break. 'Are we going to Odysseus' bay?'

'It's on the other side of the island.' He didn't look at her. 'I thought we would have lunch first. I know a good place.'

'Run by another friend of yours?'

His wintry expression eased a little. 'No one can have too many friends, *pedhi mou*.'

'No,' she said quietly. 'I'm sure that's true.'

She'd had friends, she thought, at school and later at university, but over the last few traumatic years, when Gina had been her priority, she'd lost touch with most of them. That was something she would start to rectify as soon as she got home. She might even use one of the internet sites that reunited people. It would all be part of her fresh start— her new life. Once she had laid the ghosts of the past...

'You are sighing,' Andreas said. 'What makes you sad?'

'I didn't realise I was.' Zoe hesitated. 'Perhaps all this wonderful sun and scenery reminded me that this is only a holiday, and that there's a long winter ahead at home.'

'But winter also has its pleasures, Zoe *mou*,' he said. 'If you have the right person to share them with.'

But I shan't have you... Her hands gripped together, white-knuckled, at the sudden pain of it.

Oh, dear God, she thought. How can I be feeling like this? I never meant it to happen.

Was this how her mother had felt all those years ago? she asked herself with a kind of desperation. And was this why she had never returned—never accepted possession of the house that had been given to her? Because she was suddenly overwhelmed—terrified by the force of her own emotions?

And so she'd opted instead for safety—security in England, with only the picture she'd painted to remind her of what she'd left behind.

And I, she thought, I shall only have a few photographs.

She was aware of Andreas' swift, sidelong glance, and hurried into speech. 'I've just realised I forgot to take my camera up Mount Edira. How stupid of me. I could have got some marvellous shots.'

'Another time, maybe,' he said. 'When perhaps you will trust me enough, *pedhi mou*, to tell me what you are really thinking.'

To which, Zoe decided in confusion, there was really no answer. Or not one that she dared to give.

They had the Bay of Odysseus all to themselves.

Zoe's brows lifted as she surveyed the deserted crescent

of sand. 'Did you arrange for everyone else to stay away?' she asked, not altogether joking.

Andreas smiled at her, unfazed. 'People usually come here by boat,' he explained. 'To swim and to dive. But there are no trips on Sundays.' He paused. 'As you must have noticed, it is not particularly accessible unless you have a four-wheel drive.'

'And not even then,' Zoe said, wincing at the memory of the bone-jolting ride through olive groves and citrus orchards, ending in the descent of a track like an Alpine black run.

'Also, it is not seen as a family beach,' he added. 'It shelves very deeply and quickly about fifty yards out, and, if you are not a strong swimmer, you are soon out of your depth.'

His warning came too late, Zoe thought, suppressing a bubble of hysteria. She'd been out of her depth since the moment she'd set eyes on him. And agreeing to spend the day with him—accompanying him to this silent and solitary place—was madness.

She said quietly, 'Then I shall have to be careful.' She paused. 'But if it's dangerous, why would anyone come here?' She glanced around. 'And there are certainly no concessions for tourists,' she added wryly.

'They come for the legend.' Andreas pointed to a large flat rock, gleaming white in the sun, jutting out into the sea at one end of the cove. 'They like to dive from the place where Odysseus is supposed to have rested before beginning the final leg of his journey to Ithaca.'

'You sound sceptical.'

He shrugged. 'He was on board a friendly ship, with a fair wind. Why hesitate when Ithaca was within reach?'

She looked down at the rough ground. 'Maybe he encountered yet another willing nymph.' Her voice sounded almost stifled.

'The story does not mention one.'

She swallowed. 'Then perhaps, after all those setbacks,

e was simply scared of being happy again with the people
e loved. Petrified that something else would go wrong.
And he decided he needed a breathing space.' She paused.
I suppose you would have sailed straight on.'

'When what you want most in the world is within reach,'
e said softly, 'why hold back?'

He went back to the Jeep, and began to unpack the rug,
he sun umbrella and the cool-bag from the back, leaving
er to stare after him, her heart thumping against her ribs
n mingled excitement and unease.

She turned and began to walk down the beach, feeling
he burn of the sand through the soles of her canvas shoes.

It was bakingly hot, the sea still and almost colourless,
he horizon a distant shimmer.

She had not expected to be alone with him here, she
hought. It might be off the beaten track, but it was justly
famous beauty spot. Besides, the taverna, where they'd
aten a wonderful lunch of freshly grilled fish and salad,
ad been equally remote, clinging to the edge of a cliff, but
lmost every table had been occupied.

She lifted a hand, pushing a strand of sweat-dampened
air from her forehead, recalling the boisterous welcome
hey'd received from Takis, the owner, a large, bearded
han with a booming laugh. He'd clapped Andreas cheer-
ully on the shoulder as he'd shown them to their table,
nd subjected Zoe to a long look that had combined frank
ppreciation with curiosity.

But when he'd made some jovial comment in his own
anguage, he'd encountered a frosty glance from Andreas
hat had sent him speeding back to his charcoal grill.

And when she'd enquired what Takis had said to pro-
oke such a reaction, Andreas had returned coolly and dis-
hissively that it was unimportant, and asked her if she
vould like some wine.

Clearly one was allowed to trespass so far and no further,
he thought. And maybe she should remember that.

When she turned back the sun umbrella was in place, the

rug was spread beneath it, and Andreas was stripping o his outer clothing to reveal brief swimming trunks.

She halted, feeling her mouth go dry. It was easier, sh thought, struggling for detachment, not to look at him.

He went past her, running with lithe grace, and plunge into the sea, his body cutting the water like a knife, wit scarcely a splash.

Last time, of course, this had been her signal to leav but today there was nowhere to run. They were isolate and alone together.

Yet so we were on Mount Edira, she reminded hersel and he didn't touch me.

But that was then, she thought as she began to unbutto her shirt. And this is now... And what am I most scare of, anyway: that he'll lay a hand on me—or that he won'

When he returned she was stretched out in the shado of the umbrella, sunblock applied, her hair tucked into h white cotton hat, sunglasses in place, and her attention ap parently concentrated on the book she was reading. Eve if her whole body was tingling in awareness of him, sh appeared cool, and that was what mattered.

He picked up his towel, and began to blot the moistu from his skin. She knew that he was looking down at he the dark eyes travelling slowly over her body. 'Are yo going to swim, Zoe *mou*?'

'Later, perhaps.' She kept her tone light. 'I tend to kee out of deep water.'

There was a smile in his voice. 'And you are neve tempted to throw caution to the winds?'

'Rarely.' The words on the page danced in front of h in a meaningless jumble. 'I like to keep life simple—an safe.'

'I too prefer to avoid complications,' he said. 'But som times they are inevitable.'

He stretched out beside her, close but not touching. Ver much at his ease.

He said softly, 'I am sure that is a fascinating book, *ped mou*, but I would be grateful if you could put it down. Because we need to talk, you and I.'

Zoe hesitated, then complied reluctantly. She said, 'What do you want to talk about?'

'About you, *matia mou*—what else?'

Her laugh cracked in the middle. 'Not a very interesting subject.'

'Ah,' he said. 'But I disagree. You see, Zoe *mou*, you intrigue me. So, I wish to know exactly what brought you here to Thania. And this time I want the truth.'

CHAPTER SEVEN

ZOE sat bolt upright, and stared at Andreas. He was lying propped up on one elbow, very much at his ease, the dark eyes slightly narrowed, the firm mouth cool and unsmiling as he looked back at her.

The silence seemed to echo between them. The whisper of the sea only a few yards away seemed suddenly like muted thunder to her heightened senses. Her skin tingled under his unwavering gaze.

He said, 'I am waiting for you to answer, *pedhi mou*.'

She swallowed. 'I—I don't know what you're talking about.'

'You disappoint me.'

She spread her hands defensively. 'I came here on holiday. So do a lot of other people.'

'Not that many,' he said. 'Compared with other islands. And they come in couples, or family groups.' He paused. 'There are few beautiful girls travelling alone.' His faint smile did not reach his eyes. 'So, you must see you are something of an enigma, Zoe *mou*.'

'I don't see why.' She lifted her chin. 'It was a spur of the moment booking. My friends had already made their travel plans. And I—I needed a break. I told you why.'

'Yes,' he said. 'You have known great sadness, and I am sorry. All the more reason, I would have thought, to seek company.'

'I'll try and remember that,' she said. 'Next time.'

'But I ask again,' he went on. 'Why this island of all others? And what brought you to the Villa Danae? You understand why I am intrigued.'

'No,' she said. 'I don't.' She touched the tip of her

104

ongue to her dry lips. 'I'm surprised you don't set up some
pecial immigration desk where the ferry docks. Interrogate
everyone who comes here about their background and mo-
ivation. Or would that dent the Greek reputation for hos-
•itality?'

Andreas shrugged a shoulder. 'Most of the people who
ome here are just looking for a quiet holiday in the sun.
There is no need to question them. But from the first, Zoe
mou, you have made me wonder. You are a mystery I have
vet to solve.'

'And what about yourself?' She flung back her head,
leliberately confrontational. 'You're hardly the simple man
of the soil you claim to be. Not when you stride about,
outting the fear of God into people, like the uncrowned king
of the island,' she added hotly.

'Not quite king,' Andreas drawled. 'Heir to the throne,
naybe.'

In the sudden deafening silence, Zoe heard herself swal-
ow. She said with controlled calm, 'I—see. Then I don't
suppose you're even called Andreas Stephanos—are you?'

'Those are my names,' he said softly. 'But there is an-
•ther. My last name is Dragos.'

'Of course it is.' She tried to smile. To conceal the fact
hat anguish had settled like a stone in the pit of her stom-
ich. 'Brother—cousin—nephew of Steve Dragos the ship-
oing tycoon by any chance?'

His mouth tightened. 'His son.' He paused. 'And, like
ourself, Zoe *mou*, an only child.'

'You mean we actually have something in common?'
Her laugh cracked in the middle. 'But that's the only sim-
larity. Nobody jumps when I walk into a place. Or ever
vill.'

She shook her head, almost wonderingly. 'Sherry wanted
o warn me, I see that now, but her husband wouldn't allow
t. After all, the young master must be allowed to have his
un.' She gave him a burning look. 'What a fool I've been.'

'Ah, no,' Andreas said quietly. 'I have never, from the

first moment we met, thought you were a fool, *pedhi mou*.
But I must ask you not to treat me like one, either,' h
added levelly.

'I think,' she said. 'The less I have to do with you, M
Dragos, the better.' She reached for her shirt, angrily awar
that her hands were shaking. 'I'd like to go back to m
hotel, now, please.'

'Thania is only a small island,' he said musingly. 'Bu
to walk such a distance in this heat? I don't think yo
would make it.'

'You mean you're not prepared to drive me back?' He
voice quivered with outrage.

'Certainly,' he said. 'But later. After we have spent som
time together, Zoe *mou*, without fear of interruption. An
when you have answered my questions,' he added softly
'Because something tells me you are still not being com
pletely honest.'

'You dare to say that?' Zoe almost choked on the words
'After the way you pretended to be a gardener?'

'There was no pretence. I enjoy gardening. And, if yo
recall, I said I had other duties.' He shrugged again. 'If yo
had asked me, I would have described them to you.'

'Yes,' she said smoulderingly. 'Just like you told m
your name—with the salient bit held back.'

'Well, perhaps.' He had the gall to grin at her. 'It wa
good, for once, to be with a woman who did not know wh
I was, and did not care. Someone who did not even wis
me to pay her attention. But the game is over now.'

He sat up. Moved slightly so that he was closer. Clos
enough to touch, she realised, dry-mouthed.

'So, what salient bits are you holding back, *matia mou*?
he asked softly. 'What is your interest in the Villa Danae—
which, you must acknowledge, you could not afford to ren
or buy?'

'I—saw a picture of it once,' she said. 'A water colou
painted by an artist I—knew. A view of the terrace.' Sh

hrugged. 'I wanted to see if the real thing matched the
mage.'

'I could almost ask the same of you, Zoe *mou*.'

She bit her lip. 'That's—not fair.'

'You think not?' There was a faint note of derision in
is voice. 'You truly expect me to believe that a picture
rought you here? I did not know such a thing existed.'

'You don't think the Villa Danae is worth painting?'

'Every island in Greece has its share of artists,' Andreas
aid slowly. 'But usually they try to capture the light—the
olour of the sea. And most would choose an ancient tem-
le to paint rather than a modern house.'

'So, it's a one-off,' Zoe said steadily. 'Maybe that's why
t caught my imagination.'

'I would also be interested to know how this artist gained
ccess,' he said, with a touch of grimness. 'I must tell my
ather that our security should be overhauled.'

'Why bother him with it? It was all a long time ago, and
t won't happen again.' She encountered an ironic look, and
lushed. 'Well, I certainly shan't be going back. You're
ight—the house is out of my league.' *And not just the
ouse...*

There was a pain inside her like an iron fist clenching,
nd she drew a deep breath, 'But I hated seeing it empty,
o I let myself dream for a while.' *So many dreams...*

She paused. 'Now I'm only sorry I ever went within a
mile of the place,' she added in a small wintry voice. 'So
an you call off the inquisition, please?'

'But if I am not allowed to ask questions, how can I
earn all the things I wish to discover about you, Zoe *mou*?'

He spoke gently, with a hint of laughter in his voice. The
udden change of tack caught her completely off guard, and
rought a swift warmth to her face that owed nothing to
he sun. Because this was no confrontation over a house.
This was simply a man and a woman alone together. A
ituation as old as time and as compelling.

She said, stumbling a little, 'What do you want to know?'

'Everything.' His eyes met hers. Held them. Making her aware of the smile in their dark depths. And the smoulder of heat, controlled but palpable. Somehow, he seemed to have moved even nearer, and she realised that if she did no more than turn carelessly her skin would brush his.

'Rather a crowded agenda for an afternoon on the beach.' She managed to speak lightly, in spite of the hectic plunge of her heart against her ribs.

'I learn quickly. And besides, you have all my attention *matia mou*.'

Was that supposed to make her feel any better? Zoe wondered breathlessly. She looked away, picking up a handful of sand, and letting it drift through her fingers.

'Actually, there isn't all that much to tell. I had a very ordinary, happy childhood, did reasonably well at school, and got a decent degree afterwards.' She forced a smile. 'Pretty dull, really.'

'On the contrary, Zoe *mou*. A happy childhood is a gift from the gods.' There was an odd, almost bitter note in his voice.

She glanced at him quickly, noting the taut line of his mouth. 'You can't have lacked for much.'

'Materially, no, as you would expect,' he admitted flatly. 'But—in other ways…' He paused, then said with an effort, 'Unlike you, I saw little of my parents. My father was always busy—never in the same place for more than a few days at a time. And my mother was rarely well enough to be with me. She spent a lot of her life in hospitals and clinics, or searching for new treatments in Europe and America.'

'I'm—sorry.' Zoe hesitated. 'What was the matter with her?'

'I do not believe she was ever strong.' His tone was sombre. 'She found pregnancy an ordeal, and giving birth to me a nightmare. It was certainly a trauma that always seemed to stay with her throughout her life. She had constant problems with depression, and she suffered various physical symptoms over the years, too. Endless tests were carried out, but they always proved inconclusive.'

His mouth twisted. 'With hindsight, I suspect she was simply allergic to marriage—especially to marriage with a strong, demanding man like my father,' he added wryly. 'Someone who wanted a woman to stand at his side, and give him a whole nursery full of children.'

He sighed. 'I wonder sometimes which of them was the most unhappy.' He sent her a dry look. 'So you see, *pedhi mou*, I had everything I could want—except what I really wanted.'

Zoe stared at him, seeing not the cool, sexy man who'd imposed himself on her life with such casual assurance, but the boy he'd once been, existing in some bewildered, lonely vacuum.

She heard herself say his name. Put out a hand, and touched his bare shoulder, letting her palm linger on its smooth warmth. She felt the strong muscles tense beneath her touch, then Andreas captured her fingers with his own, and carried them to the faint roughness of his cheek, before brushing them swiftly with his lips.

She was lanced, almost torn apart with the sudden force of her need. She looked down at the lean, brown fingers clasping hers, and imagined them cupping her breasts, or gliding down to part her thighs. Discovering every sweet, intimate secret she had to offer. She thought of his mouth on hers. Their bodies locked together in mutual possession.

She felt her nipples blossom to heated peaks against the confines of her bikini top, and almost before she knew what she was doing her free hand was searching for the clip, and releasing it, allowing the tiny garment to fall away from her body, revealing the beauty of her small round breasts.

Her eyes met his in mute offering. She was burning, melting with the desire to be in his arms at last. To know the caress of his hands—his mouth.

She heard his harsh, indrawn breath as he looked at her
Saw the swift flare in the dark eyes.

Only to find, in the next instant, her hand released, and
Andreas suddenly turning away—deliberately distancing
himself, she realised with shock and disbelief.

'What's wrong?' Her voice was a stranger's, small and
husky, stumbling over the words it was forming. 'Don't—
don't you—want me?'

He said, over his shoulder, 'You are temptation itself
pedhi mou. But this is not the time or the place. So be good
enough to cover yourself.'

For a moment, she knelt beside him, stricken, staring at
the long line of his bare back. But even as she tried to
make her fumbling fingers obey him, anger began to build
in place of the agonised wrench of humiliation at his re
jection of her.

She removed her top completely, and dropped it onto the
sand in a gesture of total bravado.

'Isn't it time you joined the twenty-first century, M
Dragos?' She managed mockery, edged with contempt
'After all, I saw plenty of girls sunbathing topless on the
town beach the other day. Don't you think your reaction is
just a tad extreme?'

'The women you refer to make their own choices.' His
tone bit. He did not look at her. 'They are not, however
alone with me here.'

'No,' she said. 'And how fortunate for them.' She got to
her feet, grabbing her towel and bag. 'But as we seem to
be stuck with each other, all I can do is remove mysel
from your immediate vicinity.'

She stalked off, down the beach, making for Odysseus
rock, her head held high. The slab of stone scorched the
soles of her feet as she spread out her towel, but she refused
to allow her discomfort to show, certain that Andreas would
be watching.

Well, let him look, she thought, biting her lip. Just as
long as he didn't realise she was actually dying of self

consciousness, parading around without her bra. Because
topless sunbathing was something she'd never indulged in.
Even with Mick, she'd been shy—reserved about naked-
ness, and she was beginning to regret her defiant gesture,
which now seemed plain silly.

Face it, she told herself. You're not cut out to be one of
Odysseus' nymphs.

And any form of sunbathing was out on this rock, anyway, she thought, biting her lip. There was no shade at all,
and even with high-factor sun lotion she'd be risking getting badly burned.

'Oh, damn you, Andreas Dragos,' she whispered under
her breath. 'You pushed me into this, and now I have to
deal with it.'

She was also furiously aware that there were tears prick-
ing at her eyelids. And she was not, under any circumstances, going to let him see her cry. Allow him to know
that he had the power to hurt her so badly that she could
have moaned with the pain of it.

There seemed little alternative but to go for a quick
swim. It would cool her, and calm her down. Besides, drops
of sea water would be good camouflage for any tears that
managed to escape.

She trod, wincing, to the edge of the rock, steadied herself, stood poised for a moment, then dived in.

As she launched herself she thought she heard Andreas
calling something to her.

But if it's an apology, it's too late, she told herself, gasping at the shock of the cool water against her overheated
skin, and the endless green darkness waiting for her.
Andreas had not exaggerated, it seemed. This was far, far
deeper than she was accustomed to.

She turned, kicking her way back to the dazzle of sunlight above her, grateful when she broke the surface at last,
gasping for air.

Without even glancing in the direction of the beach, she
broke into her steady crawl, and headed off determinedly

down the small bay. She would do the equivalent of a cou
ple of lengths, she decided, then return to that gridiron o
a rock, and plaster herself in sunblock.

She was a competent swimmer, but not a particularly
strong one, and the Ionian Sea, she soon realised, was no
small-town swimming pool. One length, not two, would be
quite enough, she decided, discovering that she did not care
for the sensation of knowing that, for the first time ever
she was completely out of her depth in water. Never before
and never again, she promised herself grimly as she turned
to swim back.

But she soon found that getting back to the rock, or even
inshore, was more of a problem than she'd anticipated
There was a definite current, quiet and insidious, which was
pulling her out even deeper, and preventing her from mak
ing any real headway as she battled against it.

She was beginning to get tired, too, but there was no
point in turning onto her back and floating, because that
would simply add to her problems.

She could see Odysseus' rock, shining in the sunligh
like a beacon, but a beacon that seemed to be getting furthe
away, despite her best efforts. The drag of the current ap
peared to be getting stronger, or was it just that she hersel
was becoming weaker?

She swallowed a mouthful of sea water, and came up
spluttering, trying to tread water, suddenly afraid.

She hadn't even realised she was no longer alone unti
strong hands took hold of her, and Andreas' voice said
curtly, 'I have you now. Relax, don't struggle and I'll take
you in.'

She wanted to tell him with dignity that she knew bette
than to resist when her life was being saved, but she go
another mouthful of sea water and choked instead.

Besides, she thought, recovering, there was nothing re
motely dignified in being towed back to land like a piece
of flotsam.

'We are at the rock,' his voice told her breathlessly a

last. 'Turn yourself, and hold onto it with both hands, and I will pull you up.'

Zoe clung on, gasping, as he lifted himself lithely out of the water. Then his hands were under her armpits like steel clamps, drawing her up beside him.

She wasn't sure whether she wanted to burst into tears first, or be sick.

She said in a voice she hardly recognised, 'I don't know how to thank you...'

'Thank me?' he came back at her hoarsely. His eyes were sparking with anger, his mouth set grimly. 'Thank me, you little fool? *Otheos*, you could have drowned. Didn't you hear me shouting, telling you not to dive from the rock—that it can be dangerous?'

'I—I couldn't hear what you said.' Her teeth were chattering suddenly as the realisation of what might have happened washed over her again.

He muttered something under his breath that she was glad not to understand, and enveloped her without ceremony in her towel, which he had snatched up.

She'd wondered what his hands would feel like on her body, and now she knew, and they were not tender, or gentle or even remotely loverlike. They were harsh, vigorous, and extremely thorough, but she began to feel alive again, and less like a piece of wreckage.

And when he'd finished he picked up her bag, and slung it over one shoulder, then lifted Zoe, towel and all, into his arms, and carried her back to the shelter of the sun umbrella. Where he set her on her feet.

He handed her a bottle of water. 'Drink some of this.'

She was glad of its coolness against her burning throat. She poured some of the water into her cupped hand and splashed it on her stinging eyes.

Her bikini top was still lying where she had dropped it. She bent and retrieved it, trying to huddle into it under the concealment of the slipping towel.

He said levelly, 'Isn't it a little late for such modesty?'

He took the towel from her shoulders, and tossed it to one side, then fastened the clip of her bra himself. 'Nor was there any need to remove this,' he added quietly. 'My imagination had already told me how you would look without your clothes.'

She turned to face him, but found it was beyond her, so stared down at the sand instead.

She said in a low voice, 'I'm sorry. I—I lost my temper, and put us both in danger.'

'From now on,' he said, 'you will swim only from the beach at the villa. It is shallower there. And, then, only when I am present.'

She shook her head, wearily. 'I'd have thought I was the last person you'd want around.'

'No, *pedhi mou*.' He spoke more gently. 'You know that is not true.'

'I don't think I know anything,' she said. 'Not any more.'

She'd been so determined not to cry in front of him, but suddenly the tears were there, just the same, running down her face, dripping off her lashes and the tip of her nose. And she was powerless to prevent them.

'Ah, no,' he said, and his arms went round her, drawing her to him. 'No, there is no need for this, Zoe *mou*. We are both safe.'

He stroked the damp tangle of her hair, murmuring to her in his own language, while Zoe leaned against him, resting her cheek against the wall of his chest, absorbing the cool, fresh scent of the sea on his skin, the strong beat of his heart, as she tried to control her little, shuddering sobs.

She felt a strange kind of lassitude stealing over her, and her legs were shaking so badly that, if Andreas had not been holding her, she thought she would have slipped down to the sand at his feet. And stayed there for ever.

It's shock, she told herself. Delayed shock, that's all.

And knew that was only part of it.

She thought 'I don't understand,' and only realised she had spoken aloud when he answered her.

'What do you find puzzling, *pedhi mou*?'

'What we're doing here,' she said. She turned her head a fraction so that her mouth rested hungrily against his skin. 'Why you're even with me, when you don't—' Her voice faltered. 'When you don't seem to want me...'

His hands gripped her shoulders, putting her away from him as he looked gravely down at her, the dark eyes searching hers with strange intensity.

'Is this truly what you think?' he asked softly. 'Is this what you expect of me—a few hours of pleasure for you to giggle over with your girlfriends during that long English winter?'

'No.' Her mouth trembled. '*No*. But the truth is I don't know what to expect—or what's happening to me. And that scares me.' She took a step backwards, wrapping her arms round her body. Trying to close herself off from him. Establish some physical and emotional independence, but knowing at the same time that it was way too late for that. That she was lost.

She said, her voice breaking huskily, 'Oh God, I did not—*not*—come here for this.'

'You think I did?' He laughed harshly. 'You are wrong, Zoe *mou*. I had my life in place. I knew its rules and obligations. And you, believe me, were never part of the plan.'

Her voice was little more than a whisper. 'Then let me go—Andreas, please. Let me go—now.'

'You could do that?' He stared at her. 'You could walk away.'

Her mouth twisted in a painful travesty of a smile. 'I could—try.'

'Ah, no, *matia mou*,' he said unevenly. 'You know better than that. And never think that I do not desire you—because I do, more than you will ever know.' His voice deepened to a new intensity. 'But it would be too soon, and you must be aware of that, too. We have known each other only for hours, rather than weeks, months and years. And we need more time—if only to come to terms with what has happened to us. Time to learn about each other, and reach acceptance.'

'But we don't have that sort of time,' Zoe objected raggedly. 'I'm here on holiday, and when it's over I have to go back to England, to my flat and my work.' She shook her head wretchedly. 'However much you dress it up, it can only ever be a temporary affair.'

'Only,' he said, 'if that is what you want, Zoe *mou*. So, be truthful. Is it?'

Mutely, Zoe shook her head.

'Then there is no problem,' Andreas said. 'Because that is not my wish either. You see, I do not just want your body, *agapi mou*.' He framed her face gently in his hands. 'I need your heart, your soul, and that sweet, stubborn mind that will not allow you, even at this moment, to trust me. And no less will do.'

He smiled ruefully, 'And this is also why I dare not trust myself to touch you more than this. Because I am determined to behave well.'

Her voice shook. 'Andreas—there's something I have to tell you.' Her eyes searched his anxiously. 'There—there was someone else—once. I—I'm not a virgin.'

His brows lifted. 'You think that makes some difference?'

'Well—doesn't it?'

'Is he still important in your life?'

'God, no.' She thought for a moment, frowning a little. 'I can barely remember what he looked like.'

'Good,' he said. 'Then put him from your mind.' He stroked the curve of her cheek. 'If it is the moment for confessions, then maybe I should tell you that I am not a virgin either,' he added wryly.

She was startled into a giggle.

'That's much better,' he approved softly. 'I began to think you would never smile again.'

There would never be a better moment to be totally honest with him, and Zoe knew it. To tell him why she had come to Thania, and what had taken her to the Villa Danae.

But she was scared. Frightened in case she saw the tenderness fade from his eyes, and anger harden his mouth.

And in case he believed her acknowledged longing for him was motivated by self-interest rather than passion, now that she knew his true identity.

She thought, I couldn't bear that. I can't take the risk—not yet. Perhaps not ever.

Because, she realised with sudden, startling insight, the villa doesn't matter any more, or anything that may have happened in the past. All I care about is Andreas, and our future together, and I don't want it muddled by old mysteries. So, I can just tear up the paperwork, and be free of it all.

'Hey,' Andreas said softly. 'Where are you, Zoe *mou*? Suddenly, you've gone from me.'

'I think I'm still a little stunned.' She met his gaze steadily, her eyes unclouded, feeling as if a great weight had been lifted from her shoulders. 'But I've gone nowhere. I'm here with you, and that's the only place I want to be.' She reached up and kissed him on the cheek. 'Andreas *mou*,' she added, her lips trembling into a smile. 'See, I'm learning Greek.'

He pulled her against him, making her burningly aware of his need for her. 'And I cannot wait to become your teacher,' he muttered roughly into her hair.

'Must we—wait?' She whispered the words against his skin.

'Yes,' he said. 'And yes, again, for all the reasons I have already given and a hundred more.' He put her away from him, his mouth twisting ruefully. 'Which is why I think we should continue our tour as soon as we're dry—find somewhere with other people, *pedhi mou*. Where my self-control will not be under such strain.'

Her smile became mischievous. 'I think that comes with the territory.' She paused. 'So where is there less temptation?'

'I can't think of a single place,' Andreas admitted unevenly, after a pause. 'But the Silver Caves are public enough, and have tourists. We'll go there.'

'Yes,' she said. 'It might be best.'

'Ah,' he said softly. 'My lovely girl, do not look at me like that.'

Zoe was trembling as he drew her back into his arms. He whispered her name, looking deep into her eyes, then his lips came down on hers for the first time, exploring its contours with infinite gentleness, restraining any more passionate demand with iron control.

And she wanted more—wanted it so badly that it was anguish to remain passive in his embrace. She needed to twine her arms round his neck, part her lips for the intimate invasion of his tongue, let her hands caress the long, hard lines of his back. Then pull him down to the sand, offering herself with unresisting joy, knowing the delight of his body naked against hers at last.

She was melting—scalding with desire, pressing closer to him with a little pleading murmur. Candidly testing the power of his restraint.

His breathing was ragged as he released her, the dark eyes glittering hotly, his hands lingering reluctantly on her skin, savouring its texture, the racing heat below its surface.

He said hoarsely, 'And now we go, *agapi mou*, and at once, or I cannot answer for the consequences.'

He turned away, reaching for his clothes, and Zoe, with an aching, silent sigh, realised she must do the same.

The entrance to the caves was narrow, half sandy track, half steps leading downwards, but there were plenty of guiding lights on the walls, which glimmered like mother-of-pearl in their glow.

At the bottom there was a tiny wooden jetty, where the rowing boats were moored. The silver gleam of the water had an otherworld quality that was almost eerie, and Zoe was quite glad to be part of a queue of sightseers, and not on her own.

She was still shaking inside from the memory of Andreas' kiss, her lips throbbing with heat, her entire body pulsing with the force of the emotions he had awakened in her.

Think about something else, she adjured herself as the woman guide launched into a commentary about the history of the caves and their discovery. But how was that possible when she was with the man she wanted with such desperation, her senses reacting almost frantically to the warmth of his body, the essential male scent of him?

When it was their turn, she sat beside Andreas in the bow, aware of little but his arm holding her lightly, while their boatman sent them skimming across the surface of the lake.

The power of the cave's echo was being demonstrated with gusto from the other boats, with screams of simulated terror, and sinister booming laughs reverberating round the walls.

'You know the legend?' Andreas murmured quietly in her ear, during an infrequent lull.

'Yes, I read about it. A little spooky for my taste.'

He smiled. 'You don't want to try it? To call my name and see if I will be true to you?'

'It's not necessary. Anyway, I'm not superstitious.' Zoe bent her head, and made a business of dabbling her fingers in the water. But not for long. 'God, it's like ice.' She snatched her hand back.

'Then I'll call to you instead.' He was clearly undeterred by her lukewarm response.

'No,' she said quickly, aware of a sudden, inexplicable unease. 'Don't, Andreas, please.'

His brows rose. 'You don't dare have your good faith tested, *pedhi mou*?'

'It's just a silly story,' she said. 'And, besides, there are all these people around.' She managed a laugh. 'I'd feel such a fool.'

'Then we will come back some evening, when we have the place to ourselves, and the cave will give us its blessing,' he said. 'As a man of Thania I must obey the tradition before I marry.'

Zoe started so violently that the boat rocked, and the boatman growled a warning.

She said breathlessly, 'You're talking about *marriage*?'

'Zoe *mou*,' he said patiently. 'Have you listened to anything I have said to you? I thought I had made it clear I want you to share my life, not just my bed.'

'Andreas.' Her face warmed frantically. She dropped her voice to a whisper. 'The boatman will hear you.'

'He speaks no English, and he knows better than to listen, or repeat what he has heard.' He paused. 'Why do you still doubt me, *pedhi mou*?'

She said slowly, 'Because it's all happening so fast.' She paused. 'And girls like me don't usually marry men in your position. You must know that.'

His mouth twisted. 'Ah, you think you're too good for me, perhaps? You could be right. See, I admit it.'

Her hands gripped together tightly in her lap. 'Oh, please be serious. I'm sure it can't be this simple—that you're expected to propose to someone suitable. Make a—a dynastic marriage.'

'It has been mentioned.' He shrugged. 'But I have always insisted that I would make my own choice, *matia mou*.' He smiled at her. 'And although I did not know it, I was waiting for you.'

'I don't think I altogether believe that.' Zoe's flush deepened, and her mouth curved almost shyly. 'But I like to hear you say it.'

'You still doubt me?' he asked reproachfully. 'Maybe I should ask the echo to judge me, after all.'

'No,' Zoe said vehemently, as he half turned towards the corner of the cave. 'Please, darling. Not now. We'll come back another time, as you said.'

He looked back at her, his brows lifting. He said gently, '*Pedhi mou*, it's just a legend. Why does it disturb you so much?'

She tried to laugh. 'I keep thinking—suppose we call each other's names, and there's only silence. I—I don't want to tempt providence.' She gave a slight shiver. 'And it's cold down here, too.'

'You wish to go?' She nodded jerkily, and he signalled to the boatman to take them back to the jetty.

They were quiet on the drive back to Livassi. Andreas was frowning slightly, his fingers tapping the wheel with a touch of impatience as he drove. Zoe stole glances at him, wondering what he was thinking. Could he already be having regrets about declaring himself so recklessly? she asked herself with an inward shiver.

When they drew up outside the hotel, she said with a catch in her voice, 'Will I see you tonight?'

'No, *pedhi mou*. I have things to do, and people to talk to, my father among them.' He paused. 'But I will see you in the morning. We will spend time at the Villa Danae together, and talk and make some plans. At what time shall I come for you?'

'I'll make my own way there.' She wrinkled her nose. 'After all, we don't want to cause any more gossip than necessary.'

'Soon,' he said, 'the whole world will know.' He took her hand and kissed it, his lips swift and sensuous against her fingers. 'Until tomorrow, *agapi mou*. Sleep well, and dream of me.'

As the Jeep pulled away Zoe stood on the hotel steps,

lifting a hand to wave him goodbye, and paused, the real-isation that she didn't want him to go suddenly overwhelm-ing her in a wave of utter desolation.

As if, she thought, her heart thudding, something were telling her that it was over. That it was the end of her happiness, and she would never see him again.

She called his name, wanting to summon him back, her voice high and frightened, but the Jeep was already gone, leaving just a wisp of exhaust fumes lingering in its wake.

And then, as she had dreaded, there was only silence.

CHAPTER EIGHT

ZOE was thankful that neither Stavros nor Sherry were in reception to witness her making such a fool of herself. In fact, there seemed to be no one around at all, suggesting that they were all in the kitchen getting the preparations for dinner under way.

'What did I think I was doing?' she asked herself, grimacing. 'Screaming like a banshee after a man, who couldn't possibly have heard me anyway.'

Because that was what had happened, and there was nothing more to it, so there was no need to feel so—so doomed.

'You're just being totally absurd,' she told herself as she walked through to the courtyard and sat down at a table.

Yet it was little wonder that she should be in such a state of turmoil. Her whole life seemed to have taken some quantum leap into the unknown, and she was still reeling from the effects.

Which was why she'd wanted Andreas to come back, she reasoned. She needed the reassurance of his physical presence—the caress in his voice as he called her his own—the strong shoulder for her to rest against. The long fingers clasping hers. And the sweet heart-pounding magic of his mouth possessing hers.

But instinct warned her that she would be unwise to cling too closely, or become too dependent on him. That he had a life totally outside her own experience, and responsibilities that she couldn't even begin to comprehend yet. And that there would be times when that life would take him away from her.

That was probably one of things he wanted to discuss

with her tomorrow. To spell out exactly what marriage to him would entail.

It wouldn't be easy, she knew, but she would cope. And she would stand beside him, rather than drag him back.

Part of her attraction for him, she suspected, was the fact that she earned her living, and lived and travelled alone. Quite a change, in all probability, from the spoiled, sheltered girls who were part of his own world.

Maybe, too, he still sensed there was something she was hiding from him, and found this intriguing.

But no longer, she decided with steely resolution. She knew now that she had to tell him everything. That it wasn't enough to tear up the paperwork and call it quits. Because that would not bury the past. And, unless she was completely honest with him, the gift of the Villa Danae to her mother would always be there in the back of her mind, hanging over their lives like a distant shadow.

And she wanted no shadows, she told herself, smiling. No secrets, either. Just their voices, united, echoing together down the years to come. And she'd been a fool not to trust the legend of the Caves of Silver.

'You want something?' She looked up with a start as a harsh voice intruded on her reverie, and, to her surprise, found Uncle Stavros standing beside the table.

'Oh—just some lemonade, please.' Sherry, she knew, made jugs of it, fresh and tangy with real fruit, each day and kept them in one of the kitchen refrigerators.

He grunted and went off, leaving Zoe wondering, not for the first time, just what she had done to upset him.

Well, now was her chance to find out, she decided as he returned with her tall glass of lemonade and set it down in front of her.

'I've seen you before, haven't I?' Zoe tried her most disarming smile on him—the one she kept for awkward parents. 'Up in the square the other day—and this morning.'

He gave a jerk of the head in ungracious acknowledgement, and turned to leave.

'Excuse me.' Zoe was inspired by her new-found confidence. After all, she was going to marry Andreas Dragos. 'But is something wrong?'

'*Ne.*' He swung back to her, the heavy brows drawn together angrily. 'You, *thespinis*, you are wrong. You should not have come here, and it is best you leave soon, before more trouble is made.'

If he'd slapped her, she could hardly have been more shocked.

She said, 'I—I don't know what you're talking about.'

'You think I do not remember—I—Stavros?' He smote himself on the chest. 'You thought I would not see her in you, the child of the little Gina?'

Zoe said very carefully, 'If you're talking about my mother, I know that she stayed here once, a long time ago.'

'Yes,' he said harshly. 'She and that other one, her sister.'

Zoe blinked. 'You're saying that Aunt Megan—came here—to Thania, too?' She shook her head. 'I—I didn't know.'

'There is much that you do not know.' He paused. 'Go, *thespinis*. Go before more harm is done. More sorrow caused.' He leaned down towards her, his face forbidding. 'Andreas Dragos is not for you.'

She gasped, hot colour pouring into her face. 'I think that's my business—and his. You can't say that.'

'It is said.' For a fleeting second, Zoe thought she saw a glimmer of compassion in the fierce eyes. 'Now, the matter is closed. Finished.'

He turned and stumped away, leaving Zoe staring after him, too stunned to challenge him further.

Her throat was dry and burning, but when she tried to pick up her glass of lemonade her hand was shaking so much that the liquid splashed onto the table. And the sharp scent of the lemons was suddenly acrid—nauseating.

She leaned back in her chair, heart pounding as she struggled for self-command.

She had not been too overwhelmed by unexpected happiness to realise that her relationship with Andreas might not meet with universal rejoicing. That there would be those who would think she was not a worthy wife for him, and who would not scruple to say so.

And reason suggested that there might well be serious opposition from Andreas' family, and from his father in particular.

But she had not expected such a direct and personal attack from someone who was not even a member of the Dragos clan. She wasn't even sure whether she was being warned—or threatened.

Her immediate thought was—Andreas. She had to see him—tell him what had happened. Needed him to comfort her—to assure her that she had nothing to fear.

But it occurred to her, suddenly and shockingly, that she didn't actually know how to find him. She presumed that he was living at the Dragos residence, but even that was not certain. Nor did she know where it was, she thought, swallowing. This was the man who wanted to marry her, yet she didn't even have his address or telephone number.

She felt the same sense of unease as she'd experienced just ten minutes earlier when his Jeep had pulled away. The same desolate conviction that he'd gone from her life, and nothing would ever be the same again.

Which was ludicrous, she reminded herself forcefully. Because she was seeing him tomorrow morning at the Villa Danae, and then she'd be able to tell him everything. Pour out her heart, and all the doubts and fears that were pressing on her.

He'd told her to trust him, and she would have to do so. Trust him to fight for her, and their future. Because anything else was unthinkable.

She went up to her room, and showered and changed into a sleeveless dress in blue chambray, trying to banish the taut, anxious face she saw in the mirror with blusher and eye-shadow, but, all the same, not convinced she had succeeded.

She rinsed out her bikini, and went to hang it on the balcony rail. As she did so she heard the loud throb of an engine overhead, and, looking up, she saw a helicopter swinging low over the port before heading out to sea.

She put her hands over her ears to block out the sound. It seemed too noisy—almost alien, in fact, for such a small island. But, no doubt, it was simply passing over on its way to somewhere else, she thought, glad when the whirr of the rotors faded, and peace returned.

Most of the guests were already eating when Zoe returned to the courtyard. She glanced around her, only realising when her heart lurched in disappointment how much she had been hoping that, in spite of everything, Andreas would have decided that he could not stay away after all. That he would be there, waiting for her. And that she'd delayed her own arrival for that very reason.

But the good news seemed to be that Uncle Stavros was not there either.

As she took her seat Sherry arrived with the menu, and a basket containing bread and cutlery.

Zoe gave her a determined smile. '*Kalispera.*'

The other girl nodded jerkily, and did not meet her eyes. 'The veal stew is good tonight.'

'Then I'll have that, please, and my usual red wine.' Zoe kept her tone equable, but her pulses were jumping.

When Sherry returned with the wine, and the usual bottle of water, Zoe put a detaining hand on her arm. 'Sherry,' she said in an undertone. 'What's going on?'

'You tell me. You're the one dating the heir to the Dragos millions, as I guess you know by now.' Sherry positioned herself so that her back was turned to the rest of the courtyard. Her voice was low and worried. 'For God's sake, Zoe, have you any idea what you're getting into?'

'I've fallen in love,' Zoe said quietly and simply.

'Then you'd better fall out again, and pretty damn quick,' Sherry said tersely. She paused, her tone becoming almost pleading. 'Let me call your company rep on Kefalonia— get you a swift transfer out of here, before you get your heart broken.'

'You're so sure that will happen?' Zoe bit her lip. 'Suppose Andreas loves me, too. What then?'

'He won't be allowed to.' There was an awful finality in Sherry's voice. 'I don't know what's going on, but I've gathered that much at least, and it's not good.' She shook her head. 'Hell, Zoe, you don't know the power these people have—men like Steve Dragos. And believe me, you don't want to know. Just put the whole thing down to experience, and get out, while the going's good.'

Her face was suddenly wan. 'Even I've come in for some stick. Stavros's uncle was here earlier, shouting at him for accepting your reservation, and saying he should throw you out. Telling him that all English women are nothing but trouble, and that he was a fool to have married one. And he's always been so sweet to me before,' she added unhappily.

'Oh, Sherry, I'm sorry. He had a go at me, too, earlier.' Zoe straightened her shoulders. 'But I will find out what's going on, I promise, and get Andreas to sort it all out.'

'If he can.' Sherry gave her a quick tight-lipped smile and went off.

Zoe ate her meal without appetite that evening. Her instinct told her not to wait until the next day, but find Andreas tonight. Let him deal with the problems that seemed to be mounting up like thunderclouds, before the threatened storm broke and swept them away.

On the other hand, she didn't want to panic unnecessarily either.

She would have liked another word with Sherry, but it was clear that the other girl was keeping out of the way, and Zoe could not blame her. She decided to make things easier by opting for an early night.

She undressed, put on her nightgown, and lay on top of the bed trying to read, but she was unable to concentrate. The room felt stifling, but there was a coldness deep inside her that she was unable to dispel.

She felt totally bewildered by the way everything in her life had changed so diametrically. Only a couple of hours before, she'd been happier than ever before, caught up in her own special fairy tale. Now, she seemed to be living through a waking nightmare, unable to make sense of anything that was happening to her.

Not one person wished her well, she realised, her throat tightening wretchedly, or thought that her relationship with Andreas stood any chance of survival.

And she had to know why. Was it just the disparity in their social standing—the fact that he was probably a millionaire many times over, and she was just a teacher? Or could it be the difference in nationalities?

Nothing she could think of was enough to provoke the strength of reaction that she'd encountered.

She switched off her lamp, and lay, her arms wrapped round her body, staring into the darkness.

Darling, she whispered silently. My darling. Wherever you are, think of me now. I need you so much—and I'm so scared.

It was going to be another scorching day, and Zoe was glad to reach the shelter of the olive groves.

For a moment, she regretted not bringing her bikini and towel. But she was here to talk, she reminded herself, not swim and sunbathe, so she was businesslike in a blue denim skirt, and a crisp short-sleeved white shirt. There would be plenty of time for leisure in the sun later—when everything was out in the open at last.

She'd brought the deed of gift with her, together with the documentation to prove who she was. He would probably be angry because she'd said nothing before, even though she'd had plenty of opportunity, but, she acknowledged, that was a risk she'd have to take.

If he really loves me, he'll forgive me, she told herself. And if he doesn't... Well, she wouldn't think about that possibility, she thought, shivering.

She'd assumed that Andreas would be there already, waiting for her. She went eagerly up the terrace steps, but it was completely deserted, and so was the beach.

He must be in the house, she decided. But when she tried the main door, it was locked. In fact, there was no access anywhere, she discovered as she did a complete circuit of the building. Everything was closed up and shuttered. As if it, too, had turned against her, she thought, then derided herself for her over-vivid imagination.

She couldn't even say Andreas was late, because they hadn't specified a time to meet. He obviously had a lot of stuff to catch up on, she told herself, with a shrug. After all, she had no real idea of his workload. It was one of the many discoveries about him she was going to make over the days—months—years ahead.

He'll be here, she told herself. All I have to do is be patient—and wait a little.

She found a patch of shade, and sat down in it, stretching her legs in front of her, and fanning herself with her hat.

She took the papers out of her bag, and checked them through. She'd got copies of her birth certificate and her mother's will for verification purposes. And once she'd told him the truth about her purpose in coming to Thania, she would tear all the documents up in front of him. Relinquish all claim to the house.

She looked at her watch, and grimaced, then took out her ill-used book with renewed resolution. She couldn't just sit, straining her ears for the sound of his step, or every moment would drag like an hour.

But the next time she looked at her watch, she realised, startled, that an hour had indeed gone by. Before too long she thought, we'll be running out of morning, and into afternoon.

She got to her feet, and stretched, then went to the edge of the terrace and stared down at the beach, her eyes searching the crescent of sand in case he'd arrived there by another route. But she was still quite alone.

She was conscious of a faint stirring of anger. For a man in love, this was pretty cavalier treatment. Well, she decided, she would give him another ten minutes.

But one ten minutes was soon followed by another, and eventually another hour had passed, still with no sign of him.

If she'd been scared the night before, she was frankly petrified now, and close to tears.

'Oh, where is he?' she asked herself. 'What's happened?'

She snatched up her bag, and walked back the way she had come, fighting her misery and uncertainty every step of the way.

Stavros was on the phone when she entered the hotel's reception area. She stood waiting for him to finish his call, and he rang off, giving her a wary look. 'Can I help you, *thespinis*?'

'I hope so.' She was proud of how composed she sounded. 'Can you tell me, please, how to get to Mr Dragos' house?' She lifted her chin. 'I need to see Andreas quite urgently.'

There was a silence, then he said, 'Andreas is not there, *thespinis*. He is in Athens. The helicopter came for him, and he left yesterday evening.'

She said huskily, 'He *left*? Without telling me? When he'd arranged to see me today? I don't believe it.'

Stavros looked more uncomfortable than ever. He said, 'He telephoned here before he went—and left a message for you. To say that he had been called away.'

'And you didn't think to give it to me?' Zoe's voice rose. 'What kind of a person are you? And what sort of hotel is this, withholding guests' messages like that? I actually went to meet him. I've been waiting all this time...'

'I did not wish to do it.' His voice was miserable. 'It was my uncle. He thought it would be better—kinder if you thought Kyrios Andreas had simply—gone. That you would believe he had chosen this way to end things between you, and you would leave in turn.'

'Then you're wrong,' she said. 'Because I know he would never do that. And how dare your uncle interfere in what doesn't concern him?'

'He meant it for the best, *thespinis*. He is fond of Kyrios Andreas—as if he were his own son.'

'And clearly he thinks I'm not good enough for him,' Zoe said curtly.

'I don't know, Kyria Zoe.' Stavros stared down at the polished counter in front of him. 'He says only that you and Kyrios Andreas cannot be together, but he will not give a reason.'

'Well, when Andreas returns, I intend to be here, waiting for him, however long it takes, and to hell with your uncle's disapproval.' She paused. 'Did the message say when he planned to come back?'

'No, *thespinis*. Just that he had been urgently called away.'

'Fine.' Zoe turned to go to her room. 'If any other messages come, please see that I get them at once,' she threw at him over her shoulder.

And heard him sigh. 'Yes, Kyria Zoe.'

But it was to be her sole moment of triumph, because there were no more messages. Three days limped silently by, and eventually her pride would not allow her to ask any more.

It seemed likely that Andreas would simply stay out of the way in Athens for the remainder of her holiday, thus avoiding any awkward moments or potentially distressing scenes.

But why did he do it? she asked herself over and over

again. Why pretend that he had fallen in love with me? Was it just some sick game to alleviate his boredom with island life?

If so, she thought, it must have given him a laugh a minute to see how easily she'd succumbed to his spell.

It was not easy to fill her days, but she managed it somehow. Succeeded, too, on the surface at any rate, in overcoming her sense of personal humiliation at having been dumped with such insulting ease. In spite of everything, she was not going to be driven away, she told herself with resolution.

She had braced herself too for a certain amount of covert amusement at her plight from the hotel. Instead she found herself treated with quiet friendliness.

She mentioned the subject only once to Sherry. 'I suppose everyone thinks I asked for this.'

'Nobody thinks that,' Sherry assured her, giving her a comforting pat on the shoulder. 'But I was always worried about you.' She hesitated. 'I know Andreas is gorgeous, but a hell of a lot of women have thought so, too.'

'Yes,' Zoe said quietly. 'I can imagine.'

Only she didn't want to imagine anything of the kind. It was too painful to have to admit she'd been just another item on a long list.

So, she hid her ever-present hurt and bewilderment somehow, and kept her smile in place, and her head high as she made herself join in some of the trips and activities organised by the tour company and the hotel itself.

At the same time, she was careful to avoid any of the places she'd visited with Andreas. The memory of that one, wonderful day when she'd believed herself loved was still too raw for that. His image was engraved on her mind, etched deep into her consciousness. Superimposed on everything she did by day. Coming between her and the mercy of sleep that she yearned for at night.

She could not handle any further reminders of him.

And she did not, under any circumstances, go back to the Villa Danae.

On the fifth day, she took a ferry trip to Kefalonia, exploring the shopping streets of the capital, and taking a short coach tour round the island's major beauty spots. And there were even brief moments when she found herself able to relax, and enjoy what she was seeing.

One day, I shall heal, she thought. I may even come back to Greece. But not yet.

It was early evening when her ferry docked. She came ashore slowly feeling tired, but almost tranquil.

There was a car parked directly outside the hotel entrance, and there were two men in dark glasses standing on the steps, talking to Stavros. Businessmen, by the look of their smart suits, Zoe noted casually. And the car was pretty glamorous, too.

As she approached all three men turned to look at her, and she halted, their scrutiny awakening a sudden unease.

'Miss Lambert?' One man approached her, while the other opened the car's passenger door. He was smiling, and his English was perfect. 'My employer, Mr Dragos, would like you to join him for dinner tonight.'

Zoe's lips parted in a soundless gasp. She said icily, 'Please thank Andreas for me, and tell him I'm not accepting any invitations for the foreseeable future.' She paused, deciding to ignore the fact that a horrified Stavros was sending her frantic signals. 'I'm sure he'll understand,' she added with cutting emphasis.

'You are mistaken, Miss Lambert.' The smile was unchanged. 'It is Mr Stephanos Dragos, the father of Andreas, who wishes you to dine with him. He is looking forward to meeting you, so—if you could come with us, please?'

'But I've been out all day,' Zoe protested, aware that she was being propelled courteously but inflexibly towards the car. She indicated the creases in her blue chambray dress. 'I—I need to change.' *I also need to lock myself in my room and refuse to come out.*

'You look fine, Miss Lambert.' There was an implacable note in his voice. 'This is purely an informal occasion.'

'Are you just going to stand there, and let one of your guests be—hijacked like this?' Zoe sent her stormy appeal to Stavros.

'Mr Dragos wants to see you, Kyria Zoe.' He spread his hands helplessly. 'Also, he has a very good chef,' he added.

'Great,' Zoe said furiously as she was handed into the passenger seat.

'That, of course, makes all the difference. If I don't come back, don't hesitate to let my room,' she flung at him as a parting shot.

She sat beside the driver, quivering with temper, her hands clutching her bag so tightly that its strap cut into her flesh.

The road they took led past the Villa Danae, and continued to hug the coastline. Zoe had just given up trying to calculate how far they had travelled when the car turned down a side road, eventually coming to a halt outside a pair of imposing iron gates. The driver sounded his horn, and a security guard appeared as if from nowhere, and opened the gates for them to proceed.

As the gates clanged shut behind them Zoe felt her mouth go dry, and began to regret the jibe about not coming back. Sherry's comment about the power Steve Dragos could wield was another uncomfortable memory.

They were travelling along a drive now that wound through a large garden, with spreading lawns, and cypress trees. When the house came into view, she saw that it was much older than the Villa Danae, and probably twice the size, its pale walls festooned with flowering vines and other climbers.

There were several vehicles parked in front of the house, and Andreas' Jeep was among them. Zoe felt her throat muscles contract at the sight of it.

She thought, I can't go through with this. I can't...

But the car was stopping, and she was being helped out

and escorted towards the entrance. She halted, shaking off
the officious hand holding her arm.

She said between her teeth, 'Kindly let go of me.'

It was cool inside the house. Steve Dragos had air con-
ditioning that worked. Zoe hoisted her bag onto her shoulder, and buried her hands in the pockets of her dress to
hide the fact that they were trembling.

A manservant in a pale grey linen jacket hurried to open
double doors, and Zoe found herself in a spacious low-
ceilinged room, furnished with sofas and armchairs grouped
round a massive stone fireplace.

There was only one occupant. Andreas, tall in an immaculate dark suit, was standing, hands on hips, staring out
of the window. Zoe checked at the sight of him, her heart
hammering frantically.

He turned slowly and looked at her, his face unsmiling
and set in lines of harsh weariness.

'*Kalispera.*' His voice seemed to come from a hundred
miles away. He sounded like one polite stranger greeting
another, she thought in swift anguish.

She lifted her chin. She said huskily, 'Why have you
done this? Why have you had me brought here?'

'It was not my wish,' he said. 'But—my father's.' There
was an odd hesitation in his voice. He paused, then added,
'He will not be long. He is resting after the flight from
Athens.'

'Is that all you can say?' Her tone had a ragged edge.
'You don't think I deserve some explanation?' Her eyes
met his in naked appeal, her pride splintering. 'You said—
I thought you—cared for me...'

'I care,' he said quietly. 'Nothing can ever change that.'

She said, her voice little more than a whisper, 'And if I
asked you to leave this house with me now—to go together
to the Caves of Silver and call out our names to the echo—
what would you say?'

He bent his head, almost defeatedly. 'I would say—no.'

She almost cried out with the pain of it, but forced herself to steady her voice. 'Did you ever—really want me?'

And saw him wince. He said, 'It no longer matters. Everything has changed. You must understand that.'

'I don't understand anything,' she said. 'Andreas, tell me, please—what's going on? Have you been told to give me up? Is that it?'

'I had no choice.'

'Everyone has a choice.' She went swiftly across the room to him. 'And I choose you.' She seized his hands, wanting to touch them with her lips, to place them on her breasts, but he pulled away almost violently. Stepped backwards from her, his dark face a mask of anguish, his breathing harsh.

He said, 'I cannot touch you, Zoe, and I cannot allow you to touch me. It is over.'

She heard the doors behind them open, and half turned.

A man was standing watching them. He was wearing dark trousers and a quilted crimson jacket, with a silk scarf folded at his throat, and his jutting brows were drawn together in a faint frown as he surveyed them. He was tall, with silver hair, and a strong, rugged face that had once been handsome.

Even across the room, Zoe could feel the aura of power that accompanied him. Sense the dark magnificence of his presence.

She thought almost inconsequentially, In forty years, Andreas will look like this—only I shall not see it.

When he spoke, his voice was deep, and a little hoarse, as if he was trying to suppress some emotion.

'So,' he said. 'You are Gina's child, come to me at last. Stavros was right. You are the image of her, *pedhi mou*. I would have known you anywhere.'

Zoe stiffened. She said coldly, 'I'm afraid that I can't return the compliment.' But she knew it wasn't true. Because every instinct was telling her that this was the man in the photograph that her mother had secretly treasured for all those years.

She glanced at Andreas, standing like a statue, his face deliberately expressionless. She thought suddenly, I don' want to be here. I want to put my hands over my ears— and run.

He said, 'Then let me introduce myself. My name is Stephanós Dragos—and I have the honour to be your father.'

'No.' Her voice cracked on the word. She turned on Andreas, face and voice fierce with shock and horror. 'Tell me it's not true.'

But the look of agony in his eyes gave her all the confirmation necessary. A look that she knew would stay with her until the end of her days. A look of knowledge and renunciation that said all hope was lost for ever. Consigning them both to private but separate hells.

And it was the last thing she saw as a pit of whirling darkness opened in front of her. She tried to say Andreas' name, but the darkness was all around her, consuming her and she gave herself up to it.

CHAPTER NINE

SHE became aware of things. Softness beneath her. Light beyond her closed eyelids. Voices speaking quietly. Something cool, damp and infinitely comforting touching her face.

She forced her heavy eyes to open, staring around her in dazed incomprehension. She was lying on a bed in a lamplit room, and a man she had never seen before, someone with a thin, kind face and a small neat beard, was standing beside her.

He said, 'So you are with us again, Kyria Zoe. That is good.' His hand closed round her wrist, checking her pulse rate.

'Who are you?' Her voice was a thread.

'My name is Vanopolis. I am Mr Dragos' personal physician.'

Her mind stirred, beginning to collect images—memories. A voice saying impossible words. A man's eyes saying goodbye for ever.

She moved feebly. 'I feel sick.'

'Lie still,' he said. 'It will pass.'

'What—what happened?'

'You fainted,' he said. 'But fortunately Mr Dragos was able to catch you as you fell, so you were saved any physical injury.'

'Mr Dragos,' she echoed. 'But he was on the other side of the room.'

'I meant the younger Mr Dragos,' he said. 'Andreas—your brother. He brought you here.'

For a long moment, she stared up at him, absorbing what

139

he had said. Realising that it was not just a nightmare to be forgotten as the sun rose. And that her life was in ruins.

She thought, I wish I were dead.

She felt tears stinging on her face like drops of ice, and turned her head away so that he should not see her cry.

When she could speak normally, she said, 'I'd like to leave here now, please.'

'It is better that you remain,' he said. 'You have had a shock, and your father wishes you to stay under my care tonight. Your hotel has been informed.'

'And I have no say in the matter,' she said, with sudden fierceness. 'My whole life has been turned upside down. I don't even know who I am any more, and I can do nothing. Is that what you're telling me?'

He hesitated. 'I am sorry that you should have found out in such a way. I wished the news to be broken more gently.'

Zoe sat up, pushing her hair back from her face, feeling the room dip slightly, then steady. She said, 'It would have made no difference, Dr Vanopolis. There's no way such a thing could ever have been made acceptable.'

He sighed. 'Rest now, Kyria Zoe. Would you like some tea to be brought? Or food?'

'No,' she said. 'I want to talk to Andreas. Will you ask him to come here, please?'

He said gently, 'Perhaps it would be better for you to talk to Kyrios Stephanos first.'

'No.' Zoe thumped the mattress with her fist, her eyes blazing. 'Andreas. Or I swear I shall walk out of this house and never come back, and to hell with your Kyrios Stephanos.'

He sighed again, but went to the door. Zoe lay back on the pillow. She still felt faintly nauseous, and her head ached, but her mind was clear. And for the first time she took a good look at her surroundings.

It was a large room, beautifully set out with highly polished if old-fashioned furniture. The bed she lay on was wide and comfortable, with a heavily embroidered coverlet

The shutters were drawn, and in the light from the lamp on the night table she saw a book, lying open, face own, and a pair of discarded cuff-links. There was a leather suitcase in one corner, its contents spilling out onto the floor, and a man's jacket and tie were draped across the arm of a high-backed chair. A cupboard door was ajar, and she could see other male clothing hanging inside.

She felt her whole body begin to shake in frightened awareness.

The knock at the door was barely perceptible. Andreas came slowly into the room, remaining near the doorway, his face in shadow.

Zoe pulled herself upright, staring across at him, her eyes enormous in her pallid face.

She said huskily, 'This is your room, isn't it? Your bed. You brought me—here.' Her voice cracked and broke. 'Oh, God, Andreas, how cruel is that?'

He said with a terrible weariness, 'It was the nearest room, and you were ill. I—I did not think beyond that. Forgive me.'

She closed her eyes. 'What are we going to do?'

'There is nothing,' he said. 'I am my father's son. You are my father's daughter.' His voice was cool, remote, as if he had rehearsed the words so often that all feeling was gone from them. 'That is the only consideration.'

'When did you—know?'

'My father was telephoned in Athens by an old friend,' he said. 'Someone who had known about the original affair, because your mother was staying at his hotel when it began.'

'Stavros?'

'Yes,' he said. 'Stavros. As soon as he saw you, he realised who you were. And when he saw us together, he feared what the truth might be.' He shrugged. 'I suppose we should be—grateful to him.'

'Should we?' Her voice was low. 'I—I'm afraid I haven't reached that stage yet.'

'No.' There was a note of savagery in his tone. 'No have I.'

He moved forward. Pulled the high-backed chair forwar and sat in it, still keeping a careful distance, impatientl pushing the discarded clothing onto the floor.

She heard herself say automatically, 'Andreas—you jacket. You'll ruin it…' and stopped, appalled, as she sav him flinch.

He said bleakly, 'You speak as if you were my wife, Zo *mou*. Who is the cruel one now?'

'Oh, God.' She buried her face in her hands. 'I can't d this.' Her voice was stricken. 'I have to get out of here— go back to England.'

'No,' he said. 'I am the one who is leaving. I am return ing to Athens tonight. You must stay, at least for a while My father wishes to make the acquaintance of his daughte and he has waited a long time to do so. Whatever you feelings, *pedhi mou*, you cannot deprive him of that.'

Her voice trembled. 'Did you know about my mother— about their relationship?'

'I thought I knew about all my father's women.' His fac looked as if it had been sculpted from rock. 'My mothe saw to that. "I am dying and your father has a new whore." I lost count of the times she threw that at me when I wa a child. But these were girls he kept in Paris, Rome an New York. Thania was his refuge. My mother hated it, an never came here. And on Thania there was no one, unti he met her—your mother—and loved her.'

He paused. 'And after her, I think, no one—anywhere.

He looked down at his hands, clenched tautly in his lap 'My mother screamed that he was building a house o Thania for some foreign bitch.

'I can remember her laughing when it stayed empty, yea after year. Laughing at the idea that this woman he love so desperately would return to him one day, so that the could be happy together at last.'

'She was happy,' Zoe said chokingly. 'Happy with he

usband—my father. The man whose name is on my birth
ertificate, who brought me up, and looked after me. Why
would he have done that for another man's child?'

'Perhaps, because he was a good man, and cared for her,
too. She seems to have been a woman who could inspire
love.'

Zoe's throat tightened. 'Yes,' she said. 'Yes, she was.'
She drew a quivering breath. 'We were—a happy family.
Or I thought we were.'

He said quietly, 'As my family, of course, was not.'

She said thickly, 'If your father was so in love with my
mother—so endlessly devoted, why didn't he get a divorce
and marry her?'

'He tried,' Andreas said quietly. 'But although my
mother did not care about living with him as his wife, she
liked the money and social position. She enjoyed her position as a patron of the arts—her high-profile work for
various charities, when her health permitted, of course,' he
added bitterly. 'My God, she used illness like a weapon.
Even as a child I could see that.

'As his ex-wife, her status would have suffered, and she
knew it. So, she became hysterical—threatened suicide. She
had made an attempt once before, it seems, not altogether
seriously, but my father could not take the risk.'

He paused, his face sombre. 'It was a hideous situation,
and it affected your mother very badly. She felt torn between her love for my father, and the mounting problems
that their liaison was causing. Because although she was
willing to make a life with my father as his mistress, there
was no certainty that my mother would have left them in
peace.

'And in the end she could not risk it either, and—she
left. She went back to England, and made him give a solemn promise that he would never follow.'

'Even though she was expecting his child?' Zoe demanded incredulously. 'He let her go?'

'Neither of them were aware then that she was pregnant,'

Andreas said quietly. 'And he did not simply—abando
her, *pedhi mou*. He could not have done that. He kept hi
word about following her, but he wrote to her constantly
pleading with her to return to him. He went on building th
house for her, as a pledge for their future.

'And when she wrote back, telling him there was to b
a child of their love, he was overjoyed. He replied instantly
begging her to come to him, sending an airline ticket—
money. But they were returned unused, without explana
tion, and he had no further contact with her.'

Zoe gasped. 'And he just allowed that to happen?'

His mouth tightened. 'He had been seriously overwork
ing—trying to compensate for the loss of his belove
woman—living on hope. This was a blow he had not ex
pected, and as a result he suffered a kind of breakdowr
He was ill for several months, and when he recovered hi
first act was to write to her, imploring her to reconside
But all his letters were returned, unopened. Your mothe
had moved, and left no forwarding address. She seemec
indeed, to have disappeared without trace.

'And when, eventually, he tracked her down, she wa
already married, and he had the additional pain of knowin
that she had called his child ''Zoe'', the name he had onc
told her he would choose if he had a daughter.'

He sighed. 'Even so, he wrote one last letter, telling he
that he loved her still, and would wait for her always.'

He leaned back in the chair, his face tired and drawr
'And I, Zoe *mou*, had to put my own feelings aside, an
tell him, a sick man, that all hope was gone.'

'What did he say?' she asked huskily.

'For a while, nothing. Then he said that it was no sur
prise, because he had been grieving for her from the da
she went from him. But that she had left him—you. An
you had come to find him.'

Zoe shook her head. 'She never mentioned his name
she said wearily. 'There was just—the picture. A paintin

f a house she never even saw.' She spread her hands.
How could she do that?'

'He sent her drawings—many photographs. And she
new where it was to be built. Her imagination must have
upplied the rest.' His mouth twisted bitterly. 'Maybe she,
oo, could not—completely—give up their dream.'

She said in a low voice, 'Instead, they destroyed ours.'

'You knew that he had given her the house,' he said.
Why did you not tell me?'

'I was going to—that morning we were supposed to meet
here. I intended to hand back the papers,—tell you I
vanted no part of it, and that we should bury the past.' Her
augh cracked in the middle. 'Oh, God, what a joke. What
hellish, tragic joke.'

She paused. 'Did you never suspect who I was?'

'How could I—when I never knew you existed? My fa-
her always grew angry when I tried to discuss the Villa
Danae with him. He refused even to tell me the nationality
f his lover, let alone her identity. And my mother only
alled her "the foreigner". The possibility of a child was
ever mentioned. Then, that morning in Athens, he poured
ut his heart to me—held nothing back. The phone call
rom Stavros had alarmed him, of course. He realised he
ad to put a stop to our relationship at once, so only frank-
ess would do.

'Even then, I did not believe him. God forgive me, I
hought it was a ploy to push me into another marriage he
ould be planning for me. He had to show me photographs
f her—even that last letter before I could accept the truth.'

'She should have told me,' Zoe said numbly. 'Why
idn't she tell me?'

'Maybe she also wished to forget the past. Wanted you
o go on believing in your happy family.'

'Yes.' She wrapped her arms round her body, her face
nguished. 'Oh, why did I ever come here?' She bit her lip,
ending him a swift, remorseful glance. 'You knew, didn't
ou, that I was hiding something?'

'Yes,' he said gently. 'But so was I, Zoe *mou*.
thought—I convinced myself that it was just part of th
game of love that we had begun to play. And that, soor
we would have no secrets from each other.' He pausec
'And now, God help us both, it is true.'

'He was a married man,' she said with intense bitternes:
'He had no right to fall in love with her.'

'I do not think he had a choice, Zoe *mou*. No more tha
I had when I watched you coming down the stairs toward
me, and all I could think was—"Here she is, at last."'

She bent her head, a solitary tear making its way dow
the curve of her cheek. 'Andreas—don't.'

'No.' He got to his feet. 'It will be better, I think, if w
do not meet alone again.' He walked across and picked u
his travel bag, thrusting his errant belongings back insid
it, and zipping it shut. He turned and looked at her. 'W
are fortunate, perhaps, that we do not have more to regret

'One kiss,' she said desolately. 'Oh, Andreas, God won
punish us for just one kiss.'

He paused at the door, his face haggard, his eyes burnin
into hers. 'No, *pedhi mou*?' The harsh mockery in his voic
seared across her skin. 'I think we are being punished a
ready—now, and every day for the rest of our lives.'

The door closed quietly, and he was gone.

A lifetime later, she heard the whine of a powerful er
gine, and the throb of propellers as the helicopter departec
taking him far away from her.

Zoe turned over, burying her face in the pillow he ha
slept on, and lay, unmoving, until the sound died away
She felt totally disorientated when she awoke the nex
morning.

Not long after Andreas' departure, the housekeeper ha
arrived and, tactfully ignoring her tear-stained face, ha
chivvied and coaxed her gently to another room in a di
ferent part of the house. It had come as no real surpris
either, to find that her luggage had been brought from th
hotel, and unpacked. To see that her very ordinary nigh

ress had been fanned across the bed's sumptuous satin
over, or that an enticingly scented bath was being run for
er by a maid.

What's the point of being a multimillionaire if you can't
ave a magic wand when you need to? she had wondered
ith irony, realising she was being given an object lesson
1 how the other half lived.

Left alone, she'd walked over to the window, and drawn
ack the filmy drapes, staring out into the darkness. If only
ere were a magic wand to mend a broken heart, she'd
ought, or wipe out memory, so that she could forget the
mile in Andreas' eyes, and the warm strength of his body
hen he'd held her in his arms. And, most of all, the prom-
e in his kiss.

A promise that could never be fulfilled, but which would
aunt her for ever just the same.

'Kyria Zoe.' A tap on the door brought Dr Vanopolis.
Your father is anxious about you.'

Her mouth curled. 'He's all heart.'

He said with slight reproof, 'He wishes you to know that
e will not intrude on you tonight, but asks that he may
ee you in the morning, when you are rested, and calmer.'

'Rested?' Zoe challenged ironically. 'Calm?' She shook
er head. 'Tell me, Doctor, are you licensed to perform
rontal lobotomies?'

His faint frown held compassion as well as concern.
Would you settle for a sleeping tablet instead? I will leave
ne on the night table for you to take after your bath.'

Thanks to the medication, she'd actually managed to
leep, but her dreams had been troubled and disjointed.

And now the night was over, and she had to face the day
head. And the inevitable confrontation with the man who
laimed to be her father.

She stared at herself in the mirror, trying to discern some
aint vestige of Steve Dragos in her appearance. But as far
s she could see, there was none.

I'm like my mother, and that's all there is to it, she thought.

The chambray dress had been removed, along with other items from the wardrobe, for laundering, so she settled for her denim skirt and a white top with short sleeves and a scooped neck.

After all, she wasn't out to impress anyone. She was a schoolteacher on holiday, and that was all.

The manservant from the night before was waiting at the foot of the stairs to conduct her into the dining room. Zoe took a deep breath, thrusting her hands into her skirt pockets, then walked in.

Stephanos Dragos was seated alone at the head of the large table, glancing through an array of international newspapers, but he pushed them aside and rose as soon as Zoe entered. He was wearing a shirt in Sea Island cotton, and a pair of cream linen trousers, and there was a vigour and determination about him that was almost tangible this morning.

A marked contrast to the grey-faced man who had destroyed her life with a few incredible words only a few hours ago, she thought.

'Kalimera.' He pulled out a chair, indicating that she should sit next to him.

She returned an unsmiling 'Good morning' and took a seat further down the table.

His brows rose slightly, but he made no comment. 'May I pour you some coffee? Or there is tea if you prefer it. And the rolls are freshly baked.' He signalled to the maid waiting by the massive sideboard to serve her.

'Just orange juice, please,' she said. 'And coffee. I'm not hungry.'

'But you must eat,' he said. 'Or you will make yourself ill.'

She looked back at him coolly, and levelly. 'Mr Dragos, I'm sick at heart already, and food will do nothing to cure that.'

There was a silence, then he spoke curtly in Greek to the maid who served Zoe, then scuttled out of the room.

Steve Dragos settled back in his chair, the dark eyes examining Zoe unblinkingly. He said, 'If you have everything you need, then we will talk.'

'There isn't a great deal to say.' Zoe drank some orange juice. 'You had an affair with my mother, and I was the result. I was happier not knowing about this. That covers it for me.'

'You have no curiosity about the past?'

'Once I did. That's why I came here, because I found the papers giving my mother the Villa Danae. I thought I needed to know about that, but I was wrong.'

'You speak of an affair,' Steve Dragos said, after a pause. 'But it was more than that. Your mother was the love of my life, and I lost her.'

Zoe put down her glass, her mouth curling. 'How history does tend to repeat itself.'

He was silent for a moment, then he said quietly, 'I thought there was little more I could learn about guilt or unhappiness, but I was wrong.

'I can make no excuse for loving your mother, little one. Nor can I apologise for it. Every word she spoke, every smile, every gesture was a blessing to my life.

'But, believe me, I never meant that hurt should come to you or to my Andreas.'

She looked down at the spotless linen cloth. 'In that case, you'll understand why I can't stay here. Why I need to go home.'

'This is your home.'

'No!' Zoe said in a stifled voice. 'It's not, and it never can be. That is—just not possible.'

'Not yet, perhaps,' he said. 'But one day you will feel Because my blood runs in your veins, *pedhi mou*.'

'Does it?' Zoe shook her head. 'If that was true, I'd feel *here*.' She pressed a clenched fist to her breast. 'I'd be aware of some connection between us—but I don't...'

'I can be patient,' he said. 'I have learned to be. An one day you will accept me as your father.'

She flung her head back in open challenge. 'There a tests that can decide that, Mr Dragos.'

'You doubt me?' The heavy brows snapped togethe 'Then perhaps you will believe your own mother.'

He reached into the breast pocket of his shirt and e tracted a sheet of paper, discoloured and fragile with fol ing.

Zoe took it reluctantly, and scanned the few faded line There was no question it was Gina's writing, and it sa simply that she was well, and happy and expecting h child. It ended with her love.

'And this was the last time she ever wrote to you?' Sh shook her head. 'It makes no sense.'

He said heavily, 'I have told myself the same a thousar times. And I blame myself, too. I should have gone Britain, insisted that she come to me. But I had made h a promise, and, by some oversight, left no loophole,' added cynically. 'So I could not follow without breaki my word, which she would not have forgiven.' He pause 'And the next I heard of her, she was married.'

He gave her a piercing stare. 'He was good to her, th man?'

'Yes, he was wonderful to us both.' She swallowe 'That's why I can't believe that he or my mother cou have lied to me about something so important.'

He was silent for a moment. 'Did she never talk of n at all?' There was an odd note in his voice that Zoe re ognised, shocked, as wistfulness.

'No.' She tried to speak more gently. 'I think she'd p that part of her life strictly behind her. But she kept yo photograph, and she painted a wonderful picture of th house you built for her.'

'And which you have now inherited.'

'I came across the papers by accident, and wondered.

he swallowed. 'But the Villa Danae was never hers in any
al sense. And it isn't mine either.'

He said quietly, 'But I wish you to have it, *pedhi mou*.'
s she began to protest he lifted a silencing hand. 'Use it
; you wish. Stay there sometimes. Sell it. Give it away.
he choice is yours.'

'That's—very generous.'

'You are my daughter. I would give more, if you would
low it. Acknowledge our relationship publicly.'

'Oh, no.' Zoe bit her lip. 'It's too soon. I—I need time.
have to think about this—all the implications.' She looked
him. 'You must understand that.'

'I shall try.' He pushed his chair back and rose. 'Come,
t us walk in the garden together.'

As they paced along the terrace he said quietly, 'Andreas
d not have to tell me she had gone from me. I felt it a
hile ago.' He glanced at her. 'Does it hurt you when I
beak of her?'

'No,' she said. 'How could it? We—we both loved her.
accept that at least.'

'Do you want to know how we met?' He sighed remi-
scently. 'It was all because of a sprained ankle. I was
riving back to this house, when I saw a young woman
tting at the side of the road, nursing her foot. I could see
he was in pain, so I stopped the car and offered assistance.
he did not wish to be taken to the clinic, so I brought her
ere, and my housekeeper bathed and bandaged her injury.'

'A romantic story.' Zoe forced a smile.

'But that was not your mother,' he said softly. 'It was
er sister. I gathered she had hurt herself when she stormed
ff after some quarrel, not for the first time.'

'Nothing new there,' Zoe said before she could stop her-
elf.

'No?' His mouth thinned slightly. 'I can believe it, al-
ough Gina was always loyal. I sent a message to Stavros
the hotel that his English guest was safe, and—Gina
me to collect her.' He was silent for a moment, then said

with difficulty, 'I loved her the moment I saw her. Whe
she came into the room, she made the sunlight pale. A
she confessed later it had been the same for her.

'I did not hide that I was married, but our feelings we
too strong. We became lovers within days. I persuaded h
to move here to this house, with her sister—to stay on wi
me here when the holiday was over. I could not belie
such happiness existed.'

'Did Aunt Megan stay, too?'

'No.' That shadow crossed his face again. 'She we
back,' he said shortly.

I'm surprised she didn't take the first plane out, Z
thought, picturing her aunt's cold, self-righteous face.

She had a lot to think about when she was finally alo
in her room that night. She was still determined to lea
as soon as possible, but she couldn't pretend the day ha
been all bad.

In fact if she'd spent it as his daughter-in-law instea
she'd have enjoyed his company, she thought, sadness
raw ache inside her.

It had been established that she would call him 'Steve
He objected to Mr Dragos, and she couldn't manage 'Pap

Maybe there would come a time when they could
friends, but accepting him as her father was beyond h
Even if she wanted a closer relationship, Andreas wou
always be between them, and she knew it.

She thought broodingly, I really need to get out of he
But that was not as simple as she'd hoped. Because Ste
had no wish to see her go, and was swamping her wi
kindness. One morning at breakfast, she found a flat velv
case beside her plate, containing an exquisite string
matched pearls. And when she tried to demur, he told h
shortly that they were a mere trifle.

In addition a car and driver were always at her dispos
if there was anywhere she wanted to go.

He even suggested flying her to Paris or New York
buy a whole new wardrobe of clothes.

'I'm a teacher,' Zoe protested with finality. 'I don't need esigner gear. There's nowhere I could go to wear it.'

And he sought her company constantly, and not just to lk about Gina. He wanted to know about Zoe herself— e steps she'd taken to achieve her career—her ultimate mbitions.

Whatever doubts she might still harbour, he was clearly onvinced that she was indeed his long-lost daughter, and e wanted to know every last detail of the life she'd led way from him.

And when she said her holiday would soon be over, he pplied charming but unremitting pressure on her to stay onger.

'You have made my convalescence a thing of joy, *pedhi ou*,' he told her, reminding her none too subtly of his cent heart attack.

And she couldn't deny she was tempted. It was pleasant) live in a beautiful house where the linen was changed ach day by unseen hands. Where doors opened as if by agic as she approached. Where she was served delicious ood that she hadn't had to prepare, and where her every him was indulged as never before.

Not that she had many whims, she admitted silently. But e knew there was a whole queue of people waiting for er to develop some.

But fighting the temptation to go with the flow was the ertain knowledge that Thania was no place in which to rget Andreas.

She dreamed of him each time she closed her eyes at ight. Each time she turned a corner, or a door opened, she xpected to see him there.

It was driving her mad. But back in her own environ-ent, there was work to distract her, and a new job to apply r. A completely fresh start, she thought, and she would ever need it more.

'I think I'll go into Livassi this morning,' she remarked

one breakfast time. 'Buy some souvenirs to take home wit
me—presents for people.'

She'd half expected Steve to enter some objection, b
he gave her a preoccupied smile.

'A good idea, dear child. I have some matters of busine
to take care of this morning, but we will spend time t
gether after lunch, *ne*?'

'Of course,' she said.

As they drove into Livassi she told Iorgos, her driver,
take her to the Hotel Stavros first.

After all, she'd been scooped out of the place without s
much as a by your leave, and, although she was sure th
hotel had been fully recompensed, she still felt she'd lik
to have a brief word with Sherry—offer some kind of e
planation. Although finding something feasible would n
be easy.

When Zoe walked into reception, she found Sherry b
hind the desk, her eyes on stalks.

'I don't believe it,' she breathed. 'I was going to tak
my courage in both hands and call you today. There
someone here, wanting to see you.'

For one sweet, painful moment, Zoe's heart lurche
Then she had herself under control again. 'For me? A
you sure?'

'He's having breakfast in the courtyard even as w
speak, if you want to go out there.' Sherry leaned close
lowering her voice. 'Is it really true—what Stavros' unc
has told him?'

Zoe sighed. 'Steve Dragos seems to think so, but for n
the honest answer is I—don't know.' She shook her hea
'I don't feel I belong there.'

'And you truly had no idea when you arrived?'

'None,' Zoe said. 'Or I wouldn't have come.'

'Oh, come on,' Sherry said bluntly. 'Finding you'
Steve Dragos' daughter is going to change your whole life

Zoe's smile splintered. 'It already has.'

'Oh, honey, I'm sorry.' Sherry patted her consolingl

But you must realise they'd never have let Andreas marry
you anyway. He's well and truly spoken for. Her name's
Nina Mandrassis, and her father is one of Steve Dragos'
biggest shipping rivals. A serious merger is being planned,
and not just at boardroom level, according to my Stavros.

'And she had this huge birthday party in Athens a couple
of days ago, and there's a photo in yesterday's paper of
them together, with her clinging to his arm. The caption
said that the announcement of their engagement is expected
at any moment.'

She gave Zoe a smile mingling anxiety and compassion.
'I'm sorry, love, but sometimes it's better to be prepared
for things.'

'Yes,' Zoe said quietly. 'I'm sure you're right.'

But nothing, she thought as she turned away, *nothing*
could prepare her for news like that. Oh, Andreas, how
could you? she wept inside. Yet, to be fair, he was only
doing the sensible—the expected thing, as she must do herself.

She walked into the courtyard, and stopped dead, her
eyes widening in total incredulity, as she realised who was
rising from his table to greet her with a sheepish grin.

'Hi, Zoe,' said George. 'It's really good to see you.'

CHAPTER TEN

'GEORGE,' said Zoe. 'What the hell are you doing here?'

Sherry had brought fresh coffee and left them to talk wit
a glance at George that suggested faint approval.

Someone available, in my league, and not a blood rela
tion, Zoe mentally translated with bitter accuracy.

'I've come to take you home,' George said portentousl
He produced a pair of airline tickets from his wallet wit
the air of a conjuror performing a difficult trick, then sa
back as if awaiting applause.

'Have you gone mad?' Zoe stared at the tickets, the
back at his pink face. 'George—I'm on holiday. That
what people do in the summer. And the tour company giv
you a return ticket.'

George fidgeted. He looked, Zoe thought with detach
ment, totally out of place in his crisp shirt and immaculatel
pressed shorts. What was more, a discreet glance under th
table revealed he was wearing socks with his sandals.

'I know, Zoe,' he said. 'But your aunt Megan wasn
very happy about you coming here, and she insisted I brin
you back. She even paid for the airfares.'

'Now I know you're crazy,' Zoe said flatly. 'Aunt Mega
doesn't care if I live or die.'

'That's where you're wrong,' George said, pouring him
self some more coffee. 'Because when I mentioned Thani
she became almost hysterical. My mother had to find th
medicinal brandy.'

'You mentioned? How did you know where I was?' Zo
demanded.

George looked slightly abashed. 'Oh, I happened to b

atting to Adele's sister at the travel agents' one day, and
he told me where you'd gone.'

'You were checking up on me?' Zoe's voice rose. 'How
are you?'

'I wouldn't put it quite like that,' George returned de-
nsively.

He produced a handkerchief, and dabbed at his forehead,
asting a dubious look around him. 'It isn't quite as prim-
ive as I expected,' he confided. 'But it wouldn't be my
hoice. I've never felt such heat.'

'Well, don't worry about it, George,' Zoe said crisply.
You've got your ticket home. Use it. I'll leave when I'm
eady, and it won't be at Aunt Megan's behest. She has
ome bloody nerve,' she added furiously.

George gave her an uneasy look. 'Look, Zoe, I dare not
o home without you. She was saying the most dreadful
hings—claiming you'd get involved with some Greek
hap.' His already flushed face went a deeper shade of pink,
nd he lowered his voice. 'That you'd end up in the most
rightful mess. I've never seen her in such a state. Mother
vas quite shocked.'

'She must have been—to allow you to come all this way
vithout a chaperon. But I'm afraid she'll have to get used
o it.' Zoe pushed back her chair, and rose, anger simmering
nside her. 'Because I've been invited to stay on for a while
onger, and I'm seriously considering it. Have a nice day,
George.'

'Oh, don't rush off.' He looked as if he'd been slapped.
Not when I've come all this way to see you.' He gave her
 look of entreaty. 'Have dinner with me tonight—please?'

Clearly, she was going to be wined, dined and talked
round, Zoe thought caustically. But at the same time she
elt a modicum of sympathy for George, trapped between
hose two harridans in England and her own displeasure,
lthough, admittedly, he'd brought it on himself.

He desperately needed to develop some backbone, she
hought. If it wasn't already too late.

'All right,' she capitulated reluctantly. 'I'll meet you he
at eight. And now I must go.'

She had told Iorgos to meet her in the square, but one
she had bought a piece of local pottery for Adele her sho
ping was complete, leaving her with time to kill.

She made her way to the *kafeneion* she'd used befor
and ordered a Coke. The backgammon players were alread
deeply engrossed under the trees, but she hardly gave the
a glance. She was too preoccupied with George's extrac
dinary arrival, and the reasons behind it.

Clearly Aunt Megan was terrified that she would di
cover the truth about her parentage. That was the only e
planation.

But she's never concerned herself about me before, sl
thought, slowly. So why start now?

Especially when the last thing she needed was anoth
mystery.

She was counting out the money for her drink when
gruff voice said, *'Thespinis,'* and she looked up to se
Uncle Stavros standing beside her.

'You have something else to say?' She could not kee
the antagonism out of her voice, and he sighed.

'Just that I regret I have had to cause you unhappines
Kyria Zoe.' He shook his head. 'So much wretchednes
over so many years. When will it all end?' He paused. 'Ma
I sit? Drink coffee with you?'

'If you wish.' Faintly bewildered, she watched him si;
nal to the waiter.

When the tiny cups of dark fluid were set in front o
them, he said, 'I wish to tell you, *thespinis*, that I wa
saddened to hear of your mother's death. She was a ver
wonderful young woman. Kind as well as beautiful.' H
sighed again. 'Any man would have been proud to lov
her, and my friend Stephanos—he gave her his worship.'

'Yes,' Zoe said more gently. 'I think he did.'

'They should have been together. Yes, he was marriec

it his wife gave him nothing. Why did she not come back, *espinis*?'

'Because she married, too. Made a life for herself.'

'Then I am wrong,' he said, half to himself. 'It was not ecause of that other one.'

Zoe put down her cup. 'Are you talking about my aunt Megan?'

'Pardon, *thespinis*. I do not mean to offend.'

'No,' she said. 'I—I need to know. They were on holiday gether, weren't they?'

'Two beautiful girls, *po, po, po*.' He sighed gustily. 'But ith the older one, the beauty was in the face, not in the eart. Underneath there was all this rage—this bitterness.'

'Even then?' Zoe shook her head. 'Why on earth did my other decide to go away with her?'

'Perhaps, because she wished her sister to be happy. But very day there were quarrels. Many times I saw your other fighting tears, and it made me angry also to see ow she made allowances—how she forgave so many unrgivable things.'

His face was sombre. 'It was good when the woman, ur aunt, went away. She had caused such problems, I eared what more might come.'

'But why?' Zoe stared at him. 'Why should she do such ings?'

He leaned towards her, his voice low and fierce. 'Beause she was jealous, Kyria Zoe. Because she too was in ve with my friend Stephanos. And he never looked at er.'

was a day for shocks, Zoe thought, staring out at the sea. he hadn't gone back to the house, because she knew she eeded quiet and privacy in order to think. She'd rememered the taverna on the cliff where Andreas had once taken er for lunch, and had persuaded Iorgos to drive her there, istead.

He was in the bar, enjoying a cheerful conversation with

the owner, and eating *souvlaki*, while she sat alone, toyin
with some grilled fish and a glass of white wine, trying
come to terms with Uncle Stavros' revelations.

It was hard to visualise her harsh, vindictive aunt swe
away by overwhelming passion. Yet, she recalled, Stev
Dragos had met her first—rescued her, in fact, and take
her to his house. Had Megan read too much into a simp
act of kindness—of *philoxenia*, the Greek love of th
stranger?

And then he'd added insult to injury by falling in lov
with her younger sister—the girl who'd always had th
ability to draw people to her.

Something the other sister clearly lacked.

And had she really carried that sense of injury for s
many years?

Remembering her violent reaction to the painting, Zo
could well believe it, and found herself shivering.

But it did not explain why her aunt had gone to th
extreme measure of dispatching George to bring her hom
Unless it had something to do with the 'problems' to whic
Stavros had so darkly referred.

There must be something she doesn't want me to fir
out, even now, she thought. But what?

Some kind of confrontation with her aunt now seeme
inevitable, however much she might shrink from the pro
pect. Although there was no guarantee, of course, that M
Arnold would tell her anything—least of all the truth.

I'll cross that bridge when I come to it, she shrugge
mentally.

But this new twist had finally decided her not to dela
her return after all, even though Steve would be disap
pointed.

Maybe when I know the whole truth, I'll be able to pu
it behind me, once and for all, and get some peace, sh
thought with more optimism than conviction.

On impulse, she got Iorgos to drive her round the islan

ne last time. To say goodbye, she thought. Because in-
tinct told her that she might never come back.

She would sell the Villa Danae, and if Steve would not
ke the purchase price from her, then she would give it to
harity.

She wanted it finished, she thought wearily. All ties sev-
red.

And she would have to make it clear to Steve that when
ey met in the future, it would have to be on neutral ter-
tory.

When she arrived back at the house, Andoni, her father's
najor-domo was waiting for her, clearly excited about
omething. 'Kyrios Stephanos wishes to see you, *kyria*. He
as been waiting.'

He was in the room he used as a study, seated behind
is desk.

He rose as she entered. 'You have been gone a long time,
edhi mou. I was concerned.'

She shrugged. 'I decided to have lunch out, and do some
ightseeing. Is there a problem?'

'Perhaps. Yes, I think so.' He looked longingly at the
ox of cigars on his desk, then averted his gaze. 'We have
nexpected visitors, my child. I learned this morning that
'etros Mandrassis was on his way to Thania to discuss the
nerger of our two lines. He has now arrived, and his daugh-
er Christina is with him.'

He paused. 'Also Andreas,' he added flatly.

She was very still, staring past him with eyes that saw
othing.

She said, 'Then I'll move back to the hotel.'

'Unfortunately, *pedhi mou*, you must remain here.' Face
nd voice were implacable, reminding her suddenly that
his was a man who gave orders and had them obeyed
vithout question. 'I am sorry to insist, but I need your
resence at dinner tonight.'

'But I'm dining in Livassi tonight.' She confronted him
vith assumed calm. 'An old friend's in town.'

'Then you must postpone this engagement.' She hear
the authentic note of steel. 'Mandrassis dotes on his onl
child, and she has complained to him that she feels ne
glected, because Andreas has been here on Thania instea
of paying court to her in Athens.'

His mouth tightened. 'Also he has heard—rumours o
another attachment, and this has caused offence. As a re
sult, the merger is in danger.

'I need to set his mind at rest to secure it. Therefore
wish you to attend the dinner party tonight, and allow m
to introduce you as my daughter.'

'No,' Zoe flared at him. 'I'm just not ready for that—t
be announced as your bastard to complete strangers.'

He winced. 'If there is shame, it should be attached t
me, not you, *pedhi mou.*'

'And, anyway, you can't risk me being identified a
Andreas' passing fancy.' Zoe lifted her chin. 'Well, I hav
another solution. May I invite a guest of my own tonight?

'A man?' He frowned swiftly.

'Yes, as it happens, which should silence any lingerin;
doubts about me.' She paused. 'He's on holiday, so h
won't have a dinner jacket.'

'Then I will make it clear it is to be an informal occa
sion.' He thought for a moment. 'It could be an answer.
He glanced at her, his frown deepening. 'So who is thi
man? What is he to you?'

'A friend,' she said. 'And a colleague from work. Noth
ing more.'

'He would like it to be more, perhaps?' His dark eye
were shrewd, and he grunted with satisfaction at her reluc
tant nod.

'Perhaps,' she said.

'Then there is no need to emphasise the working rela
tionship,' he ordained briskly. 'Telephone him, my child
Make the invitation.'

George, however, did not seem overwhelmed by hi;
good fortune.

'I thought I was going to have you to myself,' he returned, a touch sulkily.

'Do this for me,' Zoe said levelly, 'and I'll reconsider flying back with you.' *In fact, given half a chance, I'd leave now.* 'Is it a deal?'

'Oh,' he said, cheering. 'In that case—OK.'

'Thanks, George, you're a treasure. I'll send a car to pick you up in a couple of hours.'

'You will?' He sounded startled. 'Zoe—who are these people?'

'Oh, just a couple of multimillionaires with their heirs and successors,' she said lightly. 'The usual crowd. See you later, George.'

And as he began to make choking sounds she rang off.

Later that evening, she found herself wishing she'd accepted Steve's offer to update her wardrobe. There was nothing on her hanging rail that could compete with a shipping heiress, she thought with disfavour as she took down her black dress. At least she had her pearls to add a much-needed touch of glamour.

Her hands were shaking so much, she could hardly apply the modicum of cosmetics that was all she ever used. But tonight, she needed all the camouflage she could get.

She blotted out the sleepless shadows with concealer, and smoothed blusher along her cheekbones. She darkened her lashes with mascara, and applied a soft pink lustre to her mouth.

She'd aimed to appear cool and sophisticated, but instead she looked scared and vulnerable, she realised with a pang as she took a last look in the mirror.

As she emerged from her room she walked straight into Steve, who was waiting outside.

'You look beautiful,' he said. He drew her arm firmly through his, and led her towards the stairs. 'I am a proud man tonight.'

She said huskily, 'I'm—not sure I can do this.'

'You are a brave girl,' he said. 'I believe in you. Now let us go down to greet our guests.'

But the only person waiting in the *saloni* was Andreas. He was standing by the open French windows, staring into the garden, an untouched glass of ouzo in his hand.

He swung round as they entered. 'Kyria Lambert.' His smile was crooked. 'I had not expected this pleasure.'

'Nor had I.' Her heart felt as if it were going to burst against her ribcage. She made herself smile somehow. 'How—how are you, Andreas?'

'Trying to take this merger to its conclusion,' he said. 'As I am sure you know.' He paused. 'My father tells me you have invited a guest of your own tonight.'

'Yes,' she said. 'I hope you have no objection.'

He drank some ouzo, watching her over the rim of the glass. 'How could I? After all, I have no right to object.'

There was the sound of voices from the hall, a girl's rich giggle. Andreas stiffened, muttering something that sounded like an obscenity under his breath, then swung back to resume his moody scrutiny of the garden.

Zoe realised with shock how desperately she wanted to take him in her arms, to draw his head against her breasts and tell him that everything would be all right.

But I can't, she thought. And, anyway, it wouldn't be true. Not now, not ever.

And she swallowed, bracing herself mentally as Petros Mandrassis came into the room with his daughter. He was a fleshy man with small cold eyes, which he allowed to rove over Zoe's body, and she hated him on sight.

Christina was small, and petulantly pretty, with a mass of glossy dark hair, and a figure that already bordered on the voluptuous.

Give her a few years and she'll be fatter than her father, Zoe thought, pain prompting her to cruelty as the girl crossed the room to Andreas and slid her arm through his, looking up at him with a pouting smile.

'Petros, my friend.' Steve moved forward. 'Allow me to

resent Zoe Lambert, the daughter of an old friend, who is
onouring me with her company for a few days.'

Petros Mandrassis spoke in a grating voice. 'I am
harmed, *thespinis*.'

His daughter murmured something in her own language
o Andreas, and laughed. He inclined his head courteously,
ut his face was a mask of ice.

Zoe took the drink she was handed and stood holding it,
s if she were clinging to some wreckage. She was thankful
o her heart when the double doors opened again to admit
George.

He was wearing chinos, and a shirt that just failed to be
asual, and carrying a sports jacket over his arm. He looked
ot and uncomfortable, and as if he would rather be anywhere than here.

Zoe went to him quickly, reaching up and kissing him
riefly on the lips. 'Darling,' she said. 'It's so lovely that
ou're here.'

She added in an intimate murmur that could be heard all
ound the room. 'Remember that question you asked me a
ittle while ago, before I came to Greece? Well, I've had
ime to think, and I know that I'm ready to answer it now.
So, when we're alone, you can ask me again.'

'Gosh, Zoe.' He turned brick-red, his face a picture of
astonishment and pleasure. 'It's true what they say about
absence, eh?'

She took his hand and led him round the room, introducing him to everyone in turn, smiling with a radiance
that made her facial muscles ache. Not looking at Andreas
s the two men shook hands with the usual polite murmurs.

'It seems I am to wish you joy,' Andreas said softly.

'Looks like it,' said George. 'You could knock me down
with a feather, actually. I never thought I'd talk her round.'

Andreas smiled charmingly. 'Clearly you know all the
ight words to say.' He looked at Zoe, and it was like being
eared with a cold flame. 'You must be sure to invite me
o the wedding. When is it to be?'

'Well, we haven't quite got to that—' George began, bu
Zoe cut in quickly.

'I thought next Easter,' she said. 'And it's kind of yo
to take such an interest, *kyrie*, but I'm sure you'll be fa
too busy with your own arrangements to bother with mine

'Oh, I think I shall be married long before that.' Andrea
still held her gaze with his.

'Terrific,' she said. 'I've never seen a more perfect cou
ple.' She turned to George, treating him to another burst c
radiance. 'Darling, you need a drink.' And she whisked hi
away.

'Arrogant-looking devil,' George muttered in an unde
tone. 'Don't think I'd want him as a friend.'

'Well, don't worry on that score,' Zoe advised hi
shortly. 'Do you want ouzo, or white wine?'

'Is ouzo that cloudy stuff that tastes of aniseed.' H
pulled a face. 'I'd better stick to wine.'

He began a catalogue of small grumbles about his Gree
experiences, from the smell of the drain he'd encountere
by the harbour to his failure to raise the temperature of hi
shower above tepid.

'You're not implying the two are connected in som
way.' Zoe tried to joke him out of it.

'God, I hope not.' He sounded horrified. 'Do you thin
I should mention it to that Sherry person? She's married t
a Greek, you know, although he seems quite pleasant.'

'Yes,' she said a touch wearily. 'He is. And, no, George
I wouldn't say a word. After all, you'll soon be safely bac
in England.'

'That's true,' he said, brightening. He put an awkwar
arm round her and squeezed.

Zoe was thankful to her heart when Andoni announce
that dinner was served.

But to her horror she found she had been placed next t
Andreas, with a glowering Christina opposite. George, re
calling his company manners, applied himself to her pains
takingly, but either she did not speak English well enoug

to understand him, or considered him not worth her notice, because he received little response.

Zoe made two comments praising the food, to which Andreas acceded with cool civility, and then relapsed into silence. It was, she thought, safer that way.

But she could not escape the reality of his physical presence. She found herself terrified that his sleeve might brush her bare arm. That their hands might touch as they both reached for the salt or more bread.

She was trapped in a morass of small but potent fears.

When the leg of lamb that comprised the main course was served, conversation became general, and she was able to relax a little.

'I must say that it's wonderful to be somewhere with air-conditioning,' George announced buoyantly. 'My room was like an oven last night. I didn't bother with the coverlet at all, and I almost found my pyjamas too much.'

There was a silence, eventually broken by Andreas.

'Indeed,' he said, very gravely, and Zoe did not have to look at him to know that little devils were dancing in his eyes. 'You did not consider, maybe, taking them off?'

'Certainly not,' said George. 'Sleeping in pyjamas is much healthier.'

Andreas lounged back in his chair, eyelids drooping, a smile playing about his mouth. 'But also a little constricting,' he said silkily. 'Don't you find?'

George looked surprised. 'No,' he said. 'Not really.' And he began to eat his lamb.

As soon as conversation round the table restarted, and under cover of a noisy discussion between Steve and Petros Mandrassis, Zoe said quietly and fiercely, 'Stop it.'

'I did not start it.' Andreas, the picture of courtesy, poured more wine into her glass. 'Tell me, Zoe *mou*, do you honestly intend to marry that fool?'

'That is none of your business.'

'If so, take some advice,' he went on as if she had not

spoken. 'Leave George folded under the pillow, and sleep with his pyjamas. You will get more response that way.'

Her voice shook. 'You bastard.'

He laughed. 'Hardly an appropriate name—under the circumstances.'

She gasped. 'I—hate you.'

'You are wise,' he said harshly. 'I am trying very hard to do the same.' He saw Christina staring at them across the table, her eyes narrow with suspicion, and raised his glass to her in a smiling toast. She laughed back at him, apparently mollified, and he turned back to Zoe, offering her the dish of potatoes, every inch the attentive host.

He was still smiling, but the look in his eyes pierced her to the bone. He said very softly and evenly, 'There is not an hour of the day that I do not think of you, *matia mou*. Not a night that I do not dream you are in my arms, and wake in torment. I loathe myself for the feelings I still have for you, but I cannot drive them from my soul. I am in this—hell, and you are not with me.'

The quiet voice stopped. And in another second Andreas had joined in the conversation with the two older men.

While Zoe sat rigidly in her chair, pretending to eat, and praying for the evening to end.

CHAPTER ELEVEN

As THE plane circled above Heathrow George said, 'Zoe—are you serious about wanting to marry me?'

It was the question Zoe had been dreading all day. She'd expected him to ask it during the helicopter flight to Athens; while they were waiting at the airport for the upgrade to first class that Steve Dragos had arranged for them, and ever since the plane had taken off.

Maybe the champagne they'd been served had loosened his tongue at last.

She turned and looked at him with compunction. She said gently, 'Darling George, you know as well as I do that if I said "Yes" your mother would have talked you out of it within twenty-four hours.'

He sighed. 'I don't know why she's like that.'

Because she's a miserable, selfish witch, who's scared stiff of losing you.

Zoe thought it, but did not say it.

Aloud, she said, 'But there's one thing I'm sure of. One day you're going to meet someone, love her so much that nothing your mother says will make the slightest difference, and you'll walk off into the sunset together.'

'What about a sunset for you, Zoe?' He paused. 'It's him, isn't it? That arrogant Greek guy I met last night.'

'No,' she said. 'I thought so once—but not any more.'

'But it's hit you hard,' he said. 'I can tell. He was watching you almost all the time. So, why's he marrying Tina Whatsit?'

'Because she's got a shipping line,' Zoe said. 'And I have a degree in English. They're hardly comparable.' She

169

paused. 'You didn't seem too happy when we were taking off at Athens, George. How are you about landing?'

'I'd rather not,' he said, losing some of his colour.

Zoe took his hand and held it until the plane was safely on the ground.

She thought, It's over. I'm home and safe. And I can teach myself to forget.

When dinner was over, they'd gone to the *saloni* for coffee, and Zoe had stayed close to Steve, reasoning it was the safest place to be. She'd wanted no more exchanges with Andreas, she'd told herself, digging her nails into the palms of her hands. She'd still been able to feel the reverberations along her nerve-endings from the last one.

She'd been afraid even to glance in his direction. She'd felt her skin warm with awareness each time she'd heard his voice.

George had left comparatively early, and she'd made a business of accompanying him to the door, and lifting her mouth for his awkward kiss. She'd gone to her own room shortly afterwards, pleading a headache, and encountering a coolly cynical glance from Andreas as she'd done so.

She'd been woken a couple of hours later by the sound of a low-voiced but furious row being conducted in the garden below her bedroom by Andreas and his father, and had realised she was thankful she didn't know what they were saying.

In the morning, Steve had proved unexpectedly amenable when she'd announced she would be leaving with George to catch the afternoon flight to London. In fact, he had done everything possible to smooth her departure, as if he'd recognised it was time for her to go. That it was better—safer that way.

She had not, however, seen Andreas, even to say goodbye, and didn't know whether she should feel glad or sorry.

'He has taken my Christina to see the famous Silver Caves,' Petros Mandrassis informed her, the small eyes glittering with satisfaction.

But would he call her name to the echo? Zoe wondered sadly.

The actual moment of leaving the house was unexpectedly emotional. Steve held her for a long time, then traced a cross upon her forehead.

He said, 'I will write to you, my child, and we will talk on the telephone, *ne*? And we shall see each other again, soon.' He paused. 'Not here, perhaps, but in Paris, maybe, or Rome?'

'Yes,' she said. 'I—I'd like that.' She forced a smile. 'Papa.'

And left him smiling.

She was unutterably weary when she finally reached her flat. She stepped over a pile of mail in the hall, most of it junk, tossed her case into a corner, and went into her tiny kitchen. She made herself some tea, opening a carton of long-life milk from the refrigerator, and carried it through to her bedroom. She took off her clothes, dropping them to the floor.

Tomorrow she would pick them up, and open her letters, and throw away dead flowers, and unpack.

But for now, she just needed to get into bed.

After the heat of Greece, there was a chill to the sheets, and she huddled them round her. She turned her head slightly, and looked up at her mother's picture, remembering the rustle of the dead bougainvillea under her feet as she'd climbed the steps, the sharp scent of the pelargoniums, and the ever-present whisper of the sea.

Maybe the picture was too harsh a reminder of all that she'd lost, and she should take it down. But tomorrow was soon enough to decide that, she thought, and was asleep before her tea had cooled sufficiently to drink.

She spent three days cleaning and tidying the flat, dealing with correspondence, doing the laundry, and shopping for food.

On the fourth day she took the pottery vase she'd bought

in Livassi and went to see Adele. The cottage next doo
was sold, and the new owners were already in residence
with fresh paintwork on the doors and window frames to
prove it.

'You're back early,' Adele commented, making coffee
after the vase had been unwrapped and admired.

She set a beaker down in front of Zoe. 'I told you these
small islands were too quiet. You should have tried Corfu.'

'Next time, perhaps,' Zoe said lightly.

'Did you get to see any of the places your mother saw?'

'I think it's all changed a lot since she was there—and
Aunt Megan.' She paused. 'Have you seen her lately?'

'No, but they're all grumbling about her at the Garden
Club. They say she was impossible at the last meeting—
falling out with everyone.'

On the way home Zoe called at her aunt's house. She
rang the bell, and knocked, but there was no reply, although
she was convinced there was someone at home.

She must have known I'd come looking for her, and
taken evasive action, Zoe thought as she turned away.

When she reached home she wrote a cheque for her share
of the ticket her aunt had bought, and put it in an envelope
with a brief note of thanks.

Two days later it was posted back, torn to pieces.

Steve wrote to say that he was missing her, and that there
had been some rain. He telephoned, too, and she thought
he sounded sad. She wondered if the date for Andreas's
wedding had been fixed, but he did not mention it, and she
could not bear to ask.

His lawyers in Athens sent documentation confirming
that the Villa Danae now belonged to her, and she wrote
back, asking them to place it on the market, and detailing
what they should do with the money it fetched.

She bought educational journals, and studied the em-
ployment columns. She applied for several jobs in various
parts of the country, and was interviewed for two of them.
She was offered the second, a post in a city school with a

headmaster who was battling successfully to move out of the doldrums, and up the league tables, and accepted it.

She found a renovated terrace house a few streets away from the school, and applied for a mortgage.

Everything was going according to plan—except that it all seemed to be happening at some great distance. Someone who looked like her, and spoke like her, was performing all these actions, but she herself was standing on the sidelines, observing and uninvolved.

The autumn term started, and she began to work out her notice. She and George ate their sandwiches together, and once a week went out for a drink after work.

'Mother doesn't seem to see so much of your aunt Megan these days,' he told her on one of these occasions. 'Not since she made that scene over you being in Thania.'

Zoe shrugged. 'I don't see her either. I've been to the house twice, but if she's there she won't answer the door. And Adele says she's resigned from nearly all the groups she belonged to. It's as if she's turning into a recluse.'

'I know the feeling,' he said glumly. 'I saw in the paper they're starting line-dancing classes. Do you think I should join?'

She grinned at him affectionately. 'Go for it, George,' she told him. 'What have you got to lose?'

By the end of September, the weather was colder, with high winds and heavy rain.

'Lousy forecast for the weekend,' the bus driver remarked as he pulled up at her stop on Friday afternoon.

Lousy weekend anyway, thought Zoe, her arms aching under the weight of the briefcase full of marking that she was carrying. She couldn't run because of it, and she was drenched and cross by the time she reached the flat.

She peeled off her wet mackintosh, and lit the gas fire before sitting down to look at the small pile of envelopes waiting for her. There was one with a Greek stamp, and she opened that first. It was from Steve's lawyers, stating there had been an offer of the full asking price for the Villa

Danae, and that, if it was acceptable to her, they would
prepare the paperwork.

So, that was the end of that, she thought, and sat for a
long time, staring at the steady blue flame of the fire, and
hoping it had been bought by someone who would live in
it and love it.

She was just about to start on preparations for her evening meal when the telephone rang.

'Miss Lambert?' It was not a voice she recognised. 'I'm
sorry to bother you, but I'm a bit concerned about your
aunt, Mrs Arnold, and I didn't know who else to speak to.'

'I don't understand,' Zoe said. 'Who are you?'

'My name's Ferris, and I clean for her. She always pays
me on Fridays, only she was out this morning, and when I
went back just now she didn't answer the door. And I know
she's there because the drawing-room light's on, and the
curtains aren't drawn—and, Miss Lambert, she's sitting
there rocking herself back and forwards, and she looks
ghastly. The place is a mess, too. There's things broken,
and even a chair pushed over.

'It made me feel really frightened. I thought of calling
the police, and then I remembered you, and I don't think
she's got anyone else.'

'No,' Zoe said. 'I don't think she has.' She thought for
a moment. 'I'll get a cab, and come straight away, but
there's no guarantee she'll let me in either. It may have to
be the police.'

As soon as she got there she could see why plump, sensible Mrs Ferris had been so alarmed. Aunt Megan looked
like a crazy woman, her hair all over the place, staring in
front of her, her mouth open and moving as she rocked.

Everything seemed to be locked, but Zoe realised the key
had been left on the inside of the conservatory door.

Oh, God, she thought as she picked up a stone and
smashed a pane. Aunt Megan's pride and joy. She unlocked
the door and went in, Mrs Ferris following uncertainly.

'Shall I come with you, miss?'

'No, I'll talk to her first. But if you could make some tea it would be good.'

She stopped at the drawing-room door, thinking that she would rather be anywhere but there, then tapped lightly and went in.

Aunt Megan was still in the same chair, hugging herself, and keening in a low voice.

Zoe went over to her, stepping over fragments of mashed porcelain and torn paper, and knelt beside the chair, avoiding a crumpled newspaper, and a big leather-covered book lying on the floor at Mrs Arnold's feet.

She said gently, 'Aunt Megan, it's Zoe. What's wrong? Has someone broken in?'

Her aunt turned her head slowly, and looked at her. 'Broken,' she said hoarsely. 'Yes—all broken, all those years ago. And never mended. And now it's too late.'

'I don't understand,' Zoe told her. 'Please tell me what's troubling you. I'd like to help.'

'No one—no one can help me. Because they've all gone now. I thought—one day—I would go back. I'd see him one last time. But the girl went instead, and I knew she'd tell him that I lied to him. And then he wouldn't want to see me.

'And I couldn't have that, because I always thought I'd be able to tell him—how I felt. Make him look at me as he used to look at her. And now it's too late. All too late.' She was crying, huge, slow tears that trickled down her face and dripped into her lap.

Zoe swallowed. She felt as if she were tiptoeing through a minefield. But she had to ask, just the same.

She said, 'Aunt Megan, do you mean Steve Dragos.'

'Stephanos!' The older woman glared at her, then subsided. 'Such a beautiful name, and he was so handsome too—like a Greek god. I'd hurt my ankle, you know, and he lifted me up, held me in his arms. I knew there and then that I wanted him to go on touching me for the rest of my life, but he never did so again.'

She looked down at Zoe. 'Because she came, and it was all different. He was still kind to me, but he only looked at her.'

She shook her head. 'She left him, you know, because he was a married man, and his wife wouldn't divorce him. I would never have left. I would have stayed with him always, if he'd asked me. I wouldn't have cared.'

She wrung her hands together. 'Why did he never ask? Why didn't he want me instead of her?

'And then she told me that she was going back to him because she was having his child. And I thought of them together, making the baby, and I couldn't bear it. So I laughed, and said, "Then that makes two of us." I told her that he'd been sleeping with me too all the time. That one woman would never be enough for him.'

Zoe said, 'And she—believed you?'

'I was her sister. Her older sister who took care of her. And he was a rich man, who was unfaithful to his wife. She knew there'd been others before her. I think she was secretly afraid that he wouldn't be able to stop his womanising, no matter how much he loved her.

'And I'd been ill with a tummy bug. I let her think I was sick because I was pregnant. Yes, she believed me, because I was confirming all her doubts, all her worst fears about him.

'I remember she said, "I must think" and she went away from me out of the house, into the street, and a car knocked her down. She wasn't badly hurt—just cuts and bruises—except for the baby, of course. Stephanos' baby.'

Zoe was scarcely breathing. 'You mean my mother had a—miscarriage?'

'She was weak,' said Megan Arnold. 'She let his baby die. If she'd been strong like me, a little accident like that would have made no difference. I would have given him children. I didn't care that they would have been bastards. But she cared. It was always the moral high ground with Gina. She blamed herself for loving him. She expected t e punished for it.' She smiled, suddenly, gloatingly. 'And punished her.'

Zoe felt icy cold. Her teeth began to chatter. 'What did he say when she realised you weren't having a baby.'

'I told her it had been a mistake, but that next time I'd make sure.' She giggled almost girlishly. 'She believed that, too. Convinced herself that he wanted me more than her.' She shook her head. 'It made her quite ill. But she stopped reading his letters, even though he wrote and wrote to her. Not a word to me—just to her, although I pretended I got letters.

'She moved right away—got a job, and met someone else. Oh, he wasn't like Stephanos, but he loved her, and she knew she could trust him always, so she settled for that. And then she had you. The perfect little family, and I hated her for that.'

She sat upright. 'I went back to Thania. I saw Stephanos at his house. I told him that I'd always loved him. That I'd be anything he wanted—do anything that he wanted. I think I even went on my knees to him. But he took no notice. I don't think he even realised what I was saying. He just wanted to ask about—her. And about his baby.

'At first, I was going to tell him about the miscarriage, because I wanted to hurt him as he was hurting me. And then I realised that it would upset him far more to think he had a child that he would never be allowed to see. So I told him that Gina had a little girl, and she'd married someone else, so that his child would have a name. And that he never wanted to see him again.'

'How could you?' Zoe said slowly. 'How could you do those things—tell those lies—ruin two people's lives?'

'Because I saw him first,' said Megan Arnold. 'And he should have wanted me, not her.' She began to cry again. 'Everyone always wanted her. Even when I got married, my husband thought she was wonderful. And now he's gone, and so has she.'

She looked down at the crumpled newspaper, an moaned softly. 'And so has my Stephanos.'

Zoe's lips parted in a soundless gasp. 'What are yo talking about?' she demanded hoarsely.

'He's dead,' the older woman said tonelessly. 'Very sud denly. A heart attack. I read it in the paper—in the busines section. I was looking for the share prices, and I saw i I've lost him for ever.'

Zoe spread out the paper, smoothing the creases wit shaking hands. She found it almost at once. It was quite long piece, beginning with his funeral, which had take place in Athens the previous day, barely forty-eight hour after his death. It listed his commercial achievements, var ious philanthropic efforts he'd been associated with, an stated that the running of the Dragos companies would nov be taken over by his only son, who had already taken cor trol. It added that a proposed merger with the Mandrassi shipping line would soon be finalised.

As she shuffled the pages together she suddenly sav Andreas' face. It was superimposed above an item in th gossip column, briefly profiling the new head of the Drago Corporation.

'Once a well-known jet-setter, Andreas Dragos ha moved away from his playboy image over the past tw years,' she read. 'His forthcoming marriage will no doul provide him with additional stability.'

The door opened, and Mrs Ferris came in with a tray 'The kettle's gone wrong. I had to boil a pan on the stove She gave Megan Arnold an anxious look. 'Is she all right What happened?'

Zoe looked at the motionless figure. She said gently 'She's had a bereavement.'

The doctor came, and then an ambulance, and Au Megan was taken off to a private hospital.

Zoe paid Mrs Ferris, and cleared up the mess in th drawing room. Then she sat down in another chair, and rea both the newspaper pieces again.

I wish I could have been told, she thought sadly. I wish
I hadn't had to hear about it third hand like this—especially
like this.

Yet it all seemed to have been dealt with at phenomenal
speed. He'd died, and two days later he'd been buried. Even
if she'd known about his death, it was doubtful whether
she could have made it in time. And did she have any right
to be there anyway, under the circumstances? For one thing,
she was probably the last person Christina Mandrassis
would want to see.

Besides, journalists would have wanted to know who she
was, and what connection she had with the deceased, so
she couldn't blame Andreas for keeping her at a distance.
In his shoes, she would probably have done the same.

And her instincts had been right all along, it seemed. She
had liked Steve Dragos—could probably have grown to
love him, but she'd always been convinced, in her heart,
that she was not his child.

She folded the newspaper carefully, and slipped it into
the big leather book for safe-keeping. As she opened it she
realised that it wasn't a book, but an old-fashioned photograph album.

There were snaps from childhood and school-days, and
here were lots of Gina, riding a bicycle, bathing in the sea,
perched high in the branches of a tree, her face always
glowing with happiness.

The look of a girl, thought Zoe, who trusts life. Who
believes it won't let her down. A girl who would never
think that the older sister who'd recorded all these happy
moments could ever be the cause of her betrayal and heartbreak.

She went on slowly turning the pages, until at last she
reached the holiday in Thania. Her aunt had taken great
trouble with these photographs, every one of them carefully
named and also dated, she noted with irony.

If I'd only known the date of the holiday, she thought,
it would have been clear proof that I couldn't possibly be

Steve Dragos' daughter. I was born at least eighteen month
later.

And Andreas and I would have been free to love on
another.

As it is, I'm alone—and he's about to embark on a mar
riage of economic convenience. And neither of us are goin
to be happy.

Sighing, she put the album away, and left the room t
find a piece of cardboard to cover the hole in the conser
vatory door. Then she telephoned for another taxi and wer
home.

Some time in the distant past, she'd been planning a
evening meal, she thought as she climbed the stairs to he
flat. As she reached her landing she fumbled for the ligh
switch, and the bulb came on, revealing a tall figure leanin
against her door.

She clapped a hand over her mouth, stifling her scream
as Andreas detached himself and came towards her. H
looked grey with fatigue, but the ghost of his old smil
curved his mouth as he held out his arms to her.

'Matia mou.'

She said something incoherent that might have been hi
name, and flung herself forward.

He received her hungrily, and his mouth came down o
hers. There was no gentleness in his kiss. No restraint ei
ther. The lips that parted hers were deeply and passionatel
sensual, and they demanded an equal response.

His hands parted the damp cling of the raincoat to fin
her breasts, stroking her nipples to exquisite arousa
through the thin woollen shirt she was wearing, and sh
moaned her pleasure into his mouth, her entire body melt
ing with her need.

When at last he raised his head, they were both breath
less.

He said hoarsely, 'Your key, *agapi mou*, or I shall tak
you here.'

Somehow they unlocked the door, and stumbled inside, already shedding their clothes as they went.

When she was naked, Andreas lifted her onto the sofa, and knelt beside her, kissing her body, his mouth hot and urgent. His tongue lapped at her breasts, turning the engorged peaks to flame.

At the same time, his hand was caressing her belly, moving down over her quivering thighs, and parting them. Her body arched under the exquisite intimacy of his touch, demanding more.

He was murmuring to her in his own language, his voice low and languorous, as his fingers continued their intense erotic play. She could feel the last vestiges of her control slipping away, and then suddenly her body imploded, consuming her totally with wave after wave of pure pleasure, so that she was gasping and laughing and crying out, all at the same time.

Andreas said her name huskily. She felt him strip off his remaining covering, then he lifted himself over her, and entered her, and she enfolded him rapturously, her whole body alight with the warmth and strength of him inside her, her hands clinging to his shoulders, her slender legs locked round his waist in total surrender.

It was a lovemaking born from a stark and compelling need, and Zoe answered every powerful thrust with passionate completeness, her body as wild and driven as his own.

Nothing in her limited experience had prepared her for this fierce glory. For the frantic necessity to take as well as give. For his mouth on hers, and the hot, sexual invasion of his tongue.

Deep within her, she sensed the inexorable build of delight beginning again, and felt her body quiver and shatter once more into a renewal of rapture.

And at the height of her pleasure, as she was overwhelmed by sensation, she heard him cry out in his own release.

Afterwards they found a wonderful peace together. Zoe took him to her bed, and held him in her arms while he slept. Later, she dozed, too, and he woke her with kisses and made love to her again, slowly and very gently, his body worshipping hers.

And finally, they talked, because there were things to be said, and questions to be answered. And the revelations of the evening to be discussed.

Eventually: 'So,' she said. 'When did you realise that we weren't brother and sister after all?'

'Not until you began the sale of the Villa Danae,' he said. 'And the lawyers showed me the copy of your birth certificate. I knew when your mother had lived on Thania and the dates did not match.'

'And yet you said nothing?' Zoe reared up indignantly. 'You let me go on thinking that we were lost to each other?'

Andreas pulled her back into his embrace. 'I did it for my father's sake,' he said gently. 'He wanted to believe it so much, *matia mou*. You were this wonderful gift that he'd waited for throughout the long years. That's why he wouldn't consider the medical tests that the lawyers recommended, because he refused to admit there was even a remote possibility that he could be mistaken. You were his beloved Gina's daughter, therefore you must be his, too. I—I could not take that away from him.'

He paused. 'The doctors had already told me that he could have another attack at any time, which would almost certainly be fatal. I wanted whatever time he had left to be happy. And he was, my honey girl. He thought of you— spoke of you often. Blame me for it, if you will.'

'No,' she said. 'I understand, and I'm glad. I remember the way he said goodbye to me. I think he knew he didn't have much time left.' She paused. 'I'm sorry I wasn't at his funeral.'

'It would not have been a good experience for you. Our funerals are very noisy, emotional affairs. I had to steer myself to endure all the aunts and cousins screaming and crying. Far better, *agapi mou*, to remember him as he was.' He paused. 'Your mother's letter was buried with him.'

'Thank you for that.' She kissed his shoulder. 'I think it was that letter that made him so sure I was his child—and Aunt Megan's lies, of course.'

Andreas' arms tightened round her protectively. 'That evil bitch.' His voice was almost murderous. 'She might have harmed you. You should not have had to face her on your own, *pedhi mou*.'

'I wanted to hate her,' Zoe said soberly. 'But in the end, I couldn't. She was just sad, and—hopeless. It made me see how dangerous love can be when it gets—twisted like that.'

There was a smile in his voice, 'And now you also know how good it can be.'

'Oh, yes.' She stretched herself against him, her smile widening as she felt his body's instant response.

'Zoe *mou*,' he said. 'Have a little mercy, or I may not survive until our wedding.'

She said, faltering a little, 'You're going to marry me? But how?'

'The usual way,' he said. 'With a church and a priest. And as quickly as possible,' he added, stroking her stomach. 'I wanted you too badly even to think of protection, so there could be consequences.'

'Don't you want us to have babies?'

'Yes,' he said. 'But I am selfish enough to want my wife all to myself for a while, too.'

'Andreas,' she said, after a pause. 'You—you don't have to marry me.'

She felt him tense. 'What nonsense is this?'

'You're engaged to Tina Mandrassis. The merger depends on you marrying her. I—I know that. So, I thought of the Villa Danae. My mother never lived there, but I could—if you wanted. And belong to you for as long as you wanted.'

'But you are selling the Villa Danae, *matia mou*, and tl
new owner would not allow such immorality under h
roof.'

She lifted her chin and looked at him with suspicic
'You seem to know a lot about him.'

He grinned at her. 'An entire lifetime,' he agreed lazil

She gasped. 'You—*you* bought the Villa Danae. B
why?'

'So that we could live there together. It needs people-
children—love to bring it to life. I think we can do th;
And I suggest we sell my father's house. It has few hap]
associations for me.'

'But what about the merger?' she demanded.

His hand began to caress her breasts. 'I am more inte
ested in a different kind of merger,' he whispered.

'Darling,' she said. 'Be serious.'

'You think I'm not?' He captured her hand, and carri
it to his body. 'But you obviously will not let tl
Mandrassis merger drop, so let me tell you what I told n
father—that I intend to marry only for love. And I did n
and never could love Tina Mandrassis. And the only tin
I gave the idea of an arranged marriage any real thoug
was when I thought you were forbidden to me, and I w
at my lowest ebb. I tried to tell myself that without yc
nothing mattered, but even that could not persuade me
marry for convenience. So, I decided I would remain si
gle.'

'And celibate?' Zoe inquired dulcetly.

He grinned. 'I would have tried. But I don't think it is
condition that would suit either of us, my angel.

'As for the merger,' he went on. 'Mandrassis needs
more than I do, and I suspect he will proceed even witho
me as a son-in-law. And don't worry too much about tl
beautiful Tina. She inherited a lot of money from h
mother, so she won't lack for offers.'

'And I'm bringing you nothing,' Zoe said wistfully.

His smile was wicked. 'You think not, *matia mou*.' H

and strayed with delicate precision. 'I shall have to jog our memory.'

'I have total recall, thank you,' Zoe said severely, trying ot to wriggle and failing miserably. She sighed. 'I didn't ink it was possible to be so happy.'

Andreas bent his head and kissed her slowly and tenerly.

'And this is only the beginning,' he whispered. 'My ve—and my wife.'

MILLS & BOON®

Mills & Boon have been at the heart of romance since 1908… and while the fashions may have changed, one thing remains the same: from pulse-pounding passion to the gentlest caress, we're always known how to bring romance alive.

Now, we're delighted to present you with these irresistible illustrations, inspired by the vintage glamour of our covers. So indulge your wildest dreams and unleash your imagination as we present the most iconic Mills & Boon moments of the last century.

Visit **www.millsandboon.co.uk/ArtofRomance** to order yours!

MILLS & BOON®

Why not subscribe?
Never miss a title and save money too!

Here is what's available to you if you join the exclusive **Mills & Boon® Book Club** today:

* *Titles up to a month ahead of the shops*
* *Amazing discounts*
* *Free P&P*
* *Earn Bonus Book points that can be redeemed against other titles and gifts*
* *Choose from monthly or pre-paid plans*

Still want more?
Well, if you join today we'll even give you
50% OFF your first parcel!

So visit **www.millsandboon.co.uk/subscription**
or call **Customer Relations on 0844 844 1351***
to be a part of this exclusive Book Club!

*This call will cost you 7 pence per minute plus your
phone company's price per minute access charge.